Praise for

PANIC

"PANIC is a sleek, smart thriller that combines a family tragedy, international intrigue, and the redemptive power of love... There is no question: Jeff Abbott is the new name in suspense." —Harlan Coben

"A superior, fast-paced thriller... White-knuckled suspense that's extremely hard to put down."

—*Publishers Weekly*

"PANIC is a ride down the roaring rapids. Jeff Abbott has put together a hell of a page-turner."

—Michael Connelly

"Engrossing... with skilled handling of riveting action sequences, plot twists, and camera angles, all converging at breakneck speed, Abbott whips these simple ingredients into a near-perfect thriller that may indeed result in physical distress akin to panic for anyone trying to put the thing down before the last bullet flies. Fans of Harlan Coben, Lee Child, Joseph Finder, or John Grisham—anyone who enjoys a wild ride on a bumpy road—can cheer the arrival of our latest master of the fine art of the page-turner. Highly recommended." —*Booklist* (starred review)

"Outstanding...genuinely moving...Abbott hits full stride early on and never lets up. Readers who thrive on a relentless narrative pace and a straight line to the finish won't be disappointed." —*Publishers Weekly* (starred review)

"Breathless fun...You really do keep turning page after page." —*Cleveland Plain Dealer*

"Deliciously crafty...heart-pounding thrills...a stunner... *Adrenaline* has all the hallmarks of a career-changer. It should launch him into the Michael Connelly or Dennis Lehane stratosphere...Abbott sets a merciless pace, but he never lets speed hinder his writing...glorious sensory acumen...with just the right amount of snarky wit." —*Dallas Morning News*

"Extremely compelling...a thriller that will get even the most jaded reader's pulse racing...a grand slam home run...*Adrenaline* rivets the reader from the very first paragraph, and Capra proves to be a character with enough skills and depth to be extremely compelling...Everyone will want to see what Abbott, and Capra, have up their sleeve next." —Associated Press

"Thrilling." —*New York Daily News*

"Exhilarating...Confirms Abbott as one of the best thriller writers of our time...This is a book that's getting a tremendous amount of buzz; everyone's talking about it. I think Jeff Abbott's the next Robert Ludlum. And I think Sam Capra is the heir apparent to Jason Bourne...The most gripping spy story I've read in years...It just grabs you. Great read!" —Harlan Coben

"*Adrenaline,* like its namesake hormone, is all about pace, and a high-speed pace at that. A word of caution: Don't start reading [it] just before bedtime!" —*BookPage*

"Engaging from the first paragraph, terrifying from the second page, *Adrenaline* accomplishes what most modern thrillers can't. It makes us care about its characters even while we're speeding headlong down the ingenious rabbit hole of its plot. Well done!" —Eric Van Lustbader

"Engrossing…flows rapidly from page to page…definitely a page-turner…wonderful descriptive writing…Abbott's demonstrated ability creates a highly recommended 5-star book." —*Kingman Daily Miner* (AZ)

"The title of this book pretty much sets the pace for this action-packed thriller. Within its pages are all the best aspects of a very enjoyable good-versus-evil plot: intrigue, spies, double crosses, foreign locales, technology used for nefarious purposes, a good-hearted hero, and the obligatory nasty bad guys." —*Suspense Magazine*

"Sam Capra is the perfect hero—tough, smart, pure of heart, and hard to kill. And *Adrenaline* is the perfect thriller. Taut and edgy, with breakneck pacing and perfect plotting, it's a breathless race from the shocking, heart-wrenching opening sequence to the stunning conclusion. Jeff Abbott is a master, and *Adrenaline* is his best book yet." —Lisa Unger

"Hero Sam Capra likes to unwind with parkour, leaping from building to building, clambering up walls and hurtling through space across the urban landscape…The sport's a fitting metaphor for Abbott's style, tumbling from page to page with the frantic inevitability of Robert Ludlum…It all works beautifully." —*Booklist*

PANIC

JEFF ABBOTT

GCC

GRAND CENTRAL
PUBLISHING

NEW YORK   BOSTON

Copyright © 2005 by Jeff Abbott

All rights reserved. In accordance with the U.S. Copyright Act of 1976, the scanning, uploading, and electronic sharing of any part of this book without the permission of the publisher is unlawful piracy and theft of the author's intellectual property. If you would like to use material from the book (other than for review purposes), prior written permission must be obtained by contacting the publisher at permissions@hbgusa.com. Thank you for your support of the author's rights.

Grand Central Publishing
Hachette Book Group
237 Park Avenue
New York, NY 10017

www.HachetteBookGroup.com

Printed in the United States of America

OPM

Originally published in 2005 by Dutton.

First Grand Central Publishing Edition: May 2013

10 9 8 7 6 5 4 3 2 1

Grand Central Publishing is a division of Hachette Book Group, Inc. The Grand Central Publishing name and logo is a trademark of Hachette Book Group, Inc.

The Hachette Speakers Bureau provides a wide range of authors for speaking events. To find out more, go to www.hachettespeakersbureau .com or call (866) 376-6591.

The publisher is not responsible for websites (or their content) that are not owned by the publisher.

For Peter Ginsberg

FRIDAY

MARCH 11

1

———◦◎◦———

THE PHONE AWOKE EVAN CASHER, and he knew something was wrong. No one who knew him ever called this early. He opened his eyes. He reached across the bed for Carrie but she was gone, and her side of the bed was cool. A note, folded, on the pillow. He reached for it but the phone continued its insistent shrill, so he answered.

"Hello."

His mother said, "Evan. I need you to come home. Right now." She spoke in a low whisper.

He fumbled for the bedside lamp. "What's the matter?"

"Not over the phone. I'll explain when you get here."

"Mom, get real, it's a two-and-a-half-hour drive. Just tell me what's wrong."

"Evan. Please. Just come home."

"Is Dad all right?" His father, a computer consultant, had left Austin three days ago for a job in Australia. He made databases dance and sing for big companies and governments. Australia. Long flights. Evan had a sudden vision of a plane, scattered across the outback or Sydney Harbor, ripped metal, smoke rising. "What's happened?"

"I just need you here, okay?" Calm but insistent.

"Mom, please. Not until you tell me what's going on."

"I said not on the phone." She fell silent, he said nothing, and the uncomfortable tension of an unexpected standoff rose for ten long seconds until she broke it. "Did you have a lot of work to do today, sweetheart?"

"Just edits on *Bluff*."

"Then bring your computer with you, you can work here. But I need you here. Now."

"What's the big deal about not telling me?"

"Evan." He heard his mother take a steadying breath. "Please."

The naked, almost frightening neediness—a tone he had never heard in his mother's voice—made her sound like a stranger to him. "Um, okay, Mom, I can leave in an hour or so."

"Sooner. As soon as possible."

"All right then, in like fifteen minutes or so."

"Hurry, Evan. Just pack and come as fast as you can."

"Okay." He fought down a rising panic.

"Thank you for not asking questions right now," she said. "I love you and I'll see you soon, and I'll explain everything."

"I love you, too."

He put the phone back in the cradle, a little disoriented with the shock of how the day had started. Now wasn't the time to tell his mother that he was in love. Seriously, crazily in Romeo-and-Juliet love.

He opened the note. It simply said, *Thanks for a great evening. I'll call you later. Had early morning errands. C.*

He got in the shower and wondered if he'd blown it last night. *I love you,* he'd told Carrie, when they lay spent in the sheets. The words rose to his mouth without thought or effort, because if he'd weighed the consequences, he would have kept his mouth shut. He never said the L word first.

Before, he had told only one woman he loved her, and that had been his last girlfriend, hungry for his reassurance, and he'd said it because he thought it might be true. But last night was different. No *might* or *maybe*; he knew with certainty. Carrie lying next to him, her breath tickling his throat, her fingernail tracing a line along his eyebrow and she looked so beautiful, and he said the big three words and they felt as true in his heart as anything he had ever known.

Pain flared in her eyes when he spoke and he thought, *I should have waited. She doesn't believe it because we're in bed.* But she kissed him and said, "Don't love me."

"Why not?"

"I'm trouble. Nothing but trouble." But she held him tight, as though she were afraid he would be the one to vanish.

"I love trouble." He kissed her again.

"Why? Why would you love me?"

"What's not to love?" He kissed her forehead. "You have a great brain." He kissed between her eyes. "You see the beauty in everything." He kissed her mouth and grinned. "You always know the right thing to say . . . unlike me."

She kissed him back and they made love again, and when they were done, she said, "Three months. You can't really know me."

"I'll never know you. We never know another person as much as we like to pretend."

She smiled, snuggled up close to him, pressed her face to his chest, put her mouth close to his beating heart. "I love you, too."

"Look at me and say it."

"I'll say it here to your heart." A tear trickled from her cheek to his chest.

"What's wrong?"

"Nothing. Nothing. I'm happy." Carrie kissed him. "Go to sleep, baby."

And he did, and now, in the hard light of day, she was gone, the whispers and the promises gone with her. And this distant note. But maybe this was for the best. She was nervous. And the last complication he needed was explaining a mysterious family disaster.

He tried Carrie's cell phone. Left her a voice mail: "Babe, I've got a family emergency, I've got to go to Austin. Call me when you get this." He thought, *I shouldn't say it again, it scared her off,* but he said, "I love you and I'll talk to you soon."

Evan tried his father's cell phone. No answer. Not even voice mail picking up. But his dad's phone might not connect in Australia. He put the plane-crash scenario out of his mind. He followed his clockwork morning regimen: fired up his computer, checked his to-do list, checked his news feed: no disasters reported in Australia. Perhaps this was a disaster on a smaller scale. Cancer. Divorce. The thought dried his throat.

He clicked on his e-mail, shot off a message to his dad saying, *Call me ASAP,* then downloaded his e-mails. His in-box held an invitation to speak at a film conference in Atlanta; e-mails from two other documentary filmmakers who were friends of his; a pile of music files and a couple of his mother's latest digital photos, all sent by her late last night. He synced the music to his digital player; he'd listen to the songs in the car. Mom thrived on obscure bands and tunes, and she'd found three great songs for his earlier movies. He checked to be sure he had all the footage he needed to edit for his nearly completed documentary on the professional poker circuit. Made sure that he had the raw notes for a talk he was supposed to give at the University of Houston next week. He slid his laptop, his digital music player, and his digital camcorder into his backpack. Evan packed a bag with a weekend's worth of clothes his mother hated for him to wear: old bowling shirts, worn khakis, tennis shoes a year past their prime.

His watch said seven fifteen. It was not quite a three-hour drive from Houston to Austin.

Evan locked the door behind him and headed to his car. This wasn't the day he had planned. He fought his way through the morning snarl of Houston traffic, listening to the music his mother had sent last night. He wanted Spanish-flavored electronic funk for the opening scenes of his poker-player documentary, and no songs he'd heard yet sounded right, but this music was perfect, full of drama and energy.

He tapped his fingers to the beat as he drove and kept waiting for his cell to ring, his father or Carrie calling, his mom calling to say all was suddenly fine, but his phone stayed silent all the way to Austin.

2

His mother's front door was locked. Mom kept her photography studio out in a garage apartment, and he decided she must have retreated to the comfort of film, primer, and solitude.

He unlocked the door with his key and stepped inside. "Mom?" he called out. No answer.

He walked toward the back of the house, toward the kitchen. He had bought his mom her favorite treats, peach pastries from a bakery she adored on the way from Houston, and he wanted to put up the food before he headed to her studio.

Evan turned the corner and saw his mother lying dead on the kitchen floor.

He froze. He opened his mouth but did not scream. The world around him went thick with the sound of his own blood pounding in his throat, in his temples. The sack of peach pastries tumbled to the floor, followed by his duffel bag.

He took two stumbling steps toward her. Her throat was puffed and savaged, her tongue distended, and the kitchen air held the unmistakable stink of death. He saw a silver gleam of wire wrapped around her throat.

An empty kitchen-table chair stood next to her, as though she might have been sitting in it before she died.

Evan made a low moan in his throat, knelt by his mother, brushed a tangle of her graying hair from her face. Her eyes were wide and swollen, unseeing.

"Oh, Mom." He put his fingers over her lips: stillness. Her skin was still warm.

"Mom, Mom!" His voice rose in grief and horror. Evan stood. A wave of dizziness buckled his legs. The police. He had to call the police. He staggered around her body to the kitchen counter, where her breakfast still sat: a coffee cup with a lipsticked edge, a plate dotted with plum-jelly drips and a scattering of English-muffin crumbs. Evan reached for the phone with a shaking hand.

Metal hammered the back of his head. He dropped to his knees, his teeth biting into his tongue, the tang of blood in his mouth. The world started to crumple into dark.

A gun pressed against the back of his head; the perfect circle of the barrel was cool in his hair. A nylon rope looped over his head and tightened around his throat with a yank. He tried to jerk away but the gun cracked hard against his temple.

"Be still," a voice said. "Or you're dead." It was a young man's voice. Amused, saying *dead* in a cruel singsong. *Day-ed.*

Hands grabbed his duffel bag from the edge of the kitchen, pulled it out of his line of vision. A robbery.

"Just take it," Evan whispered. "Just take it and go." He heard the rustle of rummaging: his computer, his camera, being removed from the bag. His laptop's powering-up chime sounded, louder than his own ragged breathing. Then long seconds of silence, fingers tapping on a keyboard.

"What do you want?" he heard himself ask.

No answer.

"My mom, you killed my mom—"

"Hush now." The gun kept Evan's face tilted forward, almost touching his mother's dead jaw. Evan wanted to twist around, see the man's face, but he couldn't. The noose tightened, pulling savagely into Evan's throat.

"Got it," another voice said. Male, older than the first. Arrogant, cool baritone. Then the whisper of fingers on keyboard. "All gone."

Evan heard a pop of chewing gum close to his ear. "Can I now?"

"Yes," the other said. "It's just a shame."

Steel cracked against Evan's head. Black circles exploded before his eyes, edging out his mother's blank, dead stare.

Evan awoke. Dying.

He couldn't breathe because the rope scorched his throat and his feet danced in empty space. A plastic trash bag covered his head, making the world milky gray and indistinct. He grabbed at the rope, choked out a cry as the noose strangled him.

"You took breathing for granted, didn't you now, sunshine?" The younger man's voice, cold and mocking.

Evan kicked his feet. The countertop, the chair, had to be there to take his weight, to save him. He scissored his legs with what strength he had left because there was nothing else he could do.

"Kick twice if it hurts bad," the younger voice said. "I'm curious."

And a blast filled his world. Shattering glass. Gunfire. A second of silence. Then the younger man yelling and screaming.

The rope swung. Evan attempted to inch his fingers under the choking, killing cord. Then another rattle of gunfire boomed huge in his ears and he fell, hit the floor, plaster and splintered wood dusting him. The loose length of the gunshot-torn rope landed across his face.

He tried to breathe. Nothing. Nothing. Breathing was a forgotten skill, a trick that Evan no longer knew. Then his chest hitched with sweet air. Drinking in oxygen, drinking in life. His throat hurt as if it had been skinned from the inside.

Evan heard another eruption of shots, the sound of weight crashing into shrubbery outside the windows.

Then an awful silence.

Evan tore the plastic bag free from his face. He blinked, spat blood and bile from his mouth. A hand touched his shoulder, fingers prodded at him.

"Evan?"

He looked up. A man stared down at him. Pale, bald, tall. Around his father's age, early fifties.

"They're gone, Evan," Bald said. "Let's go."

"Ca-call..." Every syllable was fire in his mouth. "Call...police. My...mother. He..."

"You got to come with me," Bald said. "You can't stay here. They'll be hunting you now."

Evan shook his head.

Bald reached down, worked the broken rope off Evan's neck, hauled him to his feet, herded him away from his mother's body.

"I'm a friend of your mom's," Bald said. He held a wicked-looking shotgun. "Gonna get you out of here."

Evan had never seen him before. "My mother. The police. Call the police. There was a man...or two..."

"They're gone. We'll call the police," Bald said. "Just not here." He propelled Evan fast toward the back door with a shove to his back.

"Who are you?" Evan said, fighting the panic rising in his chest. A man he didn't know, with a big gun, who didn't want him to call the police.

"We'll talk later. Can't stay. I need your—" But he didn't finish, as Evan left-hooked Bald's jaw, without analysis or grace, his muscles still primed with fear and grief. Bald stumbled back, and Evan ran out the front door he'd left unlocked.

"Evan, stop! Come here!" Bald yelled.

Evan bolted into the damp spring air. The pounding of his sneakered feet against the asphalt was the only sound in the quiet of the oak-shaded neighborhood. He glanced behind him. Bald sprinted from the house. Shotgun in one hand, Evan's yellow duffel in the other, jumping into a weathered blue Ford sedan parked on the street.

Evan tore across the graceful yards, expecting a bullet to shatter his spine or his head. He saw an open garage door and veered into the yard. *Please, be home.* He jumped onto the front porch, leaned against the bell, pounded the door, shouting to call 911.

The blue Ford sped past him.

An elderly man with a military burr opened the door, cordless phone already in hand.

Evan ran back into the yard, yelling at the neighbor to call the police, trying to catch the Ford's plates.

But the car was gone.

3

WALK ME THROUGH THIS MORNING one more time," the homicide detective said. His name was Durless. He had a kind, thin face, with the gaunt healthiness of a long-distance runner. "If you can, son."

The investigators had kept Evan away from the kitchen, but had brought him back into the house so he could identify anything that was out of place or missing. He stood now in his parents' bedroom. It was a wreck. Four suitcases lay thrown against the wall, all opened, their contents spilled across the floor. They didn't belong here. But his mother's favorite photos, which did belong on the walls, lay ruined and trampled on the carpet. He stared at the pictures behind the spiderwebs of smashed glass: the Gulf of Mexico orange with sunrise, the solitude of a gnarled oak on an empty expanse of prairie, London's Trafalgar Square, lights shaded by falling snow. Her work. Broken. Her life. Gone. It could not be, yet it was; the absence of her seemed to settle into the house, into the air, into his bones.

You cannot afford shock right now. You have to help the police catch these guys. So have shock later. Snap out of it.

"Evan? Did you hear me?" Durless said.

"Yes. I can do whatever you need me to do." Evan

steadied himself. Sitting out on the driveway, crumpled with grief, he'd given the responding officer a description of Bald and his car. More officers had arrived and secured the house with practiced efficiency, strung crime-scene tape along the front door and the driveway, across the shattered kitchen window where Bald had fired his shotgun. Evan had sat on the cool of the cement and dialed his father, again and again. No answer. No voice mail. His father worked alone, as an independent consultant, no employees. Evan didn't know anyone he could call to help him locate his dad in Sydney.

He'd left a message for Carrie on her cell, tried her at her apartment. No answer.

Durless had arrived, first interviewing the patrol officer and the ambulance crew who had responded to the initial call. He'd introduced himself to Evan and taken his initial statement, then asked him to come back into the house, escorting him to his mother's bedroom.

"Anything missing?" Durless asked.

"No." And through the haze of shock Evan knelt by one opened suitcase: it lay choked with men's pressed khakis, button-downs, new leather loafers, and tennis shoes.

All in his sizes.

"Don't touch anything," Durless reminded him, and Evan yanked his hand back.

"I've never seen these suitcases or clothes before," he said. "But this bag looks like she packed it for me."

"Where was she going?"

"Nowhere. She was waiting for me here."

"But she had four packed bags. With clothes for you. And a gun packed in her bag." He pointed at a gun, tossed atop one of the clothes piles spilling from a suitcase.

"I can't explain it. Well, the gun looks like my dad's Glock. He uses it in target shootings. It's his hobby." Evan wiped his face. "I used to shoot with him, but I'm not very good." He realized he was rambling and he shut up. "Mom...must have not had a chance to get to the gun when the men came."

"She must have been afraid if she was packing your dad's gun."

"I just don't know."

"So. Let's go through it again. She called you this morning. Around seven."

"Yes." Evan again walked Durless through his mother's frantic phone call insisting he come home, his coming straight from Houston, the men attacking him. Trying to dredge up any detail that he'd forgotten in giving his initial account.

"These men that grabbed you in the kitchen—you're sure there were two?"

"I heard two voices. I'm sure."

"But you never saw their faces?"

"No."

"And then another man came, shot at them, blasted the ceiling, cut you down from the rope. You saw his face."

"Yes." Evan rubbed a hand across his forehead. In his initial statement, still trembling with shock, he had said it was a bald man, but now he could do better. "In his fifties. Thin mouth, very straight teeth. Mole on his"—Evan closed his eyes for a minute, picturing—"left cheek. Brown eyes, strong build. Ex-military, possibly. About six feet. He looked like he might be Latino. No accent in his voice. He wore black pants, a dark green T-shirt. No wedding ring. A steel watch. I can't tell you anything more about his car except it was a blue Ford sedan."

Durless wrote down the additional details, handed them to another officer. "Get the revised description on the wire," he said. The officer left. Durless raised an eyebrow. "You have an exceptional eye for detail under stress."

"I'm better with pictures than words." Evan heard the low voices of the APD crime-scene team as they analyzed the carnage in the kitchen. He wondered if his mother's body was still in the house. It felt strange to stand in her room, see her clothes, her pictures, know she was dead now.

"Evan, let's talk about who would have wanted to hurt your mom," Durless said.

"No one. She was the nicest person you could imagine. Gentle. Funny."

"Had she mentioned being afraid, or threatened by anyone? Think. Take your time."

"No. Never."

"Anyone with a grudge against your family?"

The idea seemed ridiculous, but Evan took a deep breath, thought about his parents' friends and associates, about his own. "No. They argued with a neighbor last year about the guy's dog barking all night, but they settled it and the guy moved away." He gave Durless the name of the former neighbor. "I can't think of anyone who wishes us ill. This has to be random."

"But the bald man saved you," Durless said. "He, according to you, chased the killers off, called you by name, claimed he was a friend of your mom's, and tried to get you to leave with him. That's not random."

Evan shook his head.

"I didn't get your dad's name," Durless said.

"Mitchell Eugene Casher. My mother is Donna Jane Casher. Did I tell you that already? Her name?"

"You did, Evan, you did. Tell me about the relationship between your parents."

"They've always had a strong marriage."

Durless stayed quiet. Evan couldn't bear the silence. The accusing silence.

"My dad had nothing to do with this. Nothing."

"Okay."

"My dad would never hurt his family, no way."

"Okay," Durless said again. "But you see I have to ask."

"Yeah."

"How you get along with your folks?"

"Fine. Great. We're all close."

"You said you were having trouble reaching your dad?"

"He's not answering his cell phone."

"You got his itinerary in Australia?"

Now he remembered. "Mom usually keeps it on the refrigerator."

"That's great, Evan, that's a help."

"I just want to help you get whoever did this. You have to get them. You have to." His voice started to shake and he steadied himself. He rubbed at the raw rope burn on his neck.

Durless said, "When you talked to your mom, did she sound afraid? Like these guys were already here in the house?"

"No. She didn't sound panicked. Just emotional. Like she had bad news to tell me, but didn't want to tell me over the phone."

"You talk to her yesterday, or the day before? Tell me about her mental state then."

"Perfectly normal. She mentioned taking an assignment in China. She's a freelance travel photographer." He pointed at the cracked frames, the photos distorted under the broken glass. "That's some of her work. Her favorites."

Durless cast his gaze along London, the coast, the prairie. "Places. Not people," he said.

"She likes places better than faces." It had been his mother's joke about her work. Tears crept to the corners of Evan's eyes, and he blinked. Willed them to vanish. He did not want to cry in front of this man. He dug fingernails into his palms. He listened to the snap of cameras in the kitchen, the soft murmurs of the crime-scene team working the room, breaking down the worst nightmare for his family into jotted statistics and chemical tests.

"You have brothers or sisters?"

"No. No other family at all."

"What time did you get here? Tell me again."

He looked at his watch. The face was broken, hands frozen at 10:34. It must have happened when he fell as the rope broke. He showed the stopped watch to Durless. "I didn't really notice the time. I was worried about my mom." He wanted the comfort of Carrie's arms, the reassurance of his father's voice. His world set to right.

Durless spoke in a whisper to a police officer standing in the doorway, who left. Then he gestured at the luggage. "Let's talk about these bags she had packed, for both of you."

"I don't know. Maybe she was going to Australia. To see my dad."

"So she begs you to come home, but she's getting ready to leave. With a suitcase for you, and with a gun."

"I...I can't explain it." Evan wiped his arm across his nose.

"Maybe this crisis was all a ruse to get you home for a surprise trip."

"She wouldn't scare me for no good reason."

Durless tapped his pen against his chin. "And you were in Houston last night."

"Yes," Evan said. Wondering if now he was being asked for an alibi. "My girlfriend stayed with me. Carrie Lindstrom."

Durless wrote down her name and Evan gave him her contact information, the name of the River Oaks dress shop where she worked, and her cell phone number.

"Evan. Help me get a clear picture. Two men grab you, hold you at gunpoint, but then don't shoot you, they try and hang you, and another man saves you but then tries to kidnap you and takes off when you run." Durless spoke with the air of a teacher walking a student through a thorny problem. He leaned forward. "Help me find a line of thought to follow."

"I'm telling you the truth."

"I don't doubt you. But why not just shoot you? Why not shoot your mother, if they had guns?"

"I don't know."

"You and your mother were targeted, and I really need your help to understand why."

A memory crowded back into his head. "When they had me on the floor . . . one of them started up my laptop. Typed on it."

Durless called in another officer. "Would you go find Mr. Casher's laptop, please?"

"Why would they want anything on my computer?" Evan heard the hysteria rising in his voice and fought it back down.

"You tell me. What's on it?"

"Film footage, mostly. Video-editing programs."

"Footage?"

"I'm a filmmaker. Documentaries."

"You're young to be making movies."

Evan shrugged. "I worked hard. I finished college a year early. I wanted to get into film school faster."

"More money-making blockbusters."

"I like telling stories about people. Not action heroes."

"Would I know any of your movies?"

"Well, my first movie was about a military family who lost a son in Vietnam, then a grandson in Iraq. But people probably know me for *Ounce of Trouble*, about a cop in Houston who framed an innocent man for a crime."

Durless frowned. "Yeah. I saw it on PBS. The cop killed himself."

"Yeah, once the police investigation into his activities started. It's sad."

"The guy he supposedly framed was a drug dealer. Not too innocent."

"Ex–drug dealer who had served his time. He was out of the business when the cop came after him. And there was no supposedly about it."

Durless stuck his pen back in his pocket. "You don't think all cops are bad, do you?"

"Absolutely not," Evan said. "Look, I'm not a cop basher. Not at all."

"I didn't say you were."

A different kind of tension filled the room.

"I'm very sorry about your mom, Mr. Casher," Durless said. "I need you to come downtown with us to make a more detailed statement. And to talk to a sketch artist about this bald man."

The officer dispatched to retrieve the laptop stuck his head back in the door. "There's no laptop out here."

Evan blinked. "Those men might have taken it. Or the

bald guy." His voice started to rise. "I don't understand any of this!"

"Neither do I," said Durless. "Let's go downtown and talk. Get you to work with an artist. I want to get a sketch of the bald man out on the news fast."

"Okay."

"We'll go in a minute, all right? I want to make a couple of quick calls."

"All right."

Durless escorted Evan back outside. The local TV stations had arrived. More police. Neighbors, mostly stay-at-home moms, watching the activity, their children wide-eyed, the mothers keeping the kids all close.

He turned his back on the chaos. Tried his father again on his cell phone, no answer. He dialed Carrie's apartment. No answer. He dialed the dress shop where she worked.

"Maison Rouge, this is Jessica, how may I help you?" Chirpy and cheery.

"Is Carrie Lindstrom in? I know she's not working until two, but—"

"I'm sorry," the woman said. "Carrie called in and resigned this morning."

4

EVAN HAD NEVER FELT SO ALONE. A shiver took hold of him and he willed himself to calm down. He had to find Carrie and his father. He'd left messages for Carrie; surely she'd call back soon. Her quitting her job stunned him, and a sick twist roiled his gut. *She left you a note, she quit her job, maybe she doesn't want anything more to do with you.* He didn't want to consider the possibility. So he focused on finding his father. An itinerary, penned in his father's tight, precise handwriting, wasn't on the refrigerator in its usual spot, but he found it folded underneath the phone. The itinerary listed a number for the Blaisdell Hotel in Sydney.

"Mitchell Casher's room, please," Evan said to the clerk.

The night clerk—it was almost four in the morning Sydney time—was pleasant but firm. "I'm sorry, sir, but we don't have a guest by that name."

"Please check again. C-A-S-H-E-R. Maybe they registered him wrong, put Mitchell as the last name."

A pause. "I'm very sorry, sir, we don't have a guest here named Mitchell Casher."

"Thanks." Evan hung up. He looked at Durless. "He's not where he's supposed to be. I don't understand this at all."

Durless took the itinerary. "Let us find your dad, Evan. Let's get a statement and a description while your mind's fresh."

Fresh. *It's not likely I could ever forget,* he thought. Evan leaned back, staring up at the smoke-colored clouds through the back windshield of the police cruiser as it drove away from his house. His mind whirled in a strange, panicked dance of logic and emotion. He wondered where he would spend the night. A hotel. He would have to call his family's friends; but both his parents, though successful, tended to keep their circle of acquaintances small. He would have to make funeral arrangements. He wondered how long it would take for the police to do an autopsy. He wondered at which church he should have his mother's funeral. He wondered how it had been for his mother. If she had known. If she had suffered. If she had been afraid. That was the worst. Maybe the killers had come up behind her, the way that they had on Evan. He hoped she never knew, never suffered a pitch-black terror overpowering her heart.

He closed his eyes. Tried to reason past the shock and grief. Otherwise he thought he might just break down. He needed a plan of attack. First, find his dad. Contact his dad's local clients, see if they knew whom he worked for in Australia. Second, find Carrie. Third...he closed his eyes. Make sense of the horror as to who wanted his mother dead.

But they looked on your computer. What if this isn't about her? What if it's about you? The thought chilled him, infuriated him, broke his heart in one swoop.

The police car, driven by a patrol officer who had been a responder to the initial 911 call, with Durless sitting in the front seat, turned out of the Cashers' quiet, bungalow-remodeled neighborhood onto Shoal Creek Boulevard, a long thoroughfare that snaked through central and north Austin.

"They staged the scene," Evan said, half to himself.

"What's that?" Durless asked.

"Staged. I mean, the killers murdered my mother, then were hanging me to fake a suicide. So you, initially, would think that I killed her and then killed myself."

Durless said, "We would always look deeper than the surface."

"But it would be the first and most obvious theory."

Evan's cell phone rang in his pocket. He answered it.

"Evan?" It was Carrie.

"Carrie, I've been trying to find you—"

"Listen. You're in danger. Serious danger. You need to get your mother and come back to Houston. Immediately."

"My mother's dead, Carrie. She's dead."

"Evan. Oh, no. Where are you?"

"With the police."

"Good. That's good. Stay with them. Babe, I am so sorry. So sorry."

"What danger?" Her first words rang in his head. "What do you know about this?"

Suddenly a car passed them, cut them off hard, forcing the patrol car into a manicured front lawn, a blue Ford sedan skidding to a stop, Durless yelling as the brakes threw him forward into the windshield. Evan wasn't buckled in, and the brake jam slammed him into the back of the front seat. He dropped the cell phone.

He looked through the front windshield, aware of Durless

cussing, aware of the patrol cop opening the driver's-side door.

On the other side of the windshield, the bald-headed man got out of the blue Ford. Raised a shotgun. Aimed it right at Evan.

5

EVAN FUMBLED AT THE DOOR HANDLES. But he couldn't get out of the car; the locks were controlled from the front seat. The mesh and glass trapped him.

The young officer hit the pavement, crouching down as he swung open the door. Bald jumped onto the police car's hood, then roof, pivoted the shotgun in a blur, felled the policeman with two precise blows on the side of the head with the shotgun's butt stock. The officer crumpled. Bald jumped down from the hood and leveled the shotgun through the driver's door at Durless, who bled from a gash on his nose.

"That's him!" Evan yelled. "The guy from my house!" He heard Carrie's voice calling his name, sounding tinny on the dropped phone.

"Hands where I can see them," Bald ordered in a voice of total calm. "Don't be a hero."

Durless raised his hands.

"Unlock Evan from the back."

"Durless, he's the guy!"

Durless threw himself out his door, and Bald vaulted over the cruiser, skidding across the hood. Durless landed on his back on the grass, freeing his service revolver in a smooth yank, firing. He missed. Bald slammed both feet onto Durless's chest, a brutally efficient blow that purpled Durless's face. Bald kicked away the service revolver onto the well-trimmed green of the yard.

Bald leaned down, nailed Durless with two sharp blows in the jaw.

It had taken all of ten seconds.

Evan pivoted onto his back, kicked at the window. It was reinforced; the glass held.

"No need for that," Bald said. Evan scrambled off the seat onto the floor.

Bald leaned in the driver's side, studied the controls, and popped the back door locks.

Evan leaned forward and pushed the passenger-side door open. But Bald already had the driver's-side door open, the shotgun nestled against Evan's back. Evan froze.

"You're coming with me," Bald said.

"Please, what do you want?" Evan yelled.

"It's for your own safety. Come on."

Evan was suddenly full of a determination not to go with this man. Bald had dispatched a much younger cop and Durless with shocking ease. The police might have heard the attack over the radio. Or Carrie, she might be calling 911 in Houston and reporting the attack. Or a busybody on this street might be peeking out his window, dialing for help. The cops might arrive at any second. "No. I'm not going anywhere."

Bald said, "I didn't kill these cops when I could've, you think I'm gonna kill you?"

"Who are you?" Evan spoke louder. Carrie might hear this conversation. He had to give her information to help him. "What do you want with me?"

"I want cooperation. You're dead in a day unless you come with me. I'll tell you everything. I promise. But you've got to come with me."

"No! Tell me what this is about. How do you know my mother?"

"Later." Bald seized Evan by the hair and hauled him from the back of the car. Then Bald closed fingers around Evan's throat with a practiced hand, squeezing on the rope burn. Black circles widened in the air before Evan's eyes.

Bald jammed the shotgun's barrel up under Evan's jaw. "I don't have time to coddle you."

The barrel was cold against his throat and Evan nodded.

Bald lowered the shotgun, shoved Evan toward his Ford. "You drive. You disobey me, I shoot you in the leg. Cripple you for life."

A passing car slowed—a Lexus SUV, a mom driving, a teenage boy in the passenger seat, staring at the police car in the yard. Bald raised his hand—the one not holding the shotgun—in a friendly wave. The Lexus zoomed away.

"She'll call the cops. We got seconds," Bald said.

Evan got in the driver's seat, his hands shaking. Bald slid in next to him. He rested the shotgun so that it aimed at Evan's thigh.

Evan glimpsed the unconscious officers in the rearview. "They're hurt."

"They're lucky they're breathing," Bald said.

"Let me check them, be sure they're all right. Please."

"No way. Go," Bald said, jabbing Evan with the shotgun. Evan drove the Ford off the curb, roared down Shoal Creek Boulevard.

"Turn east onto 2222," Bald said.

Evan obeyed. "What do you want with me?"

"Listen carefully to me. I'm a good friend of your mom's and she asked me for help."

"I've never seen you before."

"You don't know me, but you also don't know about your parents."

"You know so much, tell me who killed my mother."

"A man named Jargo. Done on his orders."

"Why?" Evan shouted.

"I can explain everything, once we're settled. We're going to a safe house. Turn right here."

Evan veered south onto another major thoroughfare, Burnet Road. *Safe house*. A place where the hit men couldn't find you. Evan thought he'd stepped into a mobster movie. His guts clenched, his chest ached as if it were being wrung from muscle into string. "Did you see their faces, can you identify them?"

"I saw them. Both of them. I don't know if one is Jargo or if they just work for him." Bald glanced through the back of the window.

"Why would this Jargo kill my mother? Who is he?"

"The worst man you can imagine. At least the worst I can imagine, and my imagination is pretty twisted-sick."

"Who are you?"

"My name is Gabriel." Bald softened his tone. "If I wanted you dead, I would have shot you back at your house. I'm on your side, I'm the good guy. But you must do what I say. Exactly. Trust me."

Evan nodded but thought, *I don't know you and I don't trust you.*

"Do you know where your father is?" Gabriel asked.

"Sydney."

"No, where he really is."

Evan shook his head. "He's not in Sydney?"

"Jargo may already have grabbed your father. Where are the files?"

"Files? What are you talking about?" Evan's voice broke in fury and frustration. He pounded the steering wheel. "I don't have any stupid files! What do you mean, grabbed my dad? You mean he's been kidnapped?"

"Think, Evan. Calm down. Your mother had a set of electronic files that are very important. I need them." Gabriel's voice softened. "*We* need them, you and I. To stop Jargo. To get your dad back safe and sound."

"I don't know anything." Tears burned in his eyes. "I don't understand."

"Here's where you start trusting me. We need new wheels. That soccer mom's calling the cops, no doubt. Turn here."

Evan drove into a shopping plaza that had been caught in the last economic downturn, half the storefronts empty, the others held by an Episcopal thrift shop, a used-books store, a taqueria, and a mom-and-pop office supplies store. A center on its last legs until the inevitable midtown gentrification.

But full of people, Evan thought. He could get away. Yell for help. The parking lot wasn't too crowded, but if Gabriel let him park close to a store, he could run into the shops.

"Show me you're smart." Gabriel gave Evan a cool stare. "No running, no yelling for help. Because if you force my hand, someone gets hurt. I don't want it to be you."

"You said you're the good guy."

"Good is a relative concept in my line of work. Be still, shut up, and you'll be fine."

Evan surveyed the parking lane. Two women, laughing, getting into a station wagon, carrying grease-spotted bags from the taqueria. An elderly woman with a cane hobbled toward the office supplies shop. Two black-togged twenty-year-olds window-shopped at the resale store.

"Don't test me, Evan," Gabriel said. "None of these good folks need trouble today, do they?"

Evan shook his head.

"Park next to this beauty."

Evan stopped the Ford next to an old gray Chevrolet Malibu. A sticker on the back window announced that a child was an honor student at a local high school.

"I didn't plan on your mother getting killed and me rescuing you from the police in a car that could be identified. Pop the hood, like we're jumping the battery." Gabriel stepped out of the Ford, fiddled at the Malibu's lock with a slim finger of metal, opened it, dove under the steering column for a fast hot-wiring.

Open the door. Get out and run. He's bluffing.

Evan opened the door and Gabriel was back in the car, gun at Evan's ribs. "What part of *don't* do you not get? I told you not to force my hand. Shut the door."

Evan closed the door.

Gabriel ducked back into the Malibu and put his head back under the wheel.

Leave a sign, Evan thought. He stared down at the wheel. His fingers. He pressed his fingertips against the steering wheel. Then forefinger and middle finger against the ash-tray and the face of the radio. He didn't know what else to do; it was the only trace of himself he could think to leave.

Gabriel gestured him over with the gun. Evan got into the car, behind the steering wheel. The car smelled of a sun-spoiled milk shake, and the backseat held a stack of yellowing *Southern Living* magazines.

Gabriel returned to the Ford and quickly wiped it down. Evan's heart sank. He watched Gabriel smear a cloth along the steering wheel, the doorknobs, the windows. He was fast and efficient.

But not the radio.

Gabriel left the Ford's keys in the ignition. He slid into the Malibu's passenger seat next to Evan, tossed out the leftover milk shake. Evan headed out of the lot, slow and casual, and merged into a steady stream of Burnet Road traffic.

Gabriel fished a baseball cap from where it rested on the backseat. He shoved it down hard on Evan's head. He stuck a pair of woman's sunglasses that had rested on the middle seat onto Evan's nose. "Your face will be all over the news tonight." Gabriel's lips were a thin, pale line; Evan saw, for the first time, he'd left a rising bruise on Gabriel's jaw when he'd punched Gabriel at the house. "I'd prefer no one be able to recognize you."

"Please listen to me. Really listen to me. My mom doesn't have your files, whatever it is you or this Jargo guy wants. This is a huge mistake."

"Evan, in your life, nothing is as it seems," Gabriel said softly.

The statement made no sense, but then it did. His mother, packing up bags for an extended secret trip. Her demand he return home immediately without explanation. His father not where he was supposed to be. Carrie, gone this morning, quitting her job, calling him and warning him back to Houston. *You're in danger. Serious danger.* Carrie. How would she know his life had crumbled into dust since last night?

"Get onto the highway here. Head south to 290. We'll go the back way."

Evan eased onto MoPac, the major north-south highway on Austin's west side, pushed the speed up to sixty. Soon he switched to Highway 290, which fed into the rolling Hill Country west of Austin. Suburbia fell away and there was finally countryside, and Evan found the courage to speak. "You said you'd explain the situation to me."

Gabriel watched the traffic, watched behind them.

"You promised me." Evan pushed the accelerator up to seventy. He was sick of being pushed around; a sudden awful rage burned into his skin.

"When we get settled."

"No. Now. Or I crash this car." He knew he would do it. At least take the car off the road, let Gabriel's side be torn up by the wire fencing marking property lines, render the Malibu undrivable.

Gabriel frowned, as though deciding whether to play along. "Well, you might."

"I will."

"Your mother has certain files that would be devastating to certain people. Powerful people. Your mom wanted my help in getting out of the country in exchange for those files."

"Who? What people?"

"It's best you not know specifics."

"I don't have these files." Evan rocketed past a pickup truck. Every day they handed out tickets along this highway; here he was speeding like a maniac, and he couldn't get a police officer's attention. Traffic was light and the few cars he raced behind politely moved over to the right lane.

"I think you do," Gabriel said, "but you don't know it. Slow it down and drive steady if you want to know more." Gabriel nudged the shotgun into Evan's kidney.

"Tell me everything you know about my mom. Now." Evan floored the accelerator. "Tell me, or we're both dead."

The last thing Evan saw was the speedometer inching past ninety as Gabriel slammed his fist into Evan's head, sending it smashing into the driver's window, and the world went black.

6

---◦◉◦---

STEVEN JARGO WAS KILLING MAD. He hated failure.
It was a rare occurrence, but it haunted him longer than
most men, and he despised the sensation of panic that was
a misstep's inevitable partner in his world. Work went well
or badly; a middle ground was only a theory. Panic was
weakness, a lack of preparation and resolve, a poison for
his heart. The last time he had been afraid was when he'd
committed his first murder, but that terror soon dissipated,
like smoke caught in a breeze.

But now he was scared and running, his hands scraped
raw from sliding along the rooftop of the Casher house
when gunfire had erupted in the kitchen while he was
erasing the upstairs computer. He had dropped down to
the cool of the yard, crashing into Donna Casher's rose-
bushes, thorns ripping at his hands, and seen Dezz running
out the back door, heard the shriek of the bullets, and they
had both retreated to their car parked one street away. The
noise meant police, and the police always drove fastest in
wealthier areas.

Jargo had rented an empty apartment in Austin yesterday, under a different name and for cash, and perhaps it
wasn't safe but they had no other place to go.

"At least one of them." Dezz breathed hard as Jargo drove twenty miles over the limit to a quiet, faded neighborhood on the east side of town. "Shaved head. Old like you. Mexican-looking. That's all I saw." Dezz dabbed at his head, reassuring himself that a bullet hadn't tweaked his skull. He jabbed a caramel in his mouth, chewed fast. "Didn't recognize him. I saw a blue Ford on the street. License plate XXC, didn't see the rest. Texas plates."

"Did Evan take a bullet?"

"Unknown. The attacker fired in his direction. He was almost dead from the rope. You erased the files on her system?"

"She'd overwritten her system already. She wasn't leaving anything for us to find in case we showed up."

Dezz leaned against the car window. "That guy scared the piss out of me. I see him again, he's dead." Then Dezz— small but wiry, with a look in his eyes as if he always had a fever—said, "What do we do now, Dad?"

"We fight back." Jargo parked at the condo, still watching the rearview to be sure they hadn't been followed.

"Evan didn't see us."

"But he had the files on his computer," Jargo said. "He knows."

They hurried upstairs and Jargo made two phone calls. In the first he gave no greeting, just brief directions on how to drive to the apartment, heard a confirmation, then hung up. Then he called a woman who used the code name Galadriel. He employed a group of computer experts on his payroll, and he called them his elves for the magic they could work against servers and databases and codes. Galadriel— the name came from Tolkien's queen of the elves—was an ex-CIA computer expert. Jargo paid her ten times what the government had.

He fed Galadriel Dezz's description of the attacker and the blue Ford's plates, asked her to find a match in their databases. She said she'd call him back.

Jargo put antibacterial lotion on his scored hands and stood at the window, watching two young mothers walk in the sun, carrying their babies, indulging in idle gossip. Austin embraced this beautiful spring day, a day for watching pretty moms lift their faces to the sun, not a day for death and pain and everything in his world unraveling. He studied the street. No cars parked with occupants. Foot traffic heading to a local small grocery. He watched to see if anyone watched him.

He would have to call London in a moment. He had been lied to, and he wasn't happy. Then he would make the most difficult decision of his life.

"The files are gone," Dezz said. "If Evan's alive, he can't hurt us."

"If Evan had them on his computer, I assume he saw them," Jargo said. "He can name names. It's not a risk I'm willing to take."

Dezz sat on the couch in the condo, turning over his closed Game Boy in his hands. Not playing it. Three more caramels wadded in his cheek. Jargo saw Dezz was angry and nervous, the kill interrupted before it was done. Dezz would vent all that pent-up fury on the next weak person he encountered.

He sat next to Dezz. "Calm down. We were right to run. It was an ambush."

"I'm wondering who let Mr. Shotgun know we were there." Dezz slid the blob of caramel from one side of his mouth to the other.

Jargo went to the kitchen, poured himself a glass of water.

Evan resembled his mother, and that had made trying to kill him harder. Jargo thought about Donna Casher's once-lovely face, how he shouldn't have left her alone with Dezz for two minutes while he searched her computer, how he had said *I'm sorry* to her after she was dead. Dezz needed more self-control.

"The suitcases make me believe his mother told him they had to run. The files being on his computer are the why they had to run. She had to light a fire under him, get him home fast. You should have taken his laptop."

Dezz opened up the Game Boy, twiddled the controls. Jargo let him, although he found the *ping-ping* noise of the game annoying. The electronic opiate, the cheek full of candy, calmed the young man. "Sorry. It meant getting shot. It doesn't matter, the files are gone."

"Evan talks to the police," Jargo said, "and we're mortally wounded."

"He doesn't have proof. He didn't see our faces. They'll think it's a robbery interrupted."

The radio, tuned to local news, began a story about two police officers attacked and a witness in a morning homicide abducted from their custody. Dezz folded the Game Boy shut. The reporter said two officers were beaten and injured and gave a description of Evan Casher and a bald-headed assailant.

Jargo drummed a finger against his glass. "Evan's alive and our friend let him speak to the police before snatching him back. I wonder why."

Dezz unwrapped another caramel.

Jargo slapped the candy from his hand. "My theory is Donna knew she was in danger, and she hired protection. That's who attacked us." He gave Dezz a hard stare. "You're sure she didn't spot you trailing her?"

"No way. I was extremely careful."

"I told you not to underestimate her."

"I didn't. But if this guy's just hired muscle, why does he grab Evan back? The job's dead. No need for him to risk his neck."

Jargo frowned. "That's a very good and a rather unsettling question, Dezz. Clearly he thinks Evan has something he wants."

Dezz blinked. "So what do we tell Mitchell about his wife? Or do you just kill him and not bother with explanations?"

"We tell him that we were too late to save her. That a hired gun killed her, kidnapped his boy. Mitchell will be devastated—easy to manipulate."

Dezz shrugged. "Fine. Next step?"

"Consider who Donna might ask for help. That's the kidnapper. Find him, we find Evan, tell him we can take him straight to his father. That's the shortest distance between two points."

A knock on the door. Three fast raps, then two slow. Dezz went to the door, his gun at the ready.

The pattern repeated itself, then a voice said, "Girl Scout cookies."

Dezz opened the door. Broke into a smile. "Hey, Girl Scout."

Carrie Lindstrom walked in, her face tired, her dark hair gathered into a ponytail, wearing jeans and an untucked T-shirt. She looked around the room. "Where's Evan?"

Jargo sat her down, told her what had happened, described Bald based on the news report and Dezz's fleeting glance. "You recognize the rescuer?"

"No. Evan doesn't know anyone who fits that description, at least in Houston."

Jargo gave her a hard stare. "Carrie. You were supposed

to find those files if Evan had them. They were on his computer. I saw them myself. You didn't do your job."

"I swear...they weren't there."

He liked the shock and fear in her eyes. "When did you last look for them?"

"Last night. I went to his place, we watched a movie, drank wine. I asked him if I could check my e-mail. He said yes. I looked, there were no new files on his system. I swear."

"You spent the night with him?"

"Yes."

"Was he any good?" Dezz asked. Amusement in his voice.

"Shut up, Dezz," she said.

Jargo said, "So how did he get away from you in Houston?"

"I went to go get us breakfast. I stopped by my place and I got caught in bad traffic coming back. When I got back to his house, he was gone. He left a message with my voice mail that he'd had an emergency, he'd gone home."

"I accessed your voice mail this morning. Heard his message to you."

Carrie's jaw trembled. "You accessed my messages. You don't trust me to report to you."

"Carrie. I heard nothing from you this morning. For almost two hours. If I hadn't tapped your voice mail, I wouldn't have known Evan was heading to Austin and Donna might be running. It's good I did, because otherwise we wouldn't have known. Her street's hard for surveillance and she apparently hired muscle to help her run. You cost me an hour of time today that I needed by not reporting his movements to me."

"I didn't check my messages. I'm sorry. I—"

"The files I found were placed on Evan's system this morning," Jargo said. "So I believe you. Lucky for you."

"You said you would get Evan and his mom to safety," Carrie said.

"You're losing your perspective," Dezz said. "Sleeping with him wasn't a good idea."

"Don't be a jerk." She turned to Jargo. "Where is he?"

"Kidnapped."

"Did you kill his mother?" Her voice was thin.

"No. She was dead when we arrived. Evan came in and we subdued him and searched his laptop. Found the files and erased them. But then we were attacked, and I assume it was Donna's killer, returning to the scene for some reason." Jargo watched her face, seeing if she bought the lie.

She crossed her arms. "Who would have taken him?"

"Anyone who knew his mother had the files. She must have tried to cut a deal for them with the wrong people."

"Evan doesn't know anything," she said.

"I think he fooled you. His mother sent him those files this morning, he saw them, he knows you're not really his sweet lover girl." Jargo fought down the urge to hit her, to ruin that porcelain-perfect face, to shove her right through that glass window. "He ditched you and ran, and you let him, because you're dumb, Carrie."

She opened her mouth, as if to speak, then closed it.

"Carrie. One chance. Are you telling me everything you know?" Jargo asked.

"Yes."

"Did you call him this morning?" Asking as if he already knew.

"No," she said. "Do we go hunting for him or not?"

Jargo watched her. Decided what to say. "Yes. Because

the other possibility is that it's the CIA who grabbed Evan. They have the most to lose. They had every reason to kill his mom." He let the words sink in. "Just like they killed your parents, Carrie."

Carrie's poker face didn't change. "We have to get Evan back."

"Tall order," Dezz said. "If the CIA has him, we'll never find him."

"The more worrisome angle is the Agency killed Donna," Jargo said. "And then the gentleman who grabbed Evan had another agenda entirely. Then we're fighting on two fronts."

Carrie opened her mouth, then shut it.

"You're worried about him," Dezz said.

"In the way you worry about a dog that's gotten lost," Carrie said. "A neighbor's dog, not yours."

"We'll see if Galadriel can get a trace on the bald man or Evan. See if they surface anywhere."

"If the CIA has the files, then we need to run," she said.

Dezz grabbed her by the throat, gave a cruel squeeze with his fingers that worked the flesh around the carotid and the jugular like dough. "If you'd done your job and kept him in Houston, this wouldn't have happened."

"Let her go, Dezz," Jargo said.

Dezz released her and licked his lips. "Don't worry, Carrie. All is forgiven."

Jargo's cell phone rang. He went into the other room to answer it, shut the door behind him.

Carrie sat huddled on the couch.

Dezz leaned down and massaged the feeling back into Carrie's neck. "I'm watching you, sunshine. You messed up."

She slapped his hand away. "That's not necessary."

"He got under your skin, didn't he?" Dezz said. "I don't get it. He's not better-looking than I am. I'm gainfully employed. I share my candy. Granted, I was never an Oscar nominee, but that's just a piece of paper."

"He was an assignment." Carrie stood and walked to the kitchen bar and poured herself a glass of water.

"You enjoyed playing house," Dezz said. "But playtime's over. If he's seen those files, then he's a dead man, and you and I both know it."

"Not if he's made to understand. If I can talk to him."

"Make him into you," Dezz said. "The amazing avengers of murdered parents. It could be a comic book."

"I can turn him to help us. I can."

"I hope so," Dezz said. "Because if you don't, I'll kill him."

7

CARRIE THOUGHT, *My short, sweet life is over.*

She left Dezz playing his Game Boy and went into Jargo's bedroom. He was on the phone, talking to his elves, the technical experts who worked for him. They were masters at locating information, rooting into private databases, uncovering crucial nuggets to help Jargo find what he wanted. The Ford's plates were a dead end, stolen from a car in Dallas between midnight and 6:00 A.M. this morning. But the elves now tiptoed into the Casher phone records, credit card accounts, and more, searching for a pointer to Evan Casher's savior.

Behind a closed door in the bathroom, Carrie washed and then studied her dripping face in the mirror. No pictures of her as Carrie Lindstrom existed, except for her forged passport and driver's license, and a photo that Evan had snapped before she could stop him as they drank on an unusually warm New Year's Day at a beachside bar in Galveston. That girl with the beer in her hand would soon be dead. When the elves found Evan, their next job would be to create a new persona for her. She liked the name Carrie—it was her own—but since she had used it, Jargo would make her use another one.

It had been eighty-nine days since she wormed her way into Evan's life. Jargo's instructions were simple and clear: *Go to Houston and get close to a man named Evan Casher. I want to know what films he's planning to make. That's all.*

Couldn't I just break in and search through his files, his computer?

No. Get close to him. If it takes a while, it takes a while. I have my reasons.

Who is he, Jargo?

He's just a project, Carrie.

So she got a hotel room near the Galleria, on the edge of Houston's heart. Jargo gave her forged ID in the name of Carrie Lindstrom, and she started following Evan, mapping his world.

She made her approach at his favorite coffee shop, a quiet nonchain joint off Shepherd called Joe's Java; the first week she kept him under surveillance, he went there four times. That second week she appeared at Joe's twice, once getting her coffee to go in case he did, too; the next day arriving an hour before he did, sitting at the opposite end of the café, reading a thick paperback on the history of film that she had studied so she could draw him into conversation. He preferred to sit close to the electrical outlets where he could plug in his laptop. She never saw him with a camera, only frowning over the laptop, listening to headphones; she assumed he was editing a film and having problems.

Carrie watched him. His life was dull; he spent most of his time working, attending movies, or at his house. He was four months older than she was. His hair was blondish brown, a bit too long and shaggy for its cut, and he had the unconscious habit of dragging a hand through it when he was deep in thought. He wore a small hoop earring in his left ear but no other jewelry. He was handsome but seemed unaware of it. She watched two other women check him out at the coffee shop, one giving him a boldly appraising once-over as she walked by, and Evan, lost in his work, hand snagged in his hair, never noticed. He didn't shave every day if he didn't have to, and he was on the verge of getting too old for his wardrobe, which seemed to consist of worn jeans and funky old shirts and high-top sneakers or sandals. He watched the smokers standing outside the cafe, puffing, and she decided he must have given up cigarettes once. She was careful to spend most of her time reading her book, not watching him, not being too obvious. It would work better, much better, if he made the first move.

"You're reading Hamblin? That's not a good survey," he said to her. She sat at a marble-topped table near the counter, and he was in line for another latte.

Carrie counted in her head to five, then looked up at him. "You're right. Callaway's book is better." She said this with confidence that he would agree with her. Two nights earlier, she'd followed him as he went alone into the River Oaks Theater, an art-house cinema near his home. Then she'd snuck into his backyard, disarmed his electronic alarm system with a code-breaker program on her PocketPC, eased open the lock of his door with a lockpick that had been her father's, surveyed his library of film books, spotting the Callaway as the most worn and treasured, cataloged what DVDs he owned, hunted for his weaknesses. But there were only two bottles of beer in the fridge, an unopened bottle of wine, no pot, no coke, no porn. The house was neat, but not compulsively so. His interest was his work, and his house reflected that simplicity of focus.

She did not touch his computer, his notebooks. That would come. She locked the door, reset the alarm, and left.

"Yeah, Callaway rocks. You studying film?" Evan said. The guy in front of him in the line stepped up a space but Evan, last in line, stayed put.

"No. It's just an interest."

"I'm a filmmaker," he said, trying hard not to make it sound like bragging or a pickup line.

"Really? Adult movies?" she asked innocently.

"Uh, no." He was next up to place his coffee order, and he did, turning his back on her, and she thought, *That didn't work.*

But he gave the barista his order and took the five steps back to her table. "I make documentaries. That's why I don't like Hamblin's book. He gives us short shrift."

"Really?" She gave a smile of polite interest.

"Yeah."

"Would I have seen one of your movies?"

He told her the titles and she raised her eyes when he mentioned *Ounce of Trouble.* "I saw it in Chicago," she said. "I liked it."

He smiled. "Thanks."

"I did. Bought a ticket, didn't even sneak in from another theater."

He laughed. "Oh, my pocketbook appreciates it."

"Are you making another movie now?"

"Yeah. It's called *Bluff.* About three different players on the pro poker circuit."

"So, are you in Houston to film?"

"No, I still live here."

"Why don't you move to Hollywood?"

"There's a difference?" he asked with a laugh.

She laughed, too. "Well, nice to meet you. Good luck

with your movie." She stood and headed to the counter to order a fresh latte.

"My treat," he said quickly. "If I may. I mean, you bought a ticket. It's only fair." So she smiled and let him buy her latte and she moved to sit close to him, wondering, *Why on earth could Jargo be interested in this guy?* And they talked for an hour about movies they liked and loathed, and she gave him her cell phone number.

He called the next day, they had dinner that night at a Thai place he loved; she was new to town so she couldn't suggest she had a favorite place to go. She suspected Evan was the kind of man who would simultaneously pity her loneliness and admire her guts in moving to a city where she knew no one. They talked baseball, books, movies, and avoided their personal lives. She told him she was thinking of graduate school in English and was living off a trust fund, keeping her situation intentionally vague. She tried to pay for the dinner; he slid the check to his side of the table and smiled. "But you bought a ticket."

She liked him. But over two more dates in the next five days, she hit a stone wall: he wouldn't talk about what Jargo cared about, his future movies.

She'd watched his two finished films on DVD before she'd come to Houston to lay her snares. He only talked about those movies when she asked. He never mentioned his Oscar nomination for *Ounce of Trouble*, which impressed her far more than the honor itself.

Their fourth date, she saw Dezz watching them in the restaurant. He sat alone at the bar at the small Italian eatery, drinking a glass of red wine, pretending to read the paper. Jargo watched her, through him. He left halfway through their meal.

"You're upset," Evan said, not thirty seconds after Dezz had walked past their table.

This would be a whole world easier if he were one of those men lost in himself. But Evan, when he wasn't immersed in his work, seemed to notice every small detail of her.

"No. I saw a man who reminded me of someone I once knew. An unpleasant memory."

"Then let's not dwell on it," he said.

Ten minutes later he asked her about her family. She decided to stick close to the truth. "They're dead."

"I'm sorry."

"Burglary. They were both shot. A year ago."

He went pale with shock. "Carrie, how terrible. I'm so sorry."

"Now you know," she said, "but I'd like to talk about something else."

"Sure." He glided the conversation back onto safe ground, smoothing out the awkwardness. She saw a real tenderness in his gaze toward her and she thought, *Oh, no, don't do that, you make me feel as though I'm using their deaths and I wasn't planning to tell you and I don't know why I did.* She was afraid that, having a storyteller's curiosity, he'd visit the *Chicago Tribune* website, search on her name, look for an account of the murders. And she'd had a different surname then; there would be no Carrie Lindstrom whose parents had died in a burglary. She had made a mistake, but if he never looked it up, then that was okay.

They went back to his house to watch a movie and drink wine. She knew she should sleep with him; it was time to seal the deal, insert herself deeper into his life. He didn't have a steady girl—there had been a woman last year, another filmmaker named Kathleen, who had dumped him for another guy and moved to New York. He had mentioned Kathleen only once, which she considered healthy. Evan seemed a little lonely but not needy; she could keep a closer eye on him for Jargo, for whatever odd reason. But she hesitated.

Jargo had ordered her to sleep with a man once before, six months ago; a high-level Colombian police official, married, in his late forties. But she didn't. Instead she let him pick her up in a Bogotá bar, went back to his hideaway apartment, kissed him, and slipped a knockout drug into his beer. He passed out kissing her. She undressed the official, to let him think they'd consummated their evening, and watched the man sleep. While he slept, Dezz broke into the man's home office. Two weeks later she read about a number of police officers who were on the drug cartel payrolls being arrested. She figured Dezz had stolen financial records or payoff lists. Jargo never asked if she hadn't slept with the official; he assumed she had, that she was willing to prostitute herself.

You never knew with Jargo on which side of the line between dark and light he would drop you.

But this. This she could not fake.

It'll be all right, she told herself. *He's nice and good-looking and you like him.* It would be easier, though, if she hated him, because it would only make her hate him more. She realized that with a shock as their lips met, his kisses tender and slow. She arched against him as he slid his hand over her breast, clutched his hair in her fingers.

"What's wrong?" he said.

"Nothing."

He leaned back. "You're not ready."

"You think too much." She kissed him hard again, willing

him to just not care, willing herself not to respond to his touch, his tongue. *He's just a project.*

He kissed her again but then broke it off. "Tell me what's wrong."

Oh, if I could. But I never, never will. "Nothing's wrong. Except that you haven't carried me off to bed yet."

The lie reassured him. He smiled and picked her up from the couch and they lay down on his bed and it was not like the police attaché in Colombia. She had thought, in the long, dark days of the past year, that she would never feel happiness again without pretense. But instead of being a terrible betrayal of her own self, the night with Evan broke her heart.

He's just a project, Carrie.

The next morning she called Jargo and told him that she and Evan were lovers. "I don't have any competition," she said in a flat voice. "He's giving me a lot of his time."

"Is he talking about his films?"

"No. He says if he talks too much about a movie, he's told the story, then, and he loses the passion for making it."

"Search his computer, his notebooks."

"He's not much of a note taker." She paused. "It would be helpful to know what exactly I'm looking for."

"Just find out what film projects he's considering. Sleep with him enough and he'll tell you. He's a man like any other. He likes to screw and talk about work. Men are boring that way," Jargo said. She tried to imagine Jargo performing either activity, and the picture would not come into focus.

She went back into Evan's bed and focused on him with the same energy he'd poured into her, feeling guilty and sick all at once.

"Why won't you tell me about your next project?" she

asked one afternoon after pulling him away from his video editing and into bed.

"I've got to get *Bluff* edited, it's a mess. I can't even think about the next film."

She ran a hand down his chest, his flat stomach. Nipped at his flesh below his navel with her fingertips. "No worries. I'm just interested in your ideas." She tapped his forehead, used the line that had become their tease between each other. "Don't worry. I'll buy a ticket."

And gave him the warmest smile she could conjure.

She could see in his face the decision to change a well-worn habit. He leaned back. "Well. A guy at PBS talked to me about doing a bio on Jacques Cousteau. I could get that on PBS or Discovery Channel in five seconds flat. Good for the pocketbook. But I'm not sure it's the right career move for me."

"So no idea, then."

She saw him decide to trust her, saw the smile creep across his face. "It's weird, China's Communist but they have millionaires in Hong Kong still. I think there might be a story worth doing."

"China. Too far away. I'd miss you."

He kissed her. "I'd miss you, too. You could come with me. Be my unpaid assistant."

"My dream job," she said. "So who's the lucky subject in China?" She thought this might be the seed of Jargo's interest. Evan had zeroed in on a high-ranker in Beijing who lined Jargo's pocket. But how would Jargo have known?

"There's a Hong Kong financier named Jameson Wong who might be an interesting character; he lost all his money in bad deals, and instead of rebuilding his business he's become a leading activist against the Communist government. Businessman turned campaigner for freedom."

She snuggled her face against his chest. Tomorrow she would betray his confidences, report his every word. China. This Jameson Wong guy. That was the interest point. "I'd buy a ticket. You're my brilliant boy."

"Unless I do the other project," he said. "But I think it's a dead idea."

She kept her face close to his chest. "What other one?"

"About an interesting murder case in London, about twenty-five years ago."

"Whose murder?"

"The guy was named Alexander Bast. He was kind of an über-funky cool guy, very much into the art scene, very much into sleeping with young starlets, famous for his parties. Like Wong, he lost it all. In a scandal about drugs at one of his clubs. Then someone put two bullets in him."

"I thought you preferred your subjects living."

"I do. Dead people don't talk well on camera," he said with a quiet laugh. "I thought about combining both stories. Compare and contrast two very different lives, find a common thread that gives an insight about success and failure." She heard his voice rise in excitement. "But it might not be commercial enough."

She raised her face toward his. "Don't worry about that. Make the movie you want to make."

"I know what I want to make right now." He kissed her, they made love again. He dozed and she got up from the bed and washed her face.

She made no mention to Jargo, in the days ahead, of Jameson Wong or Alexander Bast or Jacques Cousteau.

"He's focused entirely on editing his current movie," she

said the next week when she talked to Jargo. She had a cell phone that Evan didn't know about; she kept it hidden in a pocket under the driver's seat. She sat in the car, in the parking lot of a Krispy Kreme.

"Stay on him. If he commits to another film, I want to know immediately."

"All right."

"I've deposited another ten thousand in your account," Jargo said.

"Thank you."

"I wonder," Jargo said, "if you think Evan might ever consider working for me."

"No. He wouldn't. He wouldn't be good at it."

"It's an unbeatable cover. A rising-star documentary filmmaker. He can go anywhere, film about anything, and no one would doubt his credentials or his intentions."

"He's interested in the truth. That's his passion."

"And yet he's sleeping with you."

"Recruitment's not a good idea. Not now." She was afraid to argue further, afraid of what would happen if Jargo thought Evan was a danger to him.

"I want you to be prepared," Jargo said. "Because you may have to kill him."

She watched the line of cars slowly move through the doughnut store drive-through. The back of her eyes hurt. Jargo had never suggested such work to her before; mostly, before sliding into Evan's bed, she'd worked as a courier for Jargo, in Berlin, in New York, in Mexico City. Never a killer. The silence began to get dangerously long, he would get suspicious. "If you say so," she said. There was nothing else to say. "Then I should get distance. I don't want to be a suspect."

"No, you stay close. If it has to happen, you and he both

vanish. You don't stay around. You're both dead and gone, and we build you a new legend. I can probably use you more in Europe anyway."

"Very well," she said. He told her to have a good day and then he hung up. She filed her empty reports with Jargo, manufacturing innocuous lies about what Evan's next project might be, until Jargo had called her two days ago and said, "I want to know if Evan has any files on his computer that shouldn't be there."

"Be specific."

"Lists of names."

"All right."

An hour later she searched Evan's computer while he was out running errands. She called Jargo. "I found no files like that." Evan had scant data on his computer other than scripts, video footage, and basic programs.

"Check every twelve hours, if possible. If you find the files, delete them and destroy his hard drive. Then report back to me."

"What are these files?"

"That you don't need to know. Don't memorize the information or copy the files. Just delete them and make sure that hard drive can't be recovered."

"I understand." And she did. The files were what Jargo was truly worried about, probably files that connected back to Jameson Wong or the other potential film subjects.

But if Evan's hard drive was to be destroyed, she had a sinking, awful feeling that Evan was to be destroyed as well.

Carrie washed her face again. Evan was gone, stolen by a man who might be very, very bad, and soon Jargo's technical elves would find a trace of him and they would go get

Evan from the man who had taken him. The files had been sitting on his system this morning; she had left without looking for them, and if Jargo doubted her word, he would kill her. She had to win back Jargo's trust. Now.

Last night, Evan telling her that he loved her, seemed like a moment from a world that no longer existed, a pocket of time where there was no Jargo and no Dezz and no files and no fear or pretending. She wished he hadn't said it. She wanted to hit him, to push him away, to tell him, *Don't, don't, don't, you don't know anything, I can't have a life with you, I can't be normal ever again, it can't ever be, so just don't.*

She had to harden her heart now. She had to catch Evan.

SATURDAY

MARCH 12

8

EVAN OPENED HIS EYES.

He was lying on a bed. The cream-white sheets had been folded back; a thin cotton towel was spread behind his head. One of his arms was raised, bound to the bed's iron-railing headboard with a handcuff. The bedroom was high-end: hardwood floors, a rustic but expensive reddish finish on the walls, abstract art hung to precision above a stone fireplace. A sliver of soft sunlight pierced a crack in the silk drapes. The door was closed.

He had been seconds from wrecking the car when Gabriel had grabbed him and hammered him. His tongue wormed in his dry mouth. A heavy ache settled in along his jaw and neck for permanent residence. He smelled his own sour sweat.

Mom. I failed you. I'm so sorry. He swallowed down the panic and the grief, because it wasn't doing him any good.

He had to be calm. Think. Because everything had changed.

What had Gabriel said? *In your life, nothing is as it seems.*

Well, one thing was exactly as it seemed. He was completely screwed.

Evan tested the handcuff. Locked. He sat up, pushing

with his feet, wriggling his back against the headboard. A side table held a book—a recent thick bestseller about the history of baseball—and a lamp; no phone. A baby monitor stood on the far table.

He stared at the monitor. He couldn't act afraid with Gabriel. He had to show strength.

For his mom, because Gabriel knew the meat of the story as to why his mom had died. For his dad, wherever he was. For Carrie, however she was mixed up in this nightmare. She knew he was in danger—how? He had no idea.

So, what do you do now?

He needed a weapon. *Imagine the guy who killed Mom is here. What do you hurt him with? Look at everything with new eyes.* New eyes. It was advice he gave himself when he was setting up scenes to shoot. He could barely reach the side table. He managed to fingertip the knob and open the drawer. His hand searched the drawer as far as he could reach: empty. The book on the table wasn't heavy enough. The lamp. He couldn't reach it but he could reach the cord, where it snaked to a plug behind the bed. As silently as he could, keeping an eye on the baby monitor, trying to quiet the handcuff from rattling against the metal headboard, he tugged the lamp closer to him; the base was heavy, ornate, wrought-iron. But at the angle he was bound, he wouldn't be able to swing the lamp with enough force to cause serious hurt. He unplugged the cord, looped it neatly behind the table so it wouldn't catch or snag. Just in case he got a chance. Lamps could be thrown. He peered down the back of the bed, to the floor. Nothing else but miniature tumbleweeds of dust.

"Hello," he called to the monitor.

A minute later he heard the tread of feet on stairs. Then

the rasp of a key in a lock. The bedroom door opened; Gabriel stood in the doorway. A sleek black pistol holstered at his side.

"You okay?" Gabriel said.

"Yeah."

"Thanks for putting our lives at risk with your stupid stunt."

"Did we crash?"

"No, Evan. I know how to drive a car while seated in the passenger side. Standard training." Gabriel cleared his throat. "How you feeling now?"

"I'm fine." Evan tried to imagine driving from the passenger side to avoid a high-speed crash. It suggested an extraordinary level of calm under fire. "So where did you learn that driving trick?"

"A very special school," Gabriel said. "It's early Saturday morning. You slept through the night." A coldness frosted his gaze. "You and I can be of great help to each other, Evan."

"Really. Now you want to help me."

"I saved you, didn't I? If you had stayed out in the open, well, you'd be dead now. I don't believe even the police could protect you from Mr. Jargo." Gabriel leaned against the wall. "So, let's start afresh. I need you to tell me exactly what happened yesterday when you got to your parents' house."

"Why? You're not the police."

"No, I'm not, but I did save your life. I could have let you hang. I didn't."

"True," Evan said. But he watched Gabriel. The man looked as if he hadn't slept at all. Jumpy. Nervous. Like a man in need of a solid blast of bourbon. But there was nothing to be gained by silence, at least not now.

So Evan told him about his mother's urgent phone call, the drive to Austin, the attack in the kitchen. Gabriel asked no questions. When Evan was done, Gabriel brought a chair to the foot of the bed and sat down. Frowning, as if he was considering a plan of action and not caring for his options.

"I want to know who exactly you are," Evan said.

"I'll tell you who I am. And then I'll tell you who you are."

"I know who I am."

"Do you? I don't think so, Evan." Gabriel shook his head. "I'd call your childhood sheltered, but that would be a sick joke."

"I kept my promise to you. You keep yours."

Gabriel shrugged. "I own a private security firm. Your mother hired me to get you and her safely out of Austin, get you to your father. Clearly she slipped up and tipped her hand to the wrong people. I'm sorry I couldn't save her."

So he knows where Dad is.

"Go back to the attack. You were unconscious," Gabriel said. "For a few minutes, at least, between when they hit you and they strung you up."

"I don't know how long. Why does it matter?"

"Because the killers could have gotten the files I mentioned. Found them on your or your mother's computer."

"They wouldn't have been on my computer." But one of the men had accessed his laptop. He remembered now, the start-up chime, the sound of typing, telling Durless about it. "The killers, they typed on my laptop. Said something about…" He struggled to remember past the haze of trauma. "About 'all gone.' " He waited to see what else Gabriel would say.

"Your mother e-mailed you the files."

E-mailed. His mother had sent him those music files for

his soundtrack late the night before she called. But they were just music files; he'd listened to them on the way to Austin. Nothing unusual. She hadn't put anything weird in her e-mail to him. But he hadn't mentioned the e-mails to Gabriel in relating Friday morning's events; it hadn't seemed important compared to the horrors of yesterday. "My mom didn't e-mail me anything weird. And even if she did, the killers couldn't have gotten past the password."

So what did *all gone* mean?

"There are programs that can crack simple passwords in a matter of seconds." Gabriel leaned against the wall, studied Evan. "I don't have one. But I do have you."

"I don't have these files."

"Your mother told me that you did, Evan."

Evan shook his head. "These files . . . what are they?"

"The less you know, the better. That way I can let you go and you can forget you ever saw me and you can go have a nice new life." Gabriel crossed his arms. "I'm an extremely reasonable man. I want to give you a fair deal. You give me the files. I get you out of the country, provide you a new identity and access to a bank account in the Caymans, which your mother had me arrange. If you're careful, no one will ever find you."

"I'm just supposed to give up my life." Evan tried to keep the shock out of his voice.

"It's your call. You want to go back home, go ahead. But if I were you, I wouldn't. Home is death."

Evan chewed his lip. "I help you, then what about my dad?"

"If your father contacts me, I'll tell him where you are, and then finding you is his problem. My responsibility to your mother stops once you get on a plane."

"Please tell me where my dad is."

"I've no idea. Your mother knew how to get in touch with him, but I don't."

Evan let a beat pass. "I could give you what you want and you'd just kill me."

Gabriel reached in his pocket and tossed a passport on the bedspread. It bore the seal of South Africa. With his free hand, Evan opened it. A picture of him was inside—his original passport photo, the same as he had in his American passport. The name on the passport was Erik Thomas Petersen. Stamps colored the pages: entry into Great Britain a month ago, then entry into the United States two weeks ago. Evan shut the passport, dropped it back on the bed. "Very legitimate-looking."

"You need to slip into being Mr. Petersen very carefully. If I wanted you dead, you'd be dead. I'm giving you an escape hatch."

"I still don't understand how my mother could have gotten any dangerous computer files." And then he saw it. Not his mother. His father. The computer consultant. His father must have found files, in working for a client, that were dangerous.

"All you have to do is give me your password." Gabriel opened the bedroom door, wheeled in a cart, one that might be used as extra serving space for food during a brunch or a party. Evan's laptop lay on the table. Gabriel parked it close to Evan, keeping the cart between the two of them. A crack straddled the screen but the laptop was cabled to a small monitor. The system appeared to be operating normally. The password screen displayed, awaiting the magic word.

That was why Gabriel had taken the enormous risk of returning for Evan, ambushing the police car, kidnapping him. He couldn't get past the laptop's gates.

"It's on here," Gabriel said. "Your mother placed a copy on your system before she died. E-mailed it to you. She told me. She did it to ensure if she were killed, another copy of the files would be accessible to me. It was part of the deal I made with her. I couldn't risk her being caught and me not getting the files. It guaranteed I would still take care of you if she were killed." He was so matter-of-fact that Evan wanted to hit him.

Gabriel leaned closer to him. "What's your system password?"

"You're supposed to get me out of the country. So your job, technically, isn't done until you deliver. I'll tell you the password when you get me to my father."

"I've told you what the deal is, son. That's it. No room for negotiation." Gabriel retreated to the bed's edge and aimed his pistol at Evan's head. "I don't want to hurt you. Open the system."

Evan pushed the laptop away. "Contact my dad. If he tells me to give you my password, I will."

"Wax out of ears, son. I can't get in touch with him."

"If you were supposed to get me and my mom to safety, that means getting us to where my dad could find us. You must have a way to reach him."

"Your mother knew. I didn't."

"I don't believe you, Mr. Gabriel. No password."

"You don't give this to me, you spend the rest of your brief life handcuffed to that bed. Dying of thirst. Of starvation."

Evan waited, let the silence grow heavy. "You know who killed her. This Jargo guy. Who he is."

"Yes."

"Tell me about him and I'll help you. But look at it from

my side. You're asking me to run away from my life. Do nothing about my mother's murder. Simply hope I can ever find my father again. I can't just walk away not knowing the truth." He didn't believe Gabriel, anyway. His father had been impossible to find yesterday, but the police would have found him by now, wherever he was in Sydney.

"You're safer not knowing."

"I don't care about safer at the moment."

"You're stubborn." Gabriel lowered the gun, averted his eyes from Evan's.

"I know you risked a lot to save me from Jargo. I know. Thank you. I can hardly run, though, and be successful at it if I don't know who's after me. So I'll trade you the password for information on Jargo. Deal?"

After a long ten seconds, Gabriel nodded. "All right."

"Tell me about Jargo."

"He's . . . an information broker. A freelance spy."

"A spy. You're telling me my mother was killed by a spy."

"A freelance spy," Gabriel corrected.

"Spies work for governments."

"Not Jargo. He buys and sells data to whoever pays. Companies. Governments. Other spies. Highly dangerous." Gabriel licked his lips. "I suspect it's CIA data that Jargo wants."

Evan frowned. "You're suggesting, with a straight face, that my mom stole files from the CIA. That's impossible."

"Or your father stole the files, and he gave them to your mother. And I didn't say the files belonged to the CIA. The CIA simply might want the information, the same as Jargo does." Gabriel looked as if admitting this possibility was causing him a heart attack. His face reddened with anger.

"The CIA." It was insane. "How would my mother be involved with this Jargo?"

"I believe she worked for Jargo."

"My mother worked for a freelance spy," Evan repeated. "It can't be. You're mistaken."

"A travel photographer. She can go anywhere, with her camera, and not raise suspicion. You live in a nice house, Evan. Your parents had money. You think freelance shutterbugs make that much money?"

"This can't be true."

"She's dead and you're shackled to a bed. How wrong am I?"

Evan decided to play along with the man's fantasy. "So did my mother steal these files from Jargo, or from someone else?"

"Listen. You wanted to know about Jargo, I told you. He's a freelancer. People need information stolen or someone dead, and the job needs to be off the books, he's the man. The files are about Jargo's business. So he wants them back. So does the CIA, I imagine, because they'd like to know what he knows. There. You know more about Jargo than any person currently alive. Open the system."

"Can't unless you unlock me." He rattled the handcuff.

"No. Type."

"Where am I gonna go, Gabriel? You've got a gun on me. You have to unlock me sooner or later, if you're taking me out of the country. Handcuffs set off metal detectors."

"Not yet. Type it one-handed." He jabbed the gun into Evan's cheek. "I've waited years for this, Evan, I'm not waiting one more second."

Evan typed the password.

9

———◆◆◆———

I**T'S EMPTY**," E**VAN SAID**.

After it had digested the password, the hard drive's icon appeared on the screen. He searched through the system. Other than basic files, the drive was cleaned out. His video footage, his installed software programs, all were gone. The system appeared to have reverted to a factory default level. He opened the electronic trash can—empty. "Everything's gone."

All gone, the voice in the kitchen had said while the gun had dug into the back of his head.

"No." Gabriel put the gun down, grabbed Evan's throat, pushed him up against the headboard of the bed. "No, no, no. He wouldn't have had time."

"I don't know how long I was unconscious."

"This can't be. I have to have those files." Gabriel's voice rose. "They erased them." He bent back over the computer.

Evan squirmed away from him. Toward the lamp. *He may not get this close to you again. Make him think you want to help him.* "A recovery program might restore the data."

Gabriel didn't answer, tapped at the keyboard, searching for files. He looked at the empty screen as if it were the rest of his life. He kept the gun at his side, loosely aimed toward the bed. Evan crouched against the headboard, his left hand still handcuffed. The lamp was close to his right, the unplugged cord still in a neat loop on the floor.

Evan snatched the wrought-iron lamp with his free hand. It was a heavy monster, but he lifted and swung it in one awkward sweep.

The lamp's base smashed into Gabriel's arm. He fell forward, and Evan pinned Gabriel with a leg over his waist. Evan brought the lamp down into Gabriel's face. Blood welled, the base's edge cutting Gabriel in the mouth, in the chin. He howled in fury.

Evan aimed the lamp downward again, but Gabriel deflected it with his arm, threw a fist, connected with Evan's jaw. Evan dropped the lamp, snaked his arm around Gabriel's neck, wrapped both legs around Gabriel's waist. His left arm, shackled to the bed, twisted as if it would break as Gabriel struggled.

The gun. Gabriel had the gun. Where was it?

"Let go!" Gabriel said.

"I'll bite it off if you're not still." Evan closed his mouth around Gabriel's left ear. Bit down. Gabriel screamed.

"Don't," Gabriel gasped. Evan bit down again, let his teeth grind. Blood seeped into his mouth.

"Stop!" Gabriel yelled, and went still.

Evan saw the gun. Just beyond the reach of both of them, twisted in the white sheets where they rucked the bedcovers in their fight. He couldn't reach it, but if he eased up on Gabriel, the older man could. Gabriel saw it, too; his muscles strained with sudden resolve, trying to break free.

Evan bit down on the ear again and jabbed his fingers into Gabriel's eyes. Gabriel shrieked in pain. He twisted to fend Evan off, but Evan's legs kept him locked in place. Gabriel squirmed toward the gun, pulling Evan's body with him. Evan's wrist wrenched in the cuff.

He'll sacrifice the ear to get that gun, Evan thought. *Bite it off.* He couldn't.

But instead Gabriel grabbed the lamp's cord, dragged the lamp to him. He seized the lamp's body, swung it backward at Evan, the base striking Evan on top of the head, and Evan, dizzy with pain, let go of the ear. A sliver of skin stayed behind in his mouth.

Gabriel released the lamp and lurched forward. Caught the gun's barrel with his fingertips. Evan kept Gabriel's other arm pinned with his leg, pivoted—his arm twisting as if it were a centimeter away from breaking—and clutched the gun's handle as Gabriel pulled it forward. Evan wrenched the gun free and jabbed the barrel against Gabriel's temple.

Gabriel froze.

"Where's the key?"

"Downstairs. In the kitchen. You ingrate, you tore my ear off."

"No, you still got an ear."

"Listen, new deal," Gabriel said. "We'll work together to get Jargo. We'll—"

"No," Evan clubbed the gun into Gabriel's temple. Once. Twice. Three times, four. The fifth time Gabriel went limp, his temple cut and bruised. Evan jabbed the gun against Gabriel's head and waited. Counted to one hundred. Gabriel was out.

Holding his breath, Evan put down the gun. Gabriel didn't move. He jabbed his hand into Gabriel's left pants pocket, fumbled across coins, fingered the shape of keys.

"Liar," he said to the unconscious Gabriel. He pulled out a ring that held a small key and a larger key for the bedroom door. Evan kicked the man away from him, worked the small key into the handcuff lock.

The cuff sprang open. Evan rolled off the bed, his arm afire with pain. He held it close to him, unsure if it was broken or dislocated. No. Broken would be serious agony. He was sore but unhurt. He dragged Gabriel to the headboard, snicked the cuff over his wrist. Checked Gabriel's pulse in the throat. A steady beat ticked beneath his fingertips.

Evan trained the gun, with shaking hands, on the door. Waited. Steadied himself to shoot if anyone charged to Gabriel's rescue. Told himself he could do it, he had to do it. He knew how to shoot, his father had taught him when he was a teenager, but he had not fired a gun in five years. And never at a living human being.

A minute passed. Another. No sound in the house.

He noticed a small card on the bed, next to the South African passport. Forced out from Gabriel's shirt or pants in the fight. It was an ID card, government issue, worn with age and fingering. Gabriel looked fifteen years younger.

Joaquin Montoya Gabriel. Central Intelligence Agency.

The crazy freak was telling the truth. Or a partial truth. But if he was CIA, why was he operating alone?

Deep breath. He slipped the South African passport and Gabriel's ID into his back pocket. Evan went out the bedroom door, then stopped in the darkened hallway. *Be cool, be cool for your mom.* His arm and hand ached, his head throbbed, and now, the fighting done for a moment, in the darkened house, the fear rushed back into his chest.

A dim light shone from the open area downstairs; Evan was on a second floor of what appeared to be a spacious house. Thick pile carpet covered the hallway; more high-end art on the walls. The air conditioner purred a blanket of noise. From below, he heard the thin whisper of the television, its volume inched low.

He crouched, the gun out in front of him, listening.

He fortified himself with two deep breaths and crept down the stairs. *What do you do next? Keep fighting. That's the choice you made.*

But now he had nothing to bargain with to save his life. Jargo—if he was one of the men at the house—had stolen or destroyed the data. The files—if they had ever existed—were gone.

Evan reached the last stair when he thought, *You should have gagged Gabriel. He'll wake up and shout for help while you're sneaking up on any buddies downstairs.*

But he had gone too far to turn back, knowing in his heart that he wouldn't hesitate now; he could shoot anyone who tried to stop him, and he hoped he could remember to aim at legs. Unless the other guy had a gun, and then he would aim for the chest. Chests were big, he could hit a chest. Remember to take a second to aim, squeeze, prepare for the kick. If he had a second. No practice target had ever shot back at him.

Evan entered the den, gun leveled to fire. A widescreen TV stood in the corner next to an ornate stone fireplace. A commercial announced the latest pharmaceutical that you couldn't live without, as long as you risked at least ten side effects. Then the CNN theme played and the anchor started a story about a bombing in Israel.

He moved along the wall, peered into an elaborate kitchen. Empty. A lunch sat on the counter: a ham sandwich, a glass of ice water, a pile of potato chips, a Snickers bar. Lunch for himself, probably, if he'd cooperated with Gabriel.

He checked the back of the house, stopping at a marble-topped bureau with a smattering of family photos. Gabriel posed with two girls young enough to be his grandkids.

No one around. The only sounds were the air conditioner and CNN beginning a story about a bizarre homicide and kidnapping in Texas.

Evan ran back to the den and saw his face was on the TV. His Texas driver's license photo, not a bad one and true to how he looked: shaggy blond hair, high cheekbones, hazel eyes, thin mouth, the single small hoop of earring. The crawl under his face read MISSING FILMMAKER. The news announcer said, "Police investigators are still searching for Evan Casher, the Oscar-nominated documentary filmmaker, after his mother was strangled to death in her Austin, Texas, home, and an armed gunman kidnapped Casher from a police cruiser, assaulting two officers.

"Casher, the director of two acclaimed documentaries, first gained attention with *Ounce of Trouble,* a biting exposé of a corrupt police officer who framed a former drug dealer. Joining me is FBI special agent Roberto Sanchez."

Roberto Sanchez looked like a politician: perfect haircut, immaculate suit, an expression that said, *I am the most competent person on earth.* The newscaster went for the bone: "Agent Sanchez, is it possible that whoever kidnapped Evan Casher was responsible for Donna Casher's death? I mean, Mr. Casher was the only witness and then he's grabbed, right from the police."

"We're not prepared to speculate as to motives, but we are concerned about Mr. Casher's safety."

"Is there any possibility that this wasn't an abduction, per se, but that Evan Casher was taken from the police because he was a suspect in his mother's murder?" the anchor pressed.

"No, he's not a suspect. Obviously, he's a person of interest to us because he found his mother's body, and we have not had a chance to fully talk with him, but we have no reason to believe that he was involved. We would like to talk to Mr. Casher's father, Mitchell Casher, but we have not been able to locate him. We believe he was in Australia this week, but I can't share further details."

A picture of Mitchell appeared next to Evan's on the split screen. His father, missing.

"Why has the FBI taken over the investigation?" the anchor asked.

"We have resources not available to the Austin police," Sanchez said. "They asked for our assistance."

"Any idea of a motive as to the murder?"

"None at this time."

"We have also police sketches of the man who allegedly assaulted the two Austin officers and took Evan Casher," the newscaster said, and the display shifted from Evan and Mitchell Casher to a penciled drawing of Gabriel.

"Any leads on this man?" the anchor asked.

"No, none yet."

"But the Austin police found the car he used to kidnap Evan Casher, correct? A report leaked from the Austin police that the blue Ford sedan matching the description of the kidnapper's car was found in a nearby parking lot where another car had been stolen. Evan Casher's fingerprints are reportedly on the radio in the kidnapper's car. If he's selecting music, he hasn't been kidnapped, has he?" Now the anchor was trying to rewrite the news, spice it with innuendo.

Sanchez shook his head and looked dour. "We cannot

comment on leaks. Of course, if anyone has details on this case, we'd like for them to contact the FBI." The license plate of the stolen car and an FBI phone number popped up on the feed below the photo of Evan.

"In case Evan Casher has been kidnapped, what would you say to the kidnappers?" the newscaster asked.

"Well, as we would in any situation, we'd ask the kidnappers to release Mr. Casher unharmed and to contact us with any demands, or if Mr. Casher is able to contact us directly, all we want to do is to help him."

"Thank you, FBI special agent Roberto Sanchez," the newscaster said. "Our correspondent, Amelia Crosby, spoke with the former drug dealer who was the focus of Evan Casher's Oscar-nominated film."

The camera shifted to a young black man, around thirty, looking uncomfortable in a suit and tie. The subtitle read JAMES "SHADEY" SHORES.

"Mr. Shores, you've known Evan Casher ever since he did a film about how you were unjustly accused and railroaded by a corrupt narcotics investigator. What do you think could be behind Evan Casher's bizarre disappearance?"

"Oh, no," Evan said.

"Listen, first of all, that other guy—your anchor, with that freeze-dried hair—suggesting that Evan Casher could be involved in his mama's death, that is straight-out *bleeeeeep.*" The censor swooped in for the last word.

"What motive could anyone have to hurt Mr. Casher or his family?" the reporter's voice asked. "He upset a lot of people in Houston law enforcement with his documentary about you."

"No, he pointed out one real bad apple, but it's not like he indicted the whole criminal system or nothing."

"Do you have any theories on what might have led to his disappearance?"

"Well, I would think whoever killed his mama didn't want him talking about what he saw. My worry is that the Austin police done let Evan down, letting him get kidnapped. I think they ought to be looking hard at those officers, and how they let a *bleeeeep* take Evan, because a lot of police don't like to have dirty laundry aired, even when it ain't their department, and..."

The reporter started trying to talk over Shadey, to no avail.

"...that's all I'm saying is, the police got to show they're serious about finding Evan."

"Evan Casher saved your life, didn't he, Mr. Shores?"

"Look, Evan succeeds because he can be the biggest pain in the *bleeep* in the room. Evan Casher got a lot of fame and money out of my misfortune. He didn't share none of them movie proceeds with me. He made promises to me, I was gonna be famous, I could get a music career out of this movie, and that's all *bleeep*. I'm still working as a security guard." Shadey shook his head at the injustice of it all.

"You ingrate," Evan said. Using his family's tragedy as a platform for his complaining.

"He's making a new movie about professional poker, and he was supposed to introduce me to people who could help me get into that line of work, and he never did, so I'm thinking he got involved with illegal poker money, he got himself in trouble."

Shadey started to air his next grudge and the reporter briskly thanked him and shifted to the New York studio to introduce Kathleen Torrance as another prominent young documentary filmmaker. She was also Evan's ex-girlfriend from his student days at Rice, but the reporter didn't note that particular relationship, simply saying "a colleague in film." Their affair had cooled when she'd moved to New York, ended when she'd acquired another filmmaker as a boyfriend. He had not talked to her in six months, after exchanging friendly but awkward hellos at a Los Angeles film festival.

"Ms. Torrance, you know Evan Casher well," the reporter began.

"Yes." Kathleen nodded. "Very well. He's one of the top ten young documentary filmmakers in America."

"What do you think has happened?"

"Well, I have no idea. I don't think this could be related to Evan's work, as your previous guest suggested, because despite what people think, documentary filmmakers aren't really investigative journalists. Evan's films have focused on individuals in extraordinary circumstances—not on political or hot-button issues." Prompted by the reporter's questions, Kathleen gave brief descriptions of Evan's films and works. "I just hope that if whoever has taken Evan can hear me, they will let him go. He's a great guy, and I can't imagine him being involved with anything that is illicit or harmful to anyone."

The reporter thanked Kathleen and went back to the anchor, and the coverage shifted to a murder-suicide at a New Hampshire truck stop.

Evan stared at the screen. His life was being dissected on national television. His father was missing. The FBI wanted to talk to him. He hurried to the phone, picked it up, started to dial.

Then put it back down on the cradle.

Gabriel was a CIA operative, and he had put two cops

in the hospital and kidnapped Evan. If he was working on the CIA's orders, and Evan went to the police . . . what happened next? The CIA wasn't supposed to beat up cops or chain citizens to beds. So whatever had befallen his family wasn't a story that the CIA wanted in the public eye.

He needed to know more. He had a sudden terror of making a wrong move, stepping out of one prison into a far worse one.

Quickly, he checked the rest of the house. A dining room and living room. A media room with a massive TV. A laundry area. Back upstairs were four more bedrooms, one occupied by another suitcase with a few clothes unpacked. No sign anyone other than Gabriel was here.

He went back downstairs. He found a garage that held a motorcycle, a gleaming Ducati. Next to it was an old Suburban. No sign of the stolen Malibu.

Evan found the keys for the Suburban, dangling from a key holder in the kitchen. He pocketed them.

On the kitchen table was the duffel bag he'd brought from Houston. He remembered Gabriel had taken it from his house after he ran. His gear was all there. His digital music player, his camcorder, his books and notes. His clothes, which looked as if they had been searched and refolded.

He zipped up the duffel bag, carried it as he ran back up the stairs.

Gabriel was awake, one eye swelling with a purple blossom of bruise, his jaw red and scraped.

"Are you working alone?" Evan said.

Gabriel let five seconds pass. "Yes. And I'm prepared to have an honest discussion with you now about our situation."

"You're all for straight shooting when you're the one chained up, you lunatic. You don't have any credibility left." Evan waggled the ID in front of Gabriel. "You said you owned a security firm. This says you're CIA. Which is it?"

"You're in a load of trouble."

"You have information on who killed my mother, Mr. Gabriel. I have a gun. Do you see how this equation works out?"

Gabriel shook his head.

Evan leveled the pistol at Gabriel's stomach. "Answer my questions. First, where are we?"

"You won't kill me. I know it, you know it." He put his gaze to the wall, as though bored.

Evan fired.

10

GALADRIEL, JARGO'S COMPUTER GODDESS, spent the night trying to track Evan and his kidnapper. She broke into national databases. She wormed her way into the Austin Police Department's computer system, searching for traces, for reports, for the barest sign of Evan Casher. She moved through a jungle of information as patiently and efficiently as a hunter bringing down prey.

She called at Saturday's dawn with her first report.

Jargo woke Carrie on the couch and Dezz in the other bedroom. Jargo spoke at length with Galadriel, then put Carrie on the phone while he tended to private business on his phone in his bedroom.

"Evan hasn't used his credit cards or accessed his bank account. No one has. Do me a favor, hon. Look at the file I just sent you." Galadriel was a former CIA hacker, a heavyset woman who spent her hours away from the computer refining gourmet recipes and watching 1950s movies, when she believed the world had been a kinder place. She had a warm, Southern accent and sounded as if she ought to be a friend's sweet mother. "See if you see what I see."

Carrie opened the e-mail attachment, and a list of messages appeared, lifted from the Cashers' e-mail accounts:

a private account for Donna, one for Mitchell Casher's personal e-mails, and another for his work as a computer security consultant.

"I just tiptoed into their ISP's database and copied their messages. Since the boys didn't have time at the Casher house to go through their e-mails," Galadriel said.

Carrie scanned through the messages on Mitchell Casher's account. Mitchell had sent a few e-mails to his son; nothing of great interest. One update on how his golf game was progressing, a mention of a couple of vintage jazz recordings he liked and thought Evan would enjoy along with the songs in digital format, a request that Evan come home soon for a visit. A few Christmas photos done by his mother. No message appeared encoded or encrypted in any way. There were no suspicious attachments.

Donna Casher had a separate e-mail account through the same provider. More messages to and from Evan. The rest of her e-mails were mostly chatty exchanges with fellow freelance photographers. Except for Friday morning.

"She sent him four digital songs, two photos," Galadriel said. "But note the size of the photos. They're larger than they should be."

"They had the files hidden in them," Carrie said.

"I suspect one photo contained a decryption program. The other photo contained the files. So when he downloads the photos, the decryption software launches secretly and decodes the files hidden in the second photo. Buries them in a new folder deep on his hard drive, where he wouldn't look normally. And he never sees or knows that they're present."

"Please tell that to Jargo. That she could have snuck the files to Evan without him seeing them."

"But he could have seen them, hon, if he knew they were coming," Galadriel said. "You know Jargo isn't going to take the risk that he saw them."

And you, Carrie thought, *you act like you're sweet as sugar but you won't be stupid and help me when I really need it.* She wasn't fooled by Galadriel's honeyed voice. A steel-spined woman was at the other end of the line. "Are there copies on the servers that delivered the mail?"

"Cleaned off. I assume by Donna. Smart cookie," Galadriel said.

"Was Donna your friend?"

"I don't have friends in the network, honey, even you. Attachments are dangerous."

"So we have nothing to go on."

"Actually, we do. Donna had been on e-mail discussion lists for opera and books. And a group on tracing genealogies in Texas."

"Genealogy," Carrie said.

"Smart girl. Odd that Donna Casher would be interested in genealogy."

"Right. No point in tracing a family tree when you're living under a false name." Carrie jumped to the genealogy group's website and found a message index. The e-mails to the group were mostly requests from people looking for connections to particular surnames in particular counties in Texas. Every message went to every member through the genealogy list's e-mail address, which meant that every message to that address reached all subscribers. It was not the forum for a private dialogue.

"I just did a cross-check on who sent Donna e-mails within the subscriber list," Galadriel said. "Go to message number forty-one."

Carrie did. An e-mail from a Paul Granger read:

I'm very much interested in Samuel Otis Steiner family history you mentioned on genealogy forum. My
grandmother was Ruth Margaret Steiner born in Dallas died Tulsa daughter of an immigrant family from
Pennsylvania. I can supply records you requested
for the Talbott family which originated in North
Carolina, moved to TN, appeared again in Florida.
Please indicate whether you have appropriate records
or access to them. My daughter and I are visiting
Galveston soon and are interested in tracing our history back to 1849. I can be reached at 972.555.3478.

                                    Regards,
                                    Paul Granger

Carrie jumped back to the genealogy discussion list. At the
bottom of each e-mail was a link to the list's online archive.
She entered it and did a search on Samuel Otis Steiner.

She found a single posting about Steiner, from Donna
Casher approximately two days ago. She did a search on
Donna Casher's name; that single posting was the only
time Donna had ever contributed to the group discussion.
She'd simply requested information on anyone with knowl-
edge of the Samuel Otis Steiner family.

"This isn't about tracing roots, clearly," Galadriel said.
"It's a contact."

"An innocent-looking way to communicate without
arousing suspicion." Carrie studied the awkwardly worded
message. No obvious code, but the numbers might be a key.
"That number, what is it?"

"One sec." Galadriel put her on hold, jumped back on

twenty seconds later. "Hon, it's a Dallas, Texas, metro code. Got a voice-mail system. No identifier as to who it belongs to. I'll have to see if I can find it in the phone company database."

Carrie studied the e-mail again. "Eighteen forty-nine. Doesn't an end date seem odd in this context? You only want to go back so far and no further? Genealogists wouldn't stop at a particular date."

"I'm playing with the numbers, sugar. I suspect it's a code."

"One we've used?"

"I can't tell you that, honey, but I'll check."

Carrie clicked her tongue. "Eighteen forty-nine might be the key to the rest of the message. Taking the first letter, the eighth, the fourth, and the ninth, then repeat. Or the same pattern, with words."

"Too obvious an approach, dear," Galadriel said. "I'm looking at the server log for Donna Casher's e-mail account. No messages again from Paul Granger or anyone else."

"So this voice-mail account in Dallas, it's all we've got."

"Eighteen forty-nine," Galadriel said, "could be a code word itself. A warning, an instruction, and everything else in the message, other than the phone number, is camouflage. Like 1849 means *run for your life* or *we've been caught* or *go to Plan B*."

"Or *call your son, get him home, then run for your life,*" Carrie said. "Does Granger's name ring a bell?"

"No. I've checked, he's not in any of our databases. I'll check national driver's license records, but most likely it's an alias. And I've checked the message logs; no messages from Granger to Evan or Mitchell Casher."

Carrie said, "Please trace the e-mail."

"Already did. Sent from a public library in Dallas."

"So what next?"

"We have a convergence of data in Dallas. I'll see if we can connect any of our known enemies to the Dallas area." Galadriel paused. "You working this with Dezz?"

"Yes."

Galadriel made a noise in her throat. "Good luck on that, sugar."

"Thanks, Galadriel." Carrie hung up and knocked on Dezz's door. He answered after a moment, clicking off a cell phone and slipping it into his pocket.

She told him about the leads. "What are we supposed to do if we find this Granger and find the whole U.S. government right behind him?"

"Run," Dezz said. "Fast and far."

"They'll kill Evan. He doesn't deserve to die."

"What Evan Casher deserves could change from second to second. He goes public with what happened to him, he shoots us in the leg. We're lame. We'd have to shut down, at least for a year, and we can't afford that."

"It must be nice to have so little morality, you can just tuck it in your pocket."

Dezz smiled. "This from the whore. Do you need me to loan you some conscience? I've got conscience to burn."

"Evan doesn't have to die if he can help us. He'd listen to me. He doesn't know anything, he's not a threat."

"So you think."

"So I think."

"You think a lot," Dezz said. "Every brain cell firing all the time."

"News flash. Most people do."

"Most people don't, including you. You messed up, not finding those files."

She ignored him.

"Tell me true, sunshine. Does he know about the Deeps?"

"No," she said. "No, he doesn't. I'm sure of it."

She could see he didn't believe her. She poured coffee. Jargo came out of his room, pale.

"The bald man," Jargo said. "We got a positive ID from the elves, off the phone records for the voice mail and from the ID. His name is Joaquin Gabriel. He's ex-CIA. The elves are tracking back every connection in Gabriel's life to see where he might stash Evan Casher."

"Why would Gabriel want Evan? What did he do at CIA?" Carrie asked. A slow curl of horror rose up her spine.

"CIA. Oh, man," Dezz said.

"He got kicked out years ago," Jargo said.

"Maybe he got kicked back in," Dezz said.

"Gabriel cleaned up internal spills and messes," Jargo said. "He's what folks call a traitor baiter. Find the people on the inside who can bring the CIA down."

"Oh, man," Dezz said again.

"Mr. Gabriel's got a score to settle with me." Jargo's phone rang again. He listened, nodded, clicked off the phone. "Gabriel's son-in-law has a weekend house in a town called Bandera. Gabriel might run there."

"Good," Dezz said. "I'm getting bored." And he made a gun out of his hands, fired it between Carrie's eyes.

11

THE BULLET SMACKED INTO THE WALL six inches above the headboard. Gabriel jerked and flinched, his eyes widened.

"My mother is dead. My dad is missing. No more chances," Evan said. "Where are we?"

"Near Bandera."

Evan knew it was a picturesque town in the Texas Hill Country.

"It's my son-in-law's vacation house. My daughter married well." Gabriel watched the gun, not Evan.

"Are you CIA or private security?"

"Private," he said after a moment. "But I am ex-CIA, and your mother...knew of me and my work. That's why she called me. I used to do internal security. Used to. The Agency ran me out."

"Tell me how to reach my father."

"I don't have a way."

Gabriel was sticking relentlessly to that aspect of the story. Evan decided to turn the question the other way. "Does my dad know how to get in touch with you?"

"No, he doesn't. This was your mom's arrangement. I had no contact with him."

"You're lying."

"I'm not. Your mom didn't think I needed to know." Gabriel gave Evan a crooked, slightly crazy grin. "Your mother stole Jargo's files. Jargo has access to your dad because your dad works for Jargo, too. Your dad is missing. Do the math."

Evan had not thought clearly, given the pell-mell rush and chaos of the past twenty-four hours. "Jargo has my dad."

"Quite likely. I suspect he was on an assignment for Jargo when your mom decided to run. Jargo found out, grabbed your dad to keep him under control. He probably gave them your mom's computer password so Jargo could look for the files."

"I need those files. To ransom my dad from Jargo." But the files were gone, evaporated into nothing. His heart sank into his stomach. They'd gotten into his laptop fast. They knew his password. Probably from his dad, who handled the infrequent maintenance on Evan's system.

"All they'll care about now is being sure you don't know what was in the files, and that you have no copies of them." Gabriel gave Evan a sick smile. "I'm your only hope to hide from these people."

"How does Carrie fit in? She knew I was in danger, she tried to warn me."

"Who's Carrie?"

"Never mind," Evan said after a moment.

Gabriel closed his eyes. "Clearly I used the wrong approach in dealing with you, Evan. I should have trusted you."

"You think?"

"Congratulations, you've proven yourself to me. But you don't understand what's at stake. These files your mother stole, they could take down Jargo, and he's a very bad guy. I've got to have those files. They're the evidence I need."

"Against Jargo."

"Yes. To prove I shouldn't have lost my career, all those years ago. That Jargo has traitors inside the CIA working for him." Gabriel coughed. "The CIA, overall, is an organization with great, hardworking, honest people. But a few bad apples rot in every barrel, and Jargo knows the bad apples. Your mom came to me because she knew I wasn't a bad apple, Evan. She was afraid to go straight to the Agency, because she didn't want to give this information and warn Jargo. He's got people in the Agency on his payroll, people in the FBI, too. They get wind of these files, or where you're at, and they've got the same motive to get rid of you that Jargo does. They don't want to be exposed." Gabriel licked his lips. "Evan. I bet files that valuable, your mom hid another copy. Where would that be? Think. If you have another copy, I can still help you."

"Or we can just call the CIA."

"Evan. Do you think the CIA wants this news going public, that a freelance spy ring operates under their nose, inside their own walls?" Gabriel licked his lips again. "The CIA drove me out of work just for suggesting the merest possibility. Certain people in the CIA would rather kill you than let you harm the Agency's credibility. You go public, you're a dead man. They're hunting you as much as Jargo is."

The CIA. The thought made Evan's skin prickle with cold. Jargo was a killer, but he was only one man. But if these files threatened the CIA, they could find him. He couldn't hide from them forever.

"Who do I call at the CIA to tell them to stop?"

Gabriel laughed, a cold, sick sound. "You don't tell them that, son. They don't stop. They hunt you till they find you, they see what you know, and if you know too much, then they kill you. I wouldn't run to the CIA if I were you."

"So they and Jargo both want the files. Are the files lists of traitors inside the CIA who help Jargo, or agents, or names, or operations that are under way?"

"Names. See me trusting you now?"

"Of agents?"

Gabriel hesitated for a moment. "I think so."

"It either is or isn't names of agents."

Gabriel shrugged.

"What were you going to do when Mom gave you these names?" Evan steadied the gun at him. "I don't have a single reason to believe a word you've said. You could have been lying to me from minute one, and I don't think you saved me out of any debt to my mom or out of the milk of human kindness. You want those files as bad as Jargo—you could lie about what's in them and why you need them."

Gabriel kept his mouth shut.

"Fine. Play silent treatment. You can tell me about it on the way."

"Way where?"

Evan took his laptop and left the room. Gabriel didn't deserve an answer. Evan sat down in the darkened hall, put his head in his hands, weighed his options. Gabriel knew the complete truth but wasn't talking. He could stick a gun up to Gabriel's head and threaten to kill him if he didn't talk. But he and Gabriel both knew that Evan wouldn't murder him in cold blood. Gabriel saw it in his eyes.

So another tactic, and a better one that would give Evan

his dad and stop Jargo. The man behind his mother's death, if Gabriel wasn't lying.

But Evan had a call to make. His cell phone was with the Austin police, but Gabriel's phone sat on the breakfast counter.

He picked up the phone and dialed Carrie's number.

12

—◆—

THEY HAD ROCKETED SOUTH ON I-35 from Austin, veering west onto Highway 46, through the old German town of Boerne. Live oaks and twists of cedar covered the hills. The sky began to cloud.

Carrie sat in the front, Jargo in the back, Dezz drove. The highway sign read: Bandera 10 Miles.

Carrie's phone hummed in the silence. She had set it to vibrate, not ring, and she thought, *Oh, no.*

"I hear a phone," Jargo said.

"Mine." Carrie's palms went slick with sweat.

"Evan. Hallelujah," Dezz said.

"Answer it. But hold the phone so I can hear." Jargo leaned forward, put his chin over the seat, his head close to hers.

Carrie dug the phone from her purse, flipped it open. "Hello?"

"Carrie?" It was Evan.

"Sweetheart. Are you okay?"

"I'm fine. Where are you?"

"Evan, never mind me. You were kidnapped—where are you?"

"Carrie. How did you know I was in danger when you called me?"

Jargo stiffened next to her.

"Three men were at your house when I came back with breakfast for us. They said they were with the FBI, but I thought...I thought there was something fishy about them. I didn't like the look of them." She chose her words carefully, aware she had two audiences to please. "They looked like thugs trying to act like government agents. I didn't let them in the house, Evan."

"What did they want?"

"They wanted to ask you questions about your mom. Where are you, what's happening?"

"I can't really talk about it." Evan seemed to give a sigh of relief. "I just wanted to be sure you were safe."

"I'm fine, I'm just afraid for you. Please tell me where you are. I'll come, wherever it is."

"No. I don't want you involved. Until I figure out what's really happening."

"Tell me where you're at, babe. Let me help you." Jargo's hand touched Carrie's shoulder.

"Where did you go yesterday morning, Carrie?"

"You"—she closed her eyes—"you gave me a lot to think about last night. I went for a drive. Then to get us breakfast. I'm sorry I wasn't there when you woke up. I didn't mean to send a mixed message to you."

"You should leave Houston. Put space between your life and mine. I don't want you hurt by...whoever is after me."

"Evan. Let me help you. Please. Tell me where you are."

Jargo eased her closer, put his ear even closer to the phone. "I love you," she said.

A moment's silence. "Good-bye, Carrie. I really love you. But I don't think we can talk for a while."

"Evan, don't."

He hung up.

Jargo shoved her hard against the window. "You little idiot!" The glass smacked hard against her skull; the barrel of his Glock pushed against her throat.

"Should I pull over?" Dezz asked.

"No." Jargo yanked the cell phone from Carrie, read the call log, dialed Galadriel on his set, ordered her to trace the number. He hung up and stared at Carrie. "You called to warn him? You told me you didn't call him."

"No, I called to give him a reason to stay away from the FBI or the CIA if they came looking for him."

"I didn't tell you to do that," Jargo said.

"Initiative. I wanted him to shut up, about everything, until we could get to him. You didn't get to him in time. You let the police get ahold of him. But I didn't get to tell him the entire spiel. Gabriel attacked the police cruiser just as I'd gotten him on the phone."

"Why didn't you tell me?"

"Because you'd freak out, just like you're doing now. I didn't get useful information, but I didn't put us at risk."

"If the police recovered his cell phone, your phone number's on the log."

"I used a backup phone. Cheap, a throwaway. Untraceable."

"It was stupid," Jargo said.

"You want him alive so you can get the files. If his mother told him about you or the files, I didn't want him saying a word to the police about the CIA. It was to protect him and to protect you. Our interests coincided." She watched Jargo's gun, wondered if she would be dead in the second it took to see the bullet launch from the barrel.

He lowered the gun. "This is really not the time for me to worry about your loyalty. We clear?"

"Crystal clear." She gripped his arm. "The CIA killed my parents—you think I want them killing Evan? If he's with Gabriel, and we can get Evan back, let me talk to him. It'll be much easier if you let me handle it. Please."

"You think you can recruit him."

"I think I can start the process. He's lost everything. Except me. He's vulnerable. I can win him over, I know I can."

"He said he loves you," Jargo said.

"Yes. He told me that last night." She faced the front of the car.

"So you're his weakness," Jargo said with a laugh.

"Apparently."

"Him loving you should make things easier," Dezz said with a laugh. "Bring him over with a good screw, and we're set."

"Shut your stinking mouth," she said. She wanted to smash Dezz's nose in, break the teeth in his smirk.

Jargo's cell phone beeped. He answered, "Galadriel, don't disappoint me." He listened. Nodded. "Thank you." He clicked off. "The cell phone is owned by one Paul Granger."

"Same name as the e-mail," Carrie said. "How far away are we?"

"Less than five minutes," Dezz said. And then the sirens were wailing, the blues and reds of a police car flashing behind them.

13

CARRIE WAS SAFE.

Thugs trying to act like government agents, Carrie had said. Was it really the FBI? Or could it be the CIA, looking for him? How would they know about him, about his parents and their connection to these files? It didn't make sense to him, but nothing did this morning. What mattered was Carrie was safe and sound. He would have to resist the urge to hear her voice and keep her at arm's length, clear of this nightmare.

I find you and lose you, all at once, he thought. But just until he could find his dad, find out the truth of what had happened to his family. Then they could be together.

He went back to the bedroom where Gabriel was chained. Now Gabriel was sitting close to the headboard.

"My girlfriend said the FBI was looking for me yesterday morning."

"Quite possibly," Gabriel said. "What do you want me to do about it?"

"She didn't believe they were real FBI. Could they have been CIA? You pull in my mom in Austin, they grab me in Houston."

"If they wanted you, they would have grabbed you earlier

and taken you. I don't know who it was. Sorry." Gabriel rattled the chain. "Are you leaving me here?"

"I don't know yet." Evan locked Gabriel in the bedroom. He hurried down the hall. Gabriel could be lying about not having help; the CIA or any friends of Gabriel's could arrive at any moment. He ran into Gabriel's bedroom. Opened the first suitcase. A few clothes. A lot of cash. Enough to make Evan stare. Neatly bound bricks of twenties and hundreds. No ID in the bag, but the luggage tag read J. GABRIEL and an address in McKinney, a suburb of Dallas.

He searched Gabriel's other bag. A few clothes, two guns, neatly oiled and disassembled. He dumped the gun pieces in with the cash. In the corner he spotted a small metal box.

He tried opening it. Locked. Locked meant important. He needed tools to crack it open. He dumped his damaged laptop into the suitcase with the cash. Ran downstairs to the garage. He loaded the bag into the rear of the Suburban, clearing out space. He hurried back inside and retrieved the small locked box, put it inside his duffel bag, went back down to the garage, and stuck the duffel in the passenger seat.

He went back upstairs. Getting Gabriel downstairs in the handcuffs would not be easy. He would stick Gabriel in the back of the SUV, hit the road, and call Durless. He thought Durless would listen. He was probably mortified and furious at losing Evan, and then losing the case to the FBI. Evan would give him a chance to save face.

He unlocked the door and walked into the bedroom.

The bed was empty. The handcuff dangled from the bed frame. The drapes danced in the breeze allowed by the open window.

Evan ran downstairs. His own breathing, panicked, filled

his ears. CNN warbled in the den. He opened the door leading to the garage. Ducked inside. No sign of Gabriel. He edged into the dimly lit garage and over to the Suburban.

Where was Gabriel?

The garage door powered upward in sudden motion.

14

———◦◦◦———

Evan knew he would be seen in a matter of seconds. The Suburban was parked farthest from the door leading into the house. As the garage door motored up, Evan slid over the hood of the SUV, putting the Suburban between him and the rest of the garage. He huddled down close to the front right wheel. He pulled the gun he'd taken from Gabriel from the back of his jeans.

Gabriel ran into the garage.

I have his keys, he went out the window, this must be his only way back in the house, Evan thought.

Either Gabriel had seen him or hadn't and Evan would know in a moment.

Footsteps. Heading toward the door that led to the kitchen. Evan heard that door open. Then the garage door powering downward along its tracks. Gabriel cutting off his escape that way. He believed Evan was still inside the house.

Evan risked a peek above the Suburban's hood. *He's probably got more guns in the house, and he's heading for one, because he knows I've got one and now I'll have heard the garage door, wherever I am in the house.* Evan eased inside the Suburban from the passenger side, slid into the driver's seat, inserted the key into the ignition. He found the garage door opener clipped to the sun visor and hit the button. The garage door stopped.

He hit the button instantly again and the door crept up as he started the Suburban. Evan thought, *Please, let him have run upstairs already...*

The door to the house flew open; Gabriel stood in the doorway, gun in hand. The garage door still motored upward.

Gabriel slammed his fist onto the door control; it stopped. He ran past the motorcycle. Heading right for the driver's door.

Evan shifted into reverse and hit the accelerator. The Suburban roared backward, metal screeching as it scraped the lowered garage door.

Gabriel fired. The bullet pinged off the roof, his aim too high. Evan spun the wheel, slamming backward into metal in the wide stretch of driveway. In the rearview mirror he saw the stolen Malibu.

Gabriel sprinted toward the car's front, aiming at the tires, bellowing, "Stop! Evan! Give it up!"

Evan wrenched the car into drive. The Suburban rocketed forward; Gabriel screamed as he went over the hood and off the side of the car.

I hit him, Evan thought. He aimed the Suburban down the driveway, which cut down a sizable hill studded with cedars and live oaks. It looked like the Hill Country. Gabriel had mentioned Bandera. For once he'd told the truth.

The driveway snaked down to a closed metal gate that fenced the property off from a small country road. Evan pressed the other button on the garage door opener, hoping that the gate was electronic. The gate didn't budge. Then he spotted a loop of chain locking the gate shut.

He searched in the dividing console of the Suburban, then hunted on the car key ring. No extra key.

Evan grabbed the gun from the passenger seat, got out of the Suburban, left the engine running. He aimed at the hefty lock on the chain, took two steps back, and fired.

The gunshot thundered across the silence of the hills. The lock rocked, a hole blasted in its edge. He tested the lock. It held.

He heard the whine of a motorcycle. The Ducati, revving down through the driveway.

Evan steadied his aim and fired again. The bullet pierced the lock dead center. The lock fell open under his hands, and he unwound the chain, dropping the links onto the gravel at the road's edge. His breath grew heavy and loud in his ears. He shoved the gate open.

The whine crescendoed. He saw the Ducati arrowing down the driveway through a break in the trees, then roaring toward him. Gabriel raised his pistol. The warning shot kicked up dust near Evan's feet.

No place to hide. Evan, the chain in one hand, the gun in the other, slid under the Suburban at the passenger side, into the grit and gravel.

He had taken cover in panic. *Stupid, stupid, stupid*.

The Ducati stopped ten feet away. Limestone dust from the gravel coated the bottom of its wheels.

"Evan." Gabriel sounded as if he were talking around broken teeth. "Toss the gun out. Now."

"No," Evan said.

"Listen to me. Don't be an idiot. Don't run. They'll kill you."

"Back off or I'll shoot you."

Gabriel's voice lowered. "You shoot me, you're completely

alone in this world. No money. No place to go. The cops hand you right over to the FBI, and then you know what happens."

"No, I don't."

"FBI comes and collects you on behalf of the CIA. Takes you into federal custody. And then they lose you, Evan, because the government wants you and your family dead. You've become a hot potato ain't nobody touching. I'm your only hope. Now come on out."

"I'm not talking to you. I'm counting. When I hit the magic number, I'm shooting you in the foot." He wanted out from under the hot, dusty car, the heat of the engine pressing against his back.

Gabriel kept his voice calm, as though trolling his options and seeing which one would lure Evan into sunlight. "Evan, I know what it's like to have no place to go."

Evan waited.

"I know how these people work, Evan. How they'll hunt you. I can hide you from them. Or get you to a place where you could negotiate a peace settlement with them." Slowly moving, slowly circling the Suburban. "Best of all, I have a plan to get your dad back." Gabriel's voice was low, buddy-intimate.

Evan aimed at Gabriel's feet. His heart hammered against the gravel.

"Your mother trusted me, and I failed her. I feel responsible. But remember, I shot through the rope, I saved your life." Gabriel's voice dropped lower. "I'm talking with you. I'm not dragging you out by your heels to fight you."

Because I hit you with a car and because I have a gun, and you know it. You heard me shoot the lock. And you're hurt, bad hurt from hitting the car, but you still chased me down here. You need me. Because you want Jargo so bad, and I'm the bait.

"We need to go to Florida," Gabriel said. "That's where I was taking your mother. That's where she expected to find your dad." Tossing Evan a bone.

"Where in Florida?"

"We can talk about details when you come out. I've got a great idea on how to get your dad back for you."

"So let's hear your plan," Evan said. Keep Gabriel talking. Let his voice give away any sudden effort, like rushing toward the Suburban.

"Jargo wants your dad, to lure you in and ensure you can't hurt him with the files. The CIA wants your dad or those files, to nab Jargo and whoever's in the CIA that works with him. I suggest you offer deals to both sides, get them face-to-face. Then you threaten to expose both sides—Jargo as a freelance spy, the CIA as dealing with him, which is an embarrassment to them—and negotiate the return of your dad. Play them against each other. We can work out the details. But come out and let's talk."

And what does that plan buy you? Evan wondered. He could not figure out what Gabriel wanted—revenge, but against both Jargo and the CIA? It made no sense. Unless he really was ex-CIA and the disgruntled employee of the century. "All right," Evan said. "I'm coming out now. Don't shoot me."

"Toss the gun out, Evan. Flick on the safety and toss the gun out."

Evan, lying flat, aimed with care at Gabriel's foot. His hand trembled and he willed it still. *Make it count.* But the surface of the road, all rough edges of gravel, made him worry the bullet might not fly straight into Gabriel's leg. *Hurt him just bad enough so you can get away.*

He aimed. But before he squeezed the trigger, a single shot rang out. A smack of bullet slammed into flesh, and Gabriel screamed and fell to the dirt.

15

CARRIE GLANCED BACK AT THE WHIRLING sirens and lights. "It's a cop. I told you to slow down."

Dezz said, "Just be cool and follow my lead."

"Dezz," Jargo said. "Take the ticket. You're a model citizen. We leave slowly and quietly, you got me?"

Dezz pulled over and the county deputy sat behind him, lights spinning, for a minute.

"He's calling in the license," Jargo said. "Dezz, if we lose Evan over this, you're dead."

"It's all cool," Dezz said.

Carrie tensed, turning to watch as the deputy unfolded himself from the cruiser and walked up to the driver's side. *Just let us go, please,* she thought. *Please.*

Before the deputy could say a word, Dezz held his forged federal ID credentials up for inspection, saying, "Special Agent Desmond Jargo of the FBI. I'm heading to Bandera to locate a person of interest in a case based out of our Austin office."

The deputy took the proffered ID, studied it with care. He handed it back to Dezz, peered in at Carrie. "You got ID, ma'am?"

"She doesn't need it, she's with me," Dezz said. The deputy looked in the backseat at Jargo.

"Hello, Officer," Jargo said.

"They're witnesses. With me," Dezz said.

"Registration?" the deputy said.

"Did you hear one word I said to you?" Dezz said. "Special agent. On a case. In a rush. I'd simplify it further but *special* and *agent* both have two syllables."

"Cute. Registration, please, sir."

Dezz handed him the card and the deputy studied it. He handed it back to Dezz.

"Thank you. May we get on down the road, please?"

"I'm curious." The deputy was young, brash-looking, a later-life version of the smart-mouth who sat in back rows lobbing spit wads but figured out after high school that police work was steady hometown employment. Carrie didn't look at him; she looked straight ahead at the road. "What case you got of interest down here?"

"I really don't have time for a summary," Dezz said, "and it's confidential, so we're—"

"Not rushing off just yet," the deputy said.

"I'm a federal agent—"

"I heard you the first three times. But you're in our jurisdiction, and I haven't heard that you've spoken with our sheriff."

"I planned to call the sheriff shortly. We hadn't located our subject yet, and I saw no need to waste his time."

"Her time," the deputy said. "Step out of the car, sir, and we'll give her a call about your case."

"This is ridiculous."

"Sir. All due respect, you can't come down and run

ninety on our roads." The deputy leaned down close to Dezz's window. "Let's just call—"

"Let's not." Dezz's fist lashed out like a hammer into the soft of the throat, crushing the windpipe. The deputy staggered back from Dezz's window, his sunglasses askew, mouth working in circles for air. Dezz drew his gun and fired a silenced shot. It burst the forehead between the Stetson and the cheap sunglasses.

Carrie screamed. She saw a car cresting the hill, approaching them. Dezz floored the pedal; the sedan shot forward. Dezz readied his gun, steering with one hand.

"Dezz!" Jargo yelled.

The approaching car—a puttering Chevrolet, ten years old—braked at the sight of the deputy lying dead in the road, and Carrie saw the driver's face widen in shock. She was a thirtyish blonde with glasses, wearing a Walmart apron and fluffy bangs. Dezz fired twice as they zoomed past. The driver's window vanished in glass dust and a bloom of red. The Chevrolet left the road, smashed into fencing that marked the edge of a cow pasture, the front of the car crumpling like foil.

"Not. A. Word." Dezz steered back into the center of the lane and shoved the speed up to one hundred.

Jargo leaned forward and closed his hands around his son's throat.

"That was idiotic," Jargo said.

"We don't have time to mess around with cops." Dezz sounded calm, as though they'd just stopped to inspect peaches at a roadside fruit stand.

"I ordered you to take the ticket!" Jargo said. "Listen to his lecture, smile and nod, be smart."

"Dad. The only ID I had at hand was the federal. He was

calling it in, no matter what, and I couldn't let that happen. Better, tactically, to kill him now than to have to run later. It only put us two minutes behind schedule."

Jargo eased his grip off Dezz's throat, slapped the back of his son's head. "The next time you disobey, I'll shoot you in the hand. I'll ruin it. You won't ever work again. And I'll cut you off, and I'll…" Jargo fell back in the seat. He lowered his voice. "Do not disobey me."

"Yes, sir," Dezz said.

"You didn't have to kill that woman," Carrie said in a thin voice.

"I just shot out her window. So she couldn't get a look at us, spot our license plate."

Carrie fought down the urge to vomit. She couldn't show weakness around him. Not now.

Jargo said, "Let's put the unfortunate deputy and witness out of our minds. We have a job to do."

Carrie knew his request was for her benefit; the two innocents were already long gone from Dezz's mind. She checked her gun, wiped a hand across her mouth.

"Carrie, those deaths just now, they're regrettable," Jargo said. "Truly. But I can't think of them as people, you see? I can't imagine them as someone's baby, or that they had a whole and worthy life to live. You have to keep your eyes on the prize. It's the only way to stay sane."

Carrie knew he—they—were cold beyond belief. Worse than insane. They chose to murder without guilt.

Evan, please don't be at this house. Don't.

"Find a back way," Jargo said. "Pull up the GPS map for me. Just because Evan called Carrie doesn't mean he's free of Gabriel. This could be a trap, Gabriel or the CIA pulling us in."

A trap, with Evan laid as bait. She didn't want to think about that. "Evan . . ."

"Carrie, I know. You don't want him hurt. We don't, either. I have my own reasons for wanting to be sure Evan is safe." The lie—she was sure it was a lie—sounded smooth on Jargo's tongue.

Dezz pointed at the GPS screen. "There's an access road a half mile from the front entrance of the ranch. We'll go in that way."

Get to Evan first, Carrie told herself. *Find him and get him out of there before Dezz and Jargo kill him.*

The hill rose from the back ranch road in a sharp incline, limestone breaking through the thin soil in heaves and cracks, thirsty cedars and small oaks competing on the scrubby land. Dezz took the lead, Carrie the middle. Jargo brought up the rear.

Dezz stopped so suddenly Carrie nearly walked into his back.

"What's wrong?"

"I heard a hiss." For the first time Carrie heard a tremble in Dezz's voice.

"Snakes are still hibernating now," Jargo said. "No need to be afraid, little boy." Annoyance and arrogance blended in his tone; stinging still, Carrie decided, from Dezz's earlier disobedience.

"I don't like snakes," Dezz said. He took a tentative step forward. Carrie went around him to take the lead, easing down through the trees. Dezz walked as if he were navigating a minefield, one cautious step after another.

"Dezz, it's okay." Carrie wished a rattlesnake would whip its head out from under a rock, sink its fangs into

Dezz's face or leg or butt. "I think you heard the wind in the branches."

He didn't move.

"Dezz hates snakes. Reptiles. Anything that lives belly on the ground," Jargo said. "I should get him a cobra as a pet. Help him overcome his weakness."

Dezz moaned in his throat.

"Now you know how to punish him when he won't listen to you," Carrie said to Jargo. "Put a copperhead in his bed."

They heard a crash of metal, then another crash, a gunshot, a scream, the roar of an engine moving away from them.

Jargo grabbed Dezz's arm and the three hurried down an incline, then climbed up another small hill. They ran past a stable and a limestone pool, heard the rev of a second engine, heard the distant crack of another gunshot, saw a bald man racing a motorcycle down the driveway.

"Gabriel," Jargo said.

Dezz bolted, hurrying down the driveway, Jargo following. He called back over his shoulder, "Carrie, secure the house."

She didn't stop, and Jargo raised a gun toward her and said, "Do what you're told."

Evan wasn't on the motorcycle; he might be in the house. *This is my chance.* So she nodded and ran back toward the house.

Seeing Gabriel talking to a parked Suburban, Dezz hunkered down among the cedars. Jargo knelt next to him.

Evan, Dezz mouthed. *He's in the car.* Jargo nodded. They waited through two minutes of talking.

Dezz couldn't see where in the Suburban the idiot was.

But then he heard, from under the car, a clear yell: "I'm coming out..." And Gabriel training his pistol at the SUV's underside.

Dezz stood, aimed, and fired.

The bald man jerked, blood popped from his back, and he fell with a choked cry of agony.

"Don't kill Evan," Jargo whispered to Dezz. "Wound if you must. I prefer him alive to answer my questions." He gripped Dezz's arm. "Clear?"

"Totally."

Jargo frowned. "You've not had a confidence-inspiring day."

"Benefit of the doubt, Daddy." Then Dezz yelled, "Freeze! FBI!" and started down the hill. Jargo stood, glancing back at the house where Carrie had vanished. Silence. He hoped Gabriel worked alone. Traitor baiters often did; they trusted no one. It was, Jargo knew, a sad and smart way to live. He drew back into the trees to watch. In case Evan came out shooting.

Gabriel crawled for his gun, face contorted in pain. Another bullet kicked up the limestone crush by his head and he stopped.

"I told you to freeze," Evan heard a voice say. Not angry. Calm. A young voice. Almost amused. "It wasn't a suggestion. It was a strongly worded suggestion."

Gabriel said, "Him...him..."

"Evan? The cavalry's arrived," the voice called.

"Your house—" Gabriel gasped, and a second bullet hit him, this time in the shoulder. Gabriel shrieked, twisted in the dirt with a stunned look on his face. Evan could see a man's legs walking toward him.

Your house. Evan fought down the sudden surge of terror in his chest, his guts.

The voice called, "Be still now, Mr. Gabriel. You keep moving, you make me very nervous. I don't like being nervous." Then the voice brightened. "Evan? You under the car or in it?"

Evan gave no answer. That voice. It was the voice from his parents' kitchen. The voice of his mother's murderer. Rage surged up in him.

"Hey, Evan, the good guys are here. FBI. Come on out, please."

Evan didn't trust anyone who said he was FBI but who shot a wounded man.

"All's well, Evan. It's safe now. If you've got a gun, toss it out. We don't want any accidents."

Gabriel groaned and sobbed.

"Evan. I don't know what this crazy old fool told you, but you're perfectly safe. I'm FBI. My name is Dezz Jargo and"—a pause for emphasis—"I know your dad. He's sick with worry about you. We tracked Mr. Gabriel here. I need you to come out. We're gonna take you to your dad."

Jargo. Evan imagined Jargo would be an older man. This guy looked too young to run a criminal ring.

"Show me your credentials," Evan yelled.

"Well, there you are!" Dezz called kindly.

"He's a liar," Gabriel yelled, and the walking legs delivered a sudden kick to Gabriel's head. Blood and two front teeth flew free from the mouth, and Gabriel lay still. Evan couldn't tell if he was still breathing.

"Evan, come out now please," Dezz said. "For your own safety."

Evan fired at Dezz's feet.

*   *   *

Carrie moved from the garage to the kitchen. Silence, except for the television, tuned to CNN.

"Evan?" she called. "Evan, honey, it's me. Carrie. Come out."

Silence. A shiver took hold of her chest as she went into each room. Afraid she would find him dead.

He had called, he had to be free.

Unless it was a trap, and as soon as Evan called her, Gabriel killed him. She tried to think. Gabriel was ex-CIA. These files—she wasn't sure what they contained that made Jargo sweat—were of interest to Gabriel because he'd gone freelance, or he'd turned traitor, or he'd gone back to work for the Agency. Smoke and mirrors, this world was nothing but smoke and mirrors and she could not see the truth of anything except Evan lying in the bed, saying, *I love you.*

She moved through the downstairs rooms quickly, efficiently. She hurried upstairs. The last time she had seen him he was lying in bed, asleep, perfectly at peace, and now he had endured this horror. His mother dead, and she had been powerless to stop it or to protect Donna or him. His mother, strangled. Hers had been shot.

Please, Evan, be here, not down there with Dezz. Or be gone. Gone far away where I can't find you.

She tore through each room, praying to find him first.

Dezz howled and jumped at the missed shot, but he didn't retreat far. Instead he gave a twisted laugh. "Funny way of saying thanks for the save," he called. "Gabriel was aiming for you when he was telling you to come out. I saved you."

Evan waited. He thought Dezz would run for cover. It was sensible. Dezz didn't. But he didn't come any closer.

"Your father," Dezz said, "his name is Mitchell Eugene Casher. Born in Denver. He's been a computer consultant for nearly twenty years."

"So?"

"So, if I'm just FBI, I know that. But I'm his friend, Evan. His favorite ice cream flavor is butter pecan. He likes his steak medium. His favorite television show of all time is *Hawaii Five-O* and he often bores people with plot summaries. Sound familiar?"

It did. "How do you know him?"

"Evan, I have to trust you now. Your father does special work for the government. I handle his cases. I'm here to protect you. Your family has been targeted by very bad people. Including Mr. Gabriel here, who was kicked to the curb by the CIA."

The voice. He compared Dezz's voice to the voice that had spoken behind him, when he'd knelt in the kitchen, a gun at his head, his mother's dead face six inches from his. Now he wasn't sure. Those whole horrible moments fogged in a haze. He tried to remember the voice that had spoken while his mother was dead, the voice in his ears while he was dying at the end of a rope. "Be a good boy and come out. I'll share my candy with you."

"Don't talk to me like I'm four years old," Evan said.

"I wouldn't dream of talking down to the famous director."

Evan waited. A caramel wrapper dropped by Dezz's feet.

Evan thought, *If I shoot him, there is still one more. If the two of them are still together.*

"Got a friend at the house who's worried about you," Dezz said. "Carrie's here with me."

Evan thought he had heard wrong. "What?" His chest tightened. A lie. It had to be a lie.

Ten seconds of silence and Dezz said, "Sorry, Evan, stay still, I just need to take a simple precaution," and he shot out the right front tire of the Suburban. The heavy SUV sank and settled down where the tire blew.

"I can't risk you shooting me and driving off," Dezz said. "We're not doing a Mexican standoff. I want to take you to Carrie. And to your father. Come out, hands up, we call him. Get everyone back together. Nice family reunion."

Evan gritted his teeth. No. Dezz was a liar, a killer. He wouldn't believe anything he said about Carrie. These men had found invisible files on his computer, erased his computer back to a default state in minutes, found Gabriel's hideout in the middle of nowhere. Learning his girlfriend's name was nothing. It was a trick, it had to be a trick, to lure him out.

He had to get out of here. But he couldn't drive the Suburban, not with a shredded tire.

The Ducati. It stood near the front of the Suburban, where Gabriel had parked it. The Suburban faced the gate. The bike was to his right, and Dezz stood over to the left and halfway up the hill. No way Gabriel pocketed the keys when he got off the bike, ready to shoot Evan. Right?

Gabriel gave out what sounded to Evan like a long, dying sigh.

Evan would have to leave the suitcase behind, with the cash and his damaged laptop inside. He had the South African passport that Gabriel had shown him in his pocket and Gabriel's CIA ID. The duffel bag was in the car, too. But, he remembered, on the passenger side. He played the sequence of escape in his mind. Roll out on the passenger

side of the Suburban. Ease the door open, grab the duffel—
it held the small locked box he'd taken from Gabriel, and
his film gear. Shoot at Dezz to chase him back up the hill.
Jump on the bike, go through the gate. It was probably suicide. But at least he was going down trying.

"Bring Carrie down here, let me see her, and I'll come
out," he called.

Silence for a second, and Dezz said, "You come out and
I'll bring her to you."

Dezz paced about twenty feet away. Close into the trees.
He's waiting for you to go for the motorcycle. No, Evan
decided. He was just waiting. He could see Dezz's face
now: blondish hair, thin features; he looked sick-boy sallow, junkyard mean, flat-out crazy.

Did you kill my mother? He'd heard two voices, that he
was sure of, but this was only one guy.

Stay focused. Keep your hand steady when you fire.
His father's voice in his ear, although he'd never been very
good at target practice when his father had dragged him to
the range, and he hadn't been in years. Evan wriggled out
from under the car on the passenger side, the Suburban's
chassis between him and Dezz. He opened the door. He
grabbed the duffel, put the strap over his shoulder.

Dezz ran straight for him, aiming, yelling, "Evan, great,
arms up please where I can see them, okay?"

Evan fired over the hood and Dezz's jacket sleeve jerked
as if tugged from behind. Dezz dropped to the ground
and Evan kept firing over Dezz's head until the gun emptied. He reached the motorcycle.

The keys gleamed in the bright sunlight. He cranked
the engine, squeezed into gear, spinning gravel, and shot
through the narrow opening of the gate. He did not look

back because he did not want to see the bullet coming for
him. So he did not see Jargo step from the oaks, shoot at
his shoulder, and miss, did not see Dezz stand, take careful aim, and a running Carrie shove Dezz as he fired. Evan
heard the crack of the two pistols, their echoes bouncing
around the mesquite-studded hills, but nothing hit him. He
bent over the cycle, low, the duffel killing his balance, still
holding the emptied gun in one hand, his chin close to the
handlebars, and all he saw was the road leading away from
death.

16

Evan needed a car. Fast. Dezz could come after him at any moment, thundering down and running him off the road, smearing him into jelly. A sign down the road indicated he was two miles from Bandera.

He drove into town, stopping only to tuck the emptied gun into the duffel so he wasn't flashing around weaponry. Lots of shops, a barbecue restaurant, signs for festivals happening every month. He peeled off the main road and wondered how he would go about stealing a car.

It was a strange decision. He wasn't part of the normal world anymore; he had stepped over into a shadow land where he had no map, no compass, no North Star to guide him. He had seen his face on the national news, seen himself discussed as a victim of crime. He had run over Gabriel and kept driving. He had seen Gabriel shot twice but was not heading to the police. He had escaped from the man who might have killed his mother.

The rule book of his life was in the gutter.

He drove until the houses were smaller, the edges of the lawns less precise.

Small towns. Unlocked doors, keys in cars. Right? He hoped. He parked the Ducati, pocketed the keys, slung his dusty duffel over his shoulder. A slow rain began, the sky rumbled. Most of the homes had driveways with carports instead of garages. Good. That made spotting a target car easier, and he wondered if this was how thieves approached their work. The rain chased everyone inside. He prayed no one watched him as he ambled from driveway to driveway, peering into cars, testing the doors. Everything was locked. So much for small-town trust.

He was on his eighth driveway, soaked now, approaching a pickup when the front door opened and a tough, thick-necked guy stepped out onto the home's small porch.

"Help you, mister?" he called. In a tone not exactly a threat, but not saying, *Hi, come and drink a beer with me.* "What you doing?"

The lie came to Evan's mouth so easily it astonished him. "Flyers." He pointed at the duffel bag. "Supposed to leave flyers on windshields, but it's too wet. So I was gonna stick 'em in the driver's seats."

"Flyers for what?" The giant stepped forward, giving Evan a doubting eye: his shaggy hair, the earring, the now filthy bowling shirt, begrimed with wet dirt and Gabriel's blood.

"New church in town," Evan said. "The Holy Blood of Our Lord Fellowship. Have you been saved? We give more redemption for the dollar. We use rattlesnakes in our services and—"

The giant said, "Thanks, I'm good," stepped back inside, and closed the door.

Evan headed down the street. Fast now, running in the rain. The giant either bought it or he didn't and was calling the cops.

Two more doors down, a Holy Grail gleamed in the rain:

an unlocked truck. It was a Ford F-150, red, an interior clean except for a Styrofoam coffee cup in the holder, a cell phone wedged in the seat divider, and a Teletubby doll, worn out with affection. The lights were off in the house: the mailbox read EVANS. An omen, a kiss of good luck. He tore out a piece of paper from his notebook and wrote, *Really sorry about taking the truck, the Ducati parked down the street is yours to keep, I'll call and tell you where I've left your truck.* He put the note and the Teletubby doll and the Ducati keys on the porch in plain sight, got in, started the truck, backed up. He thought the phone might be useful before the angry owner deactivated its service.

No one came out of the house.

He drove out of Bandera at modest speed, checking the gas gauge. Almost full. Luck had finally given him a break he hadn't had to fight for.

Now you're a real criminal. What would his mom say?

She'd say, *Go get the men who killed me.*

No. Revenge didn't matter—saving his father did. Florida, Gabriel had claimed, was the rendezvous point for Evan's dad. His father might already be there, if he wasn't being held by Dezz Jargo's group. Evan would drive to San Antonio—it was almost noon now—and head east. He cranked on the radio as he hit the highway. Willie Nelson implored Whiskey River to take his mind. The storm blossomed into full fury, and he pointed the truck southeast. He knew the signs would guide him into the sprawl of San Antonio. Then he could take Interstate 10 in a straight shot to Houston and beyond, across the Louisiana flatlands and bayous. Across the toes of Mississippi and Alabama and into the westward finger of Florida.

Then he could find his father. In a big, crowded state,

where he had no idea where to start looking. But he couldn't stay still.

He thought about the files. The files were the crux, the negotiating point, the key to rescuing his father. If Dezz Jargo and company believed he possessed another copy of the files and would eventually exchange them for his dad, then the files shielded his father. Kill his father, and Evan had no reason to keep the files secret.

People had lied to him before, with the cameras rolling, trying to make themselves look good. Or look smart. The best liars skirted the truth, stayed close enough to it. Maybe there were pebbles of truth in Dezz's and Gabriel's claims. The truth might lie between their tongues.

His whole body hurt, his whole body said *enough*. Concentrate on the road. Don't think about Mom, about Carrie. Just drive. Every mile gets you closer. That's what his dad had said on the long family drives. They never had other family to visit; these were always trips to the Grand Canyon, to New Orleans where his parents had lived when he was born, to Santa Fe, to Disney World once when he was fifteen, too cool for Disney but actually dying from excitement. Whenever he'd ask the inevitable childish question of how much farther, Dad would say, "Every mile gets you closer."

That's no answer, Evan would complain, and his father would just repeat the answer: "Every mile gets you closer." Smiling at Evan in the rearview mirror.

Finally Mom would say, *Just enjoy the journey.* She'd lean back from the passenger seat, squeeze his hand, which embarrassed him as a teenager but now seemed like heaven's touch made real. Typical motherly, zippy optimism. He missed her as he would an arm suddenly gone.

Your father does special work for the government, Dezz had said. Even if Dezz was a liar, this had a ring of truth, given the events of the past two days. The concept was hazy, foggy. He did not know what a spy looked like, but he didn't picture James Bond. He pictured a man with the sallow, sad face of a Lee Harvey Oswald, a custom-made silencer in his pocket from a Swiss craftsman, a trench coat easily rinsed of blood and gore, an emptiness in the eyes to show the soul had withered from living under constant stress and fear of discovery. His father read Graham Greene and John Grisham, loved baseball, hated fishing, wrote computer code, and worshiped his family. Evan had never known a lack of love.

So did your dad tell you he loved you, go get on a plane, and then go steal secrets or kill people? Did blood money pay your way through college, put food in your belly, fund chewing gum and comic books and every other treasure of childhood?

The miles of Texas unfurled, long and rainy. "Every mile gets you closer," he said under his shallow breath. Again and again, a mantra to keep away the pain and to harden his heart.

He would find out the truth. He would find his father. And he would make the people who had killed his mother pay with everything they held dear.

17

I COULD KILL YOU!" Dezz screamed at Carrie. "I had him!"

She crossed her arms. "Jargo wanted him alive. You were aiming for his head."

"I was aiming for the bike. The bike!"

"If you were aiming for the bike," Jargo said, stepping between them, "you could have shot it out when you shot the Suburban's tire, son."

Dezz's red face frowned. "What?"

"You hoped Evan would run," Jargo said. "Give you a reason to shoot him dead. Get over this jealousy regarding Carrie. Now."

"That's not true." Dezz shook his head, fished in his pocket for candy. He jabbed a caramel in his mouth. "I don't care who she sleeps with."

"Why didn't you take out the bike, then? After lecturing me about tactics earlier this morning?" Jargo said. He went over, prodded Gabriel with his shoe.

"I didn't think he'd try for the bike. Who knew he would fight back, he's just a filmmaker!" Dezz spat out the title. He whirled on Carrie. "He knew how to shoot—why didn't you warn me?"

"I didn't know he could shoot. He never mentioned it."

"Dezz," Jargo said in a cold voice. "His father is a crack shot. It's not unreasonable that he might have taught Evan about guns."

Dezz jerked off his jacket, pointed at the scorch in his skin. "Where's your concern for me?"

"I'll get you a bandage. Satisfied?" Jargo said.

Carrie kept her voice cool. "If you want to know with certainty what Evan knows, and how big a threat he is, you need him alive. I can find him. He has few friends, few places to hide."

"Where will he go, Carrie?" Jargo asked. He was calm, unruffled, kneeling to check Gabriel's pulse.

"Think about it from Gabriel's perspective. He is ex-CIA. He not only has a bone with you, but with the Agency. If we assume he's operating alone, he'll have wanted to maintain total control over Evan. He stole him from the cops. That means he would have warned Evan off the cops, off the authorities." She hoped she'd made a good case and went for the close. "He'll go to Houston. He'll look for me. He has friends there."

Dezz jabbed his gun against her chest. It was still warm, the heat spreading through the material of her blouse. "If you hadn't let him head to Austin yesterday morning, we'd be in a lot better shape."

She gently moved the gun away from her. "If you thought before you acted—"

"Be quiet. Both of you," Jargo said. "All of Carrie's theorizing aside, he may be heading straight to the Bandera police. Gabriel's alive. Let's take him and get out of here."

They loaded Gabriel in the back of the dented but drivable Malibu, wiping down and abandoning their own car behind a dense motte of live oaks. Gabriel had two bullet wounds, one in the shoulder, one in the upper back, and he was unconscious. Carrie took a medical kit from the car they were leaving behind and tended to his injuries.

"Will he live until we get back to Austin?" Jargo asked.

"If Dezz doesn't kill him," Carrie said.

Dezz got into the car, jerked the rearview mirror to where he could see Carrie in the back, Gabriel's head in her lap.

"I could kill you," he said again. But now there was just the hurt of the denied child, the tantrum fading into pout.

It was time, she decided, to start playing a new hand. "You won't," she said calmly. "You'd miss me."

Dezz stared at her and she saw the anger begin to fade in his face. She allowed herself to breathe again.

"Go eat dinner," Jargo ordered them when they returned to the Austin apartment. "I need peace and quiet for my talk with Mr. Gabriel."

Carrie did not like the sound of that announcement but she had no choice. She and Dezz walked down the street, under the arching shade of the oaks, to a small Tex-Mex restaurant. It was crowded with young, hip attendees from the massive South by Southwest music and film festivals that dominated Austin every mid-March. Her heart went into her throat. Evan had talked about coming to the festival until just last week; *Ounce of Trouble* had debuted at South by Southwest a couple of years ago, and he loved the craziness, the energy, the deal making. He loved seeing all the new movies at the cutting edge of cinema, the heady rush of thousands of people who loved to create. But the edits on *Bluff* nagged at his mind, undone, so he had decided to skip this year's events.

Crowded around the tables were young people who reminded her of Evan—talking, laughing, their minds focused on art rather than survival. He should be here with her, watching movies, listening to bands, his mother alive. Instead she watched Dezz signal the hostess with two fingers and she followed him to a booth. Carrie excused herself to go to the ladies' room, left him playing with the sugar packets.

The ladies' room was busy and noisy. In the privacy of a stall, Carrie opened a false bottom in her purse. She removed a Pocket PC, tapped out a brief message, and pressed Send. The PDA tapped into the wireless server in a coffee shop next door. She waited for an answer.

When she was done reading the reply, she blinked away the tears that threatened her eyes and washed her face with trembling hands. She came out of the ladies' room, half-expecting Dezz to have his ear pressed to the door, and then she could simply kill him on the spot. But the hallway held only a trio of laughing women.

She returned to the booth. Dezz dumped his sixth sugar packet into his iced tea, watching a mound of sweetness filter down past the cubes into the tea. She considered him: the high cheekbones, the dirty-blond hair, the ears that protruded slightly, and instead of being afraid of him she pitied him. For just one bent moment. Then she remembered the deputy and the woman on the highway, him shooting at Evan, and disgust filled her heart. She could shoot him, right here in the booth. His hands were nowhere near his gun.

But instead she sat down. He had ordered iced tea for her as well.

"Sometimes," he said, not looking at her, "I really hate you and then I don't."

"I know." She sipped at her tea.

"Do you love Evan?" He asked this in a soft, almost childish whisper, as though he'd spent his day's ration of bravado and bluster.

There was only one answer she could give him. "No. Of course not."

"Would you tell me if you did?"

"No. But I don't love him."

"Love is hard." Dezz poked his straw into his sugar hill, stirred it down to nothing. "I love Jargo and look how he talks to me."

"That deputy. That poor woman. Dezz, you understand why it was a terrible mistake. How you put us at further risk." She had to treat it like a tactical error, not a human tragedy, because she was not sure that his unfinished jigsaw of a brain understood sadness and loss.

"Yeah. I know." He crumbled a tostada, flicking the fragments across the table, stuck his finger in the salsa, licked it clean. The waitress came and took their orders. Dezz wanted *tres leches* cake first, but Carrie said no, dessert after dinner, and he didn't argue.

Her hate for him did not ease, but she wondered what chance he had ever had, with Jargo as a father. "Where did you go to school, Dezz?"

He looked at her in surprise, unaccustomed to a personal question. She realized he never regularly spoke to anyone other than Jargo and Galadriel. He had no friends. "Nowhere. Everywhere. He sent me to school in Florida for a while. I liked Florida. Then New York, and I didn't even know if he was alive or dead for three years, then California for two years. Then I was Trevor Rogers. Trevor, isn't that a name that suits me? Other times he didn't bother with school. I helped him."

"He taught you to shoot and strangle and steal." She kept her voice lower than the Tejano music drifting from the speakers, than the laughter from the tables.

"Sure. I didn't like school, anyway. Too much reading. I liked sports, though."

She tried to imagine Dezz playing baseball without taking a bat to the opposing pitcher. Or three-on-three basketball, occupying the court with boys whose fathers did not teach them how to disarm an alarm system or slice open a jugular. "You don't do this often, do you? Just sit and eat with another human being."

"I eat with Jargo."

"You could call him Dad."

He sucked a long draw on his sugar-clouded tea. "He doesn't like it. I only do it to annoy him."

She remembered her own father, her clear and unabated love for him. She watched Dezz swirl the tea in his mouth, look up at her, then look down back to his drink in a mix of contempt and shyness. She saw, with aching clarity, that he believed she was probably the only woman he could talk to, that he could hope for.

"I'm still mad at you," he said to his tea glass.

Their plates arrived. Dezz forked a chunk of beef enchilada, looped a long string of cheese around his fork, and broke the thread with a flourish. He tested out a smile. It chilled her and sickened her all at once. "But I'll get over it."

"I know you will," she said.

*   *   *

The apartment was quiet and dark. Jargo had rented the two adjoining apartments as well to ensure privacy. He set a small digital voice recorder on the coffee table, between the knives.

"No objections to being recorded, do you, Mr. Gabriel? I don't want to trample on your constitutional rights. Not the way you did on other people's in years gone by."

Gabriel's voice was barely a creak, faded from blood loss, pain, and exhaustion. "Don't you talk to me about what's moral or decent."

"You hunted me for a long time. But your license got revoked." Jargo selected a small knife and a long blade geared for holiday duty. "This big beauty is designed to cut turkey. Rather appropriate."

"You're nothing but a traitor."

Jargo inspected the knife, ran its edge along his palm. "That line is awfully tired. Traitor baiter. Baiting isn't a very strong action. Catching is more impressive." He came closer to Gabriel. "Who are you working for these days? CIA or Donna Casher or someone else who wants to bring me down?"

Gabriel swallowed. Jargo held up the thin silver of the small blade, raised an eyebrow. "This one's not for turkey. It's for sausages."

"You'll kill me regardless if I talk or not."

"My son didn't leave me much of you to work with. But it's your choice whether the end is fast or slow. I'm a humanitarian."

"Screw you."

"Not me. Your daughter. Or your granddaughters. She's, let's see, thirty-five, very rich husband, living in Dallas. I'll send my son up to her showcase home. Dezz'll rape her, make rich hubby watch, tell them the reason their wonderful lives are being cruelly abbreviated is her father, then gut them both." He paused and smiled. "Then I'll sell your granddaughters. I know a reclusive gentleman in Dubai. He'll pay me twenty thou for them. More if I don't break up the set."

Gabriel's eyes moistened in terror. "No. No."

Jargo smiled. Everyone but him had a weakness, and that made him feel so much better and secure in his place in the world.

"Then let's chat like the professionals we are so your family gets to enjoy their storybook life. Who are you working for?"

Gabriel took two deep breaths before answering. "Donna Casher."

"What exactly were you supposed to do for her?"

"Get fake IDs for them, get her and her kid to her husband. Then get all three of them out of the country. Protect them."

"And your payment was what?" Jargo moved closer with the larger knife, brushed its edge along Gabriel's jaw.

"Hundred thousand dollars."

Jargo lowered the knife. "Ah. A cash basis. Would you like a drink to kill the pain? Kentucky bourbon? Mexican tequila?"

"Sure." Gabriel closed his eyes.

"And I heard you were off the sauce. Shame to backpedal. Well, you can't have a drink. Not yet. I don't believe that hundred thou was the whole payment, Mr. Gabriel."

"Please, don't hurt my girls. They don't know anything."

Jargo leaned close to Gabriel, studied Gabriel's face as

though admiring the deftness of a painting, and flicked out his hand. A shred of cheek parted from Gabriel's face. Gabriel gritted his teeth but didn't scream. Blood dripped from the cut, in a slow ooze.

"I'm impressed." Jargo got up, went to the bar, opened a bottle of whiskey. Sniffed at it. "Glenfidlich. Mother's milk, during your glory days at the Company. At least what I heard in the rare moments I gave you any thought." He poured a stream onto Gabriel's cut. "The drink you wanted. Enjoy."

Gabriel moaned.

"Now. An old spook like you, a hundred thousand won't keep you in Fritos and Ripple." He produced a piece of paper from his jacket, held it up. "We traced this e-mail from you to Donna Casher. Decode it for me."

The old training died hard. "I don't know what it means."

Jargo flicked the blade along the ear's surface, scored blood from the lobe. Gabriel jerked. "With two bullets in you, your mouth ruined, this doesn't hurt much. You want me to dig the bullets out for you?" Jargo grinned.

Gabriel shuddered.

"See, Donna Casher turning to an ex-CIA drunk is truly the million-dollar question. Why you? I believe you were willing to take a bigger chance. For more than money. Tell me. For your family's sake." Jargo leaned down, whispered into the man's devastated ear. "Buy their safety."

Gabriel's chest heaved. He cried. Jargo restrained himself from cutting the man's throat. He hated tears. They lessened a person so.

Gabriel found his breath. "The message meant she was ready to run."

"Thank you," Jargo said. "Running with what?"

"Donna had a list."

Confirmation. "A list."

"Of a group of people. Inside the CIA...running illegal, unauthorized operations. Hiring out assassination and espionage work to a freelance group of spies she called the Deeps. She had your CIA clients' names, she had account information on how they had paid for your services. Like I always suspected."

"And never proved," Jargo said. "Describe the data, please."

"This freelance group, the Deeps, she said they had clients inside the CIA. Inside the Pentagon. Inside the FBI. Inside MI5 and MI6 in England. Inside every intelligence agency in the world. Inside the Fortune 500. Inside governments, all high-ranking people. Any time someone needs a dirty job, forever off the books...they come to you."

"They do," Jargo said. "You can see why my clients wouldn't appreciate you taking their names in vain." He brought the knife closer to Gabriel's throat. "Did Mitchell Casher know about your arrangement to be his wife's bodyguard?"

"She said he didn't know about her having this client list, or her wanting to run. He was on an assignment for the Deeps—for you—and she said we would meet him in Florida in three days. That was his reentry point after his assignment overseas. She wanted me with her when she talked to him. To convince Mitchell they had no choice but to run. I was to pose as a CIA liaison, tell him they were getting immunity and new identities in exchange for the data. Then they'd run, the whole family, together."

"Donna made this a fait accompli."

"She didn't want to give her husband a choice. She was burning their every bridge."

"Where was she running to?"

"I just had to get the Cashers safely to Florida. They would run from there. Anywhere. I don't know. Didn't Donna tell you this before you killed her?"

"Dezz killed her. In a rage. Because she would not speak. She was stronger than you. And she had better training." He wiped blood off the knife. "And so she summoned Evan to Austin."

"Donna planned to explain to him they had to run—tell him the entire truth. That she worked for your network, she wanted you brought down, that she would give me the data to bring down every one of your clients. Then we were driving to Florida. She wanted to avoid airports."

"Lucky for him you arrived." Jargo brought his face close to Gabriel's. "This client list and some related files were on Evan's computer. We saw it. We erased it. You're telling me he didn't know he had the files?"

"I don't know if he knew or not. I'm telling you what his mother knew. He . . . he doesn't seem to know much."

"Does he know or not?"

"I don't . . . think so. He's dumb as a stump."

"No, he's not dumb." Jargo ran the tip of the blade along Gabriel's chin. "I don't believe you. Donna cleaned the files off her computer. She sent a backup to Evan's computer. But she would need the files to convince Evan of the need for them to vanish. You don't simply just go and run away from your life. So Evan must have seen the files. And taken the precaution of making a copy and hiding it."

"He doesn't know."

Jargo jabbed the knife into the bullet wound in Gabriel's shoulder, and Gabriel's eyes bugged, the veins popped on his neck. Jargo clamped a hand over Gabriel's mouth, twisted the knife, let the scream run its course under his fingers, removed the knife, flicked away the blood.

"Are you sure?"

"He knows," Gabriel gasped. "He knows. I told him. Please. He knows your name. He knows his mother worked for you."

"He fought you."

"Yeah."

"Beat you."

"He's thirty years younger than me."

"Given your reversal of fortune," Jargo said, "I think you'd like for Evan to bring me down."

Gabriel met Jargo's stare. "You won't live forever."

"True. Where were you supposed to meet Mitchell in Florida?"

"Donna knew the location, I didn't. He wasn't expecting her. She was intercepting him on his way home."

"Where will Evan run? To the CIA?"

"I warned him off the CIA. I didn't want—"

Jargo stood. "Ego, ego, ego. You wanted the files for yourself. To bring me down. Humiliate the CIA. It would ruin them, you know. Revenge. See where it's gotten you?"

"I've kept my promise."

"Tell me. Do you often respond to any crank who contacts you to help you in your vendetta against the CIA? She must have offered you proof of her credentials. A taste for what was to come."

Gabriel looked into Jargo's face and said, "Smithson." Smiled as Jargo went pale. "I've told you everything I know."

Jargo struggled to keep his emotions from surfacing on his face. How much had Donna told this man? Jargo pretended as if the name Smithson meant nothing to him. "Evan left a large amount of cash behind in your son-in-law's Suburban. But no IDs. Presumably you didn't plan on the Cashers flying out of Florida under their own names. I need to know the identities on the documents you created for Evan."

Gabriel closed his eyes. As though steeling himself for the answer.

Jargo sipped at the whiskey, leaned over close to Gabriel, and spat whiskey onto Gabriel's facial gash.

Gabriel spat back.

Jargo wiped the string of saliva from his cheek with the back of his hand. "You'll give me every name Evan's got documentation for. And then we'll go—"

Nowhere. Gabriel whipped his head downward and to the right. Jargo still held the long silver blade of the knife in his hand, and Gabriel pounded his throat onto the point with one breathless blow.

"No!" Jargo jerked away, letting go of the knife. It wedged in Gabriel's neck. Gabriel collapsed to the floor, eyes clenched shut, and then his breath and his life unfolded out of him.

Jargo slid the knife free. He tested for a pulse; gone.

"You can't know. You can't know." In a fury, he started kicking the body. The face. The jaw. Bone and teeth snapped under his heel. Blood splattered across the calfskin. His leg started to get tired, his pants were ruined, and the rage drained out of him and he collapsed to the soiled carpet. *Smithson.* How much had Donna told Gabriel or told her son?

"Did you lie to me?" Jargo asked Gabriel's body. "Do you know our names?" He couldn't risk it. Not at all. He had to assume the worst. Evan knew.

He could never let his clients know they were in danger. That would start a panic. It would destroy his business, his credibility. His clients could never, ever know such a list existed. He had to bring Evan down now.

He cleaned the blood from the knife and called Carrie's cell phone. "Get back here. We're leaving for Houston. Immediately."

No debate now. No discussion. Evan Casher was a dead man, and Jargo knew he had just the perfect bait to grace a trap.

SUNDAY

MARCH 13

18

SUNDAY MORNING, shortly after midnight, Evan finally let himself weep for his murdered mother.

Alone in the cheap Houston motel room, not far from the shadow of the old Astrodome and the distant hum of cars speeding along Loop 610, the lights off and the bed weathered with hourly use, he lay down, alone, and memories of his mother and his father flooded his mind. The tears came then, hot and harsh, and he curled into a ball and let them come.

He hated to cry. But the moorings of his life had been shorn away, and the grief throbbed in his chest like a physical pain. His mother had been gentle, wry, careful as a craftsman about her photos. Shy with strangers but expansive and talkative with him and his father. When he was little and would beg to sit in her darkroom and watch her work, she would stand over her photo-developing equipment, a lock of hair dangling in her face, singing little songs under her breath that she composed on the spot to keep him entertained. His father was quiet, too, a reader, a computer geek, a man of few words, but when he spoke every word mattered. Always supportive, insightful, quick to hug, quick to gently discipline. Evan could not have asked for kinder and better parents. They were quiet and a little closemouthed, and now that quirk loomed large in his head. Because now it meant more than computerish solitude or artistic introversion. Was it a veil for what lay beyond, their secret world?

He'd believed he knew them. But the burden of a hidden life, lived just beyond his eyes, was unimaginable to him.

Because they didn't want you hurt. Or because they didn't trust you.

Ten minutes. Crying done. No more, he told himself. He was done with tears. He washed his face, wiping it dry with the paper-thin, worn towel.

Exhaustion staggered him. He had driven straight into San Antonio, changed the license plates off the stolen pickup, trading with a decrepit-looking station wagon in a neighborhood where it seemed less than likely the police would get a prompt phone call. He drove the speed limit on I-10, heading east, winding through the coastal flatlands and into the humid sprawl of Houston. He stopped only for gas, eating Slim Jims and guzzling coffee, paying with cash when he had to refill the tank. He found a cheap motel—cheap in that the hookers shook their moneymakers a block away—and booked a room for the night. The clerk seemed to resent him—Evan supposed they didn't get much demand for more than an hour or two in the room. Evan palmed the room key and drove the truck—too nice for the lot—past an old woman smoking cigarettes in a doorway, past two whores chatting and laughing in the parking lot. He locked the door behind him. There was no furniture other than the bed and a worn TV stand, bolted to the floor. The TV brought a fuzzy picture and offered only the local Houston channels.

All gone. The words spoken by one of the killers in the

kitchen. The file they killed his mother for had been on his computer. Somehow.

Gabriel said she'd e-mailed the files. Assume it was true, since she'd sent him a large e-mail late the night before she called him. So she must have hidden a program inside the songs, tucking these hidden files on his laptop in a place he would never look. He wasn't a computer geek, he didn't explore the innards of his laptop, he didn't browse through his library or preference files. But the data would be there, a backup for his mother or insurance for Gabriel, and Evan would have never thought twice about receiving a set of music files.

Music files.

He dug his digital music player out of the duffel. Evan always synced his music files with his digital music player, and he had Friday morning, so he could listen to the music during the drive to Austin. So potentially he still had the file—still encoded, but not lost. If he could move the correct music file to a new computer, it might automatically re-create the files his mother had stolen.

If it was in a digital photo—those he didn't back up. It would be lost forever.

He would need a computer. He didn't have enough cash for one, and he did not dare use a credit card. Tomorrow's problem.

Outside, a woman cussed, a man laughed and asked her to love him until tomorrow, then the same woman laughed with him.

He dug out the small, locked box he had taken from Gabriel's house. A single wire hanger dangled in the closet; he tried to pick the lock with its bent end, feeling ridiculous. Got nowhere. He walked down to the motel office.

"Do you have a screwdriver I can borrow?" he asked the clerk.

The clerk looked at him with empty eyes. "Maintenance'll be here tomorrow."

Evan slid a five-dollar bill across the counter. "I just need a screwdriver for ten minutes."

The clerk shrugged, got up, returned with a screwdriver, took the bill. "Bring it back in ten or I'll call the cops."

Customer service, alive and well. Evan headed back to his room, ignoring a "Hey, sweetheart, you need a date?" from a prostitute at the edge of the parking lot.

Evan broke the lock on the fifth try. Small, paper-wrapped packages spilled out, and Evan hurried back to the office in case the grumpy clerk made good on his threat. The clerk didn't look over from his TV basketball game as Evan slid the tool back across the counter.

The low groans of a couple sounded through the thin walls when he went back into the room. He didn't want to hear them and he cranked on the TV. Evan opened the first package. Inside were passports from New Zealand, held together with a rubber band. He opened the top one: his own face stared back at him. He was David Edward Rendon, his birthplace listed as Auckland. The paper looked and felt appropriately high-grade government authentic; an exit stamp indicated he'd left New Zealand a scant three weeks ago.

He picked up another New Zealand passport from the spill of papers. His mother's picture inside, a false name of Margaret Beatrice Rendon, the paper worn as if it had flown a lot of miles. A South African passport in the name of Janine Petersen. Same last name as his African identity. A Belgian passport for his mother as well, her name now

Solange Merteuil. He picked up another Belgian document. His picture again, but with the name of Jean-Marc Merteuil. He opened the second package: three passports for Gabriel, false names from Namibia, Belgium, Costa Rica.

The next package held four bound passports at the bottom of the pile, looped together by a rubber band. He flipped them over, freed them from the band. South Africa. New Zealand. Belgium. United States. Opened them. And inside each, his father's face stared up at him. Four different names: Petersen, Rendon, Merteuil, Smithson.

Odd. Three for him, three for his mother, but four for his dad. Why?

In the final package were credit cards and other identity documentation, tied to his family's new names. But he was afraid to use the cards. What if Jargo could find him if he charged gas or plane fare or a meal? He needed cash, but he knew if he made an ATM withdrawal from his accounts, the transaction would register in the bank's database, the security tape would capture his image, and the police would know he was back in Houston. *So what if they know you're in Houston? You're leaving for Florida.* But he was still reluctant to go to a bank.

He tucked the passports back into the bag.

The awful question wormed in past his fatigue: *Was Jargo waiting for me at Mom's?* If Jargo wasn't expecting Evan, then they were after his mother and Evan had simply arrived at the wrong time. But if they were . . . how had they known he was coming? He had talked directly to no one but his mother. He could phone in an anonymous tip to the police, suggest they look for bugs on her phone. Or on his. He had called Carrie, left her a voice mail. They could have intercepted that message.

You're ignoring that Carrie quit her job that morning. She vanished without telling you. Did she know about this?

The thought dried his throat. *Don't love me,* she had said. But that couldn't mean regret. That couldn't mean she was preparing to betray him. He knew her, he knew her heart. He could not believe Carrie would have any voluntary involvement in this horror. It had to be a phone tap. Which was an entirely scary prospect of its own. Gabriel had called Jargo a freelance spy—assume that was true, then Jargo could tap phones. But if it wasn't, then Jargo was working for a bigger fish. The CIA. The FBI.

He needed money. He had the Beretta he'd fired at Dezz, but he had no ammo left. He needed help.

Shadey. He could call Shadey. The falsely accused man who had been at the heart of his first documentary. Shadey had griped about Evan plenty on CNN, but he was tough and smart and resourceful.

Evan paced the floor, trying to decide. He suspected if the police were serious about finding him, Shadey might be under surveillance. And Evan was a little afraid of Shadey. He had been wrongly persecuted by a vengeful cop, but he wasn't a saint. He was a risky choice as an ally. He craved attention, and from his TV interview he acted as if Evan had done him wrong. He might turn Evan over to the police immediately and grab a headline for himself.

But Evan had no one else to ask.

He doused the lights. Played back every moment he had spent with Carrie Lindstrom over the past three months, when she had stepped into his life. When he slept, he did not dream of her, but of the noose tightening around his neck as his mother lay dead below his feet.

A harsh buzzing woke him. Forgetting where he was,

he first thought it was his old alarm clock, and that Carrie was in the bed with him, and all was right with the world. But it was the stolen cell phone from the truck. Probably the owner, calling to chew him out for stealing the phone. It was 6:00 A.M. Sunday morning. He picked up the phone; the display screen didn't reveal a number.

He clicked on the phone. "Hello?"

"Evan. Good morning. How are you?" a voice said. It had a soft Southern drawl.

"Who is this?"

"You can call me Bricklayer."

"Bricklayer?"

"My real name's a secret, son. It's an unfortunate precaution I have to take."

"I don't understand."

"Well, Evan, I'm from the government, and I'm here to help you."

19

---◆◉◆---

"HOW DID YOU GET THIS NUMBER?" Evan whispered. Outside was still and quiet, except for the infrequent hum of traffic; the lovers next door slept or, more likely, had concluded their business and crept back into the empty night.

"We have our ways," Bricklayer said.

"I'm hanging up unless you tell me how you got this number."

"Simple. We recognized Mr. Gabriel from the police description. We know Mr. Gabriel seized you for, well, let's call it his version of protective custody. We know he was in Bandera because of a credit-card charge he made. We know he has a family member with a house that has been occupied, damaged, and abandoned as of yesterday. We know Mr. Gabriel is missing. We know a truck with a cell phone in it was stolen from Bandera. We arranged with the owner and the cell phone company to keep the phone activated. So we could talk to you, if you or Mr. Gabriel was in possession of the phone. And I see that you are."

Evan got up and began to pace the room.

"May I speak to Mr. Gabriel?" Bricklayer asked.

"He's dead."

"Oh. That's unfortunate. How did he die?"

"A man named Dezz Jargo shot him."

A long sigh. "That's very regrettable. Are you injured?"

"No. I'm fine."

"Good. Let's proceed. Evan, I bet you're scared and tired and wondering what you ought to do next."

Evan waited.

"I can help you."

"I'm listening." He wondered—they had found him because of a stolen phone. Could they be tracing the call, turning a satellite miles above to shift its lens onto Texas, onto Houston, onto this seedy nowhere?

"You and I have a mutual problem. Jargo and Dezz."

Evan blinked. "Dezz is Jargo. Jargo's his last name."

"Clarification, Evan. I say Jargo, I mean a man we know as Steven Jargo. Dezz is his son. Of course, those aren't their real names. No one knows what their real names are. Probably even they don't."

"His son." He'd had it wrong. Dezz and Jargo. So there were two. Son and father. "They killed my mother."

"Dezz and Jargo will kill you, too, if they get a chance. We don't want you hurt, Evan. I want you to tell me where you're at, and I'm gonna send a couple of men to pick you up. Protect you."

"No."

"Evan, now, why say no? You're in terrible danger."

"Why should I trust you? I don't even know your real name."

"I understand your reticence. Truly. Caution is the hallmark of an intelligent mind. But you need to come in under our wing. We can help you."

"Help me by finding my dad."

"I don't know where he is, son, but if you come in, we'll move heaven and earth to find him."

It sounded like an empty promise. "I don't have the files you all want. They're gone. Jargo and Dezz destroyed them." He picked up his music player. Perhaps not. But if he simply gave them the files, they could use them how they wanted, destroy them, and make him vanish. He would only trade them for his father. Nothing else.

Bricklayer paused, as though contemplating unexpected news. "Jargo won't leave you alone."

"He can't find me."

"He can and he will."

"No. You want what he wants. These files. You'll kill me, too."

"I most certainly would not." Bricklayer sounded offended. "Evan, you're emotionally exhausted. It's understandable, given your horrible ordeal. Let me give you a number, in case we get disconnected. I loathe cell phones. Will you write the number down?"

"Yes," and Bricklayer fed him a number. He didn't recognize the area code.

"Evan. Listen to me. Jargo and Dezz are very dangerous. Extremely."

"You're preaching to the choir." He risked a guess. "Are you with the CIA?"

"I loathe acronyms as much as cell phones," Bricklayer said. "Evan, we can have substantive talks when you come in. I personally guarantee your safety."

"You won't even tell me your name." Evan paced the room. "I could buy time by talking to the press. Telling them the CIA is offering to help me. Give them this number."

"You could go public. I suspect, though, that Jargo will kill your father in retaliation."

"You're saying he has my father." Evan waited.

"It's most likely. I'm sorry." Bricklayer sounded like a mortician, gently agreeing that, yes, it was a beautiful casket. "Let's move forward, so we can work together to get your dad home. Would you meet with me? We can meet in Texas; I assume you're still in the state—"

"I'll consider it and call you back."

"Evan, don't hang up."

Evan did. He switched off the phone, dropped it on the bed as if it were radioactive. If Bricklayer could triangulate on the phone, the government could just bust the door down.

He pulled on a change of clean clothes he'd packed in the duffel. He spread his cash in front of him. He had ninety-two dollars. A camcorder, a cell phone, a Beretta with no ammunition.

He couldn't face Shadey or the sweet-talking Bricklayer or Dezz and Jargo without being armed. It would be suicide. But he didn't think gun shops were open on Sundays, and he couldn't go into one anyway, not with his picture all over the news as a missing man. Pawnshops? He didn't want to part with the camera suddenly; he wished he could have gotten Dezz on film. That would have been leverage. Selling the camera was a last resort.

You could buy all sorts of things on the street. Drugs. Sex. Why not ammo?

He closed his eyes. Thought out ways he could acquire ammo for a particular gun. One idea came to mind, crazy, definitely daring, but it played on the only common wish he knew how to grant with the skills and resources he had.

Evan ventured into the early-morning damp. Down low on his head, he wore a baseball cap that had been in the rear seat of the stolen truck. He bought the Sunday *Houston Chronicle* out of a vending machine in front of a decrepit coffee shop. His face and his father's face were on the cover of the metro section, an old publicity photo his mother had shot after *Ounce of Trouble* had made the short list for the Oscars, where his hair was shorter and he wore nerd-boy eyeglasses. He didn't need glasses but he'd decided they made him look smarter, more artistic. It had been a shallow affectation; his mother had teased him about how seriously he took himself, and now he felt embarrassed. The paper said his father was also considered missing; no record existed of anyone named Mitchell Casher having flown to Australia from the United States in the past week. No mention or picture of Carrie.

Carrie's here with me, Dezz had claimed in his creepy singsong voice. Evan had not believed him. If Carrie had been kidnapped, it would have been in the papers.

Or would it? She had quit her job. She wasn't with him. Who would report her missing? But if she had been taken, she wouldn't have been able to call him and warn him before Gabriel's attack. So where was Carrie? Hiding? He ached to talk to her, to hear her soothing voice, but he couldn't go near her, he couldn't involve her again.

He folded the paper under his arm. Pay phones were a dying breed with a cell phone wedged in every pocket and purse, but he found one two blocks down at a convenience store where the lot smelled of Saturday-night beer. A gangly kid lounged near the phones, chewing on a grape Pixy Stix, watching Evan with all the suspicion and arrogance of a prison guard.

He might do. Evan picked up a phone, dropped in the required coins.

"'Spectin' an important call on that phone," the boy said in a low murmur. Giving Evan a narrowed stare.

"Then they'll get a busy signal for a minute."

"Find another phone, son," the kid said.

Evan stared at him. He wanted to pop the kid in the sneering mouth and say, *You picked the wrong guy to mess with today*. But then he decided he didn't need another enemy. He had learned one thing as a filmmaker: everyone wanted to be in a movie.

Evan didn't put a smile on his face because smiles weren't always good currency. "You an entrepreneur?"

"Yeah, that's me. I'm a mogul."

Evan grabbed the Beretta tucked in the back of his jeans, under his shirt, and he jammed it into the kid's flat stomach. The kid froze.

"Calm down. It's unloaded," Evan said. "I need bullets. Can you get them for me?"

The kid let out a long wheeze. "Man, forget you. I might've if you hadn't been a jerk just now."

"Then I'll make my call." Evan let his fingers drift back to the filthy keypad.

"Wait, wait. What is it?" The kid put his back to the street and examined the gun. Evan kept it in a tight grip. "Beretta 92FS ... yeah, I bet I can score a few sweet mags for you. Friend of a friend. Cash basis."

"Of course."

"Lemme make a call on your coins," the kid said.

Evan handed him the receiver. The kid punched numbers, spoke in a low tone, laughed once, hung up the phone. "An hour. Be here. Cash. Four mags, fifteen rounds each, three hundred dollars."

He didn't know ammo prices, but he suspected the quote

was higher than what he would pay in a gun shop or online. But the street didn't ask questions. "I don't need that much ammo."

"Won't deal less. Otherwise not worth getting out of bed, son."

Evan didn't have three hundred dollars, but he said, "I'll be back here in an hour."

Now that he had a customer, the kid nodded. Ambled off across the lot, sliding a fresh Pixy Stix out of his pocket, tearing off the top, and dumping the purple powder onto his tongue.

Evan walked four blocks until he found another convenience store. He wore the sunglasses he had found in the stolen pickup and he bought hair-coloring dye, a pair of scissors, a giant coffee, and three breakfast tacos thick with fluffy eggs and potato and spicy chorizo sausage for breakfast. It didn't get him closer to three hundred dollars. He swallowed the crazy urge to show the clerk the gun tucked in the back of his pants to see if that would produce three hundred bucks. The clerk rang him up. Watching Evan when she gave him the change.

Fear slammed into his stomach like a fist. Was this what paranoia was?

He hurried back to the motel. Evan locked himself in. Devoured the breakfast tacos and finished the black coffee while he read the directions on the hair dye. It would take only thirty minutes to set.

He cut his hair, locks falling into the sink. He had never given himself a haircut before and it looked really bad until he muttered, "Screw vanity," and he hacked it into a not-as-bad burr. He removed the small hoop earring from his left ear. The earring seemed too young for him now; it was time to grow up. Then he dyed his hair, sitting on the bathroom floor, refining his plan while the black color set. He laughed when he saw himself in the mirror, but it was serviceable. He didn't look exactly like the picture in the paper. But he still looked like himself.

He had about eighty bucks left and ten minutes before the kid showed up with the ammunition. He drove back to the store where he had met the kid, parked at the edge of the oil-pocked lot. He went inside the store. An old lady bought orange juice and a can of pork-and-beans and shuffled out the door. Evan waited until she was gone and approached the clerk. This clerk nodded along with a Sunday-morning evangelical-church service and slurped coffee. She was an older lady, dour, with a stray eye.

"Excuse me, ma'am. That tall kid who hangs out by the phone," Evan said. "Mr. Pixy Stix. Is he a problem for you?"

"Why you care?"

"He warned me off using the phone. I bet he's using it for drug deals."

"He don't buy enough Pixy Stix to pay rent."

"So if I get him to quit hanging out here, you won't be heartbroken? You wouldn't feel you have to call the police right away?"

"I don't want no trouble."

"He'll never know what hit him."

"What do you care what he's doing? I never seen you in here before."

"My aunt just moved in down the street, and that kid smarted off to her when she was using the phone, and old ladies should be able to make phone calls without hassle."

"So tell the police."

"That's a temporary solution. The police come, then they go. My idea is longer-lasting."

The clerk studied him. "What are you doing?"

"I'm going to hang out at the phone and wait for him."

"Why? You buying?"

He held up the duffel and showed her his camcorder. "No. I'm selling."

The kid returned, five minutes late. But not alone. His companion was a thick-necked young woman with a toughness etched in her face. She stood bigger and taller than the kid, and a similar set to their eyes and their frowns suggested she might be an older sister. She carried a shopping bag from Goodwill in her hand. They arrived in a new Explorer and parked at the end of the lot.

Evan stood by the phones with the duffel over his shoulder, the digital camcorder wedged in place in the duffel. He left the zipper gaping open enough so that the lens could get a clear shot. The woman didn't like that he had the duffel. Tension deepened the frown in her face.

"Hey," Evan said.

"Drunk barber got ahold of your hair, son," the kid said.

"The makeup director wanted me to have a more street look," Evan said, and waited to see what they would say.

The kid just frowned as if Evan were crazy—and then the woman said, "Let's go to the back of the store."

"Actually, there'll be a phone call coming in for you here in a minute. We should just wait right here." Evan put a bright, fake smile on his face.

"Excuse me?" The woman was running the show now, not the kid.

"Here's the deal," Evan said. "I'm a scout for a new

reality show, it's called *Tough Streets*. HBO next fall. We put people who don't have any street smarts in neighborhoods where they've never been before. Picture soccer moms and suburban dads trying to cope in the Fifth Ward. Whoever can accomplish a set list of goals, well, they move on in the competition. The grand prize is a million bucks."

The woman stared at Evan, but the boy said, "I got an idea for a show. You put me in River Oaks, let me live in luxury, and film that all the livelong day."

"Shut up. You buying or not?" the woman said.

"Did you bring the ammo?" Evan asked.

"Yeah."

"I'm buying. But we're test-driving this as one of our challenges. I just wanted to see how easy it was to buy ammo on the street. While taping." He raised the camcorder, with its lens cap off and recording lights aglow, out of the duffel. "Smile."

"No, no, no!" the woman said, and she shielded her face with her fingers.

"Wait. Wait." Evan switched off the camcorder. "I'm not getting you in trouble. I just had to test the challenge. Ma'am, you're an original. You're what we're looking for on *Tough Streets*."

"Me. On TV." She brought her hands down from her face.

He held up one hand as though framing her face. "I think you'd be great. But you don't have to be on TV if you don't want to be."

"Big Gin gonna be a star." The kid laughed.

Big Gin froze. "What is this?"

Evan held up his hands. "The contestants all have street guides as partners in the game, because you and I know that they won't have a chance without them. Dumb people from suburbia."

"Like you," Big Gin said.

"Yes, like me. You're beyond telegenic. The strength in your face. The confidence of your walk, your talk. Of course the street guide shares half the prize money—"

"A half million. You're kidding," Big Gin said.

"—unless you have a record," Evan finished his sentence. "We could not hire anyone with a record. The lawyers are insistent about that."

"Buying ammo would get you a record," Big Gin said.

"Well, the contestants wouldn't truly be buying real ammunition. Just blanks. The lawyers are insistent about that, too."

"She's never been convicted," the kid said.

"Shut up." Big Gin looked at Evan in a way he'd seen in film-deal meetings: a player who's wondering if she's the one being played.

"This is bull," the kid said. "You got three hundred bucks for the ammo, or not, 'cause we ain't staying if you don't."

"Shut up," Big Gin said to him.

"Um, I cannot give you three hundred bucks," Evan said. "That would mean we've conducted an illegal transaction, and we couldn't hire you then for the show, Ms...."

"Ginosha," she said.

"Don't tell him your name," the kid said. "He doesn't have the money, let's go."

Evan had a leftover card in his wallet from a screening and cocktail party he'd been at last week in Houston. One was from a producer with a Los Angeles production company called Urban Works, a guy named Eric Lawson. He handed Big Gin the card. "So sorry. Meant to give this to you earlier."

"Whoa," she said. "You for real."

"Yeah."

"Where's your camera crew? Why just you?"

"Because this is guerrilla TV. We don't bring camera crews out here when we're scouting for talent and locations. It would not be reality TV then, would it?"

Big Gin studied the business card, as though it held a doorway to a long-held desire.

"So who's calling on the phone?" she said.

"One of the talent scouts," Evan said. "He'll pretend to be the suburban contestant you have to help. But I want to film you from back over here, near this side of the lot. Just talk off the top of your head, show me how you can improvise. I've got a mike built into the phone already, but I want a distance shot of you. Here, young man, I'm sorry, what's your name?"

"Raymond." The boy examined the business card but with a critical glare.

"You come over here and stand by me, out of the shot."

Raymond frowned but not at the business card. "Why can't I be in the shot?"

"It's my shot," Big Gin said.

"Well, Raymond, frankly, you didn't act interested," Evan said. "You didn't think I was legit."

"Sure he did," Big Gin said. "That's just the way he talks. He's cool now, he's not disrespecting."

"Raymond, you know, we have to win over the young audience as well," Evan said. "Our target demographic includes teenage girls."

Raymond, holding the bag with the ammunition, tented

his cheek with his tongue, gave Evan another frown, but went and stood by the phone, calculated a pose, stood his best side.

"Excellent. But I don't like the bag being in your shot. You look like you're shopping." Evan took five steps back.

Big Gin picked up the bag of ammo clips, brought them over to Evan, put them at his feet. "We ought to be compensated for our time if you ain't buying."

"Oh, absolutely. Of course this is basically your private audition, and you didn't have to stand in line, and"—he put the camcorder up to his eye—"I go down to the community center, I got folks lining up around the lot to try out."

Big Gin gave him a look in the lens. "What do I do?"

"Let your natural personality shine through." Evan was fifteen paces from them now, worried about the boy, whose suspicions had not flagged for one moment. The duffel and the bag of ammo sat between Evan's feet. The stolen cell phone lay wedged in his back pocket.

"Act natural. Don't look at me." Evan reached behind him, pressed the dial button of his pocketed phone. It was already keyed to the pay phone's number.

One ring. "Look at the pay phone, let it ring three times, let me get the film rolling." But Evan was the one rolling, grabbing the duffel and the ammo, running backward toward his truck. Two rings. Raymond still stared at the phone, but Big Gin couldn't resist the lure of the camera's eye. She spun as Evan jumped into the truck. He'd left the key in the ignition. He wrenched the car into reverse, saw Big Gin shout and run after him. He tore out into the street, into a hail of horns of oncoming traffic.

Raymond, now sold on the idea of TV stardom, answered the phone. "Is this part of the audition?" he asked.

"I've taped you dealing for a week," Evan lied into the phone. "You show up at that phone again, I give the cops the tape." In the rearview mirror Big Gin stormed out into traffic, shooting him the finger, winded in a short run.

"That's illegal!" Raymond hollered. "You nothing but a thief."

"Complain to the cops. Thanks for the ammo. We've made a fair trade—I'll be quiet and I'll keep your bullets."

Raymond's reply got cut off when Evan thumbed off the phone. Evan floored the accelerator in case Big Gin came after him in their shiny new Explorer. He hoped Big Gin and Raymond had been more honest than he had. He opened the bag. Four magazines. He tried to fit one into the Beretta. It smacked in clean and true.

Now he could go find Shadey.

20

———◆◆◆———

EVAN DROVE THE PICKUP TRUCK PAST the gated community's wall. The condos stood behind wrought iron and imported stone. The building lay at the edge of the Galleria district, Houston's Uptown, crammed full of high-end shops and eateries and condominiums catering to both the aged oil money and the young high-tech rollers. This particular enclave was called Tuscan Pines, but tall Gulf Coast loblollies, less romantically named than European evergreens, shaded the lot. Across the street stood high-end office space and a small boutique hotel. Evan parked in the office lot.

He waited. He expected to see police cars. But instead a parade of Mercedes and BMWs and Lexuses came and went out of the gate. After another hour Shadey walked out of the security guard's box, headed toward a beat-up Toyota, got in, and puttered out of the complex. Evan followed him as he headed down Westheimer, toward River Oaks and the heart of Houston.

He stopped next to Shadey at the first light. Waited for Shadey to look over at him. Shadey was a typical Houston driver who didn't mess with glancing into other lanes.

Evan risked a honk.

Shadey looked over. Stared as Evan smiled, as he recognized him under the black hair.

I need to talk to you, Evan mouthed.

No, Shadey mouthed back. He shook his head. Blasted through the red in a sudden sharp left turn.

Evan followed. He flashed his lights. Once. Twice. Shadey made two more turns and drove behind a small barbecue restaurant. Evan followed him.

Shadey was at his window before Evan had finished parking. "You stay away from me."

"It's nice to see you, too," Evan said.

Shadey shook his head. "It's not nice to see you. No way nice to see you. I got an FBI agent I'm supposed to call if I see your smiling face."

"Well, I'm not smiling, so you don't have to call."

"Just go, man. Please."

"I'm not a suspect, I'm not a fugitive. I'm just missing."

"I don't care about what you calling yourself. I don't need trouble in my life."

"You complained on national TV that I didn't set you up in movies or as a musician."

Shadey glared at him. "Hey, man, I was just making myself available to interested parties. You never know who's watching the news."

"Well, since you told a couple of lies about me, you can help me and wipe the slate clean. I need cash."

"Do I look like an ATM?" Shadey lowered his sunglasses so Evan could see his eyes. "I'm a security guard, I don't got cash."

"I know you can get cash, Shadey. You have connections."

"No more. Get your unconnected self on your way."

"It's funny how being cleared of a crime creates this

wave of gratitude," Evan said. "Considering you didn't even have a good lawyer when I met you."

"I don't owe you forever, Evan."

"Yes, you actually do. Without *Ounce of Trouble* you're still in jail, Shadey, and, yes, you owe me forever."

Shadey closed his eyes. "You're in trouble. I don't do trouble anymore. I help you, I'm a felon."

"No. You're a friend."

"Spare me, man."

"I pissed off the wrong people, just like you did years ago, and they're trying to kill me to make a problem go away. I need cash, I need a computer."

"Make yourself a movie. Explain it to the world." Shadey shook his head. "I'm sorry, no way, no how."

"You know what, you didn't deserve me, as an advocate or a friend. I'm sorry I bothered. You live your life of freedom. Free to complain. Thank me when you think of it."

Shadey stared at him. Pushed his sunglasses back into place.

Evan started the pickup's engine. "If people come around looking for me, tell them you haven't seen me. But don't be surprised if they kill you just to cover their trail." He started to put the car into reverse and Shadey put his hand on the door. Evan stopped.

"I already got a call. After I was on CNN. A lady. Said her name was Galadriel Jones. She said she worked for *Film Today* magazine. Said if I heard from you or could tell her where you was, exclusivelike, I'd get fifty thousand in cash. Under the table."

Evan knew *Film Today*. It was a small, influential trade-press publication, and he didn't believe for a second a reporter would pay fifty thousand dollars to a tipster; an industry magazine couldn't afford it.

"How did this woman sound?"

"Too-sweet nice."

"Did she give you a phone number?"

"Yeah. Said not to call the magazine's number, said to call her number."

"They're playing you for a fool, Shadey. They won't pay you. They'll kill us both. The people who killed my mom, I think they've got my dad. The only way you're safe is if you help me."

Shadey cracked knuckles, cussed under his breath. Leaned in close to the window. "I don't like gettin' played. By either them or you."

"I'm the one being straight with you. I've always been straight with you, no matter what you think. Please help me."

Shadey gave Evan a hard stare. "You remember where my stepbrother's house is, over in Montrose?"

"Yeah."

"Meet me there in two hours. You ain't there when I arrive, I ain't waiting, and we never saw each other, we never talked, and you never come look for me again." He got back into his car, waited for Evan to back out, then peeled out of the parking lot.

Evan drove in the opposite direction, watching for cars that were watching him.

The next theft: a computer.

He couldn't go to Joe's Java, where he'd met Carrie—too many people there knew him. He remembered an independent coffee shop called Caf-fiend near Bissonnet and Kirby, usually with a big Rice University undergrad clientele. As a visual-arts student just a few years ago, he'd edit film on his laptop, leaving it at the table because there were always nice folks around and he was just up at the counter getting coffee, he could keep an eye on it. But he'd turned his back on it plenty. Laptop users could be complacent.

Shadey might not show with the money, much less with a computer. He had already stolen a truck that was someone's pride and joy; he could steal a computer. Shame welled in him. He needed something, he'd steal it. It would hurt an innocent person to steal and he still cared about that. But his survival was at stake.

He wondered as he walked into the coffee shop, *Who am I becoming?*

He put on the sunglasses he had found in the stolen pickup, ran a hand over his shortened black hair. The shop was busy, nearly every table taken, and a steady business of people buying coffee drinks to go.

A new line of computers stood on a counter running along one wall, Internet-ready. He wouldn't have to steal one—at least not to do half of what he needed. His next serious crime could wait.

He got a large coffee, surveyed the crowd. No one paid him any attention. He was anonymous. He put his back to the room, the sweat dampening his ribs. He opened a browser on one of the computers. He was the only one using the store-provided systems; most people had brought their own.

He went to Google and searched on "Joaquin Gabriel." No clear match; there were quite a few men named Joaquin Gabriel in the world. Then he added "CIA" to the search terms and got a list of links. Headlines from the *Washington Post* and the Associated Press.

VETERAN SPY'S CLAIMS ARE "DELUSIONAL," CIA SAYS. And so on. Most of the articles were five years old. Evan read them all.

Joaquin Gabriel had been CIA. Before the bourbon and paranoia got hold of him. He was charged to identify and run internal operations to lure out CIA personnel who had gone bad—a man known as a traitor baiter. Gabriel launched a series of increasingly outrageous accusations, condemning CIA colleagues for collaborating with imaginary mercenary intelligence groups, of running illegal operations both in America and abroad. Gabriel accused the wrong people, including a few of the most senior and honored operatives in the Agency, but his claims were hard to swallow given his alcoholism. And complete lack of evidence. He left, abruptly, with a government pension and no comment. He had moved back to his hometown of Dallas and set up a corporate security service.

Why would his mother trust this man—a drunken disgrace—with their lives?

It made no sense. Unless Gabriel had been dead right in theory. Mercenary intelligence groups. Freelance spies. Consultants. What he claimed Jargo was.

That's why Mom went to Gabriel. She knew he would believe her; this was the evidence that would vindicate him, redeem his career.

He had another idea. The names on his father's passports. Petersen. Rendon. Merteuil. Smithson. *You also don't know about your parents.* Gabriel meant more than the usual unimaginable life of his parents before he was born or their hidden dreams and thoughts. More than regrets of youth or unfulfilled hopes or an ambition never mentioned to him but allowed to die in isolation. Something bad.

Petersen. Rendon. Merteuil. Smithson.

First he did searches on Merteuil. Most of the links referenced Merteuil as the surname of the vicious aristocratic schemer from the French novel *Les Liaisons Dangereuses*, variously played in film adaptations by Glenn Close, Annette Bening, and Sarah Michelle Gellar. He wondered if that meant anything, an alias based on a deceitful character. But then he found a reference to a Belgian family with that surname, killed five years ago in a Meuse River flood. The dead Merteuils had the same names as those on his family's Belgian passports: Solange, Jean-Marc, Alexandre.

Rendon produced a bunch of results, and he specified the search more carefully on the name in his alias: David Edward Rendon. He got a website rallying against drunk driving in New Zealand and listing a long history of people killed in accidents as meat for the argument for stiffer penalties. A family had been killed in a horrific crash in the Coromandel mountains east of Auckland. James Stephen Rendon, Margaret Beatrice Rendon, David Edward Rendon. The three names on the passports.

He searched on the Petersen names. Same story. A family lost in a house fire in Pretoria, blamed on smoking in bed.

Dead families hijacked, he and his parents readied to step into their identities.

The coffee in his gut rose up like bile.

It was the nature of a good lie to hug the truth. He was Evan Casher. He was supposed to be, in addition, Jean-Marc Merteuil, David Rendon, Erik Petersen. Every name was a lie waiting to be lived by his whole family.

Except the one name that didn't have a match in his mother's or his fake passports, the extra passport for his father. Arthur Smithson.

Searching the name produced only a scattering of links. An Arthur Smithson who was an insurance agent in Sioux Falls, South Dakota. An Arthur Smithson who taught English at a college in California. An Arthur Smithson who had vanished from Washington, D.C.

He clicked on the link to a story in the *Washington Post*. It was a report on unsolved disappearances in the D.C. area. Arthur Smithson's name was mentioned, as well as several others: runaway teens, vanished children, missing fathers. Links offered the original stories in the *Post* archives. He clicked on the one for Smithson and found a story from twenty-four years ago:

Search for "Missing" Family Suspended
by Federico Moreno, Staff Reporter

A search for a young Arlington couple and their infant son was called off today, despite a neighbor's insistence that the couple would not simply pull up stakes without saying good-bye. Freelance translator Arthur Smithson, 26; his wife, Julie, 25; and their two-month-old son, Robert, vanished from their Arlington home three weeks ago. A concerned neighbor phoned Arlington police after not seeing Mrs. Smithson and the baby play in the yard for several days. Police entered the house and found no signs of struggle, but did find that the Smithsons' luggage and clothing appeared to be missing. Both the Smithsons' cars were in the garage.

"We have no reason to suspect foul play," Arlington Police Department spokesman Ken Kinnard said.

"We've run into a brick wall. We don't have an explanation as to where they are. Until we receive more information, we have no leads to pursue."

"The police need to try harder," said neighbor Bernita Briggs. Mrs. Briggs said she routinely babysat for Mrs. Smithson since Robert was born, and that the young mother treated her as a confidant and gave no indication that the family planned on leaving the area.

"They had money, good jobs," Mrs. Briggs said. "Julie never said one word about leaving. She was just asking me about what curtains to pick out, what patterns to get for the nursery. They also wouldn't leave without telling me, because Julie always teased me as being a worrywart, and if they just took off and left, I'd be worried sick, and she wouldn't put me through grief. She's a kind young woman."

Mrs. Briggs told police that Smithson was fluent in French, German, and Russian and that he did translation work for various government branches and academic presses. According to Georgetown University records, Mr. Smithson graduated five years ago with degrees in French and Russian. Mrs. Smithson worked as a civilian employee of the navy until she became pregnant, at which point she resigned.

The navy did not return calls for this story.

"I wish the police would tell me what they know," Mrs. Briggs said. "A wonderful family. I pray they're safe and in touch with me soon."

The archived story offered no picture of the Smithson family. No further links to indicate that there was a follow-up story on them.

Another family, dead like the Merteuils in Belgium, the Petersens in South Africa, and the Rendons in New Zealand. But not dead. Vanished. Unless this Washington Smithson was now the Smithson selling insurance in South Dakota or the Smithson teaching Shakespeare in Pomona.

What had Gabriel said during their wild car ride out of Houston? *I'll tell you who I am. Then I'll tell you who you are.* Evan thought he was crazy. Maybe he wasn't.

He stared at the name of the vanished child. Robert Smithson. It meant nothing to him.

He jumped to a phone-directory website and entered the name BERNITA BRIGGS, searching in Virginia, Maryland, and D.C. It spat back a phone number in Alexandria. Did he risk the call on the hot cell phone? Bricklayer would know, no doubt accessing the call log. No. Better to wait. It might put her in danger if Bricklayer knew he was calling her.

He wrote down Bernita Briggs's phone number. He left, conscious of the barista's eyes on him. Wondering if this was paranoia, settling into his skin and bones, taking up permanent residence in his mind, changing who he was forever.

21

THE HOUSE STOOD ON THE EDGE of the Montrose arts district, on a street of older homes, most tidy with pride, others worn and neglected. Evan drove by Shadey's stepbrother's house twice, then parked two streets over and walked, the duffel over his shoulder. The cap and shades made him feel like a bandit waiting outside a bank. A For Sale sign stood in the overgrown yard, a full sleeve of brochures awaiting curious hands. Every drape in the house lay closed, and he imagined the police waiting, or Jargo handing a suitcase full of cash to Shadey, or Bricklayer and government thugs smiling at him behind the lace. He remembered interviewing Shadey's stepbrother, Lawan, here for *Ounce of Trouble*; Lawan was a smart, kind guy, quiet where Shadey was loud, ten years older. Lawan managed a bakery, and his house always smelled of cinnamon and bread.

Evan waited at the street corner, four houses down.

Shadey was ten minutes late. He came alone, walked up to the front door, not looking at Evan. Evan followed a minute later, opening the front door, not waiting to knock. The inside of the house smelled now of dust instead of spices and flour. No one was living here.

"Where's Lawan?" Evan asked.

Shadey stood at the window, peering out to see if anyone had followed Evan. "Dead. Two months ago. The AIDS caught up with him."

"I'm really sorry. I wish you had called me."

Shadey shrugged. "When was the last time you called me, just to see how I was?"

"I'm still sorry."

"You don't have to be. Back to biz, son."

Evan waited.

"I scrounged up green for you. But you get caught, you keep my name out of it."

"Why are you so mad at me?"

Shadey lit a cigarette. "Why you think I'm mad?"

"On CNN. You acted like I'd ripped you off. I didn't make a lot of money on the movie, Shadey. I'm not Spielberg. I didn't promise you a career in entertainment—I couldn't make that promise."

"Being in your movie, you gave me a taste of a better life, Evan, better than what I had here. Better than what I could have gotten when I dealt." He watched Evan through the smoke. "You know, once *Ounce* came out, I wanted to make a movie. Tried writing a script. Took classes. Couldn't stitch two scenes together. No head for it."

"Why didn't you tell me? I would have helped you with your script."

"Would you? I think you were one busy white boy after *Ounce* hit big. You get into your work, you don't pay so much attention to people. You're right, I had my freedom because of *Ounce*. But you had your career because I said yes to letting you film my story. That's a debt you can't repay, either."

"Shadey. I'm sorry. I had no idea. I do owe you. Thank you. I'm sorry if I never said it before."

Shadey offered his hand; Evan shook it. "The whole damn world boils down to you owing another fool something. So it don't matter. Because now we're even. If I was mad—well, you limited my career options."

"I don't understand."

Shadey leaned forward in the quiet of the house. "I was still dealing dope on occasion, Evan. Yeah, that cop Henderson framed me, he planted the coke in my car. But I had kilos of coke riding in the trunk not three days before."

Evan stared.

"You really thought I was innocent, pure as the driven snow." Shadey shook his head. "Evan, I was driving the snow." He laughed at his own joke. "But you do your movie, I can't deal no more. My face is too well known, and I'm Mr. Innocent Wronged by the Police. You get me interested in movies, but I don't got a clue how to make 'em. So I'm a security guard. That's about all you left me. Certain times freedom is just painting yourself into a new corner you can't get out of."

"I'm sorry, Shadey."

"Don't worry about it no more." Shadey handed Evan the case. Evan sat it on the floor and opened it. Cash, a few hundred, all in worn tens and twenties.

"Count it, it's about a thousand. All I can spare."

"I don't need to count it. Thank you."

"Lawan had a laptop computer; you can have it."

"Thank you, Shadey. Thanks a lot." Evan blew out a sigh to hide the quaver in his voice. "I knew I could trust you. I knew you wouldn't let me down."

"Evan. Listen to yourself. You think I never saw the pity in your face, that I never heard that tone of voice that let me know you were doing me a life-changing favor? You ain't as smart as you want to be, Evan. Now you're the one brought low. Now you're the one needing the handout. Now you're the one that looks like something to scrape off the bottom of a shoe."

"I never pitied you."

"You didn't believe I could stand on my own two feet to get out of jail."

"You couldn't."

"The way the wheel of fortune spun, you landed on my doorstep, you helped me. But I want you to wake up and see the world how it is, because you don't know what it is to be in trouble, real trouble. I trusted you because I didn't have a choice. You trusted me when you do have a choice, Evan. You got other friends you could've run to, smarter than me. Don't trust unless you must. That's my motto." Shadey reached out, squeezed Evan's shoulder. "I thought about what that Galadriel Jones said to me. If you came around, she said call this number, and I'd have fifty thousand bucks in cash, tax-free."

"But you haven't called."

"What do you think?"

"No. Because you're all about respect, and she's trying to bribe you. Trick you."

"I pretended to listen to her. Sure I was tempted. That's over two years' salary taking shit from the snobs at Tuscan Pines. But you know, I might lie and I might steal once upon a time, but I ain't gonna be bought."

"I'm glad, Shadey. Thank you."

"Welcome."

"I need to borrow a phone. And I need to use your brother's computer. Are we safe here for a while?"

"Yeah. Less the real estate lady shows up to show the house." Shadey shrugged. "Doesn't seem likely."

Evan sweated through four rings.

"Hello?" A woman's voice, worn from a lifetime of use.

"Hello, may I speak to Mrs. Briggs?"

"Whatever you're selling, I sure don't want none."

"I'm not a salesman, ma'am. Please don't hang up—you're the only person who can help me."

This appeal to elderly ego could not be resisted. "Who is this?"

"My name is David Rendon." He decided at the last moment not to use his real name; old people were often news junkies, and he tossed out one of the false passport identities. "I'm a reporter for the *Post*."

She didn't give a reaction to this, so Evan plunged ahead: "I'm calling to see if you remember the Smithson family."

Silence for ten long seconds. "Who did you say you were?"

"A reporter for the *Post*, ma'am. I was doing a search through the archives and saw a story about your neighbors having vanished over twenty years ago. I couldn't find a follow-up and I was interested to know what happened to them, to you."

"Will you put my picture in the paper?"

"I bet I can arrange a picture."

"Well"—Mrs. Briggs lowered her voice to a practiced conspiratorial whisper—"no, the Smithsons never showed up again. I mean, that house was a dream, perfect for a new family, and they just up and walk away. Unbelievable. I'd gotten attached to that baby of theirs, and Julie, too. Arthur was a jerk. Didn't like to talk." Reticence was clearly a crime to Mrs. Briggs.

"But what happened to their house?"

"Well, they defaulted on the mortgage, and the bank finally resold it."

He wasn't sure what to ask next. "Were they a happy family?"

"Julie was so alone, you could see it in her face, in the way she talked. Scared girl, like the world had gone up and left her behind. She told me she was pregnant and I remember wondering, 'Why is there dread in this sweet girl's face?' Happiest news you could get, and she looked like the whole world crashed down on her."

"Did she ever tell you why?"

"I considered that she wasn't happy in her marriage to that cold fish. Child might have anchored her down."

"Did Mrs. Smithson ever suggest that she might want to run away, go live under a new name?"

"Good Lord. No." Mrs. Briggs paused. "Is that what happened?"

He swallowed. "Did you ever hear them mention the name Casher?"

"Not that I recall."

He had spent his childhood in New Orleans while his father completed a master's in computer science at Tulane. When Evan was seven, they moved to Austin. He thought he had been born in New Orleans. "Did they ever mention New Orleans to you?"

"No. What have you found out about them?"

"I've found pieces that don't quite fit together." He blew out a sigh. "You wouldn't happen to be a pack rat, would you, Mrs. Briggs?"

She gave a soft, warm laugh. "The polite term is *collector.*"

"Did you keep a photo of the Smithsons? Since you and Julie Smithson were so close?"

Silence again. "You know, I did, but I gave it to the police."

"Did you ever get it back?"

"No. They kept it, didn't return it to me. I suppose it might still be in the case file. Assuming there is one."

"You didn't keep another photo?"

"I think I had a photo of them at Christmas that I kept, but I don't know where it would be. They didn't travel at Christmas. No family but each other. They met at an orphanage, you know."

"An orphanage?"

"Positively Dickensian. Oliver Twist marrying Little Nell. I couldn't get to my sister's for Christmas one year because of a snowstorm, so I spent Christmas Eve with the Smithsons. Arthur drank. He didn't want me around. It embarrassed Julie, I could see, but we still had a nice time once Arthur passed out." She paused. "I just don't understand the pressure people inflict on themselves. It ages them. Me, I never worry."

An indecisive mother, a drunken father. It didn't sound like his parents. "Mrs. Briggs, if you have another photo of the Smithsons, I would be very obliged if I could get it from you."

"And I would be if you would tell me who you really are. I don't think you're a reporter, Mr. Rendon."

Evan decided to play it straight. Trust her, because he needed the information. "I'm not. My name is Evan Casher. I'm sorry for the deception."

"Who are you, then?"

This was a huge risk. He could be wrong. But if he didn't

chance it, he was hitting a dead end. "I think I'm Robert Smithson."

"Is this a joke?"

"It's not the name I grew up with, but I found a connection to my parents and the Smithsons." He paused. "Do you have Web access?"

"I'm old, not old-fashioned."

"Go to CNN.com, please. Do a search on Evan Casher. I want you to tell me if you recognize any of the pictures."

"Hold on." He heard her set down the phone, heard a computer rouse from sleep. She clicked and typed. "I'm at CNN. C-A-S-H-E-R?"

"Yes, ma'am."

He heard her clacking on a keyboard. Silence.

"Look for a story about a homicide in Austin, Texas," he said.

"I see it," Mrs. Briggs whispered. "Oh, dear."

The last time he'd checked out the website, the update included a picture of his mother and of himself on the site. "Does Donna Casher look like Julie Smithson?"

"Her hair is different. It's been so many years...but, yes, I think that is Julie." She sounded as grieved as she would if Julie were still her neighbor.

He steadied his voice. "Mrs. Briggs. I believe my parents were the Smithsons and they got into serious trouble all those years ago and had to take on new identities. Hide from their past."

"Is this you? The picture next to her?"

"Yes, ma'am."

"You look like your mother. You're the spitting image of Julie."

He let out a long sigh. "Thank you, Mrs. Briggs."

"This says you were kidnapped."

"I was. I'm okay. But I don't want anyone to know where I am right now."

"I should call the police. Shouldn't I?" Her voice rose.

"Please don't call the police. I have no right to ask it of you, and you should do what you think is right...but I don't want anyone to know where I am. Or that I know what my family's names used to be. Whoever killed my mom might kill me."

"Robert." She sounded as if her heart were breaking. "This better not be a joke."

"No, ma'am. It's not. But if Robert was my name, I've never known it."

"They both loved you very much," she said. Choking back tears.

Evan's face went hot. "You said they met at an orphanage. Where?"

"Ohio. Oh, dear, I don't remember the town's name."

"Ohio. Okay."

"Goinsville," she said with sudden assurance. "That's the town. She joked about it, never going back to Goinsville. It was so sad that they were both orphans, I remember thinking that at Christmas. And that they were so happy to have you. Julie said she never wanted you to endure what they did."

"Thank you, Mrs. Briggs. Thank you."

Now she cried softly. "Poor Julie."

"You've been a tremendous help to me, Mrs. Briggs." A terrible reluctance to hang up, to break this fragile link to his past, shook Evan. "Good-bye."

"Good-bye."

He hung up. She might have caller ID. She might have

seen the number and be calling the police right now. They might not believe her, but it would be a lead, and it would be followed.

Goinsville, Ohio. A place to begin.

Smithson. Why would Gabriel prepare a passport with his father's old identity? Possibly that information—of who the Cashers once were—was part of the payment. Possibly it was Gabriel's idea of a joke.

He found Shadey's stepbrother's laptop, stored on a closet shelf. It was a nice new system. He hooked up his digital music player to the computer, made sure it had all the same music software as his original laptop, and transferred the songs his mother had e-mailed him Friday morning.

He searched for newly created files. None, other than the songs themselves. He went through every folder, opened every file, to see if an unseen program dumped new data.

Nothing. He didn't have the files. His mother had used another method to get Jargo's treasured data on his system, or the program simply didn't execute more than once. Maybe the data was erased or ignored if the encrypted songs were copied again.

He had nothing to fight Jargo with now.

Except Bricklayer.

Shadey was watching TV downstairs. "May I have that number that Galadriel lady gave you?"

"Tell her I said hi," Shadey said. "Not."

Evan went back upstairs. Shadey followed him. Evan dialed.

Four rings. "Yes?" A nice-sounding lady, Southern accent. Calm.

"Is this Galadriel?"

"Who's calling?"

"I'm actually more interested in talking to Mr. Jargo, please."

"Who's calling?"

He wasn't going to give her enough time to trace the call. "I'll call back in one minute. Get Jargo on the line." He hung up. Dialed back in two minutes.

"Hello." Now a man's voice. Older. Cultured.

"This is Evan Casher, Mr. Jargo."

"Evan. We have much to discuss. Your father is asking for you. He and I are old friends. I've been taking care of him."

Jargo had his dad. Evan sank to the floor. "I don't believe you."

"Your mother is dead. Don't you think such a tragedy would make your father surface and run home to you, if he could?"

"You killed my mother." Now he'd found his voice again.

"I never harmed your mother. That was the work of the CIA."

"That makes no sense."

"I'm afraid it does. Your mother worked for the CIA on an infrequent basis. She came across information that would irrevocably damage the Agency. America's enemies already believe our intelligence operations are on the ropes; these files would be the CIA's death knell. The CIA will kill you to keep those files secret."

"I don't care about these files. You and your son killed my mother."

A pause. "You know I have a son?"

"Yes." Let Jargo believe that he had information that could make Jargo worry, make Jargo wonder how much he knew. "His name is Dezz."

"How do you know he's my son?"

He thought it might be unwise to name Bricklayer as his source. "It doesn't matter." Evan's head started to throb. "Let me talk to my dad." At these words, Shadey sat on the floor across from him, a scowl of worry on his face.

"I'm not prepared to do that yet, Evan," Jargo said.

"Why?"

"Because I need an assurance from you that you'll work with us. We came to that house outside of Bandera to help you, Evan, and you shot at us and ran away."

"Dezz killed a man." Now Shadey raised an eyebrow at Evan.

"No. Dezz saved you from a man who was using you so he could fight his own war against the CIA. The CIA would then use you to try to get us and your father. You're nothing but a pawn to them, Evan—pardon the melodrama—and they're prepared to slap you all over the chessboard."

It fit in with what he had learned about Gabriel; at least, a bit.

"If I give you the files, will you give me my dad? Alive and unharmed."

He thought he almost heard the barest sigh of relief from Jargo. "I'm surprised to hear you have the files, Evan."

The files were real. Here was confirmation. Sweat broke out under his arms, in the small of his back. He had to be very, very careful now.

"Mom made a backup and let me know where they would be." The lie felt just fine in his mouth.

"Ah. She was a very smart woman. I knew her for a long time, Evan. Admired her greatly. I want you to know that because I never, ever could have harmed Donna. I'm not your enemy. We're family, in a way, you and I. I respect how you've protected yourself thus far. You have much of your parents in you."

"Shut up. Let's meet."

"Yes. Tell me where you are and I'll take you to your father."

"No, I choose the meeting place. Where is my father?"

"I'll trust you, Evan. He's in Florida. But I can get him to wherever you are."

Evan considered. New Orleans was between Florida and Houston, and he knew the city, at least the part around Tulane where he had spent his early childhood. He remembered his father walking him through the Audubon Zoo, playing catch with him on the green stretches of Audubon Park. He knew the layout. He knew how to get in, get out. And it was very public.

"New Orleans," Evan said. "Tomorrow morning. Ten A.M. Audubon Zoo. Inside the main plaza. Bring my dad. I'll bring the files. Come alone. No Dezz. I don't like him, I don't trust him, I don't want him near me. I see him and the deal is off."

"I understand completely. I'll see you then, Evan."

Evan hung up.

"What have you gotten yourself into and what do you think you're doing?" Shadey asked.

"Documentary lesson number one. Show characters in conflict. You remember at the courthouse—I got your mama to wait out on the steps when Henderson's mom came out. Put two mothers fighting for their sons, in direct opposition, together. Fireworks."

"But what if he's bringing your dad?"

"He wouldn't let me talk to him. He won't stick to the deal. He's trying to convince me that the CIA killed my mother. I'm sure he and Dezz did."

"You saw their faces."

"No."

"Then how are you sure?"

"Their voices...I heard their voices. I'm sure." Pretty sure, he thought. But not one hundred percent sure.

"So what now?" Shadey asked.

"I can't find my dad dodging bullets, running all the time. I played this by their rules, now I'm playing it by mine." He hoisted the camcorder out of the duffel bag. "These folks stick to shadow. I'm dragging them out into the light."

"And you gonna do all this by yourself?" Shadey said.

"I am."

"No. You're not. I'll go with you."

"I'm not guilting you, it's not your fight."

"Shut up. I'm coming. End of discussion." Shadey folded his big arms. "I don't like these people trying to play me. And I figure I need to get you back in debt to me."

"All right." Evan picked up the cell phone. Punched the number Bricklayer had given him.

"Bricklayer. Good afternoon. It's Evan Casher. Listen carefully because I'll say this once and just once. You want these files, meet me in New Orleans. Audubon Zoo. Front plaza. Tomorrow. Ten A.M." He clicked off as Bricklayer started to ask questions.

"You stirring the pot," Shadey said.

"No. I'm putting it on to boil."

22

———◆———

LATE SUNDAY NIGHT, Jargo's chartered plane landed at Louis Armstrong International. Jargo hurried Carrie into a suite at a hotel close to the Louisiana Superdome. Carrie watched the Sunday-night tourist crowd ambling for Bourbon Street. Jargo sat on the couch. He had said little en route to New Orleans, which always made Carrie nervous. Dezz had flown early Sunday morning to Dallas, planning to break into Joaquin Gabriel's office to find any records of Evan's new passports. He was due to arrive in New Orleans at any minute.

"My son," Jargo said into the silence.

Carrie kept watching the tourists. "What about him?"

"He loves you. Or rather, he feels toward you what he believes love to be, which is a sad mix of possession, anger, longing, and utter awkwardness."

"I wonder whose fault that is."

"I ask only that you not be cruel to him."

"He's threatened to kill me before."

"Only words." As if words didn't matter.

"He's..." She searched for the term. *Crazy* might be appropriate, but it was not a word she could use with Jargo. "Troubled."

"He lacks confidence. You could give it to him."

Her skin went cold. "How?"

"Pay extra attention to him."

"I'm not sleeping with him."

"But you'd sleep with Evan Casher. For the good of our network."

"I'm not sleeping with Dezz."

The hotel phone rang. Jargo didn't look at her; he punched the speakerphone button.

"Good news and bad news. Which you want first?" Galadriel said on the speakerphone.

"Bad news," Jargo said.

"Evan's off the grid," Galadriel said. "No sign of credit card use, no police report yet that he's surfaced. You won't be able to grab him before your meeting, unless he's stupid enough to use his credit card for a hotel or restaurant."

"He's not stupid," Carrie said.

"Did you pull all stolen-car reports for the five-county area?" Jargo asked.

"Yes. Finally I was able to get it. The most likely candidate is a pickup truck, a one-year-old Ford F-150, stolen from a driveway in Bandera. A note with the keys to a Ducati motorcycle were found on the porch."

"Are the locals tracing the Ducati?"

"That I don't know," Galadriel said. "Sorry."

Carrie watched Jargo. "CIA or FBI trace it back to Gabriel, they'll arrive back at that house. Start asking questions."

"I'm not worried," Jargo said. "What's of more interest is if they don't trace the Ducati."

"I don't understand," Carrie said.

"Sure you do. The Bandera authorities don't trace it, it's

because the investigation's been shut down. Because our friends at the FBI and at the CIA don't want the motorcycle traced, don't want the truck theft pursued."

"Because they're looking for Evan now themselves," Carrie said in an even tone.

Jargo nodded at her and said, "So that's the bad news. What's the good?"

"I got a partial decode on the e-mail message that Donna Casher received from Gabriel," Galadriel said. "He used an English variant of an old plain-language SDECE code abandoned back in the early seventies. The name for the code was 1849." SDECE was French intelligence. Carrie frowned. 1849. The same as the date in Gabriel's e-mail to Donna. Telling her what code to use.

"Odd choice," Jargo said.

"Not really. One assumes Donna contacted Gabriel in a hurry, and they needed a common code base from which they could both easily work."

"So what's the message say?" Carrie resisted the urge to hold her breath. She didn't look over at Jargo.

"Our interpretation is READY ON MAR 8 A.M. DELIVER FIRST HALF OF LIST UPON ARRIVAL IN FL. SECOND HALF WHEN YOU ARE OVERSEAS. YOUR HUSBAND IS YOUR WORRY."

"Thank you, Galadriel. Please call me immediately if you get a trace on Evan." Jargo clicked off the phone.

Carrie studied the tension in Jargo's shoulders, his face. She had seen the kicked-to-chunks remains of Joaquin Gabriel and knew this man was on a lethally short fuse. She chose her words carefully. "The Cashers were to rendezvous in Florida. Where?"

"We grabbed him in Miami, returning from a job in Berlin.

He must have broken protocol and let Donna know his itinerary," Jargo said. "She must have promised Gabriel the final payoff delivery when the family was overseas and hidden."

"*Second half.* Sounds like two deliveries," Carrie said. "What else did she have beside the account files?"

Jargo's face darkened. "Half the files first, half the files when they were safe." He looked to Carrie as if he were scared and furious and trying to suppress his rage.

"Jargo. What are these files?"

A knock at the door. Carrie checked the peephole and opened it. Dezz stepped in. He didn't look happy. "Nothing in Dallas. Gabriel's office is under surveillance."

"Locals or federal?"

"Locals. But it's got to be at the request of the Agency, probably asked via the Bureau," Dezz said. "I couldn't get close to see if there was any info on Evan's aliases in his office. They've connected Gabriel with this case."

"You didn't answer my question, Jargo. What are these files?"

Jargo didn't look at her. "Donna Casher stole our client list."

Dezz said, "There's no such list."

"She amassed a list. A brilliant insurance policy." Jargo turned to Carrie. "Either through Gabriel or his mom, Evan knows all about us now. He just promised me the files in exchange for his dad. He knows Dezz is my son. He knows about us, Carrie. He's seen more than the client files. Maybe files on us."

"So we have to meet him," Carrie said.

Dezz said, "Let us take Evan, Dad. You go back to Florida, break out the knives, make Mitchell talk. See if he knows where the client list is."

Jargo rubbed at his lip. "But I'm sure Mitchell had no idea Donna betrayed us. He wouldn't have gone on a mission for me if his wife was about to stab me in the back and then return the moment I summoned him back to Florida. It put him straight in our hands, left his family defenseless."

"He could hardly say no to you," Dezz said.

"Sure he could. He could have argued a reschedule. I respect his opinion. He could have easily run from us, and he didn't."

"You're blinded by affection for Mitchell," Dezz said. "It's not very appealing."

"I can't afford sentiment. Even when I really wish I could." Jargo closed his eyes, rubbed his temples.

For the first time Carrie saw a light that wasn't cold and hateful in Jargo's gaze. For the first time since Jargo had told her a year ago, *I know who killed your parents, Carrie, and they will kill you, too. But I can hide you. You can keep working for me, I'll take care of you.*

"Carrie. Did Evan ever mention New Orleans to you? They might have told him where to run if he ever got into trouble. Or if something ever happened to them."

"I'm sure they never gave him any kind of escape plan, because he didn't know his parents were agents. If he'd had a hint of the truth, he would have found out long ago. That's who he is." She shrugged. "He told me he was born in New Orleans, but he hasn't lived there since he was a child. I assume you know that already."

Jargo nodded. "Evan specifically asked you not be at the meeting, Dezz."

"He doesn't like me? I'm hurt."

Jargo gave Dezz a stern glare. "We're not having a repeat

at the zoo tomorrow. You will be calm and you will do as you're told."

Dezz chewed a caramel and stared at the carpet.

"What is Mitchell Casher to you?" Carrie asked Jargo. "You seem worried about him as much as frustrated with him."

"I would like for him to contact his son for me. To bring him in. He refuses. He doesn't trust me."

"Obviously. You're holding him prisoner."

"I'm convinced he wasn't part of Donna's scheme now. But I can't yet convince him of my good intentions toward his son."

"I wonder why," Carrie said. "Since you don't plan to honor your deal with Evan."

"He won't be expecting to see you, Carrie. You're the element of surprise," Jargo said. "I can't let Evan walk away from that meeting. Once we have the files, Evan's a done deal. You know that. He'll talk. He won't keep his mouth shut. It's the kind of man that he is. You said it yourself."

"The Audubon Zoo is a very public place. Major attraction," Carrie said. "Too many people. Too contained. He made a smart choice. You won't be able to grab Evan there, Jargo."

"Not grab. Kill," Dezz said.

"Not there you can't," Carrie said.

"No. We'll get him to leave with you. He'll be thrilled to see you," Jargo said. "Take him someplace private. Where just the two of you can talk. Then you can kill him."

MONDAY

MARCH 14

23

Evan didn't expect the children.

Monday morning at ten Evan imagined the Audubon Zoo would be nearly empty, but a good-sized crowd trickled to the gates as the zoo opened. The small parking lot, on the edge of Audubon Park, held two buses of schoolkids from a Catholic academy and three minivans sporting the logo of a retirement community. Then there was the usual spill of tourists, which New Orleans never lacked.

Evan paid his admission to the zoo. He wore his dark glasses and baseball cap. Few twentyish men were in the crowd. He spotted Shadey, paying in a different line, wearing an Astros ball cap and sunglasses. Keeping his distance, walking with Evan's duffel slung over his shoulder.

The zoo, Evan noticed, wasn't a place where many people walked alone. Families and couples and herds of students with harried teachers. He circled, keeping his gaze moving across the crowd.

No sign of his father. Or Dezz. He had no idea what Jargo looked like. He saw no sign of a squad of guys in dark glasses that might work for Bricklayer, with earpieces and trench coats. They wouldn't be so obvious.

Evan darted through the swell of the opening-gate

crowd. Last night, in the cheap motel rooms he and Shadey had scored near the French Quarter, he had downloaded a map off the Audubon Zoo's website and memorized it. Every way in, every way out. The zoo backed up to the green sprawl of Audubon Park on one side, to an administration building, side roads, and a Mississippi River landing on the other. The map was general. He suspected there were routes for animal handlers and zoo employees that were not shown.

He remembered strolls here with his father, his hand in his dad's, his other hand holding a sticky, melting ice cream. He loved the zoo. He headed in the direction of the main fountain in the plaza, with statues of a mother elephant and her calf cavorting in the spray. He walked a slow, measured pace along the palm-lined brick pathway, glancing behind him, as if he were taking in the sights and were in no hurry. Schoolkids milled around him, a teacher attempting to herd them to his right where the real elephants ambled in the Asian Domain, others eyeing a restaurant to his left, although it was too early for burgers and shakes. He was a man enjoying a day at the park, the gentle best of the Louisiana spring before the swamp-native heat and humidity melted the air.

A long, curving bench near the fountain sat empty. Schoolkids and families drifted toward the elephant pen. Most of the early crowd passed him, moving beyond the fountain for the zoo's carousel and the Jaguar Jungle exhibit.

Evan spotted a man walking toward him. Eyes locked on him. Tall, a handsome face, hard blue eyes like chips of ice. Hair streaked with gray. Wearing a dark trench coat. Rain loomed in the skies, but Evan believed the man had something hidden under his coat. That was fine. Evan had something hidden under his raincoat, too. Not a gun. Shadey had the gun, because if either Jargo or Bricklayer grabbed Evan, they'd simply relieve him of the weapon. He had his music player in his pocket, and he would say the files were on it. No argument. No searching. He'd just give it to them, let them worry about decoding it if they could.

He watched. No sign of his father.

"Good morning, Evan," the man said. Baritone. The same voice he'd heard in his kitchen, heard on the phone.

"Mr. Jargo?"

"Yes."

"Where's my dad?"

"Where are the files?"

"Wrong. You first. Give me my dad."

"Your father doesn't really need rescuing, Evan. He's with us, of his own free will. He's worked for me for years. So did your mother."

"No. You killed my mother."

"You're confused. The CIA killed your mother. I would have saved her, given the chance. Please look over to your right."

Evan did. There was a small playscape, then by the restaurant a patio of tables and chairs for diners. Dezz and Carrie stood at one of the canopied tables, Dezz with his arm looped around Carrie's shoulder. She looked pale. Dezz grinned at Evan.

Evan's heart sank into his gut. *No.*

Carrie's gaze locked on Evan's.

"But Carrie, she's another matter. My people found her when they came to your house in Houston to help protect you the morning your mom was killed. We couldn't leave her for the CIA to kill as well, so we brought her with us."

Jargo made his voice a slow soothe. "This has all been a terrible, wretched mistake, Evan."

They'd found her. It could explain Carrie's behavior after he'd left for Austin. They'd forced her to quit her job so she wouldn't be missed, forced her to call him to see where he was when he was in the car with Durless.

"Carrie is a true innocent, Evan. I think she's a fine young woman. I don't wish her any harm. I'd like to let her go, and I will, as soon as you give me those files. You and Carrie can talk privately. Then I can take you to your father. He's desperate to see you."

Evan opened his mouth to speak, but nothing came out. He stared at Carrie. She shook her head, ever so slightly.

"Yes or no, Evan."

Evan kept waiting for the government to descend on them. Bricklayer might be lurking nearby, watching the drama play out, seeing who broke the standoff. But he couldn't wait forever.

Evan said, "Carrie walks out of here, free and clear. She tells that security guard over there she's very sick, she needs to go to a hospital. Right now. An ambulance takes her away. When she's safe, she calls me on a number I give her. Then you get my dad on the phone and I talk to him, and then, and only then, do I give you the files."

"I'm a great believer in compromise, Evan." Jargo held up a small device—a handheld computer, a PDA—next to Evan's ear, thumbed a control.

"Evan," his father's voice said. Mitchell Casher sounded tired, sounded desperate. "The danger you're in is not from Jargo or any of his people. It's from the CIA. You've made a mistake in not trusting Jargo. The CIA killed your mom. Not Jargo. Please cooperate with him."

Jargo clicked off the voice recorder. "I've satisfied one of your requirements."

"I said a phone. Not a recording. He could have said all that under duress. You could have put a bullet in his head when he was done talking."

"Let me assure you, I would never hurt your dad," Jargo said in a low voice. "I don't want to hurt you. You don't want to come with me, fine. You and Carrie can just walk out of here once I have the files."

"As if I could trust you."

"That's your call," Jargo said with a quiet shrug. "If you want to trust the CIA not to kill you once you're back on the streets, that's your call, too. Give me the files, and you and Carrie can walk out of here together if you choose. Have your wonderful life together, although I think the CIA will keep that wonderful life exceedingly brief. Or you can come with me and I'll take you to your father, and I'll protect you from those murderers."

"You promised me my father. You can't tell me that he didn't want to come here and see me."

"Your father's face is all over the news right now. You and he are the most prominent missing people in the country. He wasn't comfortable with traveling. Not when the CIA is hunting him as much as they hunted your mother."

"I don't believe you. We had a deal. You're changing it."

"The world changes all the time, Evan. Only fools don't change with it."

"Well, your world just changed. Look over by the elephants," Evan said.

"I don't have time for games."

"I'm not playing one."

Slowly Jargo made a quick survey over the scattered crowd around the elephant pen, looked back at Evan.

"Thanks for the nice profile shot," Evan said. "You're being filmed. On digital, with a high-powered lens that provides me pristine prints of your face and of Dezz's face."

"I don't believe you."

"I have friends in the documentary world all over this country. You hurt or kill me or Carrie, you're on the evening news, and you won't be able to spot the hidden camcorder before my friends get away. I told you my demands for giving you the files. Let me talk to Carrie. Now."

Jargo beckoned with a single finger and Carrie hurried over to them. Dezz stayed put.

"Evan," she said.

"No touching." Jargo raised an arm, kept her back.

"Are you all right?" Evan asked in a low voice.

She nodded. "Fine. They didn't hurt me."

"I'm so sorry," he said.

She opened her mouth to speak, then shut it.

"She leaves, just as I described," Evan said.

"You're not very smart," Jargo said. "You showed too much of your hand. I would have been willing to let Carrie go once you gave me the files. But film of me? No. I'll need that as well."

"When she's gone." Evan narrowed his stare. "Soon as Carrie's safely away, I'll give you the film and hand you a music player that has the files stored on it. I don't have copies. Understood?"

"No. Give me the files and the film, then she walks. If you've got a camera on us, I certainly am not going to harm you, if that's what you're so wrongly worried about. Then we can all part ways, if you're so determined not to see your dad," Jargo said.

Carrie broke free from Jargo, closed her arms around Evan. Sobbed into his shoulder. He embraced her, smelled the soft peach scent of her hair, kept his stare locked on Jargo.

"Trust me," Carrie whispered into Evan's ear. Then she pulled a small gun free of her coat and jabbed it under Jargo's chin. "Tell Dezz to walk away or I shoot you through the neck."

Jargo's eyes widened in shock.

She pulled Jargo in front of her and Evan, putting him between them and Dezz. "It's okay, Evan. We're getting out of here. He's got a gun in his pocket. Take it."

"Carrie…"

"Do what I tell you, babe," Carrie said. Evan did, pulling a gleaming pistol free from Jargo's coat. He risked a look the other way—toward where Shadey actually stood, under the awning at the edge of the food court. With a duffel, one side cut out, the camera resting inside.

Dezz, now hurrying forward, stopped, fifteen feet away from them, staring at the small gun pressed into his father's neck. Carrie moved the gun down, pressing into Jargo's back, where it wasn't so visible.

"Back off, Dezz!" Carrie shouted. She lowered her voice to a whisper. "Evan, if he comes any farther, shoot him."

Evan, still stunned, nodded.

"Evan. You're making a mistake," Jargo said. "I'm the one who can help you. Not this liar."

Dezz's mouth worked, watching his father, and he ran ten feet to one side, grabbed a young mother pushing a stroller with a fussing toddler. He jabbed a gun into the young woman's throat, yanked her around, put her between himself and Evan. The young mother's face blanched in shock and terror.

"No!" Carrie said.

"I'll trade you!" Dezz yelled.

Another woman saw the gun in his hand, shrieked for security, began to run.

Carrie shoved Jargo to the ground in a hard sprawl. "Run, Evan," she said.

Dezz pushed his hostage away; she grabbed her baby and fled. Dezz ran toward Evan and Carrie. Pistol out, readying to aim.

Screams erupted around them. Carrie fired past Evan. Dezz ducked behind the bench and shrubbery.

Around them, people panicked, stunned for a moment at the oddity of gunfire, then stampeded for cover or for the entrance, teachers herding kids, parents carrying children.

Jargo grabbed at Evan and Evan popped him in the jaw, sent him sprawling back over the bench.

A zoo security guard advanced toward them, yelling an order. "Down on the ground! Now!"

A bullet splintered the palm trunk by the guard's head. Dezz had fired. The guard retreated behind the thick trunk.

Carrie gripped Evan's arm. "Run. If you want to live and get your dad."

He ran with her, dodging through scrambling tourists, deeper into the zoo. He glanced back. No sign of Shadey; he would blend in with the retreating crowd, escape. Evan had told him to make sure whatever footage he got of Jargo made it to safety, no matter what happened to Evan.

"The entrance," Evan said. "It's the other way—"

"I know," she said. "But they can cut us off. This way."

He didn't argue. He was the faster runner and he clutched her arm.

Dezz moved through the fleeing crowd, pursuing fast. Gun drawn, people veering away from him in every direction, giving him a clear path. Jargo followed. A man wearing a Tulane sweatshirt made a lunge at Dezz, and Dezz hit him hard across the face with the pistol. The man went down. Dezz and Jargo didn't slow down, Dezz handing Jargo a second pistol.

Evan and Carrie ran past the singsong of the zoo's carousel, firing up for its first ride of the day, and onto a tram path where the Swamp Train looped around the zoo. The next section held animals from South America. Evan looked around for an Exit sign. Or a building where they could hide. They kept running, onto a wooden walkway. It bordered an algae-topped pond for a flock of flamingos on the right and pine-studded land for llamas and guanacos on the left. A family with three kids stood at the walkway's halfway point, admiring the flamingos, snapping photos.

"Over the railing," Evan said. They couldn't run past the family, who would be caught between Carrie and Evan and their pursuers.

Carrie bolted over the wooden divider, dropped down into the exhibit. A small herd of llamas watched them with disinterest. The ground, groomed to look like Louisiana's best approximation of the pampas, was hard and dusty, and they ran to a dense grove of pines near the exhibit's back perimeter.

"Get the trees between you and them," Carrie said. They ducked into the short maze of pines. A bullet smacked against the trunks.

"Over the fence," he said. They climbed in a fast

scramble, toppled over the barrier onto an unpaved trail behind the exhibit. The musky smell of wolves in a neighboring exhibit filled their noses. They ran down the service path. Maintenance buildings lined one side, the back of the South American exhibits the other. Tried the doors. Locked.

Through the foliage and the fencing, Evan saw Jargo running past the family on the wooden walkway, spotted Dezz following in their tracks through the South American grounds.

Trying to catch Evan and Carrie between them.

"Keep your head down." Carrie grabbed at the back of his head. "Security camera up ahead, don't want it to catch your face."

He obeyed. They ran, eyes to the ground. The service road dead-ended. A glass and stone building to their right held a family of jaguars. A re-creation of a Mayan temple, Jaguar Jungle was a major attraction of the zoo.

They clambered over the padlocked fencing at the dead end, dropped onto a stone visitors' path by the jaguars, who lounged behind thick glass. One yowled at them, baring curved fangs.

Jargo huffed into the Mayan plaza, saw Carrie, fired. A bullet pinged against the Mayan stone carvings. The jaguars raised a ruckus of snarls and snaps.

Carrie and Evan sprinted through dense growth and stone paths, past another faux temple with spider monkeys, past a children's archeological-dig play area. They stumbled down a creek lined with thick bamboo, hurried back up the other side to the stone path. A few moms and kids ambled along and they stared.

"Crazy guy with a gun!" Carrie yelled. "Take cover!"

The moms jumped for cover in the bamboo or off the path. Jargo ran past the women, ignoring them.

"Evan!" he yelled. "I can give you your dad!"

Carrie spun and fired at him. Jargo ducked back into the bamboo. Evan ran past a sign that read No Trespassing, Zoo Employees Only, Carrie following. It had to lead to a building, he decided, a place they could barricade themselves in—Jargo would flee to avoid the police, who would be racing into the zoo now.

Evan hit a short fence, they went over it and then rushed up to another short fence, and Evan said, "Uh-oh."

Alligators. On the other side of the three-foot divider, on a bank, with a narrow gap of scum-topped water beyond, leading to the zoo's Louisiana Swamp wooden walkway, where visitors walked above the water and admired the reptiles from a safe distance. Three of the gators sunned themselves on the bank. Not five feet away from them.

Behind them, a bullet hissed through a suppressor. The shot caught Carrie high in the shoulder and she staggered and screamed. On the walkway across the water, a woman screeched for the police. Loudspeakers boomed into life, urging everyone to head calmly for the exits.

"Wrong move, Carrie," Dezz called from behind a tree. "Wrongo. Stupid. Dense."

Evan held her with one arm, aimed the gun with the other. To stand there was to die. The gators looked fat and zoo-happy and probably weren't hungry. Please. He hoped. He spotted Dezz peeking around a tree and fired a steady barrage of bullets, forcing Dezz back into the undergrowth, then helped Carrie over the fence.

"Dezz . . . hates reptiles," she said. "Afraid of them."

Evan wasn't sure he had a bullet left in the clip. He

hurried her past the resting gators. He stumbled over one's tail and it opened its white, razor-ringed mouth in a defensive hiss. But the gator started a slow waddle away from them.

Do they smell the blood? Evan had no idea.

"Go," she said. "Leave me. Get safe."

"No. Come on." Dezz would be charging toward them since Evan had quit shooting. He saw Dezz approaching, taking careful aim. Evan's gun clicked on an empty magazine. Evan and Carrie jumped into the green-frothed water. He heard a bullet scream above their heads.

Evan held Carrie's gun above the water, but he couldn't swim, help Carrie, and shoot at the same time. The distance to the wooden walkway seemed like a mile. People on the walkway scattered, mothers fleeing with children, one man hollering into a cell phone.

Dezz gingerly put a foot over the fence, his gun aimed at the gators, who seemed as uninterested in him as they had been in Evan and Carrie.

Evan kicked forward, pushing Carrie, thinking, *Dezz gets a bead on us, it's over.*

"Help us!" he hollered up toward the walkway. The cell phone man gestured at Evan to swim to the right.

A log lay between them and the walkway, and with a sudden, yet ancient horror that spasmed up from his spine, Evan saw it wasn't a log. An alligator, facing away from them, lay barely submerged. Ignoring the ruckus behind him.

Evan shoved Carrie to one side, slapped his hand on the water to draw the gator away from her. Carrie paddled toward the walkway. He heard a hiss behind him. One of the gators on the bank opened its mouth again, heckling

Dezz, and Dezz gave ground, putting one leg back over the fence. Looking scared and furious.

They can move faster in water, Evan thought, logic kicking into his brain. *Carrie's bleeding, does it draw them like a shark?* Carrie reached the wooden supports, the cell phone man offered a hand, another man steadying him, and they hauled Carrie up to the walkway.

Evan kicked away from the track Carrie had cut in the water. The log-gator orbited toward Evan. Evan swam hard, waited for the tug that would tear off his leg. He blundered close to the walkway and put up an arm. The men yanked him up. Six feet behind him, the gator wrenched its mouth open in bravado, then settled and watched him with an ageless gaze. Evan dripped water and scum and sprawled across the wood. One of the rescuers wrenched Carrie's gun from his grasp.

"Please!" Evan said. "I need that!"

"No way!" Cell Phone Man put a heavy hand on Evan's chest, pushed him to the railing. "I called the police, you stay right here!"

Evan turned toward the bank. Dezz was gone, swallowed back in the bamboo. No sign of Jargo.

"She's really shot," the other man said in shock.

Evan seized Carrie's hand, shoved Cell Phone Man to one side, ran. The men yelled at him to stop. Old swamp-style rocking chairs lined the deck, two older ladies sitting frozen in shock, clutching their purses, as Evan and Carrie ran past. At the end of the walkway stood a gift shop and, just past its door, a railing. They went over the railing; the next walkway led to a wildlife nursery, built to look like a weathered swamp shack with small boats docked in a fronting lagoon. They hurried around the back of the shack. More fencing, covered with ivy, bamboo curtaining a service road beyond.

Evan pushed Carrie up so she could pull herself over. Blood welled from her shoulder, and she gasped as she climbed. She tumbled over the ivy, falling headfirst into the blanketing thicket of bamboo beyond the fence. He jumped on the mesh and saw Jargo approaching from his right, Dezz from his left.

"Give it up, Evan," Jargo called. "Right now."

"Stay back, or that tape puts your face on the evening news."

The indecision played on Jargo's face. "You go, you'll never see your dad again."

Evan went over the fence. A bullet barked a centimeter from his hand as he let go and fell into the overgrowth.

Carrie grabbed him and they ran, hearing the *pit-pit* of bullets pocking through the bamboo curtains. Then the noise stopped. Evan was sure the two men were only stopping to climb over the fence in pursuit. They ran along a paved road that served as a tram path. Zoo employees headed away from them in a golf cart, hollering into walkie-talkies. Another fence and they stumbled along a stretch of parking lot and grassland on the border of the zoo. He checked behind them. No sign of Dezz or Jargo; they hadn't scaled the fence.

They ran along the edge of the zoo now, hearing the approaching whine of sirens.

"Are you in pain?" he asked. Stupidest question ever asked, he decided.

"I'll make it. Are you all right? Did they hit you?"

"No. I'm fine. How did you…" *Shoot your way out of there. Save me.* He looked at her as if he didn't know her.

"We're getting out of here," she said.

Beyond the expanse of the parking lot they could see the whirl of police-car lights near the main entrance.

"Here." He steadied her. "I'm getting you to a doctor."

"No doctor. Evan, you have to do what I say. I've been protecting you since day one. I'm sorry I had to lie to you." Her voice faded to a weak whisper. "I'm from Bricklayer."

He stopped in his tracks. "What?"

She reached out a hand to him, bloodied from being pressed against her shoulder. "I . . . I was supposed to protect you. I'm sorry."

"Protect me. For how long?"

She steered him off a path that cut across a swath of deep green. "Jargo thought I worked for him. He thought I would kill you for him today. But I would never hurt you. Never."

This wasn't what he'd expected. He hurried her into the truck he'd stolen from Bandera. Sirens rose.

Trust me, she had said. He nearly said, *I can't leave Shadey.* But if he told her about Shadey, and she was leading him into a trap, then Shadey would be caught in Bricklayer's net. He shut his mouth, hoped that Shadey had escaped in the melee.

He eased her over into the passenger seat, looking around frantically for Jargo and Dezz.

She collapsed, blood smearing the seat.

"Bricklayer and I are CIA, Evan," she said. "I'm not supposed to tell you, but you need to know." She gritted her teeth against the pain.

CIA. Like Gabriel. The people Jargo said had killed his mother.

He didn't believe Jargo.

"There they are," she said as he climbed into the pickup.

"The Land Rover. Silver." Jargo and Dezz, trying to wend past the New Orleans police cars that had responded. Evan didn't see Shadey anywhere in the mass of people milling in the lot. An ambulance stood, lights flashing, but paramedics weren't loading Shadey, or anyone else.

"Hold on." Evan floored the pickup across the lot, then over the expanse of lawn. Headed toward Magazine, the frontage street for the zoo that separated it from Audubon Park.

"Jargo's seen us," she said. "You're not trained for evasive driving, Evan."

"I'm a Houston driver," he said, drunk with fear and energy, and he barreled across Magazine, laying on the pickup's horn, bouncing over the curb into the greater expanse of Audubon Park. *Think. Think of what they'll try next and be prepared for that. Because you can't make a mistake.*

In the rearview he saw the Rover narrowly miss hitting another car, then follow him across the grassy yard between the parking lot and Magazine, Jargo laying on the horn.

Midmorning joggers crossing the swale of parkland stared at Evan as he revved the pickup truck along the grass, dodging the oaks. The northern edge of Audubon Park faced out onto busy St. Charles Avenue, and the neighboring Loyola and Tulane universities stood on the other side of the avenue. He had forgotten that along St. Charles everyone parallel-parked, and this morning cars filled every inch of curb bordering the park. Large concrete cylinders blocked the park's main gate from the street.

No way out.

He veered the car to the left, spotting an opening at St. Charles and Walnut, the park's far corner. It was a no-parking zone across from an old estate reborn as a hotel. The pickup lumbered as he spun out onto Walnut and hooked an immediate right onto St. Charles.

He started to panic. St. Charles was hardly a raceway. Stoplights stood every few blocks; the wide median held two streetcar tracks, with their green tubes lumbering up and down the rails, tourists leaning out to snap photos of the grand homes or of leftover, faded beads still dangling from the street signs from a passed Mardi Gras. If there wasn't a light, a crossover spanned the median, and cars making turns backed onto the avenue.

But at 10:20 in the morning, traffic wasn't a thick nest. He heard a boom, a thud. The Rover exited Audubon Park behind him, navigating an opening on the opposite corner of the park from where he had exited. Shots hit the bumper; the Rover powered up close to the back of the pickup.

"He's shooting for the tires." Carrie shivered, in shock and dripping wet, blood flowering through her blouse.

A light ahead, red. Cars stopping.

Evan swerved the truck into the streetcar median. He nicked a line of crape myrtles and put the truck on the rail tracks to avoid the metal poles that supplied the cars with electricity. He jammed the accelerator to the floor.

From his right, gunfire, a bullet smashing into the rear window. Shards of glass nipped the back of his head.

Carrie said, "Drive steady, please."

"Sure!" he yelled back. He zoomed past—no one in the median turn—the intersection with the light, and in his rearview the Rover bounded onto the median with him. Accelerated fast.

Ahead, a minivan loitered in the median, waiting for

traffic to open up. Two children in the minivan's windows stared as the pickup truck rocketed toward them, a boy pointing in surprise.

Evan spun back onto St. Charles, narrowly missing the minivan, clipping a parked car. Jolt and shatter. He could not head farther right—parked cars lined the length of St. Charles, and the front yards of many of the homes were fenced or walled in. No clear room to navigate. It was the street or the median. Bad choice versus worse.

Another shot hit the rear of the pickup truck. A line of heavier shrubs lined this stretch of the median. Evan plowed back through them, deciding he was putting fewer lives at risk there than on the street, after he went through another intersection where a car waited in the median to turn onto the westbound side of St. Charles.

Then he saw the streetcar coming toward him, occupying the left-side track, and he laid on his horn.

The streetcar driver grabbed at a radio mike and yelled into it. Evan screeched to the left, the streetcar passing between him and Jargo.

Ahead he saw two police cars, lights flashing, sirens blaring.

Evan rumbled right, aiming for the center of the median; another streetcar was approaching and he overshot, revving off the tracks and back onto St. Charles. An open intersection. He took a hard right, more to keep from crashing than from strategy, then the next left, and drove down a residential street of neat homes, cars parked on the street. Then another right.

"Turn here, here!" Carrie said.

She pointed at a corner lot, a bright yellow building, antiques in the window, a neon Open sign. He saw her idea.

The parking and exits were behind the building. He spun into the lot and stopped the car.

Waited.

The Rover, its side badly dented, shot past on the street. Evan counted to ten, then twenty. The Rover didn't return.

"What now?" Evan didn't recognize his own voice. His mouth tasted of the fake-swamp water and his hands shook.

"Police will be all over St. Charles," she said. "Take a side road that runs parallel. Get us down to Lee Circle, we can get to the interstate there. Get to the airport."

"You need a hospital."

"No hospital. Our pictures will be on the police wire soon," she said through gritted teeth.

He gently peeled her blouse away from her shoulder. He saw the small but vicious wound, touched the stickiness of the blood.

"You need a doctor."

"Bricklayer will get me help." She closed her eyes, closed her hand over his. "You don't have any reason to trust me. But we just saved each other. That means something, doesn't it?"

He didn't know what to say.

She opened her eyes. "A government plane there can take us to a place we can be safe. Where we can work on getting your dad back."

"What will the CIA do to get my dad back? He's not one of them. He's an enemy to them if he's worked for Jargo."

"Your father could be our best friend. With his help, your help, we can break Jargo." She leaned against the door. In pain. "Certain people in the CIA and Jargo . . . have an arrangement. Jargo's selling information to every country, every intelligence service, every extremist group that he can. We're trying to find his contacts inside the CIA. Get rid of the traitors. They're selling our national secrets to Jargo. I was undercover for the Agency, working for Jargo for the past year."

"Year," he whispered.

"We've never been able to identify any of his operatives other than Dezz. He has a whole network. Your parents... worked for him."

Evan swallowed past the rock in his throat. "I can't keep pretending they are completely innocent in all this, can I?"

"No one can tell you what to do. I learned that early on."

"But Jargo knows you've turned on him, and you have me. He'll just kill my father."

"No. He doesn't want to kill your dad, I don't understand why. Your father is Jargo's weakness. We have to use it against him."

Airport. Hospital. He had to choose. Trust the stranger beside him or trust the woman he loved. He started the car, eased out of the lot. No sign of Jargo. Evan drove, finally turning back onto St. Charles. He drove through Lee Circle and fed onto the highway that would merge into Interstate 10. Traffic was light. He steadied his hands.

"So. You knew me before I knew you," he said.

"Yes."

"So our relationship was a trick. A show."

"You don't understand."

"No, I don't, I don't understand how you could lie to me."

"It was to protect you." Her voice rose in half hysteria. "Would you have believed me if I'd said, 'Hey, Evan, both a freelance spy network and the CIA are interested in you, want to go see a movie'?"

"You answer one question for me."

"Anything."

"My mother. Did you tell Jargo that I was going to Austin?" His voice strained for control.

"No, baby. No. Jargo picked up my voice mail. He got the message."

If I hadn't left Carrie the message, my mom would be alive. Grief and horror rose in him like a tide. "No. Why did you have to leave that morning?"

She covered her face with her hands.

"Carrie, you answer me!" he screamed.

Her voice sounded broken. "I wanted permission from Bricklayer...to end the surveillance on you. To pull you and your mom out, get you both to safety. To forget trying to draw Jargo into the open. I had to talk to Bricklayer alone. That's where I was. When I got back, you were gone."

"And so you told Jargo."

"No. No. I acted like I didn't know where you were. I told him I hadn't checked my voice mails, I hadn't gone back to your house."

"You told him I loved you, didn't you?"

"Yes." She closed her eyes.

"You must have all had a laugh."

"No. No."

"Did you send the CIA to my house?"

"No. Bricklayer's team is very small. We're not set up for big operations. We can't reveal our existence to any possible traitors inside the Agency, because they're our targets, along with Jargo. We're not supposed to operate on American soil."

"Wow, so my family and I, we're really freaking special," Evan said. "I don't know why I should believe you now."

"Because I'm still the same woman you met a few

months ago. I'm still Carrie." She spoke after long seconds of silence. "I love you. I told you not to love me, I didn't want you to say it, but I wanted it to be true. I didn't want you hurt. That's why I wanted to pull out. I'm sorry." She leaned forward, watching the rearview, watching for the police. "Oh, Evan, this hurts."

Did you ever love me?

He made his choice. He followed her directions, stopping at a quiet aviation office near Louis Armstrong International with two cars parked in front.

"Inside. People who work for Bricklayer. Bricklayer's real name is Bedford. There's trust for you. Only three people inside the CIA know his real name."

He looked at her. He could just run. Leave her, her colleagues would find her, and he could vanish and never see her again. Never hear another lie from her lips.

He thought of that morning three days ago, waking up, loving her with both dreaminess and certainty. And she was gone. Thought of how beautiful she had been the first time he'd seen her in the coffee shop, reading that bad book on film with intense concentration. Lying in wait for him. Thought of her in his bed, the softness of her kisses on his lips. Looking at him as though her heart would burst. Maybe her loving him was a lie, but he loved her. She was the worst thing that had ever happened to him. She was the best chance to get his father home. And she had saved him now, saved him from certain death.

Evan carried her out of the car and kicked four times on the office door.

24

KEEPING A MAN IMPRISONED WAS LIKE buying a tour inside his soul. Jargo had seen men, locked in the cramped confines of his homemade jail, talk to people long dead and gone; cry and sob after days of complete silence; one unfortunate drowned himself in the toilet. Strength was often shallow; confidence was a ploy; bravery a mask.

He already knew Mitchell Casher's soul. It was a soul incapable of betraying anyone he loved. It was a soul that trusted few, but that trust ran deep as gold veining through the earth.

Jargo went inside the room. Mitchell lay on the bed, a heavy chain bound around his waist and his ankles, long enough to permit him to reach the toilet. Mitchell was unshaven, unwashed, but dignified. The room smelled of the dried-food packets he'd left for Mitchell, since he and Dezz could not stay to serve as his jailer.

He stood watching Mitchell, who did not say hello. Jargo lit a cigarette. He had not smoked in fifteen years. He pulled hard on the smoke, breathed in, coughed like a tobacco virgin. He studied the glowing ember of the cigarette.

"I'm afraid to ask," Mitchell Casher said.

"I have a difficult question for you," Jargo said, "but I really must insist on honesty."

"I've always been honest with you." Mitchell's voice was broken, worn with grief for his wife and fear for his son. He sounded like the dead Mr. Gabriel. Jargo offered him a cigarette, and Mitchell shook his head. The imprisonment would take months, years, to break him; bad news about his son would shatter him at once, Jargo knew.

"I appreciate your honesty, Mitch. Will Evan fight for you?"

" 'Fight for me'? I don't know what you mean."

Jargo sat down across from Mitchell Casher. The glow of the light, high above in the ceiling where no prisoner could reach it, was eye-achingly dim. No window graced the room; Jargo had bricked it years ago, after an unfortunate incident involving a shard of glass and the wrist of a stubborn informant within Castro's regime. But Jargo considered Mitchell not to be missing a view. Outside, the night sky of southern Florida hung heavy with clouds that resembled cancers. "Will he fight for you? Will Evan try and get you back?"

"No."

"I've been thinking long and hard about Carrie and what she's done. I don't know for sure that she is CIA; at the least she's freelance now, and she's taken Evan to sell him and his information to the highest bidder. I suspect that bidder will be the CIA."

Mitchell put his head in his hands. "Then let me go. Let me help you find him. Please, Steve."

"Find him? You and I can hardly stroll into Langley's lobby and ask for him back now, can we?"

"They'll kill him."

"Yes. But not right away." Jargo took another drag on the cigarette, and this time the tobacco soothed his nerves. *You never really forgot how to smoke,* he thought. *The way you never really forgot how to swim, to make love, to kill.*

"I don't understand."

This was the conversational equivalent of cutting a diamond. One had to be precise to get the intended effect, and there were no second chances. "Evan told me he has a list of our clients. He also knows my name, and he knows that Dezz is my son. So either he's been in touch with the CIA, or he's got even more information. Information about us. Who we are."

Mitchell's eyes went wide.

"All our clients, Mitchell. Do you realize what this could do to us? It's one thing if we all have to vanish and start over again. That's almost impossible. But our clients? We could never rebuild if the CIA got that information." Jargo brought his gaze back to the burning ember.

"I swear to you I never knew she was betraying us," Mitchell said in a hoarse voice.

"I know. I know, Mitchell. Otherwise you would have run with her. I know."

"Then please let me help you."

"I want to let you go. But you're hardly in fighting shape. You might take off and endanger the only chance I have"—Jargo paused—"of getting Evan back safely for you."

"The only chance. Tell me."

Jargo watched his cigarette burn. Waited. Let Mitchell squirm.

"Evan." Mitchell put his face in his hands.

"I haven't seen you cry since we were boys."

"They killed Donna. Imagine your son in their hands."

"Dezz would never be taken alive. You know how he is." Jargo didn't look at Mitchell. "I'm so sorry." His voice cracked. Jargo closed his hand on Mitchell's arm.

"So let me help you. Please."

"He said he had the client files, Mitchell."

"I bet he lied...Donna wouldn't have shared information with him. His finding out about us, it was her worst nightmare."

"Reality check. They were on his computer. Donna had clothes packed for him to run. He took off without waiting for his girlfriend. I think he knew. And he might know what the files are worth."

"Evan...wouldn't know how to sell the information. He wouldn't know anyone to contact. And he wouldn't hurt me."

"You never told him about your background? Not once?"

"Never. I swear, he knows nothing."

You don't know what he knows, and I'm not taking the risk, Jargo thought, but instead he said, "I'm weighing whether to attempt to get Evan back at all. If he plans on fighting for you, he won't simply hand the files over to the CIA. He'll try and strike a deal. Which may give us a window of time. But that's the risk I'm assessing."

"I don't understand."

Jargo leaned forward, whispered an inch from Mitchell's face, "You know I have operatives working for me within the Agency."

"I suspected."

"And clients within the Agency. Those people are at huge risk if Evan turns over the files. They're dead in the water." Jargo tasted the smoke again, stubbed out the cigarette in an ashtray. "My people inside the Agency have every reason to get Evan back for me. For us." He put a hand on Mitchell's shoulder.

"They won't hurt him?"

"Not if I tell them to bring him to me alive." The lie felt fine in his mouth. "But either way, we must get Evan and whatever information he has away from the Agency. Alive, so you can be together with him again."

"Please, Steve. Let me help. Let me help you find my son."

Jargo stood. Made his decision. Dug in his pocket and unlocked the chain, slipped it free of Mitchell. The links made a pool of silver on the hardwood floor.

Mitchell stood. "Thank you, Steve."

"Go get showered. I'll cook you dinner." He gave Mitchell Casher a rough hug. "How's an omelet sound?"

Mitchell seized him by the throat, shoved him hard against the wall, relieved him of his gun, angled it under his chin. "An omelet sounds great. But just so you and I are clear. Your agents. They don't hurt or kill my son. Make them understand we need him alive."

"I'm glad that's out of your system. You can let me go now."

"If they kill my son, I will kill yours."

"Let go."

Mitchell released his hold on Jargo; Jargo gently pushed his hand away. "This is what our enemies want. Us at each other's throats."

Mitchell handed him his gun. "Evan. Safe. That's nonnegotiable. I can control my son once we've got him back."

"I will do everything I can to bring him home. You realize he'll be the best-kept secret in the Agency. Resources, people, will be diverted from their normal work to help hide him and to rally against us. My eyes inside the Agency will be looking for those signs. A well-meaning idiot in the Agency will mass for a secret war against us, and we'll stop them with our own Pearl Harbor."

"Getting him back will be almost impossible."

"In a way," Jargo said, "I think it might be easy. What we need to do is convince him to come back to us."

He went downstairs to make the omelet. The curving cypress staircase was full of shadow; he did not like lights burning brightly in the lodge, even with every window carefully sealed and covered. Too much light would glow like a beacon in the vast dark and might attract unwanted attention.

The kitchen in the empty lodge was large, dimly lit. Dezz sat on a stool eating a candy bar, sullen, morose. CNN was on the TV.

"Any details of note?" Jargo asked.

"No. A few people suffered minor injuries in the rush to get out of the zoo. No arrests. No suspects. But no mention of videotape of us." Dezz chewed his candy. "When we catch them, I get Carrie. She's all mine. Ask her your questions, then give her to me. Christmas comes early this year."

"If Evan has the client list and hands it over to the CIA, then they'll up the surveillance on those targets. Not just on our clients inside the CIA, but elsewhere. But slowly. They can't commit too many resources suddenly to us without incredibly uncomfortable questions being asked."

"Your point?"

He could share with Dezz what he didn't dare share with

Mitchell. "Very few in the CIA know about us. There is a man, code-named Bricklayer, but I have not been able to determine who he is. Bricklayer is supposed to root out any internal problems in the CIA: problems such as using free-lance assassins, selling secrets, committing unapproved kills, stealing from American corporations. Basically, Bricklayer wants to put us out of business."

"Bricklayer."

"Carrie's a resource Bricklayer will have to use. That may be a blessing to us."

"How?"

"How the CIA uses Carrie will tell us how much they really know about us." He gathered the makings of an omelet from the fridge. Cooking would calm him. He chopped vegetables and he thought of a lifetime ago, a child, watching the girl who became Donna Casher standing across a sun-drenched kitchen table from him, cutting vegetables with a calm precision. She had always wanted everything exact, just so. The sun had always caught her hair in a way that transfixed Jargo, and a tinge of sadness and regret touched his heart. He wished, just once, he had told her how much he liked her photographs.

"You know, Mitchell and Donna and I, the first job we had together when we went freelance, it was in London. A hit. Really simple, it didn't require all three of us, but there was a sense of power in the three of us doing the kill together. A sense of liberation."

"Who killed whom?" Dezz asked.

"Victim doesn't matter. Mitchell and I both did the kill, although my shot hit first. Donna handled logistics." Jargo cracked eggs in a bowl, stirred in milk, dumped in the broc-coli and peppers. "Because it was our first job, we were cutting the bonds of our old life. We were so conscious in making our decisions. Before we were never encouraged to be so deliberative. We were more 'point and shoot, don't ask questions.' I fingered the bullets I was using for the longest time, like they were worry beads. Or the last shackles of a chain that we were all breaking."

Dezz ate a piece of candy.

"I just traded one set of chains for another, Dezz."

Dezz had no mind for reflection. He said, "So how are you getting Evan and Carrie back? Or at least shutting them up?"

"Carrie will tell the CIA what she knows, which isn't much. She can't betray enough to hurt us. She can give them descriptions, the apartment in Austin, but not much in terms of usable evidence."

"Get real," Dezz said. "If she's double, she might have information, files . . . she could skin you."

"She had no access."

"You don't know what she had, Dad."

Jargo kept his voice low. "You missed a prime chance to kill them both. Shut up." He dumped butter in the sizzling skillet, poured in the eggs. "I intend to cover every base. Including bases you don't even know are on the field, Dezz."

"We need to pack and run. Set up shop elsewhere. England. Germany. Greece. Let's go to Greece."

"No. I'm not dismantling years of sweat and work. My chains are still ones of my own choice, Dezz." The failure dimmed in Jargo. He was ready to roll.

"You're not going to be able to get Evan back."

Jargo finished cooking the eggs and slid them on a plate. "Take this plate and a cup of strong coffee up to Mitchell.

Be nice; he threatened to kill you a few minutes ago if I don't get Evan back safe and sound."

Dezz frowned.

"Don't worry," Jargo said in a low voice. "Soon Evan will be dead, but Mitchell won't be able to blame us."

TUESDAY

MARCH 15

25

‑‑‑◆‑‑‑

EVAN WATCHED THE PADDED WALLS, and the walls watched back—the small dents in the fabric reminded him of eyes. He imagined cameras lurking behind the fabric. He wondered what dramas they had witnessed in this room. Interrogations. Breakdowns. Death. A faded stain marred the wall, about the height of a sitting man, and he imagined how the stain had got there and why it hadn't been removed. Probably because the CIA wanted you to contemplate that stain and what it might suggest.

Two CIA men, one the pilot, flew them on the private jet out of New Orleans. Evan told them he would talk only to Bricklayer. They provided first aid to Carrie and left him alone until the plane landed in a small clearing in a forest. Then a private ambulance with North Hill Clinic written on it, with Virginia license plates, whisked them away. A medical team took Carrie, and a thick-necked security guard put him in this room. He sat and resisted the urge to make faces at the wall, sure cameras watched him. Worried about Carrie, worried about Shadey. Worried about his father.

The door opened and a man stuck his head inside. "Would you like to see your friend now?"

It occurred to Evan the man might not even know Carrie's real name. It occurred to him that he might not, either. But he said, "Thanks," and followed the man down a brightly lit hallway. The man led him down three doors, and her room wasn't padded; it was a typical hospital room. No windows, the light on the bed eerie and dim, like the glow of the moon in a bad dream. She lay in bed, her shoulder bandaged. A guard stood outside the door.

Carrie dozed. Evan watched her and wondered who she really was, in the spaces between flesh and bone. He took her hand, gave it a squeeze. She slept on.

"Hello, Evan," a voice sounded behind her. "She'll be right as rain real soon. I'm Bricklayer."

Evan put her hand down gently and turned toward the man. He was sixtyish, thin, with a sour set to his mouth but warm eyes. He looked like a difficult uncle. Bricklayer offered Evan his hand. Evan shook it and said, "I'd rather call you Bedford."

"That's fine." Bedford kept his face impassive. "As long as you don't do it in front of other people. No one here knows my real name." He stepped past Evan, put a hand on Carrie's forehead in a fatherly fashion, as though checking her for fever. Then he steered Evan into a conference room down the hall, where another guard stood watch. Bedford closed the door behind him and sat down. Evan stayed on his feet.

"Have you eaten?"

"Yes. Thank you."

"I'm here to help you, Evan."

"So you said the first time we talked." He decided to test the waters. "I'd like to leave now."

"Oh, goodness, I think that very unwise." Bedford tented

his hands. "Mr. Jargo and his associates will be hunting for you." His politeness was like an heirloom, given prominence on the table.

"My problem. Not yours."

Bedford gestured at the chair. "Sit for a minute, please."

Evan sat.

"I understand you grew up in Louisiana and Texas. I'm from Alabama," Bedford said. "Mobile. Wonderful town. I miss it terribly the older I get. Southern boys can be stubborn. Let's both not be stubborn."

"Fine."

"I'd like for you to tell me what happened since your mother phoned you on Friday morning."

Evan took a deep breath and gave Bedford a detailed account. But he did not mention Shadey, he did not mention Mrs. Briggs. He didn't want anyone else in trouble.

"I offer my deepest sympathies on the death of your mother," Bedford said. "I think she must have been an extraordinarily brave woman."

"Thank you."

"Let me assure you that her funeral arrangements will be taken care of."

"Thank you, but I'll handle her memorial when I get back to Austin."

"I'm afraid you truly can't go home again."

"Am I a prisoner?"

"No. But you're a target, and it's my job to keep you alive."

"I can't help you. I don't have these files. Telling Jargo that I did was simply a bluff to get my dad back."

"Tell me again exactly what your father said. Since he blames us for your mother's death."

Evan did, repeating his father's plea word for word, as best as he could remember. Bedford took a tin of mints from his pocket, offered Evan the tin, popped a mint in his own mouth after Evan shook his head. "Quite a story Jargo's peddling. We didn't kill your mother. He did."

"I know. I'm not sure why he cares what I think."

"He doesn't. He just wants to manipulate you." Bedford chewed his mint. "You must feel like Alice, fallen down the rabbit hole into Wonderland."

"Nothing wondrous about it."

"The fact that you survived an attack and a kidnapping is quite impressive. Mr. Jargo and his friends, they've stolen your life from you. They put a piece of wire around your mama's throat and squeezed the last breath out of her. How does that make you feel?"

Evan opened his mouth to speak and then shut it.

"It's the kind of question you ask in your films. I watched them a couple of months back. How did that fellow in Houston feel, framed by the police? How did that woman feel when her son and her grandson didn't come home from war? I was most impressed. You're a good storyteller. But just like a reporter with his soul sucked out, you have to ask the dreaded question: 'How does it make you feel?'"

"You want to know? I hate them. Jargo. Dezz."

"You have every reason." Bedford's voice went lower. "He made your mom and dad lie to you for years. I suspect it wasn't entirely their choice to work for the Deeps, at least for as long as they did."

"The Deeps."

"Jargo's name for his network." Bedford tented his hands.

"Gabriel said he was a freelance spy."

"It's true he buys and sells information, between governments, organizations, even companies. As far as we know."

"I don't understand."

"We've never been able to prove, conclusively, that he exists."

"I've seen him. So has Carrie."

"This is what we know: There is a man who uses the name Steven Jargo. He has no financial records. He owns no property. He does not travel under his own name, ever. Very few people have seen him more than once. He regularly changes his appearance. He has a young man who works with him, supposedly his son, and the son works under the name of Desmond Jargo, but there is no record of his birth, or his schooling, or him having anything like a normal life that creates a paper trail. They have a network. We don't know if it's just a few people or if it's a hundred. We suspect, from the times the name Jargo has popped up, that he has clients, buyers for his information and his services, on every continent." Bedford opened up a laptop. "I'm about to show extraordinary trust in you, Evan. Please don't disappoint me."

Bedford pressed a button and activated a projector cabled to the laptop. The image of a body, sprawled on pavestones, one arm dangling in a turquoise pool. "This is Valentin Marquez. A high-ranking financial official in Colombia, one that our government was not fond of because he had connections to the Cali drug cartels, but we couldn't touch him. His body was found dead in his backyard; four of his bodyguards were killed as well. Rumors surfaced that an American State Department official funneled money to a man named Jargo; he put a hit on Marquez. Given the political situation, this would not be an activity we want exposed: American officials illegally diverting taxpayer funds to hired killers."

Click. Another picture. A prototype blueprint of a soldier wearing a formfitting jumpsuit. "This is a project the Pentagon has been working on, the next generation of ultralightweight body armor for field troops. This blueprint was found in the computer of a senior army official in Beijing by one of our agents, who was attempting to steal data on the Chinese conventional-weapons program. We kidnapped the official, and under duress, he told us he bought the plans from a group he called the Deeps. We found an attempt was made to sell the same armor prototype to a Russian military attaché three weeks later. He refused the offer and attempted, instead, to steal the prototype from the seller. The seller killed the man, his wife, and his four children. The wife's aunt, who was visiting, survived by hiding in the attic. She got a glimpse of the killer. Her description matches Dezz Jargo's, although his hair was a different color and he wore glasses in Russia. Two months later, a major international armaments dealer made a proposal for a body armor that matched these specifications exactly. In short, Jargo works both sides of the fence. He steals from us, he sells to us."

Evan closed his eyes.

"Those are the closest cases we can tie to Jargo. We have several others where we suspect his involvement but can prove nothing."

"My parents could not have been involved with a man like that. It just can't be."

"That's what Carrie thought, I'm sure," Bedford said. "Her father worked for Jargo. Jargo killed her mom and dad. Or rather, had them killed."

Evan felt sick.

"Her real name is Caroline Leblanc. Her father ran a private security service after a long career in military intelligence. He had come to the Agency and met with me, let me know that Jargo had operatives working in the Agency and people buying his services within the Agency. I asked him to remain in place, keep working for Jargo, but report to me. Jargo found out, or Carrie's father slipped up. Jargo made her think the CIA was responsible for her father's death. But Carrie came to us after her father's death—she learned additional details that convinced her that Jargo was behind her parents' murders. At tremendous personal risk, Carrie joined us and became our double agent within the Deeps."

Evan found his voice after a moment. "Jargo killed her folks. And she kept working for him."

"Yes. It was difficult but she knew it had to be done. Carrie is our single operative who's gotten close to Jargo, although she's seen him face-to-face less than five times."

"So who sent her into my bed, you or Jargo?"

Bedford let the words die on the air. "A man like you, who looks for truth in the world, knows that life is complicated. I asked her to watch out for you. I didn't order her to kiss you, sleep with you, or care about you. She's not who you thought she was...but she's still Carrie. Does that make sense?"

He didn't know. "Why were you and Jargo interested in me?"

"I, simply because Jargo sent Carrie to watch you." Bedford cleared his throat. "He wanted to know what film you were making next."

"Film? I don't understand. Wasn't he watching me because of my parents?"

"That would be the natural assumption. But he wanted Carrie to find out about your film plans. That seems to have been the genesis of his interest in you."

"He wanted me for this network. Like Carrie."

"Possibly. But then he'd have gotten your parents to recruit you. Like how John Walker talked his friend and his son into becoming spies for the Russians."

Evan tried to imagine his parents sitting him down for that talk. The picture wouldn't form.

"But...Jargo never said a word to me about my films. He said I had files he needed. He wanted them in exchange for my dad."

"He told Carrie the files are information on his clients— the people in the CIA and elsewhere who hire him to do their dirty work. I don't know why your mother went against Jargo, but she did. We think she contacted Gabriel to extract her and you. In return, she would have given him Jargo's client list. Gabriel would have taken the list public, to shame the CIA—we fired him, because no one believed his stories that we had freelance spying occurring within the Agency—and to bring down Jargo."

"How did Mom get these files?"

"Unknown. She must have worked for Jargo."

"So Gabriel was telling me the truth. Well, partially."

"Mr. Gabriel let his personal weaknesses and biases cloud his judgment. Both here and after he left the Agency. It's very sad. I've asked the FBI to move his family to a safe location, hide them until we bring Jargo down. We told both the family and the Bureau that Mr. Gabriel gave us information on a drug cartel before he vanished."

"So...how long ago did Jargo order Carrie to get involved with me?"

"Three months."

"When did my mother steal these files?"

"I'm not sure, but we believe she contacted Gabriel last month."

"So Carrie was watching me...before Mom stole the files. That doesn't make sense." Evan stood up, paced the room. "I never thought, never talked, about making a documentary about spies or the CIA or intelligence work of any sort. Why would he tell Carrie to watch me because of my films?"

"He never gave her a more specific reason," Bedford said.

"So she's told you about what films I've made or might make."

"Yes."

"So, you must have an idea about what sparked Jargo's interest."

"Tell me what your planned subjects were."

"Hasn't Carrie reported all this to you anyway?"

"I'd like to hear it from you, Evan. Tell me everything. This might be the key to locating Jargo. We find him, we get your father back."

"Won't he just kill my dad? If my mom betrayed him, he'll think my dad did as well."

"Carrie tells me Jargo has been rather protective of your father. I'm not sure why. Now tell me about your films."

"I thought about telling the story of Jameson Wong, the Hong Kong financier. He had the franchise for a number of luxury brands in Hong Kong. But he made bad investments, got grossly overextended, lost his fortune. When he got on his feet, he started funneling money from wealthy expat Chinese to groups that support reform in China. He went from being a self-involved CEO to a real voice for democracy."

"How did you choose him?"

"I read an article about him in the *New York Times*. Is he connected to Jargo?"

"Perhaps. Continue."

"Um, Alexander Bast. He was kind of the king of the London social scene about thirty years ago. High roller, slept with lots of famous women. Renaissance man, for a partyer. Ran three famous nightclubs but also two art galleries, a modeling agency. He lost it all, I think his accountant stole it from him, and then he started a small publishing company, of all things, publishing books by Soviet dissidents. Then he was murdered in a robbery of his home."

"How did you find out about Bast?"

"Well, he was semifamous already, simply because he was such a friend to so many famous people. But I was in the UK a few months ago, lecturing at the London Film School, and I got an anonymous package indicating that Alexander Bast would be a good subject for my next film project. It included clippings about Bast, his murder, his life."

"That's rather unusual, isn't it, for someone to pitch you a film idea anonymously?" Bedford cupped his hands over his chin, leaned forward on the table.

"Everyone has an idea for a movie, I get ideas tossed to me by nearly everyone I meet." Evan took a long sip of water. "But, yes, an anonymous package, this was odd. I hadn't ever heard of Bast. But the story about him—rich party animal embraces social change—was interesting, and he was certainly an intriguing character. Most pitches are beyond boring—they just don't have meat enough for a movie."

"Did you ever find out who left the package?"

Evan shifted in his chair. "The head of the documentary department at London Film, Jon Malcolm, told me that a man named Hadley Khan had been asking him if I'd mentioned doing a film on Alexander Bast. I told Malcolm about the anonymous package I'd gotten, because it was odd."

"Hadley Khan."

"Yeah. He's from a wealthy Pakistani family based in London. I had met him at a Film School cocktail party. His family donates money to a number of London cultural interests. Malcolm told me Hadley had mentioned my work to him a couple of times, pushed for me to get an invite to speak at the Film School. I figured Hadley sent the package."

"What did he talk to you about at the cocktail party? Do you recall?"

Evan thought, let the silence take hold of the room. "I only thought about it later, when it became clear he'd sent me the anonymous package." He closed his eyes. "He asked about my next film project. I don't discuss my ideas, and I gave him the polite answer that I wasn't sure yet. And frankly, I really wasn't sure what I'd do. He told me how much he admired biography as a focus, that London was full of fascinating characters. It was all harmless and vague. But I remember his face—he reminded me of a rookie car salesman, gearing up for the pitch but lacking the spine to close the deal."

"Did you ever ask Hadley Khan about the information on Bast?"

"No. Malcolm didn't tell me about Hadley having sent me the package until I was back in the States. I e-mailed

Hadley but never got a response." Evan shrugged. "It was strange, but I found out a long time ago all sorts of people want to get close to the film business. I figured, since he had money, he probably wanted to be a producer. Get a credit on a film. It's very common. I thought he was just an amateur." Evan shook his head. "It definitely sounds more sinister now. Knowing what I know."

"Alexander Bast was a CIA agent," Bedford said. "A low-level courier. Not important. But still on our payroll until the day he died."

Evan leaned back in the chair. "Nothing in the material Khan gave me on Bast indicated he had a CIA tie."

"We don't generally advertise," Bedford said dryly.

"Bast has been dead for twenty-plus years. If there was a connection to him and Jargo, why would Jargo care now?"

"I don't know. But that has to be part of the reason Jargo was interested in you. Bast was CIA, Jargo has contacts in the CIA. You were in England before Jargo got interested in you. So was your mother."

"She had a photographic assignment for a magazine."

"Or she had work to do for Jargo."

Evan decided to broach the subject. "Jargo said your people killed my mother."

"We covered that already. He lied, of course."

"But what you're doing is illegal. Last I heard the CIA isn't supposed to operate on American soil. Yet here you are."

"Evan. You're correct. The CIA charter doesn't permit the Agency to conduct clandestine ops on U.S. soil or against citizens." Bedford shrugged. "But the Deeps are a very special case. If we bring in the FBI, we hopelessly complicate the situation. We can act and act decisively."

"*Complicate* means 'expose,' and that's what you don't

want. The fact is you have active traitors and rogues in the Agency."

"I don't want them to know we're on their trail. All our activities will come to light once the bad guys are down. We still have congressional oversight, you know."

"All I care about is getting my dad back from Jargo."

"Without the files," Bedford said, "we don't have a lot of options."

"I don't know where any of the files on the Deeps are."

"Oh, I believe you. If you knew, you would have given them to us." Bedford crossed his legs.

"My mother had to have stolen them from somewhere. If this network is as fragmented as you say, she wouldn't have easily amassed a list of the clients. She would have to steal this list. From a central source."

"I think it likely."

Evan got up and began to pace the floor. "So. Jargo gets interested in me because he hears I'm doing a film that threatens him. That means he has a connection to Hadley Khan. He inserts Carrie into my life to watch me. Then my mother steals these files... why? Why does she turn against Jargo, after so long?"

"Maybe she learned of Jargo's interest in you. It was probably a protective measure."

Evan's head spun. His mother. Set her own death in motion, trying to save him from Jargo.

"You get the client list, what do you do with it?"

"The CIA has only a few bad apples. I think Jargo knows most of them. We take them down. Jargo has to be stopped."

"And you getting a list of Jargo's other clients, that doesn't hurt you, either."

"Of course not. The British and the French and the Russians want to know about their own loose cannons. But my primary concern is in cleaning our own house. If you might help us figure out where she hid another copy of the files, that would—"

"I told you, I don't have the files," Evan said. "So we should steal the files again."

Bedford raised an eyebrow. "How?"

"Go backward from when my parents vanished from Washington all those years ago. Find another path into Jargo's organization."

"He'll have destroyed the files."

"But not their essence. He still has to have a way of tracking clients, payments made to him, deliveries he does. That information still exists. We have to crack his world."

"Stop saying *we*."

"I want my father back. I can't just sit around a hospital room forever."

Bedford leaned back. "And you think you could do it."

"Yes. If I start getting close to Jargo, he'll try and grab me. Or he'll think I'm working with you now, and he'll want to grab me to see what you know."

"Or grab Carrie."

"No. He nearly killed her. She doesn't go anywhere near him." Evan shook his head. "Where were you, by the way, in New Orleans? You sent her alone."

"Carrie is an excellent agent, but she's strong-willed."

"Oh. That's not an act?" Evan said, and permitted himself his first smile in days.

Bedford gave a soft laugh. "No, that's who she is. She risked everything to save you."

"I don't want her near Jargo."

"That's not your choice, though, is it?"

"Get another agent."

"I can't. Fighting Jargo is not official CIA policy, son, because we don't want to admit he's a problem." Bedford put the smile back on. "You're at a secret CIA clinic in rural Virginia. The locals think this is a sanatorium for rich alcoholics. On our books you're listed under a code name, which in the records is a nonexistent Croatian Muslim college student living in D.C. wanting to trade information on Al Qaeda in Eastern Europe that will, of course, not pan out. Your flight from New Orleans will be logged as me traveling back from a meeting with a journalist from Mexico who had information to share on a drug cartel that is financing terror activities in Chiapas. You see how the game is played? Until we identify who Jargo has in his pocket in the Agency, we dare not tip our hand. No one in the Agency can know we're hunting Jargo and the Deeps. According to Agency records, Carrie is assigned deep cover to an operation in Ireland that doesn't exist. You don't exist. I sort of exist, but everyone thinks I'm just an accountant who travels a lot checking Agency books." Bedford smiled again.

"Then let me find the files. You don't risk anything, and I'm the only one who you know can draw Jargo out."

"You're a civilian. Carrie goes with you."

"No."

"Because you don't trust her or because you love her?"

Evan said, "I don't want her hurt again."

"She saved your life, son. She wants the people who killed her parents to go down, and she's worked this for a year. She's an extraordinary young woman."

Evan stood up, paced the room. "I just wish...you had

been watching my mom instead of me. You had to have checked on me, on my family, when Jargo assigned Carrie to me."

"We did. Your parents had extremely good legends."

"Legends?"

"Background stories. There was nothing to make us doubt them, until we went back and found no pictures of them in the high school yearbooks they supposedly were in."

"Then why weren't you watching them?"

"We were watching your father. But very carefully. We thought he had the connection to Jargo, as Carrie's father did. These people are extremely good. They'd spot surveillance unless it was perfect."

"Once again, you didn't want to tip your hand. You left us out in the cold."

"We didn't know what was happening. We couldn't find it out."

Evan let it go. "If my dad wasn't in Australia, like Mom said…"

"He spent the last week in Europe. Helsinki, Copenhagen, Berlin. We lost him in Berlin last Thursday."

His father. Evading the CIA. It didn't seem possible.

"Either Jargo grabbed him in Germany or he returned to the U.S. without us knowing, and then Jargo nabbed him."

"If I get the files back, what happens to me and my dad?"

"Your father tells us everything he can about Jargo and his organization. In exchange for immunity from prosecution. You and your father get new lives, new identities overseas, courtesy of the Agency."

"What about Carrie?"

"She gets a new identity. Or she keeps working for us. Whatever she wants."

"All right," Evan said quietly.

"I'm surprised, Evan. I had you pegged as more self-involved."

"I find out what was in the files my mom stole, I don't just get a negotiating tool to get my dad back. I find out the truth about who they are. Who I am."

Bedford gave him a smile. "That's true. It could be the first step in having your life back."

"I don't have my laptop—it got left behind when I escaped from Gabriel's house—but I have my music player...it contained the files my mother sent, I think, but I couldn't decode the files again when I downloaded them a second time. And the player was in my pocket when I jumped in the water in the zoo. It's ruined."

"Give it to me. We'll try."

"I have a passport that Gabriel provided. South African." Evan pulled it from his shoe. "I had other passports, but they got left behind in my motel room in New Orleans." He supposed Shadey took them when he fled.

Bedford studied the passport, handed it back, gave him a critical look. "We can improve your hair color. Change your eyes. Do a new photo. It's probably best the world still thinks you're missing. You'd be besieged by the media if you surfaced right now."

"All right."

"Evan. Understand this. One mistake and you're dead. Your father's dead. And worse—the Deeps get away with everything."

26

Carrie was awake when Evan returned to her room. The guard shut the door behind him, left them alone.

"Hey. How are you feeling?" he asked. A dinner tray of comfort food sat before her: chicken soup, mashed potatoes, a chocolate shake, glass of ice water. Mostly untouched.

"You're not hungry?" He wasn't sure how to start this conversation. She had been unconscious much of the time on the fast flight out of New Orleans, and he couldn't talk to her in front of the CIA guys.

"Not really."

"Bedford said your wound wasn't too bad."

Color touched her cheeks. "More gouge than bullet hole. It caught the top of my shoulder. It's sore and stiff but I'm feeling better."

He sat in the chair, bolted to the floor, at the foot of her bed. "Thank you. For saving my life."

"You saved mine. Thanks."

Awkward silence again.

He got up and sat on the bed next to her. "I just don't know what to believe right now. I don't know who to trust." He heard Shadey's words in his head: *Don't trust unless you must.* Maybe Carrie had spotted Shadey in the crowd—recognized him from *Ounce of Trouble*—but she still made no mention to Bedford. Protecting his friend. Showing him, through her silence, that she could be trusted. He didn't dare mention Shadey's name—the room was probably bugged. He just hoped Shadey was safe and lying low.

"Trust yourself," Carrie said. Now she looked at the tangle of sheet around her waist.

"Not you?"

"I can't tell you what to do. I have no right."

"Bedford says you'll want to help me get my dad back."

"Yes."

"At great risk to yourself."

"Life is nothing but risk."

"You don't have anything to prove to me."

"You and your father are the best hope we have of breaking them. It's not a matter of force. It's a matter of subtlety. That's all I want, Jargo broken. And for you to be safe."

He leaned forward. "Listen. You don't have to play a role anymore. You don't have to pretend to love me. Or even like me. I'll be fine."

"Don't sell yourself short, Evan. You're easier to love than you think."

His face felt hot. "Why didn't you just tell me the truth?"

"I couldn't put you in that danger. Jargo would have killed you."

"And you would have lost your chance to take him down."

"But you're more important to me than Jargo." She closed her eyes. "I didn't let myself get close to anyone after my parents died. You were the first."

He held her hands. "Bedford says Jargo killed your folks."

"I don't know who actually pulled the trigger. One of the other Deeps or a hired hit man. Jargo wouldn't soil his hands. He made sure I was with him and Dezz when it happened. He wanted me to be sure that I thought the CIA was responsible."

"Tell me about your parents."

She stared at him. "Why?"

"Because now you and I do have truly a lot in common."

"I'm sorry, Evan. I'm so sorry."

"Tell me about your folks."

She let go of his hands, knotted the sheets with her fingers. "My mother wasn't involved with the Deeps. She was an advertising copywriter for a small firm that did direct mail. She was pretty and kind and funny—just a really great mom. I was an only child, so I was her everything. She loved me very much. I loved her. Jargo killed her when he killed my father. That's about it."

"And your dad?"

"He worked for Jargo. I thought he had his own corporate security firm." She took a sip of water. "I suspect he mostly did corporate espionage—finding people inside companies willing to sell secrets. Or setting up compromising situations where they were forced to sell."

"Did your mother know?"

"No. She wouldn't have stayed married to him. He lived a life we didn't know about."

"How long ago did they die?"

"Fourteen months. Jargo decided my father had betrayed him, and he killed them both. It was made to look like a robbery. Jargo stole their wedding rings, my dad's wallet."

She closed her eyes. "I was already working for Jargo. Through my dad. He recruited me."

"Why would your father have drawn you into this mess?"

She looked at him with haunted eyes. "I don't know why...I assume he thought it was good money, better than I was making. I have a degree in criminal justice from the University of Illinois, I went into police work...he told me I could make a lot more money doing 'corporate security.'" She drew quote marks with her fingers around the last two words.

"What kind of work did you do?"

"Low-level stuff. I'd be the go-between from Jargo to other agents or client contacts. I filled dead drops—you know, secret places where you leave documents and the client picks them up. I never even saw Jargo or the client's contact. I never got the location of the dead drop until the last minute, so it was much more difficult for Bricklayer to watch. I hadn't done a job for Jargo in three months when he ordered me to Houston."

"Bedford says you came to him to fight Jargo."

"I never bought the robbery story...my father was trained to fight, he wouldn't be taken so easily. I was on a job in Mexico City and I went to the embassy. They put me in touch with a CIA official, he got Bedford down fast on a plane. He asked me to stay in place, keep working for Jargo, feed them what information I could. But it was hard. I wanted out. I wanted to shoot Jargo dead. I've wanted to kill Dezz. But Bedford ordered me not to—we needed to wrap up the whole network, and their clients. I kill them, another Deep simply takes over and we're back to square one."

"I still don't see why they can't put their hands on this guy."

"Evan. He's extraordinarily careful, and he's been doing this a long time. I'd get my instructions—encoded—in what would look like an innocent e-mail. Then I'd pick up from a dead drop the materials for the client that another Deep had stolen, go to a second dead drop, often in another city or country, and leave them. If the CIA picked up whoever picked up the goods, Jargo would know his network was blown, and we wouldn't get any closer. The best the CIA could do was to replace the information I was dropping off with data that was similar but not quite right. He never uses the same e-mail twice. Never the same base of operations twice. Everything is handled through third-party companies that are simply fronts, and as much with cash as he can. He's really, really hard to stop. He's killed four people in the past few days." Tears threatened her eyes. "I thought I could do it alone, but I couldn't."

He kissed the top of her hands and put her hands back onto the blanket. "I'm going to find the files my mom stole. Jargo still has my father, I'm getting him back. Do you know where he is?"

"I think in Florida. Jargo has a safe house there, but I don't know where."

"Bedford has agreed to help me."

"Let Bedford hide you, Evan. If your dad can get away from Jargo—"

"No. I can't wait. I can't let my dad down. Bedford already said I won't be able to talk you out of this. Will you help me?"

She nodded, took his hand. "Yes. And . . ."

"What?"

"I know it's hard to trust anyone now. But you can trust Bedford."

"All right."

She put her hand on his cheek. "Lie down here with me."

"Um, I don't want to hurt your shoulder."

She gave him a slight smile. "You're just lying down, ace."

She scooted over and he stretched out next to her and held her and she fell asleep in a few minutes, her head on his shoulder.

Bedford sat watching a monitor that showed Carrie and Evan lying in the hospital bed, whispering quietly, talking. Love at twenty-four. It was the intensity of it that could frighten a man, the sureness of it, the belief that love was a lever to lift the world. He had already lowered the volume; he didn't need to hear what they said. He was a spy but he did not want to spy on them, not now.

Carrie slept and Evan stared off into space.

I wonder, Bedford thought. *I wonder how much you really know, or really suspect.*

"Sir?" A voice behind him, one of his techs.

"Yes?"

The man shook his head. "The damaged music player... we can't recover any encoded files from it. Whatever process was used, it did not leave any other files hidden inside the music files when he transferred them to the player. I'm very sorry."

"Thank you," Bedford said. The tech left, shutting the door behind him.

After a moment Bedford switched off the monitors and went down to the clinic's kitchen to make himself a sandwich.

He heard a noise behind him after he spread the mayo on the rye.

Evan stood behind him, a slightly crooked smile on his face. "I know where we can start. We can make a move that Jargo will never anticipate."

Galadriel looked at the readouts while sipping decaf and eating a chocolate doughnut. She knew she shouldn't, but stress made her crave carbs. She had hacked into the FAA database, examining every plane takeoff in Louisiana and Mississippi since Jargo and Dezz had lost Carrie and Evan in New Orleans. Every flight accounted for, recorded, logged. But no flight that led to a place where it should not. Which meant that they hadn't flown, they had driven out of New Orleans. Or they could still be in New Orleans.

But she had already been through every hospital record she could acquire, stealthily weeding through the databases, and no young woman matching Carrie's description had been admitted to a hospital in that area. She would have to widen the search, cover Texas to Florida.

She sipped her coffee, nibbled at her doughnut. Shame that Carrie was a traitor. She rather liked Carrie, although she had never met her and had only talked with her on the phone a few times. But Carrie and Evan were young and stupid, and sooner or later they'd poke up their heads, via a travel document or a credit activity, and Galadriel would see them. Then Jargo would unleash his dogs and end this particular mess.

She had an unusual protocol to follow, designed by Jargo years ago, in case he feared the network was in danger of exposure. Panic mode. She was to monitor phone lines used only for emergency communications by certain Deeps, to ensure that no one was running. She ran a program that would feed cleaned money into banks around the world.

And for some odd reason, he added another request last night: she was to track cellular phone call patterns to and from a small chunk of southwestern rural Ohio. Glean every cellular call made, incoming or outbound, then deliver the data to Jargo.

She wondered, exactly, what Jargo was looking for in Ohio. Or what conceivable danger could lurk for him on such quiet country roads and fields.

WEDNESDAY

MARCH 16

27

WEDNESDAY MORNING EVAN AND CARRIE regarded each other's new look over breakfast.

"You don't look like you," Evan said.

"Welcome to Salon Bricklayer," she said.

Evan's hair was now a rich auburn and cut in a cleaned-up military burr, his hazel eyes hidden behind brown contact lenses. He wore a dark suit with white shirt, a shift from his normal colorful clothing. Carrie's dark hair had been lightened to blond and cut short. She wore tinted glasses that made her eyes look brown instead of blue.

"Call me chameleon boy," Evan said.

"Hope and pray that this is the last time you ever have to go through a transformation."

After reviewing their plans with Bedford, Evan and Carrie boarded the small government jet that had brought them from New Orleans. They flew to Ohio, landing at a small regional airport east of Dayton.

Bedford had arranged for a car to be left for them, and while the pilot hurried to fetch it, Carrie and Evan waited under the canopy in front of the airport. Rain weighed the pewter sky, the wind blew damp and constant. Evan had an umbrella, from the plane, and he abandoned the idea of talking to her under it, even surrounded by the open lot. There might be a mike hidden inside the umbrella's shaft. There might be a mike hidden in the car. The pilot might report every word he spoke back to Bedford. He wondered how his parents had coped with the burden of endless deception. Perhaps it explained their silences toward each other, the gentle quiet of the love that demanded few words.

Goinsville—where Bernita Briggs had told him that the Smithson family, his family, was from—lay ten miles west of the slant of Interstate 71. The pilot drove. Evan sat in the backseat. Carrie's arm rested in a sling, and she seemed tired but relieved. Relieved, Evan decided, to be out of her bed, to be taking action against Jargo.

They left the CIA pilot drinking coffee and ordering a second breakfast in a diner at the edge of town, working through a thick magazine of crossword puzzles.

Evan drove into Goinsville and parked in the town square. Four junk shops angling for antiquers' dollars; an outdoor café with weathered tables, empty under the rain-bottomed clouds; an optometrist's office; a law office; a title office. A normal, anonymous town.

"Goinsville never quite got going," he said. He drove a block off the square and parked in front of a small, newer building with Goinsville Public Library in metal letters mounted against the brick.

Evan told the librarian on duty that they were researching genealogies.

The woman—small, dark, pretty—frowned. "If you're looking for birth certificates, you're out of luck before 1967."

"Why?"

"County courthouse burned down. We're the county seat. All the records went up in smoke with them. Anything from '68 on, we can do."

"What about your local newspaper?"

"On microfilm back to the 1940s," the librarian said. "We've also got old phone books—in original form, if that helps. What's the family name?"

"Smithson." First time he could claim the name as his own, first time he had said it aloud in public. *Arthur and Julie Smithson. They used to live here. They grew up here.*

"I don't know any Smithsons," the librarian said.

"My parents grew up in an orphanage here."

"Goodness. No orphanage here. Closest one would be in Dayton, I'm sure. But I've only lived here for five years."

She showed them the microfilm machines, told them to ask if they needed any help, and retreated back to her desk.

"The orphanage must be closed," he said. Or Mrs. Briggs was mistaken. Or a liar. "Start with the current phone books, look for any Smithsons. I'll start with the paper. I got to go to the bathroom, though."

She nodded and he returned to the entry foyer. Next to the restroom was a pay phone. He fed it quarters, dialed Shadey's cell phone.

"H'lo?"

"Shadey. It's Evan. I only have a few seconds. Are you okay?"

"Yeah, man, where are you?"

"I'm fine. I'm with . . . the government."

"Please be kidding."

"I'm not. Did you make it back to Houston?"

"Yes. Charged a plane ride back on my Visa, man, you owe me." But the earlier bite in his tone, when he and Evan had talked in Houston, was gone. "You sure you okay?"

"Yes, and I'll make sure you get your money."

"I...I don't mean to sound cheap. It's just now I'm scared, Evan."

"You should stay out of sight."

"I am. I called in sick at work, I'm staying at a friend's house."

"Good idea. Did you get Jargo and Dezz on film?"

"Crystal clear. Got Dezz grabbing that little mama, him shooting and missing that guard, too. That's called attempted murder in Louisiana, I do believe."

"I need you to upload the film to a remote server where I can get it. Do you know how to do that?"

"No, but my friend knows computers. Where do you want it?"

Evan gave him the name of a remote server service he'd used to back up dailies of his films, so he always had an off-site backup in case his computer was stolen or his house burned down.

Shadey repeated back the information. "I'll set up an account under my stepbrother's name. Password is evanowesme."

"Thanks. Stay low, Shadey."

"When are you coming back to Houston?"

"I don't know. Thanks for everything. I'll wire you your money."

"Man. Don't worry about it. Watch your back."

"I will. I got to run, Shadey. Stay safe. I'll call you when I can."

He walked back to the table and Carrie gave him a smile as he sat back down.

"Not much to look for in the phone books, the last twenty years," she said. "No Smithsons. I'm already on the newspapers. You start on that set."

Evan put in the microfilm to search through the town paper. He was conscious of Carrie's closeness, of the smell of soap on her skin, of what it would be like to kiss her and pretend none of this nightmare had happened.

It wouldn't ever be the same between them, he knew. The innocence was gone forever.

"Your parents could have lied to your source," Carrie said.

"It bothers you I won't tell you the source's name." He had not told anyone Bernita Briggs's name or how he'd found the information tying his family to the missing Smithsons. Bedford hadn't pressed him.

"No. You're protecting that person. I'd do the same in your shoes."

"I want to trust you. I know I can. I just don't want Bedford to know."

"You can trust him, Evan." But she went back to her search.

He started on a set of microfilmed newspapers that began in January 1968. Goinsville news was full of civic events, farm reports, pride in the school's students, and a smattering of news from the wider world beyond. He spun the film reader's wheel past car crashes, births, football reports, a saints' parade of Eagle Scouts and FFA honorees.

He stopped at February 13, 1968, when the county courthouse burned. Read the article. The fire completely consumed the papers in the old courthouse. In the following days, arson rose its head and had also been suspected in the orphanage fire three months before. Investigators were attempting to find a link between the two fires.

"Are you to the end of 1967?" he asked.

"No. Halfway through '63."

"Go to November '67. I found it. Orphanage fire."

In a few minutes, she found the newspaper account. The Hope Home for Children sheltered the illegitimate unwanted in Goinsville. The stray seeds of southwest Ohio that didn't end up at church homes in Dayton or Cincinnati apparently found root at the Hope Home. It housed both boys and girls. In November 1967, fire erupted in Hope's administrative offices, tearing like wind through the rest of the complex. Four children and two adults died of smoke inhalation. The rest of the children were relocated to other facilities throughout Ohio, Kentucky, and West Virginia.

The Hope Home never reopened. Evan went back to the courthouse fire story. Most articles written about the orphanage tragedy and the courthouse fire carried the byline of Dealey Todd.

"Let's look him up in the most recent phone book," Evan said.

Carrie did. "He's listed."

"I'll call him and see if he'll talk to us." Evan did. "His wife says he's retired, at home, and bored. Let's go."

28

<hr/>

"THOSE POOR KIDS," Dealey Todd said. He hovered near
eighty, but he wore the unfettered smile of a child. His hair
had beaten a long-ago retreat, leaving a trail of freckles
mapped across his head. He wore old khakis that needed
a wash and a shirt faded with loving wear. His den held
a rat's nest of old paperbacks and three TVs, one tuned
and muted to CNN, the others tuned to a *telenovela,* also
muted.

"Learning Spanish," he said.

"Watching pretty girls," his wife said.

Evan's throat tightened as CNN played. His face
had been on CNN repeatedly in the past couple of days,
although other stories had now bumped his from the news.
But Bedford's disguise seemed to work; Dealey Todd
hadn't given him a more curious look than he would have
given any other stranger when Evan introduced himself
and Carrie as Bill and Terry Smithson. Probably Dealey
paid more attention to the *telenovela* bosoms than he did
the news feeds.

Mrs. Todd was a bustling woman who offered coffee and promptly vanished into the kitchen to watch yet
another television.

Evan decided to play a sympathetic hand. "We think my parents came through the Hope Home orphanage, but their records were destroyed," said Evan. "We're trying to locate any other alternative source of records, and also to learn more about the Home. My parents died several years ago, and we want to piece together their early lives."

"Admirable," Dealey Todd said. "Interest in your parents. My own daughter lives down in Cleveland and can't be bothered to phone more than once a month."

"Dealey," Mrs. Todd called from the kitchen. "They don't care about that, honey doll."

The honey doll made a sour face. "Okay, the orphanage." He shrugged, returned to his smile, sipped at his black coffee. "Orphanage got built, then it burned ten years later. So you might be in for a long, difficult haul to find records."

Evan shook his head. "There has to be a source for records. Who built it? Maybe whatever charity sponsored it has what I need."

"Let's see." Dealey closed his eyes in thought. "Originally a nondenominational charity out of Dayton started it up, but they sold it to"—he tapped on his bottom lip—"let's see, I want to say a company out of Delaware. You could probably find a record of sale at the county clerk's office. But I remember they went bankrupt, too, after the fire, and no one rebuilt the orphanage."

A bankrupt owner. Who knew what had happened to the files. But Evan knew from his documentary interviews that dead ends often had left turns, just out of view. He thought for a second and asked, "How did the town view the orphanage?"

"Y'know, not that Goinsville isn't a charitable place, 'cause it is, but many folks around here weren't overjoyed with the orphanage. Kind of a not-in-my-backyard feeling. Bunch of so-called church ladies were just tight-jawed about it—"

"Dealey, honey doll, don't exaggerate," Mrs. Todd called from the kitchen.

"I thought when I retired from the paper I left editors behind," Dealey said.

Silence from the kitchen.

"I'm not exaggerating," he said to Evan and Carrie. "People didn't like in particular that young ladies in trouble could go to Hope Home and drop their precious loads. You get the sinners along with the end product." He stopped suddenly, the smile now uneasy, remembering that he was speaking of Evan's parents and grandmothers.

"Did anyone dislike the place enough to burn it?" Evan asked.

"Everyone thought it was an accident at first, the wiring. But six months after the fire, a teenager named Eddie Childers shot his mama and himself. The police found souvenirs from both burn sites—baby socks, a girl's uniform from the orphanage, family photos from the workers at the courthouse. All stashed under his bed. I'll never forget that—I was there when the officers found the stuff. And he left a note taking responsibility. He was a wild kid. Sad, very sad."

"So the records of any children born at the Hope Home were destroyed," Evan said. "Because both the orphanage and the county courthouse were gone, and the owners went bankrupt."

"Yes, basically," Dealey said. "I remember I wrote a few stories about the company that owned the orphanage after it burned...because, you know, it brought about twenty or so jobs to the town. People hoped they'd rebuild. Twenty jobs is twenty jobs."

"Well, we'll look up those stories at the library," Carrie said.

Evan thought, *This is a dead end, this is nothing. It couldn't be.* And then he thought, *That is the point: Goinsville is a dead end.* Someone wanted it to be the end of the road for anyone who ever came looking for Evan's parents. *It can't be. You can't run a business that takes care of kids and have every bit of its history vanish . . .*

"Thanks for your time," Carrie said.

"Twenty jobs," Evan said suddenly. "Hey, do you know anyone who worked at the Hope Home that might still be alive?"

Dealey bit his lip in thought. Mrs. Todd emerged from the kitchen. "Well, Dealey's cousin's wife worked at the orphanage as a volunteer. Read the kiddies stories every Wednesday, you know. Get 'em interested in books, because you know that's the key to success. I remember because Phyllis won a volunteer-of-the-year award, and my mother-in-law nagged at me for weeks to volunteer myself. She might be able to help you, or give you the names of the employees."

"Does she by any chance still live around here?" Evan asked. "I could show her pictures of my mom and dad, see if she would remember them."

"Sure," Dealey said. "Phyllis Garner. She lives five streets over."

"Phyllis is as sharp as a tack," said Mrs. Todd. "Honey doll, shame it don't run in your family."

A quick phone call determined that Mrs. Garner was home, watching the same soap opera as Mrs. Todd. They drove over the five streets with Dealey Todd to an immaculately maintained brick home, shaded by giant oaks. Mrs. Garner wore a lavender sweater set, was perfectly coiffed, and was eighty-five if a day.

Phyllis Garner gestured them to sit on a floral couch.

"I know it's been many years, ma'am." Evan showed her current photos of his parents. "Their names were Arthur and Julie Smithson."

Phyllis Garner studied the photos. "Smithson. I think I do recall that name. James!" she called to her grandson, who was puttering around in her garage. "Come help me a minute." They vanished down into a basement, leaving Dealey, Evan, and Carrie to talk about the weather and college football, two of Dealey's keen interests.

Phyllis returned fifteen minutes later, dusty but smiling. The grandson carried a box. He set it on the coffee table and left to finish his puttering.

Phyllis sat down between Evan and Carrie, opened the box, and pulled out a yellowing scrapbook. "Photos of the kids. Mementos. They'd draw me a picture and sign it *for Miss Phyllis*. One girl always signed it *for Mommy*, told me she needed to practice on me, for the day when she got herself a real mother. It broke my heart. I wanted to bring her home but my husband wouldn't hear of it, and it was the only argument I never won. My heart bled for those children. No one wanted them. That's the worst thing in this world, to be unwanted. I hope you recognize your parents in here." She flipped through pages. Phyllis Garner, radiant and beautiful and probably every orphan's dream. Evan wondered if she had been conscious of how the bereft children must have ached for her to slip her hand into theirs and say, *You're coming home with me.* It might have been less painful if such an angel had kept her distance.

She pointed at a photo of a group of six or seven children. Evan's eyes went to the children first, looking for his father and mother in every face. No. Not them. Then he noticed the man standing behind the children.

The man was short, balding, but not completely bald. He wore glasses and a thin, academician's beard. But the shape of the face, the sureness of the stance, were the same. Evan had seen the face several times, in the news clippings left anonymously for him at his lecture four months ago. The man's smile was tight, as though bottling in the scintillating personality that had made him such a force in London.

Alexander Bast.

"That man. Who's he?" Evan asked. He kept his voice steady.

Phyllis Garner flipped the picture over; she had a list of names written in tidy cursive on the back. "Edward Simms. He owned the company that ran Hope Home. He only came here once, that I recall. I asked him to pose with a group of the children. In honor of his visit. He smiled, but you would have thought I scalded him. He acted like the children were dirty. The other ladies found him charming, but I don't have to count scales to know a snake."

Carrie's hand closed around Evan's arm. Hard. She pointed wordlessly at a tall, thin boy standing near Bast. Shock on her face.

"What's the matter, dear?" Phyllis asked.

29

After a long moment Carrie said, "Nothing. I thought . . . but it was nothing."

"Are you all right?" Evan asked.

She nodded. "I'm fine."

"This was the last batch of kids that came in before the fire, I believe." Phyllis Garner laid the open scrapbook on her lap, ran her fingers along the page. "I remember they were shy at first. And of course, they were older kids, not babies. Sad that they hadn't been adopted yet. People wanted babies."

Carrie pointed at one tall, lanky kid. "He was in the picture with Mr. Simms." She kept her grip on Evan's arm.

Phyllis pried the picture out of the plastic page cover. "I wrote their names on the back . . . Richard Allan." She frowned at Carrie. "Honey, are you okay? You still look upset."

"Yes, I'm fine, thank you. You're right, it's sad, these older kids not finding homes." Carrie's voice was normal again.

"It was just so unfair," Phyllis said. "The focus on finding babies. This was an appealing group of kids. Nice-looking, bright, clearly well cared for, well spoken. At the orphanage, you'd see kids, and all the hope had died in them. Hope that they would not just find families, but have a life beyond low-end jobs. Orphans face such an uphill fight. These kids, they don't look very broken at all."

Evan flipped a page. A picture of two teenage girls, a teenage boy standing between them, brownish hair thick, a wide smile on his face, a scattering of freckles across high cheekbones, a tiny gap between his front teeth.

Jargo. His eyes were the same, cold and knowing.

"Oh," Carrie said. It was almost a moan.

Sweat broke out on Evan's back.

"Did you find your dad?" Phyllis asked brightly.

Evan looked down the rest of the page. Two photos down were two kids, a girl, blond with green eyes, memorably pretty but with a serious cast to her face. A boy standing with her, holding a football, sweaty from play, light hair askew, grinning, ready to conquer the world.

Mitchell and Donna Casher, young teenagers. Frozen in time, like Jargo.

"May I?" Evan asked.

"Of course," Phyllis said.

He loosened the picture from the plastic cover, flipped it over. *Arthur Smithson and Julie Phelps,* written in Phyllis's neat script.

"Smithson," Phyllis said. "Oh, that's it! Are they your folks?"

"Yes, ma'am." His voice was hoarse. He forced himself to smile at her.

"Honey, then you take that picture, it's yours. Oh, I'm so glad I could help."

Carrie tightened her grip on his hand. "Phyllis, did any of this last group of kids die in the fire?"

"No. It was younger kids. The older kids all got out."

"Do you remember where any of these kids went after the fire? Specific other orphanages?" Evan asked.

"No, I'm sorry. I don't even know that I was told." Phyllis leaned back in her chair. "We were told it was best for us not to stay in touch with the kids."

"May we borrow these photos? We can make copies, scan them into a computer, give them back to you before we leave town," Evan said. "It would be huge for us."

"I never did enough for those kids," Phyllis said. "I'm glad someone finally cares. Take the pictures, with my blessings."

After waving good-bye to Phyllis and Dealey, they drove toward the airport, where a computer and a scanner waited on the jet.

"My *father*," Carrie said, her voice shaking. "That boy in the picture next to Alexander Bast, it's my dad, Evan, it's my dad!"

"Are you sure?"

"Yes. Our parents knew each other. Knew Jargo. When they were kids." She jabbed at one of the photos. "Richard Allan. My dad's name was Craig Leblanc. But this is him, I know it's him. Don't go to the jet. Let's go get coffee for a minute, please."

They sat in a corner of a Goinsville diner, the only customers except for an elderly couple in a booth who exchanged laughs and moony smiles as if they were on a third date.

"So what does this mean?" Carrie studied the picture of her father as if he might have the answers. Tears sprang to her eyes. "Evan, look at him. He looks so young. So innocent." She wiped the tears away. "How can this be?"

This evil—Jargo—that had touched their lives went far

deeper than Evan had ever imagined. It intertwined his life with Carrie's even before they were born. It frightened him, made the threat against them seem like a shadow always looming over them, both of them unaware that they lived in darkness.

Evan took a steadying breath. Find order in the chaos, he decided. "Let's walk through it." He ticked the facts on his fingers. "Our parents and Jargo were all at an orphanage together. The home burned down with all its records. The kids get dispersed. Then the county courthouse burns a month later, and it's all blamed on a firebug who commits suicide. Alexander Bast, a CIA operative, runs the orphanage under a false name."

"But why?"

"The answer's in front of us, if we were looking for these kids' pasts. The records. The birth certificates. You could create a false identity very easily, using Goinsville and the orphanage as your place of birth. You can say, yes, I was born at the Hope Home. My original birth certificate? Unfortunately destroyed by fire."

Carrie frowned. "But the state of Ohio would have issued them new ones, right? Replaced the records."

"Yes. But based on information provided by Bast," Evan said. "He could have falsified records so that he could claim every orphan living at Hope Home was born at Hope Home. Maybe those kids had different identities before they came to this orphanage. But they come here and they're Richard Allan and Arthur Smithson and Julie Phelps. After the fire, they have new birth certificates in those names, forever, without question. And then you just ask for replacement birth certificates in the names of any of the dozens of kids at Goinsville."

Carrie nodded. "A whole pool of new identities."

Evan took a long sip of coffee. He couldn't tear his eyes away from the photo; his mother had been so beautiful; his father, so innocent looking. "Go back further. Back to Bast, because he's the trigger. Tell me why a London night-club owner, friend to celebrities, dabbles in an American orphanage."

"The answer is he's not just a London party boy," Carrie said.

"We know he was CIA."

"But low-level."

"Or so Bedford says."

"Bedford's not a liar, Evan, I promise you."

"Never mind Bedford. This might have been a way for the Agency to create new identities more easily."

"But they're just kids. Why would kids need new identities?"

"Because…they were part of the CIA. Long ago. I'm just theorizing."

Her face went pale. "Wouldn't Bedford know about this if the Deeps were part of the CIA's history?"

"Bedford got the job to track down Jargo only about a year ago. We don't know what he was told." He grabbed her hands. "Our folks left their lives. Quit being Richard Allan and Julie Phelps and Arthur Smithson and took on new names. Bedford might have been told it's a problem he's inherited, rather than a terrible secret."

Evan went back to the stack of photos. "Look here. Jargo with my folks." He pointed at a picture of a tall, muscular boy standing between Mitchell and Donna Casher, his big arms around the Cashers' necks, smiling a lopsided grin that was more confident than friendly. Mitchell Casher bent a bit toward Jargo's face, as though asking him a question. Donna Casher looked stiff, uncomfortable, but her hand was holding Mitchell's.

Carrie traced Jargo's face, looked at Mitchell's. "There's a resemblance with your dad."

"I don't see it."

"Their mouths," she said. "He and Jargo have the same mouth. Look at their eyes."

Now he saw the similarity in the curve of the smile. "They're both just grinning big." He didn't want to look at the men's eyes—the nearly identical squint. It couldn't be, he thought. It couldn't be.

She inspected the back of the photo. "It just says Artie, John, Julie."

He flipped over to the other picture of Jargo that Phyllis had shown him. "John Cobham."

"Cobham. Not Smithson." She clasped both his hands in hers.

"The photos are faded," he said in a thin voice. "It blurs features. Makes everyone look the same."

She leaned back. "Forget it. I'm sorry. Back to what you said. Whether Bedford knows. He must not—he wouldn't have bothered to send us here."

"So what are you going to tell him?"

"The truth, Evan. Why not?"

"Because maybe, maybe this is a CIA embarrassment Bedford doesn't know about. Bast brought these kids here, set up names for them, made it hard for anyone to ever trace their records, and he worked for the CIA." Evan leaned forward. "Maybe the CIA took these young kids and raised them to become spies and assassins."

"That's a crazy theory. The CIA would never do this."

"Don't take the CIA's side automatically." Evan lowered his voice, as though Bedford sat in the next booth. "I'm not attacking Bedford. But don't tell me what the Agency—or maybe a small group of misguided people in the Agency— might or might not do, or have done decades ago, because we don't know. Bast was CIA. He brought our parents here. For a reason."

Carrie held up a hand. "Assume you're right. But, at some point, this group took on new names and new lives, and they all went to work for Jargo. Why? That's the question."

"Bast died. Jargo took over."

"Jargo killed Bast. It has to be."

"Maybe. At the least, Jargo had a hold on our parents and maybe these other kids. An unbreakable hold. I want to go to London."

"To find out about Alexander Bast."

"Yes. And to find Hadley Khan. He knew about the connection between Bast and my parents. It can't be coincidence."

"It can't be coincidence, either, that your mom picked now to steal the files, to run. She knew you'd been approached about Bast."

"I never told her. Never. You know I don't talk about my films when I'm concepting. You were the first person I told."

"Evan. She knew. You e-mailed Hadley Khan, trying to find out why he left you that package about Bast. She could have looked on your computer. Maybe she saw Bast's name in an e-mail to Hadley. Or when she met me...maybe I reminded her of my dad. Maybe she was afraid you'd be recruited. And she just wanted a permanent escape hatch for your family."

"She spied on me." He knew it was true. "My own mother spied on me."

She reached past their cold coffee cups to take his hand. "I'm so sorry, Evan."

The photo of Bast, scattered among the pictures of their parents and Jargo a lifetime ago, smiled up at them.

They called Bedford from the plane and explained what they had found. "We want to go to London," Evan said. "My mother's last travel photo assignment was there. Hadley Khan is there. And Bast died there. Can you get the CIA office in London to get us the complete files on Bast's murder?"

"There is no record in Bast's file about this orphanage," Bedford said. "Are you sure it's him in the photo?"

"Yes. Could his record have been expunged if someone at the CIA wanted to hide his involvement?"

"Anything is possible." Bedford's voice sounded tight, as though the rules of engagement had just been rewritten. Evan could see the heightened tension on Carrie's face: *What are we dealing with here?*

"London," Evan said. "Can we go?"

"Yes," Bedford said. "If Carrie feels well enough to travel."

"I'm fine. Tired. I can sleep during the flight," Carrie said.

"I'll arrange a pickup for you in the London office. I'll talk to our travel coordinator, but I believe you'll have to have a fresh pilot. Change in Washington. And, Carrie, I'll have a doctor check you before you leave for Britain, and another doctor for when you get to London."

"Thank you, Bricklayer."

Bedford hung up. Carrie went to the restroom. Evan closed his eyes to think.

He heard Carrie return to her seat. He kept his eyes shut. The jet roared above Ohio, turning toward Virginia. Leaving a patch of ground that was the first step in the long lie of his family's existence.

He pretended to be back in the study in his Houston house, digital tape downloaded onto his computer and him threading his way through twenty hours of images, paring away all the extraneous gunk and talk from the heart of the story he wanted to tell the audience sitting in the quiet dark. He had read once that Michelangelo just took away the chunks of marble that didn't belong and found the David hiding within the mass of stone. His David was the truth about his parents, the information that would free his father.

So what was the true story, where was the subtle art under the block of marble?

He opened his eyes. Carrie sat, staring ahead of her, hunched as though caught in a chill wind.

Suddenly his heart filled with . . . what? He didn't know. Pity, maybe sadness, in that neither of them had asked to be born into this disaster. But she had chosen to stay in it. First for her parents, then for Bedford. And now for him.

The weight of what he owed her, as opposed to the confusion and pain from her earlier lies, settled onto his heart. "What are you thinking of?" he asked.

"Your father," she said. "You look like him. In your smile. In those photos, your father had a very innocent smile. I was wondering if he is scared. For himself, for you."

"Jargo's told him a thousand lies, I'm sure."

"He only has to tell one really good one."

"One wasn't good enough to fool you," Evan said.

"I wonder if our parents were ever afraid we would find out the truth and turn away from them."

"I'm sure they must have been. Even when they knew we loved them."

"But my father recruited me, he pulled me into this world, the same way Jargo did to Dezz. I still don't understand why he did it." But she sounded tired, not angry.

"We don't know he had a choice, Carrie. Or maybe he hoped if you were involved in the business, you wouldn't reject him."

"I would have loved him, no matter what. I thought he knew that."

"I'm sure he did."

She shook her head. "I just feel now, he had this whole life I never knew. A whole set of thoughts and worries and fears that he had to keep secret. It's as if I didn't know him at all. Probably that's how you feel about your dad." *Or me,* he waited for her to say, but she didn't.

He cleared his throat. "I only know I love the dad that I know, and I have to believe that's the truest part of my father, no matter what else he has done."

"I know. I feel the same. You would have liked my father, Evan."

"You must miss him."

"Seeing him in those pictures, so young...it's still getting to me." She wiped at her eyes. He moved into the seat next to hers. Put his arm around her. Brushed the tears from her cheek.

"They didn't trust us with the truth," she said after a moment.

"They were trying to protect us."

"That was all I wanted to do with you. Protect you. I'm sorry I failed."

"Carrie. You didn't fail me. Not once. I know you were in a terrible, terrible position. I know."

"But you hate me a little. For lying."

"I don't."

"If you hate me," she said, "I'd understand."

"I don't hate you." He needed her. It was a subtle shock. The knit of tragedy forever linked them, the same way his parents and her father were linked. He did not want to be alone.

He kissed her. It was as tentative and shy as a first kiss, a first real kiss, often is. He leaned back to study her, and she closed her eyes and found his mouth with her own, gently, once, twice, then he kissed her with passion. A need for tenderness mixed with a need to show her that he loved her.

She broke the kiss, rested her forehead against his. "Our families lived false lives. I did it for a year. I don't want to live a lie anymore. You cannot imagine how lonely it is. I don't want you to do it. We can just be us. I love you, Evan."

He wanted to believe. He needed to love; he needed to believe the best in her. He needed to regain what he had lost, in some small measure. The awareness was sudden and bright, a firecracker in his head. He wanted to be alone with her—away from CIA bugs, away from their parents caught as strangers in old photos, away from death and fear.

"I love you, too," he said quietly.

She settled into his arms and he held her until she slept. *We can just be us.*

Yes, he thought. *When Jargo is dead. When I've killed him.*

As the jet screamed toward Virginia, Evan didn't wonder if she was the same woman he loved. He wondered if he was still the same man she loved.

30

JARGO LAY HALF AWAKE, half asleep, waiting for the phone call that would end this nightmare. He was a boy again, sitting in a darkened room, listening to the voice of God ringing in his ears. God was dead, he knew, but the idea of God was not, of a being so powerful he held absolute sway over you, whether you breathed, whether you died. The boy he was had not slept in three days.

"The challenge," the voice said, soft, British, quiet, "is that you must make a failure into an opportunity."

Jargo-the-boy—his name had been John then, the name he liked best—said, "I don't understand."

"If you create a situation, and you lose control of it, you must be able to reimagine that situation. Turn it to your advantage."

"So if I fall off a ten-story building...I can hardly reimagine that into victory." He was thirteen and he was starting to question the whole world he had always known.

"I speak of salvageable situations," the voice said with no trace of impatience. "You live and breathe, you can manipulate people. You must construct every trap so that if the prey escape, they do not believe they were in a trap of your making."

"Why do I care," Jargo asked, "what an escaped victim thinks?"

"Stupid, stupid boy," the voice said. "You don't see it. The trap still has to be set. You have to remain unknown, no suspicion of you brought to light. I don't really think that you'll ever be ready to lead."

The phone rang.

Jargo sat up, blinking, the frightened boy sitting in the dark lingering for just a moment, then gone. He groped for the phone, clicked it on.

"I have the cellular records from your special chunk of Ohio."

"Okay," he said.

"They're uploaded to your system," Galadriel said.

"I'll tell you what I'm looking for. Calls to the D.C. metro area."

"Seven," she said after a moment.

"Get me addresses for all those numbers."

A pause. "Two residences. Five government offices, mostly congressional offices and Social Security."

"None to confirmed CIA addresses?"

"None," she said after another moment. "But we don't have a complete list of CIA numbers. You know that's impossible."

"Get me calls from or to all of Virginia and Maryland."

Another pause. "Yes. Sixty-seven in the course of the day."

"Any to Houston?"

"Fifteen."

"Get me all those addresses, for every call." His other line rang. "Hold on a minute." He answered the other phone. "Yes?"

"I think they're flying to Britain," the voice said.

Jargo closed his eyes. Down the hall he could hear the barest *zoom-zoom* of Dezz's Game Boy, the quiet of Mitchell's voice. They'd had a long day and accomplished little in trying to devise a way to draw Evan back to them. But now everything had just changed.

"From where?"

"I suspect from an Agency medical clinic in southwest Virginia. It's called North Hill Clinic. There's a private airstrip close by and the requisition is for that airstrip."

"They flew there from New Orleans?"

"I don't know. I've only seen the requisition for a plane to go from D.C. airspace to the UK. Not even sure it's them. A doctor requisitioned to meet the plane before departure, another doctor requisitioned for meeting the flight in London. If your former agent is injured...it could be her. Of course it could be an ancient Agency fart traveling with a medical condition."

"You said *meet* the plane. Where else has it been?"

"Don't know."

"You can't find another requisition for today's travel?"

"No. But it must be domestic. A tight lid is kept on domestic data, and I'm not cleared for it."

"What's the ID on the case for the flight to the UK?"

"Also classified, but joint ops with British intelligence. That's all I know." The voice started getting nervous. "You better get this under control, Jargo..."

"It's under control. Hold on." He got back on the phone with Galadriel. "I want to know if there were any cellular calls placed today from jet phones in our Ohio territory to southwestern Virginia. Cross-reference it with any known CIA or federal numbers in that area."

"I'm not sure I can trace aviation calls," Galadriel said. "I don't know if the calls are handled differently."

"Just do it. Search for satellite calls as well."

He heard the hammer of keystrokes. He waited long minutes, listening to fingers dance on a keyboard as she wormed her way into databases. Galadriel hummed tune-lessly as she worked. "Yes. Just one, if I'm reading the data correctly. Went through a transmitter near Goinsville, Ohio. To a number keyed to North Hill Clinic, due east of Roanoke, at two forty-seven this afternoon."

They had been to Goinsville.

Jargo closed his eyes, considered his narrowing options. *You must construct every trap so that if the prey escape, they do not believe they were in a trap of your making.* The hardest lesson he had ever learned, but the philosophy had kept the Deeps in the shadows, kept them alive, made them rich. He'd racked his brains all night and day today, trying to construct a way to lure Evan out into the open, lure him back into their world to simplify killing him while making Mitchell believe they were rescuing Evan.

But perhaps this wasn't a disaster. Rather, his best chance yet to rid himself of every headache, every threat.

Goinsville. They might have found nothing; what was there to find? Nothing. His life there was a past no one remembered. But they'd found something. London was the next stop in the thread. He could not ignore the possibility that Evan knew far more than his father thought he did.

Certain times called for a slow cut; other times required a final slash across the throat.

It was time to be brutal.

He got back on the other phone. "I still need your help."

"What do you want?" the voice asked.

"Want. What a concept, want." Jargo knew the pain it would cause Mitchell. He wasn't blind to suffering; pain was irrelevant. Jargo would suffer his own setback as well. But he had no choice. "I want a bomb."

THURSDAY

MARCH 17

31

⬥

THE LONDON-BASED CIA FIELD OFFICER—his name was Pettigrew, he didn't offer a first name—picked them up at a private airstrip in Hampshire. He carried himself with an impatient air. Pettigrew was closemouthed as he hurried them to a car, driving them himself to a safe house in the London neighborhood of St. John's Wood. He took his time, circling in roundabout routes, and Evan, who only knew London well enough to find Soho and the London Film School, got lost along the drive.

Pettigrew didn't speak a word to them on the way.

It was early afternoon in London, and they had, to Evan's surprise, left the rain in Ohio. The sky was clear, the few clouds thin cotton. Pettigrew shut a wrought-iron gate behind them as they went up the house's front stairs.

Pettigrew escorted them to tidy, unadorned rooms, with private baths, and they both showered. A doctor waited to change Carrie's bandage and inspect her healing wound. When they were done, they followed Pettigrew into a small dining room where an elderly woman brewed strong tea and coffee and served a lunch of cold meats, salad, cheese, pickles, and bread. Evan drank down coffee with gratitude.

Pettigrew sat down, waited until the elderly lady had

bustled back into the kitchen. "This is all damned odd. Being ordered to dig up Scotland Yard files with cobwebs on them. Taking orders from a man with a code name."

"My apologies," Carrie said.

"I have top clearance," he said. Almost peevishly. "But I live to serve. We didn't have much notice"—his tone held the acid of the long-suffering—"but here's what we found."

He handed them the first file, squiring the remaining two close to his chest. "Alexander Bast was murdered, two shots, one to the head, one to the throat. What makes it interesting is that the bullets came from two different guns."

"Why would the killer need two weapons?" Carrie said.

"No. Two killers," Evan said.

Pettigrew nodded. "Vengeance killing. To me it speaks of an emotional component to the killing. Each killer wanting to put his imprint on the act." He slid them a picture of the sprawled body. "He was killed in his home twenty-four years ago, middle of the night, no signs of a struggle. Entire house wiped down for prints." Pettigrew paused. "He worked for us for twenty-three years before he died."

"Can you give me more details about his work here?" Carrie asked. She and Evan agreed that she, being a CIA employee, would drive the questioning. An ID Bedford had provided named Evan as a CIA analyst, but he stayed quiet.

"Well, among Bast's many creative sidelines, he dabbled in art, he dabbled in sleeping with celebrities who frequented his nightclubs. Drug arrests at one of his clubs lost him his cachet, and he burned thousands of pounds trying to keep them afloat. We looked hard at him then—we don't want agents involved with illegal narcotics—but the drug dealing was simply a few of his regular customers abusing his hospitality. After the clubs closed, he focused all his energies on his publishing firm, which he owned for quite a while but had been his most neglected business. He published literature in translation, especially Spanish, Russian, and Turkish. Imported permitted books back into the Soviet Union, translated underground Russian literature into English, German, and French. So he was a valuable contact, given that he could reach into the dissident community in the Soviet Union and that he could travel somewhat freely back and forth. At first his handlers suspected he might be a KGB agent, but he checked out clean and got cleared on every follow-up. We watched him closely during his financial troubles; that's a time when an operative might be bought. But he always came out clean. He was popular with the dissident Russian community here in London."

"So what exactly did he do for the CIA?" Carrie asked.

"Couriered data from his contacts' contacts in and out of Berlin, Moscow, and Leningrad. He was handled by American embassy officers under diplomatic cover. But he was low-level. He didn't have access to Soviet state secrets. And the dissident community was not particularly useful to the Agency at that point in time—they might give us names of people who had critical access and would spy for us, but dissidents were too closely watched by the KGB. Too easy, frankly, for the KGB to infiltrate."

Evan studied the picture of Bast, murdered. Bast's eyes were wide in horrified surprise. This man had known Evan's parents. Played an unseen role in their lives. "No suspects?"

"Bast lived a high life, even after his fall. A few husbands were rather unhappy with him. He owed money. He broke business deals. Any number of people might have wanted him out of their lives. Of course, Scotland Yard didn't know about Bast working for the CIA, and we didn't tell them."

"Rather important information to withhold," Carrie said.

"I didn't personally. You needn't sound peevish."

"Of course you didn't," Carrie said with a laugh, trying to defuse the sudden tension. "You're not even forty, right? It just surprises me."

Pettigrew's voice took on a peppery tone of disapproval. "It's not good advertising for recruitment to have your assets murdered."

Carrie paged through the murder-scene photos. "The CIA must have suspected Bast was identified as a CIA agent and killed by the Soviets?"

"Naturally. But the murder looked like it coincided with a robbery, and that simply wasn't the KGB's style. Remember, Bast was a low-level asset at best. He never was an original source of valuable information. He never fed us disinformation originating from the KGB. He was just a very reliable courier and gatherer of contacts. You know, a lot of KGB archives have come to light since the fall of the USSR. There's no record that the KGB ordered him killed."

"Could we talk to his handler?" Carrie asked.

"Bast's case officer died ten years ago. Pancreatic cancer."

"The robbery," Carrie said. "What was taken? Could the killer have discovered anything that pointed to Bast's connection to the CIA?"

Pettigrew pushed another file toward them. "The Agency had an operative sweep Bast's apartment after the murder and after the police had gone through. He found Bast's CIA gear all properly hidden. Undiscovered by the police, who of course would have confiscated the stuff."

"What about his personal effects or his finances?" Evan asked. "Anything unusual?"

Pettigrew flipped through the papers. "Let's see...a friend, Thomas Khan, supplied information." He ran a finger down a list. "Bast had two separate bank accounts, he had a lot of money tied up in his publishing concern..."

"You said Khan? K-H-A-N?" Evan said. Same last name as Hadley Khan. Here was the connection from Evan to Bast. Carrie shook her head. *Say nothing.*

"Yes. I have a file on Thomas Khan as well." Pettigrew fingered the file, pulled out a sheet of paper. "Mr. Khan said Bast kept a fair amount of cash on hand, and none of that was found in the house. Khan was a rare-book dealer and said Bast often paid him for volumes with cash."

Carrie took the paper and read aloud from the report as she scanned it: "Born in Pakistan to a prominent family. Educated in England. His wife had been an Englishwoman, a high-ranking political strategist and academician who worked on defense initiatives. No trouble with the law. Conservative in political leanings, served as a director on a British foundation that pledged financial support to the Afghani rebels against the Soviet invaders. Worked in international banking for many years, but his real passion is Khan Books, a rare-book emporium, on Kensington Church Street, which he's operated for the past thirty years. He retired from banking ten years ago and put his entire focus on the bookstore. Widowed twelve years ago. Never remarried. One son, Hadley Mohammed Khan."

"I know his son," Evan said. "Hadley. He's a freelance journalist."

Pettigrew shrugged; he didn't care. His phone rang in his pocket; he excused himself with a quick wave of his hand, shutting the door behind him.

Evan made a quick survey of the files. No hint that Bast was also Mr. Edward Simms. Bedford had dug last night into incorporation databases and found that the Hope Home in Goinsville had been bought by a company called Simms Charities. The company had incorporated two weeks before it bought Hope Home, sold all its assets after the fire. If the CIA had put Bast up to buying orphanages, though, no sign remained in his official file.

Evan went back to the sheet on Thomas Khan. "Rare books, and among his specialties are Russian editions. Bast did Russian translations. So they both had contacts back into the Soviet Union. And both were involved in rebellion movements—one supporting dissident writers, the other supporting the mujahideen in Afghanistan."

"So they both hated the Soviets. It doesn't prove anything," Carrie said.

"No. It doesn't." But Evan sensed a thread here; he just didn't know how yet to grab it, follow it. He opened the file on Hadley. It was not a formal CIA file, unlike the one on Thomas Khan, who had had a London station file opened on him when he'd assisted the police in Bast's murder investigation, or on Alexander Bast, who had been a paid operative. It was the little Pettigrew's people had gleaned after Bedford's hurried request: Hadley's birth date, schooling, travel in and out of Britain, financial records. The school records were not impressive; the success and brilliance of the parents eluded the son. Hadley had spent two months in an Edinburgh detox center; he had lost two good magazine jobs and had not been published in the past six months. But the inquiry had produced new information: according to his latest girlfriend, who had been fooled by a London station assistant who'd called her this morning pretending to be a colleague of Hadley's, Hadley Khan was recently estranged from his father. The girlfriend had not heard from or seen Hadley since last Thursday, but she did not sound concerned; he was a loose-footed guy who often went to the Continent for a couple of weeks at a time. Especially after a falling-out with dear old Dad.

The photos of Hadley in the file were culled from his British driver's license; Evan remembered him from the cocktail party a lifetime ago at the Film School, his grin a shade too eager, his eyes holding a secret.

"So Hadley Khan anonymously urges me to do a film on the murder of Alexander Bast, a friend of his father, and never responds to my e-mail asking why," Evan said. "And then he takes off the day before my mother dies. Hadley never mentioned any connection between Bast and his dad in the material he gave me."

"That's very odd. It would have simplified your research." Carrie tapped Hadley's file. "We know there's a connection between our parents and Bast. And a connection between Bast and Khan. That doesn't mean a direct connection between Thomas Khan and our parents."

A chill prickled Evan's skin. "It's no coincidence that Hadley pitched the Bast story. He must have known of my parents' connection to Bast."

"He approached you, but he didn't tell you everything. So he either copped out or he was stopped from getting in touch with you again."

"I think he got scared. It's why he went anonymous. Hadley had his own agenda. The girlfriend says he and

Thomas don't get along. I wonder...if this was revenge against his father."

"It's only revenge if his father's done wrong." Carrie massaged her injured shoulder.

"Like involvement with Bast's murder?"

Carrie shrugged.

"The British authorities would have an interest, but why would Jargo care?"

They fell silent as Pettigrew returned. He assembled a sandwich from the cold meats and cheese. "My source at New Scotland Yard called. There's been no report filed that Hadley Khan is missing. No indication that he traveled out of Britain, or into any European country in the past two weeks." He took a jaw-breaking bite of sandwich. "We've called Hadley's cell phone three times this morning, and he's not answering."

"We'll pay his dad, Thomas, a visit," Evan said.

"No time like now," Pettigrew said around a still-full mouth.

"We don't alert Thomas Khan by barreling in full force," Pettigrew said as he parked a block away from Khan Books and displayed a Borough resident's parking permit—Evan guessed it had been provided to the CIA by the Brits out of professional courtesy. "I suggest Evan go in alone."

"What do you think?" Evan asked Carrie.

"Khan may run," Carrie said. "I think I should be ready to follow him." She pointed at an opposite street corner. "I can stand there. You can tail him if he comes this way, Pettigrew."

Pettigrew frowned. "We should have a team set up for surveillance. Bricklayer said nothing about this turning into an active field operation. I would have to alert the Cousins"—using the term British and American intelligence services had for each other—"we can't start tailing a guy on British soil without approval."

"Calm down," Carrie said. "I just want to be prepared."

"I'm not entirely comfortable," Pettigrew said.

"If there's a problem, Bricklayer will deal with it. No heat on you," Carrie said.

Pettigrew nodded. "All right then. If Khan bolts, you follow on foot, I'll follow in the car."

"Watch yourself." Carrie got out of the car, put on sunglasses, walked down to the corner opposite the bookstore, held a cell phone to her ear as though she were chatting with a friend.

"Be careful," Pettigrew said to Evan.

"I will." Evan got out of the car, strolled past a mix of antiques shops, high-end eateries, and boutiques. The bell on the door of Khan Books jingled as he went inside. Late afternoon on a weekday, Khan Books' only customers were a French couple exploring a display of Patricia Highsmith and Eric Ambler first editions in an assortment of languages. Evan found himself noting the exit doors, the surveillance cameras posted in the corners of the rooms.

I've changed. I feel like I have to be ready for anything at any time.

A small, wiry man, dapper in a tailored suit, with a shock of gray-chalk hair, came forward. His shoes were polished black ice; an impeccable triangle of blue silk handkerchief peeked from one pocket. "Good afternoon. May I assist you today?" His voice was quiet but strong.

"Are you Mr. Thomas Khan?"

"Yes, I am."

Evan smiled. He didn't want to be subtle. "I'm in the market for first editions published by Criterius. I'm particularly interested in the translation of *Anna Karenina* and any dissident literature published in the 1970s."

"I'll be happy to check."

"I understand the owner of Criterius—Alexander Bast—was a good friend of yours."

Thomas Khan's smile stayed bright. "Only an acquaintance."

"I'm a friend of a friend of Mr. Bast."

"Mr. Bast died a long time ago, and I barely knew him." Thomas Khan smiled in good-natured confusion.

Evan decided to gamble, toss another name into the weird ring that joined all these lives together. "My friend who recommended your store is Mr. Jargo."

Thomas Khan shrugged. Quickly. "One meets so many people. The name does not signify. One moment, please, and I'll consult my files. I believe I have multiple copies of the *Karenina* edition." He vanished into the back.

This man may have kept a secret for decades; you coming in here and tossing around names won't scare him. But then, if you're the first to toss it at him in many years... maybe you will rattle him. Evan stayed in place, watching the French couple loiter, the woman leaning slightly on the man as they hunted the shelves.

He waited. He didn't like that Khan was out of his view. Maybe the man was bolting out the back door. Jargo's name might be like acid on skin. Evan stepped behind the counter and went around the corner—cluttered with a watercooler, stacks of books, and an antique desk with a computer—and went searching for Thomas Khan.

*   *   *

Pettigrew watched Carrie pretend-chatting on her phone, keeping her gaze near the bookstore entrance. Evan went in. A minute passed; Pettigrew counted each second. Then he pulled a briefcase from the rear seat of his sedan, got out of the car, and strolled toward the entrance to the bookstore.

He saw Carrie watching him and he lifted his hand in a quick, furtive palm-up signal: *wait*. She stayed put as he headed for the bookstore.

The maze of offices in the back of the gallery led nowhere.

"Mr. Khan?" Evan called in a hushed tone as he went into the bookstore's back. It was empty. Thomas Khan employed no assistants, no secretaries, no junior booksellers in his rabbit hole of a business. Evan heard a slight sound, two sharp *thweets*, maybe an alarm peep announcing a door had opened and closed. Evan found a back exit door. He pushed it. It opened onto a narrow brick way and he saw Thomas Khan running for the street, glancing back over his shoulder.

"Stop!" Evan ran after him.

Pettigrew performed best while taking specific orders. This was the truth of his life: taking orders in school, in family, in bed with his wife. He carried out today's orders with certainty. He stepped inside the bookstore, closed the door behind him, locked the dead bolt above the key lock. He flipped the simple calligraphied sign over to Closed. No one else had left or entered the shop since Evan. He saw Evan stepping into the rear of the shop, quietly calling, "Mr. Khan?"

A couple rummaged for editions on a table. The woman murmured in French to the man, pointing out a volume's price in dismay. Pettigrew brought out his service pistol and with a hand only slightly shaking, shot them both in the back of the head. *Thweet, thweet,* said the silencer. They collapsed, their blood and brains spraying across a pyramid of volumes. Ten seconds had passed.

Pettigrew set down the briefcase. Jargo said there would be a two-minute delay once he set the briefcase's combo lock to the correct detonation sequence. Ample time for him to get out, go to the street corner, shoot Carrie in the head, escape in the confusion. He thumbed the last number of the lock into place.

Jargo lied.

32

⬥━◉◉◉━⬥

THE EXPLOSION TORE OPEN THE FRONT of Khan Books, flowering into an orange hell, sending glass and flame shooting into Kensington Church Street. Carrie screamed as the force of heat and blast hit her. A car passing in front of the bookstore tumbled and slammed into a restaurant across the street. People fled, several bleeding, others running in blind panic. Two people lay in bloodied rags on the pavement.

Debris rained down on the street, shattered chunks of brick, raindrops of glass, a sooty mist, and smoke. Carrie careened backward, into the shelter of the corner of the building, in front of a dress shop, the mannequins indistinct behind the webbed glass.

Evan.

Carrie stumbled to her feet, ran toward the inferno, stopped halfway across the street. Heat slammed against her face. Burning pages settled toward the ground in a fiery snow. One landed on her hair; she slapped at her head, burned her hand.

"Evan!" she screamed. "Evan!" Only a fierce roar answered her as thousands of books, and the structure of the building, abandoned themselves to flame.

Gone. He was gone. She heard the rising cry of police and emergency sirens. She ran down the block toward the CIA car. The door was unlocked, the keys still inside. She ducked into the car, started the engine.

Shaking, she made a mix of left and right turns, avoiding the instant traffic jams, and stopped near Holland Park. She willed her fingers to be still and dialed Bedford. When he answered the phone, at first she could not speak beyond identifying herself.

"Carrie?" he said.

"At Khan's store. There was an explosion." He was gone. Evan could not be gone.

"Calm down, Carrie." Bedford's voice was like steel. "Calm down. Tell me precisely what happened."

She hated the hysteria in her voice but her self-control broke like a rotting dam. Her parents dead, her year of nonstop deceit, worrying that Jargo would discover her at any moment, finding Evan and nearly losing him again...she bent over in the car.

"Carrie! Report. Now."

"Evan...went inside Khan's bookstore. Pettigrew followed him inside a minute later, but he signaled all was well. Then about thirty seconds later, a blast. The entire store is gone. Bombed." She steadied her voice. "I need a team here. We need to find Evan. Maybe he's still inside, hurt, but it's all on fire..." She stopped. *He's gone. He's gone.*

"Did you see Evan or Pettigrew leave?"

"No."

"Any other exit or entrance?"

"I don't know...not on the street I could see."

"Okay," Bedford said. "Assume you're under surveillance. Obviously the Deeps have targeted Khan."

"Get me a team. MI5 or CIA. Now. I need them here now."

"Carrie. I can't. We can't show our involvement. Not with a bombing in London."

"Evan—"

"I can be in London in a few hours. I need you to lay low. That's a direct order."

"Evan's dead, Pettigrew's dead, and that's just too bad, isn't it? You let him get involved, you wanted him involved because it made this hunt easier for you!"

"Carrie. Get ahold of yourself. Right now I want you safe, I want you protected. Pull back. Find a place to hide, a library, a coffee shop, a hotel. You are not authorized to talk to anyone, not even Pettigrew's superior, until I arrive and debrief you. That's a direct order. I'll call you back when I'm on the ground in the UK."

"Understood." The word tasted like blood in her mouth.

"I'm sorry. I know you cared for Evan."

She couldn't answer him. She wasn't supposed to lose anyone else she loved. He could not be gone.

"Good-bye," she said.

She hung up. She steadied the tremble that threatened to take over her hands.

She wasn't hiding in a hotel. Not yet.

She got out of the BMW. Cars and pedestrians fleeing the blast area choked the streets. She stopped at an office supplies store near Queen Elizabeth College and asked to borrow their phone book. She found the listing for Thomas Khan.

"Where is this, please?" she asked the clerk, pointing at the address.

"Shepherd's Bush. Not at all far, west of Holland Park."

The clerk gave her a look of friendly concern; the news of the Kensington Church Street blast was all over the television and radio, immediately suspected as a terrorist attack, and Carrie was begrimed and shaken. "Do you need help, miss?"

"No, thank you." She wrote down Khan's address. She could break into his house, find if he had any connection to Jargo or to the CIA. It was action. Evan was gone. She could not sit still.

"Are you sure you're all right?" the clerk called as Carrie ran out the door.

No, Carrie thought, *I'll never be all right again.*

But wait. She stopped herself, stumbling along the sidewalk, the sirens a constant buzz in the air. As soon as the police identified Khan Books as the bombing site, the police and MI5 would be poring over Thomas Khan's house. If the slightest connection pointed back to the CIA—if she was found there and questioned by British authorities—it would be a public relations disaster for the Agency. She couldn't go to Khan's. Not enough time to search before the police arrived.

Not enough time. Not with Evan. She thought of him in that first moment of talking with him, him buying her coffee: *But you bought a ticket,* teasing her about paying to see his movie. He had told her that he loved her first, but she'd known she loved him weeks before he said the words.

Carrie leaned against the car. A pall of smoke rose from the direction of Kensington Church Street. She had nowhere to go in London, no one to trust.

Evan. She shouldn't have left him alone. She should have stayed at arm's length. Her face ached with unshed tears.

I'm sorry, sorry for what I've done, sorry for what has been lost, Evan, what have I done?

Carrie made her decision. Run and hide. Wait for Bedford's call. She wiped Pettigrew's car of prints, out of habit, and walked away from it.

She did not see the men following her from across the street, staggered apart by thirty yards, all three closing in on her.

33

---❖❖❖---

Evan caught Thomas Khan's jacket sleeve just as the explosion ripped apart the bookstore. Air rushed forward, blown down the throat of the brick way by heat and force. The blast hammered Evan into Khan, shoved them both off their feet, and they sprawled onto the ground. Dust misted and heated the air.

Evan scrambled to his feet, pulling Khan with him.

"Let me go!" Khan tried to jerk free. Evan tightened his grip and dragged Khan to the street behind the bookstore. Coughing, they stumbled into a mad dash of shoppers, clerks, tourists, and neighborhood residents. A pillar of fire and smoke rose behind them. Khan twisted away from Evan's grip, but Evan manhandled him by both arm and neck and hurried him down the street. He pictured where he had left Pettigrew and Carrie. Down a block, then up another two blocks, and they would come up behind Pettigrew's BMW.

"This way," Evan said.

"Let me go or I'll scream for help," Khan said.

"Go ahead. Be an idiot. I'm with people who can protect you."

"You bombed my store!"

Rage seized Evan. He gripped Khan by the throat. "You were involved in my mother's death."

"Your...mother?"

"Donna Casher."

"I don't know any Donna Casher."

"You're connected to Jargo, you're involved."

"I don't know any Jargo."

"Wrong. You just ran when you heard his name."

Khan tried to pull free.

"Just walk home, Mr. Khan." Evan released Khan's throat. "Go on. I'm sure the police will have lots of questions as to why your business was bombed. Get your answers ready. I'll be happy to talk with them, too."

Khan stood still.

"You've got both Jargo and the CIA after you, Mr. Khan. But I'm here right now, and if you don't help me, I guarantee I will kill you. But if you help me, you're safe from everyone who could hurt you. Decide."

"All right." He held up his palms in surrender. "I'll help you."

Evan seized the older man's shoulder, hurried him along the street. They rounded a corner, raced up toward Kensington Church Street where Pettigrew was parked, fighting against a fleeing crowd.

"Who sent you?" Khan asked.

"Me, myself, and I," Evan said.

They reached a block and Evan saw the CIA BMW tear out, backward, Carrie at the wheel.

"Carrie!" Evan yelled. "Here!"

But in the chaos of noise, the rush of people and cars, she didn't see him. She spun the car and roared, awkwardly, down the street and out of sight, narrowly avoiding running pedestrians.

Evan groped for his cell phone. Gone. He'd left it in the car with Pettigrew. He shoved Khan against the brick wall of a building. "Jargo killed my mother. Your son wanted me to do a documentary about Alexander Bast and it got back to Jargo, and he panicked and started killing people. Now, you'll tell me everything about my parents and Jargo, or I'll drag you back to the flames that was your bookstore and throw you inside."

Khan's eyes were wide with terror and Evan thought, *I really could kill him.*

"Listen," Khan said. "We have to get off the streets. I have a place where we can hide." He closed his eyes.

Evan considered. Pettigrew wasn't at the wheel, didn't appear to be in the car. Carrie looked hysterical. Where was the CIA officer? Dead in the street, killed by the blast? Evan looked down the wrecked street but couldn't see in the haze of smoke.

The day had gone horribly wrong. Maybe it wasn't a good idea to haul Khan back to the CIA safe house. Evan knew Khan's offer could be a trap. He had no gun, no weapon. And no choice. He couldn't let Thomas Khan simply walk away. Evan stayed close to the man, keeping a firm grip on his arm. Khan no longer appeared inclined to run. He walked with the frown of a man dreading his next appointment.

As they walked south to Kensington High Street Khan said, "May I hazard a theory?"

"What?"

"You came to my bookstore with the CIA. Or maybe MI5. And surprise, you're supposed to be dead, along with me."

Evan gave no answer.

"I'll take that as a yes," said Thomas Khan.

"You're wrong." *No way,* Evan thought. No way Carrie could have been involved if the bomb was meant for him. She could have killed him at any point in the past few days if she were against him, and he knew she wasn't. But Bedford—he didn't want to think the old man had set him up. Pettigrew. Maybe he was in Jargo's pocket. Or he was one of Jargo's Agency clients, a shadow who wanted Jargo protected.

Evan said, "Take me to Hadley."

Khan shook his head. "We talk in private. Keep walking." Khan ran across the street, Evan still clutching his arm. Khan pointed toward a small bistro. "We need transportation. I have a friend who owns that business, he'll be sympathetic. Wait here."

Evan tightened the grip on his arm. "Forget it. I'm coming with you."

"No, you're not." Khan smoothed down his hair, straightened his suit jacket. "I need you, you need me. We have a common enemy. I'm not running off."

"There's no way I can trust you."

"You want a sign of my good faith." He leaned close to Evan, his jaw touching Evan's, whispering into Evan's ear, "Jargo's clearly after me now. I am a loose end. So are you. We have a mutual interest."

He thinks the bomb was planted by Jargo. Not the CIA. Or at least he wants me to think he blames Jargo. "Why are you sure it's Jargo?"

"I protected him long enough. But no more. Not when he's after me now. He wants war, he gets war. Wait here." He shrugged free and Evan knew he'd have to fight Khan, here on the street, to keep him close, and it would attract attention. He watched Khan hurry and vanish into the café.

Evan waited. Panicked Londoners jostled past him, a hundred people passing him in a matter of minutes, and he had never been so alone in his life. He decided that he had made a huge mistake in letting Khan walk free. But moments later Khan drove up to the curb.

"Get in," he said.

34

THOMAS KHAN HEADED SOUTHEAST ON THE A205. Evan flicked on the radio. The news was full of the explosion on Kensington Church Street. Three confirmed dead, a dozen injured, firefighters battling to bring flames under control.

"Where is Hadley?" Evan said.

"Running and hiding, just like you and me."

"Why?"

"I've hidden Hadley from Jargo. I thought my influence with Jargo could survive our...recent problems. I was wrong."

"What problems?"

"Once we're safe."

Khan exited in Bromley, a large borough of suburban homes and businesses. He navigated a maze of streets and finally steered into a driveway of a good-sized house. The driveway snaked behind the home, and he parked where the car couldn't be seen from the street.

"I suspect we don't have long," Khan said. "The home belongs to my sister-in-law. She is in a hospice. Dying of brain cancer. But soon the authorities will be looking to anyone who knows me for information."

"Like your friend who owns the coffeehouse. He can tell them you're alive."

"He won't," Khan said. "I smuggled him and his family out of Afghanistan during the Soviet occupation. I asked for silence, he will be silent. Hurry inside. Our only advantage may be that Jargo will believe us both dead."

They entered through a back door. It opened into a kitchen. A mineral smell of disinfectant hung in the air. In the den, antique furnishings blended with an eclectic and colorful mix of abstract art. Bookshelves commanded one wall. The house had a comfortable air, but already wore a heavy sense of abandonment.

Khan collapsed on the couch. Clicked on the TV with the remote, found a channel airing live footage of the bombing site. The reporter indicated the destroyed business was owned by an Anglo-Afghani, Thomas Khan. The reporters tossed out theories and speculations as to a reason for the bombing.

"They got it wrong. You're from Pakistan," Evan said.

Khan shrugged. "I have bigger worries."

Evan went to the kitchen. Hanging along a magnetic strip were a wicked assortment of knives. He picked the largest one and returned to the den. Khan looked up at him.

"Is that for me?" Khan did not act afraid.

"Only if I have to."

"You won't. Stabbing is intensely close-range and personal. Nasty. Messy. You feel the person die. A sheltered boy doesn't have enough steel in his spine."

"I'm just learning what I'm capable of. You're going to help me bring Jargo down."

"I said no such thing," Khan said. "I said we had a mutual enemy. I can hide for the rest of my life. I don't need to fight Jargo. He thinks I'm dead."

"If he's your enemy now, surely you'd rather see him taken down than worrying about him ever finding you."

Khan shrugged. "The young worry about victory. I prefer survival." He tilted his head at Evan. "I thought you would be far more interested in hearing about your parents than planning an impossible revenge on Jargo."

Evan took a step forward with the knife. "You know my mother worked for the Deeps."

"I only knew her by her code name. But I read the American news on the Web, I saw her face on a report after her murder and I knew who she was."

"You saw her when she was in England a few weeks ago."

"Yes." His voice was barely a whisper.

"Why was she here?"

"It's oddly liberating to tell you what I always kept secret. I feel like I'm shedding an old coat." Khan offered a gentle smile. "She stole data from a senior-level British researcher involved in developing a new Stealth-style fighter. He had classified information on his laptop; you know the sort of man, technically brilliant but chafes at rules. Lax about security. He meets his mistress for getaways from the lab at a small hotel in Dover. Your mother took photos of him and the mistress, although probably he'd let his affair be exposed rather than cooperate, but more importantly, she obtained copies of the fighter data during their stay. That's the real leverage. Unless you're copulating with animals or small children, sex isn't the great lever it used to be." Khan almost sounded disappointed; a man wistful for the good old days.

"So she steals the data and you sell it."

"No. I provide the logistics to support her, I arrange for the money to go into her account. Jargo handles the sell."

Logistics for support. Money. He would have to know where the money came from. *The client list,* Evan thought. This man had it. He kept his face neutral. "And who would Jargo sell this data to?"

Khan shrugged. "Who doesn't need information like that these days? The Russians, who are still afraid of NATO. The Chinese, who still fear the West. India, who wants to take a bigger role on the world stage. Iran. North Korea. But also corporations, here and in America, who want the plans. Because they want to get contracts or outmaneuver the avionics firm who designed the plane." He offered Evan a neat, practiced smile. "Your mother was very good. You should be proud. She followed me to where I kept the files, accessed my laptop, stole the data, and I never knew until last week."

"I can't find pride in her accomplishments right now," Evan said.

"Now, if we'd wanted the man dead . . . well, your father would have been sent. He's quite the able killer." Khan studied his fingernails. "Garrote, gun, knife. He even killed a man in Johannesburg once with nothing but his thumbs. Or perhaps that was simply a rumor he started. So much depends on reputation."

The knife seemed suddenly lighter in Evan's hands.

Khan made a murmur of sympathy in his throat. "I know them better than you do, yet I never knew their real names. Rather sad, really."

You're just trying to goad me. Play me into making a mistake. "Since we're helping each other, tell me what my mother stole from you."

Khan's tongue touched his lower lip. "Account numbers in a Caymans bank. She copied a file that had names linked to accounts. I didn't realize she had stolen the files, copied them, until I ran a test on my system last Thursday."

Thursday. The day before his mother died. The day, perhaps, she decided to run. She must have known Jargo and Dezz were after her. Or Khan was lying—a distinct possibility. "And she got a list of all the Deeps' clients."

Khan frowned. "Yes. She got that as well."

"And you warned Jargo?"

"Naturally. He didn't know about the client list. That was my own insurance in case things ever got ugly between him and me. But I convinced him that your mother had pieced together the list from other information Jargo knew I already had."

The other information. Khan must have it all—the name of every Deep, every financial account they used, every detail of their operations. No wonder Jargo wanted him dead. "I want a copy of every file."

"Destroyed in the bomb blast, I'm afraid."

"Don't lie to me. You have a backup."

"I must decline."

Evan stepped forward. "I'm not giving you an option." He moved the knife toward Khan's chest.

"It's shaking," Khan said. "I don't think you truly have the stomach for—"

Evan jerked forward and brought the point of his knife to Khan's throat. Khan's eyes widened. A globe of blood welled where blade met skin.

"I'm my father's son. The knife's not shaking now, is it?"

Khan raised an eyebrow. "No, it's not."

"I will kill you if you don't help me. If you help me, there's a man at the CIA who can protect you from Jargo.

Help you and your son hide. Give you both a new life. Do you understand?"

Khan gave the slightest of nods. "Tell me who this man is at the CIA. I hardly plan to turn myself over to one of Jargo's clients."

"You don't need to worry about that. Talk straight. Tell me where Hadley is."

Khan clenched his eyes shut. "Hiding. I don't know."

"He's hiding because he pitched me the Alexander Bast film project. Hadley set all this mess in motion."

" 'How sharper than a serpent's tooth.' " Khan pressed his fingertips into his temples. "It is cruel to know a child could hate you so. Did you love your parents, Evan?"

No one had asked him this, ever, not even Detective Durless in Austin, which seemed like a thousand years ago but had been only a few days. "I do. No past tense about it. Very much."

"Do you still love them, knowing what they were?"

"Yes. Love isn't love unless it's unconditional."

"So when you look at your father, you won't see a killer. A cold and capable killer. You'll just see your dad."

Evan tightened his grip on the knife.

Khan said, "Ah. The poison of doubt. You don't know what you'll see. How you'll feel. I was clumsy a few months ago. I recruited Hadley to work for me. To assist me. I trusted him, I thought he simply needed meaningful work to bring order to his life, and I was wrong. He was given a basic assignment and he barely escaped being caught by French intelligence. He promised me he would do better, but he decided that he wanted out."

"You didn't accept his resignation."

"He didn't tell me he wanted to quit. It's not a job you

leave. In learning how to do my work, he found files on the Deeps—all of them, and their children. If he went to MI5 or the CIA, he knew he would be put under protective custody and my assets would be immediately frozen. He wanted the money. So he wanted Jargo and myself exposed, but not until he could make arrangements to vanish. So he could access my accounts and rob me first." He sounded more tired than angry.

"You sound as though you've talked with him."

"I have. Hadley confessed all to me before he left." Khan gave a thin smile. "I forgave him. In a way I was almost proud of him. Finally he had shown daring and intelligence. You were the only child of a Deep involved in the media. He thought he could befriend you and subtly draw you out to expose the network. Tease you with the murder of Bast. Egg you on to investigate. Make you do the dirty work without him putting his own neck in Jargo's noose."

He's opening up too easily, Evan thought. Like a documentary subject who won't shut up, because the only way to convince is with a torrent of words. Or they need to hear themselves talk, maybe to persuade themselves as much as convincing you and the audience. *How far is he playing me?* Evan wondered. "But he didn't respond to my e-mail about the Bast package."

"A fool puts great events in motion and then grows frightened." Khan raised an eyebrow. "I'm talking freely now—is the knife necessary?"

"Yes. The orphanage in Ohio. Bast was there, Jargo was there, my parents were there. Why?"

"Bast had a charitable soul."

"I don't think that was it. Those kids, at least three

of them, became the Deeps. Did Bast recruit them for the CIA?"

"I suppose he did."

"Why orphans?"

"Children without families are so much more pliable," Khan said. "They're like wet clay; you can mold them as you see fit."

"Why did the CIA need them instead of using regular agents?"

"I don't know." Khan almost smiled, then closed his eyes. He gave a hard sigh, as though confession had lifted a burden from his shoulders.

"Tell me why they needed fresh starts, fresh names, years later. Did they leave the CIA?"

"Bast died. Jargo took command of the network."

"Jargo killed him."

"Probably. I never asked."

"Were Jargo and my folks, and the other kids from that orphanage, were they hiding from the CIA?"

"Before my time. I don't know. When Jargo took over, he gave me a job. He brought me in to run logistics for him."

"Were you CIA?"

"No. But I'd helped support British intelligence ops in Afghanistan, during the rebellion against the Soviets. I knew the basics. I retired. I wanted just a quiet life with my books. No more field work. Jargo gave me a job."

"Well, Jargo just fired you, Mr. Khan. You work for me now."

Khan shook his head. "I admire your nerve, young man. I wish Hadley had become your friend. You might've been a good influence."

The phone rang. Both men froze. It rang twice and then stopped.

"No answering machine," Evan said.

"My sister-in-law hated them."

The ringing phone bothered Evan. Maybe a wrong call, maybe someone calling for the dying sister-in-law, maybe someone looking here for Khan. "I want my father back. You want Jargo to stop trying to kill you. Do our interests coincide or not?"

"It would be better if we could both just vanish." Khan swallowed. Sweat beaded along his face and he coughed for breath.

"Give me what I need. We can lean on the clients to break Jargo. Trace their dealings back to him. He's finished, he can't hurt you or Hadley."

"It's too dangerous. Better to just vanish."

"Forget that."

"I can't think with a knife at my throat. I would like a cigarette."

Evan saw fear and resignation in the man's face, smelled the sour tang of sweat on Khan's skin. He'd overstepped. He eased up off Khan, dropped the knife from his throat. Khan put his fingertips up to the slight welling of blood, dabbed into the blotches. "Shallow wounds. Thank you. I appreciate the kindness. May I reach in my pocket for my Gitanes?"

Evan put the knife back at Khan's throat, opened his jacket. Fished out a pack of Gitanes cigarettes. Stepped back and dropped them on Khan's lap.

"My lighter's in my pocket, may I get it?" Thomas Khan's voice was calm.

"Yes."

Khan dug out a small, Zippo-style lighter, lit a cigarette, exhaled smoke with a weary blow.

"I gave you your cigarette," Evan said. "Now I want this client list."

Khan blew out a feather of smoke. "Ask your mother."

"Don't be a jerk."

"You appear to be a bright boy. Do you really think that if your mother stole the files that could identify the clients, we would leave those accounts open?" His voice was gentle, almost chiding, as though talking to a slightly dense but adored child.

Evan said, "I'm not falling into the trap. You have the accounts that the operatives—like my parents—used. That's all I need. I can break Jargo either way."

Khan laughed. "Do you think our operatives will keep working under those names, given the danger we're facing?"

"If they have families and kids like my folks or you, your suburban camouflage, they can't change."

"Sure they can. Your mother's account isn't under Donna Casher, you stupid, stupid boy." Khan shook his head. "It's under another name she used. You won't catch anything in that net. We're far too careful. We've got escape routes built in if our covers are ever blown. We've all been doing this a very long time, before you were off your mother's teat." He stubbed out the cigarette. "I suggest you leave now. I will give you half the money in your mother's account, and I will keep the rest for my silence. It is two million U.S. dollars, Evan. You can vanish into the world instead of a grave. You will not be able to get your father back. Your dying won't bring back your mother." Khan pulled a fresh cigarette out with delicacy. "Two million. Don't be a fool, take the money. Get a new life."

"But..." And then Evan saw the hole in Khan's offer. Accounts with false names. The explosion. Escape routes. The phone ringing only twice. A new life. This was a trap, but not the kind he'd expected.

Khan had all the time in the world sitting here in this house. Smiling at him. No dying sister-in-law. No Khan name attached to this house. Escape route.

"You—" Evan said.

Khan flicked the lighter again, holding it sideways, a blast of mist jetting from the lighter's end. Evan threw up his jacketed arm across his face. Pepper spray seared his eyes, his throat. He staggered and fell across the Persian rug. Pain gouged up through his eyeballs, his nose.

Khan dashed across the room, knocking a thick tome from the shelf, reaching in, drawing a Beretta free, spinning to fire at Evan. The bullet barked into the coffee table by Evan's head. He blindly seized the table, brought it up as a shield, charged at Khan, his eyes burning as if he'd had matches poked into them. Two more silenced shots and wood splintered into Evan's stomach and chest, but he rammed the table into Khan, forced the gun downward, drove him back into the oak shelves.

Pressing and pressing and pressing harder. Evan powered his legs, his arms, the agony in his face fueling him. Flattening the man into the wall. He heard Khan's lungs empty, heard him gurgle in pain; the man dropped to the floor, the gun still in his hand.

Evan dumped the table and snatched at the gun, Khan's face and fingers nothing but a blur. But Khan held on to the Beretta. Evan fell onto the older man. Khan pistoned a knee into Evan's groin, jabbed bony fingers at his clenched-shut eyes. Evan let go of the gun with one hand and punched, connecting with Khan's nose. The man's face was a haze through his tearing eyes. Evan seized the Beretta again with both hands, fought to turn it toward the cloud of the ceiling. Khan jerked it back, aimed it toward Evan's head.

The gun fired.

35

THE HEAT OF THE BULLET PASSED Evan's ear. He put all his weight and strength into twisting the barrel toward the floor. Khan jerked, trying to wrench the weapon free. The gun sang again.

Khan spasmed. Then went still. Evan yanked the gun away, staggering, clawing at his eyes.

He retreated to a corner of the room. He could barely see Khan, but he kept the gun trained on him. Evan moaned; the pain in his eyes was blinding.

No movement from Khan. He forced himself back toward the body, touched the throat. Nothing. No pulse.

Agony. Evan stumbled into the kitchen. Powered on the faucet, splashed handfuls of water on his face. The brown contact lenses Bedford had given him washed free. After the tenth handful the agony started to subside. No sound in the house but the water hissing into the sink. He rinsed his swollen eyes, again and again, the gun still in his other hand, until the pain lessened. He walked back into the den.

Khan stared up at him from the floor, three-eyed, the middle eye red. Evan checked again; the neck, the wrist, the chest, were all empty of a heartbeat.

I just killed a man.

He should be sick with fear, with horror. A week ago he would have been paralyzed with shock. Now simple relief flooded him that it was Khan lying dead on the floor and not him.

He went to the bathroom and studied his face in the mirror. His eyes hazel again and swollen almost shut. His lip was badly split and bloodied. He opened the cabinet under the sink and found a fully stocked first-aid kit. Of course there was one here; in this house was everything Khan needed.

This was Khan's escape route.

He had not thought clearly in the chaos of the bomb blast, he was so focused on getting his hands on the man who could unfold the map to his parents' lives.

Khan had screwed up in Jargo's eyes, but maybe Jargo didn't want him dead. Maybe Jargo wanted to dead-end any immediate investigation into the Deeps. Khan had walked out after Evan had said the name Jargo. Or maybe he already knew Evan's face. Then Pettigrew walked in with the bomb, or Khan triggered the bomb once he was clear of the building. Khan, with his own business destroyed, would not run to a place that would only give him a few hours' sanctuary. He would run for his escape hatch. If the Deeps had fallback identities, so did Khan, their moneyman. He'd brought Evan to a place where Khan could hide, clothe himself in a prepared identity, melt into the world. Even better, he would be assumed dead in the bookstore blast.

When Thomas Khan was assumed dead, then no one in the CIA would be looking for him.

It was no small thing to walk away from your life. And if this house was Khan's hidey-hole, his first stop in the journey into a fresh and secret life, he would have resources here to shut down his operations, money and data to cover his tracks and to step into his new identity. But if Jargo knew this was where Khan would run—and Jargo might— then Evan didn't have much time at all. Jargo could send an agent to ensure Khan had escaped the blast if Khan didn't check in.

The ringing phone. Maybe it had been Jargo calling for Khan.

Evan might not have much time at all, but he had to risk it. The answers he needed could be inside the house.

Evan checked every window and door to be sure it was locked. He pulled down every window shade, closed every curtain. Two small bedrooms, a study, and a bath upstairs, a master bedroom and bath downstairs, with den, kitchen, dining room. A door off the kitchen led down to a small cellar; Evan ventured down steps, flicked on a light. Empty. Except for in the corner, a large, black, zippered bag. A body bag.

Evan eased down the zipper.

Hadley Khan. He recognized the face—what was left of it. He had been dead for a few days. Lime powder dusted his body, to minimize the burgeoning odor of decay. Shot once through the temple. He lay curled tight in the bag, naked; long, vicious welts marred his face and his chest. His hands were missing. His mouth gaped open; there was no tongue.

I forgave him, Khan had said.

Evan stood and walked to the opposite side of the cellar and pressed his forehead against the cool stone and took deep, shuddering breaths. *Khan did it here, he tortured and killed his own son for betraying him. For betraying the family business.*

What would his parents have done to him if he'd stumbled on the truth or threatened to expose them? He could not imagine this. No. Never.

Khan's voice echoed in his ear: *I know them much better than you do.*

Evan closed the body bag. He went upstairs to the den. He dragged Thomas Khan's body down the basement steps, placed him next to his son. He went back upstairs, found a folded sheet in a bedroom closet, and covered both corpses with it.

He drank four glasses of cold water, ate four aspirin that he found in the first-aid kit. His eyes hurt, his stomach ached.

He returned to the study and tested the desk and a credenza; both were locked. Evan went back to the basement and searched Khan's pockets: no keys, but a wallet and a PDA. He powered it on; a screen appeared, asking for his fingerprint.

He dug Khan's right hand from under the sheet, pressed the dead man's forefinger against the screen. Denied. He grabbed Khan's left hand, pressed Khan's left forefinger against the screen. It accepted the print, opened to show a normal startup screen. He studied the applications and files. The PDA held only a few contacts and phone numbers: a few Zurich banks, a listing of London bookstores. There was an icon for a map application. He opened it. The last three maps accessed were London; Biloxi, Mississippi; and Fort Lauderdale, Florida. A notation on the Biloxi map, showing the location of a charter air service. Biloxi wasn't that far from New Orleans. Maybe that was where Dezz and Jargo had fled after the New Orleans disaster.

But nothing that announced, *X marks the spot where your father is.*

Except maybe Fort Lauderdale. A specific place in Florida. And Gabriel had said Evan's mother had claimed that they would meet his father in Florida. Carrie thought his father was in Florida.

Carrie. He could try to call her. Reach her through the London CIA office. Tell her he was alive. But, no. If Jargo's agents or clients within the CIA thought he was dead...no one would be hunting him. And they had known he was in London, had nearly killed him. Bedford's group had been compromised.

He wanted to know Carrie was safe; he wanted to tell her he was alive. But not now, not until he had his father back. She wouldn't go back to the house Pettigrew had taken them to, he believed; if Pettigrew worked for Jargo, it was too dangerous. She would carefully reunite with Bedford.

Evan reconfigured the password program to delete Khan's fingerprint and used his own thumbprint as the passkey. It might be useful later. He put the PDA in his pocket. Standing up, he spotted a toolbox in the corner and took it upstairs.

He jabbed a screwdriver into the desk lock with caution; after the trick pepper-spray lighter he could not take anything on face value. But there was only the click of the metal against metal.

He picked up a hammer and with four solid blows cracked open the locks on Thomas Khan's desk. In one drawer he found papers relating to the ownership of the house. It had been bought last year by Boroch Investments. Boroch must be a front for Khan; if there was no obvious connection to Khan, the police wouldn't come here. Thomas Khan wouldn't show his face if he could help it in digging his escape tunnel.

In the desk drawer he found stationery and envelopes for Boroch Investments, as well as a passport from New Zealand and one from Zimbabwe, both in false names and with Thomas Khan's pictures inside. There was a phone, in need of a charge but working. He dug out the charger from the back of the drawer and began to power up the phone. He checked the call log; the list was empty.

He forced the lock on another desk drawer. It held a metal box containing bricks of British pounds and American dollars. Beneath that an automatic pistol and two clips. He counted the money. Six thousand British pounds, ten thousand in U.S. funds. He set the cash on the desk. The side desk drawers were empty.

He attacked the credenza with a hammer, a screwdriver, and then a crowbar. Dizziness oozed into his brain, from lack of eating, from exhaustion, from the pepper spray, but he knew that he was close, so close to getting what he needed. So close.

The door cracked under the crowbar. Empty.

No, it couldn't be. Couldn't. Khan would need data files, he would need to access new accounts, erase old ones. There had to be a computer in this house aside from the PDA. Unless Khan had kept it all in his head. Then Evan was back to zero.

He searched the room. The small closet held office supplies, old suits, a raincoat. He went through the guest bedrooms—practically bare—and the downstairs bedroom. He searched carefully, knowing he was no pro, but he reminded himself to be disciplined and thorough. But he found nothing, and the chance to close his hands around Jargo's throat started to turn to smoke.

In the darkened den, he risked a reading light. The bookcase. Khan had hidden his gun behind the volumes.

Evan searched the rest of the bookcase. Nearly every inch filled with good books, leftovers from Khan's store. How could such a psychopath have such excellent taste in reading? But nothing else lay concealed behind the books. He rifled through the kitchen cabinets and pantry. He dumped canisters of salt and flour on the floor. Nothing. A freezer full of frozen dinners, but he ripped them open, dumped them in the sink, hoping a disk or CD might be hidden inside. Suddenly he was hungry and he microwaved a frozen chicken-and-noodle dinner, nauseated at eating a dead man's food. He decided to get over it.

He sat down on the floor and forced himself to calm down as he ate. The food was tasteless but filling. His stomach settled. The jet lag and the fade of his adrenaline rush swamped him, and he fought the urge to just lie down on the floor and close his eyes, slip into sleep. Maybe there was nothing more to find.

The basement. The one room he hadn't searched. He went down the darkened steps. Past the sheeted bodies. The basement was small. Square, with a stacked washer/dryer on one side and metal shelving on the other. The shelves held an assemblage of junk. More books, boxed. He went through them all. A television set with a cracked screen. A box of gardening tools, clean of mud, probably never used. A couple of cases of canned soups and vegetables and meats, in case Khan had to hide a fellow operative.

His gaze went back to the TV with its cracked eye. Why would anyone keep a small broken TV? TVs were cheap now. To repair the screen, you might as well buy a new one. Maybe Khan was driven by a sense of waste not, want not. But he had been well-to-do. A broken TV was nothing.

Evan took the TV down from the shelf. He retrieved a screwdriver and unfastened the back.

The television had been stripped of its guts. Inside was a small notebook computer and charger. Evan powered on the laptop; it presented a dialog box prompting him for a password.

He entered DEEPS.

Wrong. He entered JARGO.

Wrong. He entered HADLEY. Wrong. The CIA could crack this, but he couldn't. Even if he deduced a password, Khan might have encrypted and passworded the files on the system. He would be a fool not to take that precaution.

Evan stared at the screen. Maybe he should just take the computer and go to Langley, the CIA's headquarters. Turn himself in . . .

. . . and not save his father.

His father's face floated before him in the darkened basement, and he stared at the father-and-son bodies of the Khans. If he believed the past few days, his father was a professional killer who had stamped out lives the way others stamped out ants. But that wasn't the father he knew. It could not be; the truth could not be that harsh or that simple. He had to have the data to rescue his father.

Or, he thought, he had to create the illusion that he had the data.

The laptop. He didn't need the data, he just needed the laptop itself to barter for his father. It might hold the exact same files his mother had stolen. At the least it was a negotiating point: he could always threaten to turn over the laptop to the CIA unless his father was released. Jargo couldn't know with certainty that the files were, or weren't, on Khan's machine. Even if this didn't hold the client list, it might hold enough data—financial, logistical, personal—to destroy the Deeps.

His mother might have stolen the files from this very laptop. He tried to imagine how she had done it. She'd snapped pictures in Dover, stolen the military data. Delivered the goods to Khan. But probably not here, not in his safe spot. She'd probably handed him the stolen data and photos on a CD, in a park, in a theater, in a café. But maybe she follows Khan here after they part ways. Then...what? Khan loads the data she stole on the computer to send to Jargo. He leaves. She breaks into the house, finds the laptop. She must have software to bypass the passwords—a necessity if she routinely stole information.

If she did it—it could be done. He could steal the same files.

He tried the laptop once more. Entered BAST. Nothing.

OHIO, because of the orphanage. No.

GOINSVILLE. Refused.

He found Khan's car keys on the kitchen counter, put the laptop and the money in the car's trunk. He went back inside and put Khan's PDA, gun, and phone into his jacket pocket. He wanted to sleep, and he wanted to believe that Khan's hiding place could be his hiding place. But it wasn't safe to stay here.

Fort Lauderdale. His mother's mention of Florida to Gabriel. It was his best bet.

He got into the borrowed Jaguar. Realized he had never driven a car designed for the left side of the road and, for the first time in days, really laughed. This would be an adventure.

Nerves on edge, Evan drove into the darkness. A cold rain began to fall. He had to concentrate entirely on retraining his driving reflexes. He headed slowly, like a rookie driver, back toward London and found a decent hotel in Crystal Palace. He treated himself to a real meal of steak and fries in a small bar, drank down a pint of ale, watched a couple and their grown son laugh over lagers. He paid and went back to the hotel, lay down on the bed.

He turned Thomas Khan's cell phone back on and it chimed that there was a message. He didn't know Khan's voice-mail password. But he found a call log, listing a recently missed number.

He opened Khan's PDA and activated the Voice Memo application. Then he dialed the number on the new call log.

He could not negotiate if they all thought he was dead.

It was answered on the first ring. "Yes?" He knew the voice, his soft psychotic purr. Dezz.

"Let me speak to Jargo." Evan held the PDA close enough to record every word.

"No one here by that name."

"Shut up, Dezz. Let me talk to Jargo. Now."

Three beats of silence. "Put ourselves back together, have we?"

"Tell your father I have all of Mr. Khan's files relating to the Deeps. All of them. I'd like to negotiate a trade for my father."

"How's Carrie? Blown to bits? I'm sorry I wasn't in London to help you pick up the pieces." He stifled a giggle.

"You say another word to me, freak, and I e-mail the client list to the CIA, to the FBI, to Scotland Yard. You're not calling the shots. I am."

Silence for a long moment, and Dezz said with icy politeness, "Hold, please."

He imagined Dezz and Jargo, seeing Khan's number on

a cell phone screen, knowing now about the explosion and weighing if Evan was telling the truth.

"Yes? Evan? You're well?" Jargo. Sounding concerned.

"I'm fine. I have a proposal for you."

"Your father is worried sick about you. Where are you?"

"Deep in the rabbit hole. And I have Thomas Khan's laptop. From his hiding place in Bromley. With all his files."

A long pause. "Congratulations. I for one find spreadsheets boring."

"Give me back my father, and I'll give you your laptop, and then we're walking away from each other."

"But files can be duplicated. I don't know that I can trust you."

"You have no room to question my integrity, Mr. Jargo. None. I know about Goinsville, I know about Alexander Bast, I know he set up the original Deep network." All bluff; he wasn't sure how any of this fit together, but he had to pretend that he knew. "I have Khan's laptop and I'm giving it to you. Not to the police. Not to the press. All I want is my dad. You either take the deal or you don't. I can tear the Deeps apart in five minutes with what I've got."

"May I speak to Mr. Khan?" Jargo asked.

"No, you may not."

"Is he alive?"

"No."

"Well. Did you kill him or did the CIA?"

"I'm not playing twenty questions with you. Do we have a deal or do I go to the CIA?"

"Evan. I understand you're upset. But I didn't want Khan dead. I didn't want you dead." A pause. "If you've got Internet access, I'd like to show you a tape. To prove my point."

"A tape."

"Khan had a digital camera in his business. Did a constant feed to a remote server. We take a lot of precautions in our line of work, you understand. I just accessed the server. I can prove to you it was a known CIA operative who set off the blast. His name was Marcus Pettigrew. I suspect the CIA saw a way to get rid of you and Khan all at once, nice and neat."

Evan remembered seeing a set of small cameras mounted in the corners near the bookstore's ceiling. He said what he thought Jargo would expect him to say, "So what? So I can't trust the CIA. It doesn't mean that I can trust you."

"Watch the tape," Jargo said, "before you make up your mind."

"Hold on." Staying on the phone, Evan walked down the stairs from his room to the hotel's business center. It was empty. He fired up a gleaming new PC, set up a new e-mail account at Yahoo! under an invented name, and gave Jargo the new e-mail account's address. After a minute the attached film clip appeared in the in-box. Evan clicked it. Saw himself, from above and to the left, come in and talk to Khan. Khan and then Evan went offscreen, and here came Pettigrew. Flipping the Closed sign. Murdering two people. Leaning down to touch his briefcase. Then nothing.

"I'm not really into eviscerating my own network," Jargo said. "The CIA would be, however."

"You could have doctored that tape."

"Evan. Please. First Gabriel, now Pettigrew. Your friend Bricklayer sent you right into that death trap. Kill two birds with one stone, you and Khan. I'm not your enemy, Evan. Far from it. You've fallen in with the wrong crowd, to put it mildly, and I've been trying to save you."

Bricklayer...he knows Bedford's code name. He hated the oily concern that failed to hide the arrogance in Jargo's voice.

"That tape doesn't lie. Now who do you believe?" Jargo asked.

"I want to talk to my dad." Evan put a calculated quaver of doubt in his voice.

"That's an excellent idea, Evan."

Silence. And then his father's voice: "Evan?" He sounded tired, weak. Beaten.

Alive. His father was truly alive. "Dad, are you okay?"

"Yes. I'm all right. I love you, Evan."

"I love you, too."

"Evan...I'm sorry. Your mother. You. I never meant for you to get dragged into this mess. It was always my worst nightmare." Mitchell's voice sounded near tears. "You don't understand the whole story."

He knew Jargo was listening. *Pretend you believe him. It's the only way Jargo will give you Dad. But not too fast, or Jargo won't buy it.* He had to play his own father. He tried hard to keep his voice steady. "No, Dad, I sure don't understand."

"What counts is that I can keep you safe, Evan. I need you to trust Jargo."

"Dad, even if Jargo didn't kill Mom, he kidnapped you. How can I trust this guy?"

"Evan. Listen carefully to me. Your mother went to the CIA, and the CIA killed her. I don't know why she did it, but she did, thinking they would hide her, hide you. But they killed her"—his voice broke, then steadied—"and now they've used you to try to draw me and Jargo out."

"Dad—"

"Jargo and Dezz weren't at our house. It was the CIA. Anything else you've been told is a lie. Believe your eyes. That CIA agent in London tried to kill you. There's no plainer evidence. I want you to do what Jargo says. Please."

"I don't think I can do that, Dad. He killed Mom. Do you understand that? He killed her!" He gave his father an abbreviated account of his arrival at home.

"But you never saw their faces."

"No...I never saw their faces." He let three seconds tick by, thought, *Make Jargo think you want to believe Dad, you want to believe worse than anything, so this horror will all be over.* "I saw Mom, and then I freaked, and they put a bag over my head."

Mitchell's voice was patient. "I can tell you it was not Dezz and Jargo, it wasn't."

"How can you be sure, Dad?"

"I am. I am absolutely sure they didn't kill your mom."

Start acting dumb. "I just heard voices."

"In the most horrifying moment of your life, you might make a mistake, Evan. Jargo might threaten you to get cooperation, but it's easier than explaining to you. But he really wouldn't hurt you. They shot at Carrie at the zoo. Not you."

Not true, but Jargo had fed his father a matched set of lies. He didn't argue the point. *Now for confusion.* "But Carrie said—"

"Carrie betrayed your trust. She played you, son. I'm sorry."

He let the silence build before he spoke. "You're right." *Forgive me, Carrie,* he thought. "She wasn't honest with me, Dad. Not from day one."

Mitchell cleared his throat. "Never mind her. All that

matters is getting you here with me. Are you safe from the CIA right now?"

"To them, I'm dead."

"Then bring Jargo the files. We'll be together. Jargo will let you and me talk, work out what happens next."

Evan lowered his voice. "Say nothing. I have the laptop, but I can't get past its password. I've never seen these files Jargo wants. I'm not a threat to him." He knew Jargo was drinking in every word.

"It'll all be fine as soon as we're together."

"Dad...is it all true? What I found out about you and Mom, about the Deeps? Because I don't understand..."

"You have been very sheltered, Evan, and you are about to do more harm, ever, than good if you expose us. Do what Jargo says. We'll have lots of time, and I can make you understand."

"Why aren't you Arthur Smithson anymore?"

A pause. "You don't know what your mother and I did for you. You have no conception of the sacrifices we made. You've never made a difficult choice. You have no idea." Then Mitchell's words came in a rush, as though his time ran short: "You remember when I gave you all the Graham Greene novels, and I told you the most important line in all of them was 'if one loved, one feared'? It's true, one hundred percent true. I was afraid you wouldn't have a good life, and I wanted a good life for you. The best life. You are everything to me. I love you, Evan."

"I remember. Dad, I love you, too." No matter what he had done. Evan remembered his father giving him a bunch of Greene novels his senior year in high school for Christmas, but he didn't understand the quote. It didn't matter. What mattered was Dad was alive and he was getting him back.

"Listen closely." His father's voice was gone, replaced by Dezz's. "I'm in charge of you, now. Where are you?"

"Just tell me where I'm supposed to be to exchange Khan's computer for my father."

"Miami. Tomorrow morning."

"I can't get to Miami that fast. Tomorrow night."

"We'll arrange tickets for you," Dezz said. "We don't want the CIA scooping you back up."

"I'll handle my own travel. I'll call you from Miami. I'm picking the time and place for our exchange."

"All right." Dezz gave a giggle. "Don't run away from me this time. Now that we'll all be like family." And he hung up.

Like family. Evan didn't like the dig in Dezz's tone, and he thought of the faded pictures of the two boys in Goinsville, their similar smiles and squints. Seeing now what he didn't want to see then, the possibility that the connection between his father—a man he loved and admired—and Jargo, a brutal and vicious killer, could be a thread of blood.

Evan had decided to play dumb, to let Jargo think he would blindly rush to save his father, but now he felt dense. Graham Greene quotes that had burned up the precious time talking with his father. Digs from Dezz. It didn't make sense.

Evan erased the downloaded movie from the PC and walked back to his room. He sprawled on his bed and stared at Khan's laptop, still hiding its secrets like a willful child.

If he walked this laptop back to Jargo for his father, he'd get his dad back, he hoped, but Jargo would not be stopped. No. Unacceptable. So he had to do both. Get his father back and bring Jargo down, with no room for error.

He sat and considered the tools at his disposal, the ways tomorrow might play out.

It was a matter, he decided, of simply being the best storyteller. He needed to outdo a veritable king of lies. His first prop was this uncooperative laptop. It was time for sleight of hand.

36

SHE PICKED UP THE PHONE ON the third ring. "Hello?"

"Hello, Kathleen."

A moment of stunned silence. "Evan?"

"Yeah, it's me."

"Are you okay?"

"Yes. I saw you talking about me on CNN last weekend. I appreciate the kind words."

"Evan, where are you, what happened? I've been worried sick about you."

He wanted to believe it was true, his former girlfriend fretting over him, and he knew his request would put her to the test.

"I can't tell you what's happened or where I am. I need your help. I may be putting you in danger by asking. If you hang up now, I won't blame you."

Silence. Then she said, "What kind of danger?"

"Not so much to you, but to whomever you can get to help me."

"Spit it out, Evan." She always had a brutal directness.

"A dangerous group of people want me dead. They killed my mom, kidnapped my dad, they're looking for me.

I have one of their computers and I need access to it. But it's encrypted."

"This is a joke, right?"

"My mom's dead, do you think I'm joking?"

Four beats of silence. Her voice lowered. "No, I don't think you are."

"Help me, Kath."

"Evan, listen, go to the police."

"They'll kill my dad if I do. Please, Kathleen."

"How could I help you?"

"Because you produced *Hackerama* with Bill." Bill was the guy she'd left Evan for, a filmmaker from New York Evan actually thought was a cool guy. He'd beaten Evan out for the Oscar with his film about the culture of computer hackers.

"Yes," she said after a moment's hesitation.

"I need a contact in England. Smart and discreet, who won't go straight to the police, and is an encryption expert. I can pay them well. You, too."

She let a beat pass. "Evan. I'm not taking your money and I can't help you commit a crime."

"It's to save my dad, to save myself."

He heard Kathleen fidget.

"If you've been watching the news, you might have heard about a bombing in London today. That was this group, trying to kill me."

"You sound crazy right now, to be honest."

"I've been on the run for days. Hiding. My life is literally in your hands, Kathleen. I need help. I can't stop these people, I can't expose them in any way that the police will believe, without this evidence."

"Assuming that you're telling the truth, you're asking me to call a friend and put him or her in great danger."

"Yes. That's true. You should warn them. Be honest with them so they know what they're facing. But I'm paying. These guys always need money, right?"

"Doesn't sound like a good idea," she said, "for anyone but you."

Dead end. He couldn't blame her. "I understand. I wouldn't want an innocent hurt, either. Thanks for being willing to talk to me. And thanks for defending me on CNN. It meant a lot to me."

"Evan."

He waited.

Finally she said, "I'll find someone to help you. How can I reach you?"

"It's better for you if I just call you back. The less you know, the better."

"I'm so sorry about your mom. She was a terrific woman. And your dad . . ."

"Thank you."

"Call me back in an hour."

"Okay." He hung up. He wondered if she would call the police straightaway. He called Kathleen Torrance back in precisely an hour, using the hotel phone. Khan's cell phone was strictly for talking with Jargo.

"Evan. A hacker gave me the name of a friend of his in London. I called the friend. His hacker name is Razur. He doesn't want you to know his real name. He said he'd meet you tonight at this café. You got a pen?" She gave him an address in Soho.

"Thank you, Kathleen."

"I beg you. Let the police handle this."

"I would if I could. It's complicated."

"Will you call me back? Let me know you're all right?"

"When I can. Be well, Kathleen. Thanks." He hung up.

He went downstairs, asked the desk clerk for directions to the café Razur had suggested. He got back in Khan's car, steeled himself for driving on the opposite side of the road, and headed out into the chilling, cutting rain.

37

You were very persuasive, Mitchell," Jargo said. "I'm proud of you. That was a difficult conversation."

"I don't want him hurt." Mitchell Casher closed his eyes.

"None of us want Evan hurt." Jargo set coffee down in front of Mitchell. "I hate to criticize, but you should have told him about us long ago."

Mitchell shook his head. "No."

"I told Dezz as soon as he was old enough to understand. We get to work together. It's very nice to work with your son."

"I wanted a different life for Evan. The way you wanted a different life for all of us."

"I applaud the sentiment, but it's misplaced. You didn't trust him, so you put him in greater danger, made it more likely he could be used by our enemies." Jargo stirred his own coffee. "You seemed to win his trust back, at least to a degree."

"I did," Mitchell said in a hard voice. "You don't need to doubt him. Your tape convinced him. He's got a false ID, he's got cash, he can get back here."

"It bothers me he wouldn't let us come fetch him. Bothers me a lot. This could be a CIA trap."

"Your contacts would tell you if he'd been found."

"I hope." Jargo sipped at the coffee, watched Mitchell. "He seemed to soften toward you, but I'm not convinced."

"I can persuade my son our best interests are his best interests. You trust me, don't you?"

"Of course I do." And behind the frown of family concern, Jargo allowed himself a regretful smile. What was the opening line of *Anna Karenina*? Bast had given Jargo a copy of the book a week before Jargo had killed him. The line was arch nonsense about every unhappy family was unhappy in its own way. The Jargos and the Cashers, he decided, were truly unique in their misery.

He left Mitchell alone in his room and went downstairs to the lodge kitchen. He wanted quiet in which to think.

The boy might be lying about having Khan's laptop, but Jargo decided he wasn't. He wanted his father back too badly. He wondered if Dezz would fight so hard for him. He thought not. That was good, because to fight for what could not be won was stupid.

And he loathed stupidity. He'd lightened the world's burden of two idiots today. Khan had gotten too lazy, too complacent, too self-important. Losing him, losing Pettigrew as a client, were setbacks but not a crippling loss. He could let Galadriel take over Khan's duties; her loyalty was unquestioned, and she had no bitter offspring to get underfoot, no ego cultivated in boardrooms. Pettigrew had been slow to pay for a hit on a senior CIA official in Moscow whom he personally disliked and whose job he coveted. Khan had no involvement with Jargo's American properties; otherwise staying here at the lodge, under the empty black skies, would have been too risky.

Jargo poured a fresh cup of coffee, studied its steam. The

boy couldn't crack the laptop; at least Khan had done one thing right. And Mitchell had, if words were to be believed, snared his own child into a death trap.

He would have a Deep operative do the hit on Evan, after he had delivered the client list and Khan's laptop. Without killing Mitchell, of course: from a distance, with a high-powered sniper's rifle. He suspected Mitchell would want to talk to the boy alone. An attack staged on father and son, he decided, and poor Evan just stepped the wrong way and put his brains in a bullet's path. He liked the approach because it would stoke Mitchell's fury, make him easier to manipulate. Evan dead, Donna dead, that grief could make Mitchell even more productive in the years to come.

But he had to prepare for every eventuality, act as though meeting Evan was a CIA trap, and seal every exit. He picked up a cell phone, made a call.

Jargo then crushed a sedative into a glass of orange juice to keep Mitchell calm and took the doped drink back upstairs. He had a long night ahead of him.

38

RAZUR WAS THIN, like his sharp-edged namesake. He wore a goatee dyed platinum blond and black eyeglasses, and a Celtic cross was tattooed on the back of his neck. "Evan?"

"Yes. Razur?"

Razur shook hands with him and sat down at Evan's table, in the far back corner of the café. He tilted his head at Evan. "Your eyes look like you just smoked yourself a big chronic."

"Chronic?"

"A potent joint, mate."

"Oh." Evan shook his head. "No. You want a coffee?"

"Yeah, black. Largest they got."

The café was grimy and funky, but not too busy, a line of computers on one side of the metallic wall, young people Web-surfing while downing juices, teas, and coffees. Evan got up and ordered the drink from the barista. He sensed Razur's gaze on him the whole time. Evaluating him as a series of problems to be broken down into his constituent parts and solved. Or maybe revisiting the marijuana theory and deciding Evan's request was the result of reefer madness. Evan came back to the corner table and set a steaming cup in front of Razur.

The hacker took a cautious sip. "I'm told you're being raked over by nasty people."

"The less you know the better." Evan didn't want to get into the details of the Deeps or their entanglement with the CIA.

Razur gave a thin smile. "But you've gotten their dirty secrets."

"Yes. On a laptop. But I can't get past the password."

"I won't either," Razur said. "Without the cash."

Evan handed him a laundry bag from the hotel. Razur peeked inside at the money.

"Count it if you want."

Razur did, fast, under the table, where the bricks of cash wouldn't draw attention. "Thanks. Sorry I'm not a trusting soul. You got the system?"

"Yes." Evan brought the laptop out of a shopping bag he'd found in the back of the Jaguar.

"I'm not really into breaking the law, I'm into technical challenges, showing up the losers who think they're so smart but they aren't. Savvy?"

"Savvy."

Razur popped open his own sleek laptop, revved it up, cabled it to the Ethernet port of Khan's machine. "I'll run a program. If the password can be found in a dictionary, we're in."

He clicked keys. Evan watched as words began to rapid-fire scroll on a screen, faster than he could read them, throwing themselves against the gates of Khan's laptop fortress.

After a few moments Razur said, "No joy. We'll try it with alphanumerics thrown in at random and variant misspellings." Razur slurped at his coffee. Watched the slow, solemn rise of a status bar as millions of new combinations attempted to speak the open sesame of Khan's laptop.

"Hey, do you know much about handhelds?" Evan asked.

"Not my specialty. Low-powered buggers."

Evan pulled Khan's PDA out of his pocket, used his thumbprint to open it.

"Biometric security," Razur said. "What have you got on your to-do list, stealing a nuclear weapon?" He laughed.

"Not today. What are these programs? I don't recognize them."

Razur studied the small screen. "My. I'd like to play with these. This one's a cellular interference program—it would emit a signal to jam any cell phone in the room." He grinned mischievously, eyeing the several customers chatting on their phones. "Should we try?" Tapped the pad without waiting for Evan's answer.

Within ten seconds everyone was frowning at his or her phone.

"Ah, I think I just broke a law." Razur tapped again and the phone service seemed to return as the customers redialed and started their conversations again.

"And this one"—Razur tapped it open, studied the program with a frown—"it's like what I'm using on your laptop. But specialized. For keypad alarm systems. Most have only a four-digit password. Patch into the alarm system and it would decipher and activate the code."

"You mean it would give me the code of an alarm system on the screen so I could enter it?"

"I think that's what it's designed to do. Hmmm. This one copies a storage card or a hard drive. Compresses the data so it would fit on this PDA."

"You couldn't copy a whole computer hard drive using this, though, could you?"

"No. Not this. Too small. But another PDA, or a set of files, sure."

Maybe my mother used an approach like this to steal the files from Khan, Evan thought. "It would be fast?"

"Sure. If you grab other files along with it, no problem. Grab a whole folder, it's faster than searching and grabbing for files. If you can compress it, all the better." He handed him back the PDA, his eyebrow raised. "You steal this from the spooks?"

"Spooks?"

"Spies."

"You don't want to know."

"I don't," Razur said.

Evan watched the status bar slowly inching its progress. *Please,* he thought, *crack. Give me the files.* But they weren't just files: they were a lifetime's worth of secrets, the financial trails of terrible deceits, the record of lives snuffed out for dirty money. He had one hand to play with Jargo, and it was on these files.

Razur lit a cigarette. "I could hack a porn site while we're waiting. Cover up the tits with pictures of prominent politicians. I'm very antiporn these days. I've gone all Victorian."

Evan shook his head. "I want your opinion on an idea of mine. If we crack the password, but the files on the laptop are encrypted, would that keep you from copying them to another computer?"

"Possibly. Depends on how they're encrypted. Or if they're copy-protected."

"The program to de-encrypt the files has to be on this

laptop, right? I mean, you would need to edit files, so you would have to decrypt them first, make changes, and lock them back up."

"Yes. If the unlocking program's not on the laptop, it needs to be in a place where it can be downloaded easily. Otherwise it's like a lockbox without a key, worthless. If your bad guy stashed a custom program on a remote server, I'll dig through his cache, if it hasn't been erased, to track it, or I'll have to hack into his service provider." Razur grinned. "I detect an evil idea about to take flight."

"So we could decode the files," Evan said, running a finger along the smooth edge of the laptop, "and hide a copy. On a server where I could retrieve a copy off the Web. Then we encrypt the hard drive of this laptop again, using the same locking software and the original password. I give the bad guys their encrypted laptop, they might believe I never, ever saw the files. It's like returning a locked box to them that I never had the key for. So they think I'm no longer a real threat to them."

Razur nodded.

"Or even if they kill me, the files could still be used to cut off the balls of said bad guys. It would be my ace in the hole."

"No guarantees," Razur said, "that I can even break this system open."

"Then I think I need a Plan B." Evan toyed with the possibilities. He smiled at Razur. "I'm going to need a bit more help from you. Of course I'll pay extra."

"Sure."

"Tell me, do you play poker?"

FRIDAY

MARCH 18

39

THE MEN CAUGHT EVAN AT HEATHROW Airport early Friday afternoon. He made an effort to look like any young tourist. He wore fresh-pressed khakis and a new black sweater, tennis shoes, and sunglasses bought from Razur. His hair was still CIA-short but now it was platinum-white, courtesy of Razur's much-tattooed girlfriend. The men let him approach the British Airways counter, buying a round-trip ticket to Miami, paying with cash, even let him glide through security. He used the South African passport he stole from Gabriel a lifetime ago. He was nearly to his gate when the agents came up on both sides of him, said, "This way, Mr. Casher, please don't make a fuss," with cool politeness, and so he didn't. Suddenly walking next to him and in front of and behind him were six British MI5 officers, and they boxed and steered him with grace.

No one around Evan realized he had been plucked into custody.

The agents escorted him into a small, windowless room. It smelled of coffee. Bedford stood at the end of a conference table. Then Evan saw Carrie on the other side of the room. She rushed to him, embraced him. "Thank God you're okay."

She held him for a long minute, tight, and he gave in to her embrace, being careful of her hurt shoulder.

"I thought you were dead," she said into his neck.

"I'm sorry. I tried to stop your car but you didn't see me. I was too far away. But I knew you were alive. You're okay?"

"Yes. British intelligence had a team following us. They found me after the blast. Took me to a safe house for questioning."

She pulled back from him, kissed him quickly, put her hand on his cheek. Giddy in her relief. "What's with the Sting look?"

He shrugged. Bedford came forward, put his hand on Evan's shoulder. "Evan. We are all tremendously relieved that you're alive and well."

Another man sat next to Bedford: clipped hair, good suit, a face bland as air. "Mr. Casher. Hello. I'm Palmer, MI5."

"My counterpart, of sorts," Bedford said. "Not his real name. You understand."

"Hello," Evan said. He ignored Palmer's outstretched hand, shrugged his shoulder out from under Bedford's grip.

"Evan?" Carrie eased him into the chair next to her. "What's the matter?"

"My problem is with you," Evan said to Bedford. "You delivered us into the hands of a murderer."

Bedford went pale. "I'm sorry. We've looked at every moment Pettigrew's spent in the Agency for the past fifteen years and still haven't found the connection to Jargo."

"I know where you can get the accounts linking Pettigrew and Jargo. And maybe, just maybe, I'll give it to you. But you and I have to make a deal."

"A deal."

"I don't think you can keep me alive, Mr. Bedford. You're so worried about showing your face you don't know who to trust. I'm not waiting to be shot by Pettigrew, Part Two."

Carrie asked Bedford, "Could I talk to Evan alone?"

Bedford measured the chill in the room and gave a quick nod. "Yes. Palmer, let's you and I talk outside, please." They shut the door behind them.

Carrie took his hand. "How could you let me believe you were dead? I've spent the past twenty-four hours grieving."

"I am truly sorry. But I didn't know who other than you and Bedford I could trust. Clearly Bedford doesn't know, either. I wasn't going to phone in and walk back into the arms of another Pettigrew."

"How did you get information tying Pettigrew to Jargo?" she said.

"I got resourceful."

"Will you give it to me?"

"No. If I hand it over, my father is dead. I need your help. I have to get out of here." Evan spoke in the barest whisper. "If Jargo gets word that the CIA has picked me up, he'll call off trading me the files for my dad."

"You really have the files." She sounded stunned.

"Yes."

"I can't go against Bedford. You're not thinking straight."

"I'm so far down the rabbit hole now . . . I can't trust anyone. Jargo not to kill me, Bedford to protect me. You to love me."

"I do love you."

He was suddenly afraid the poker face he'd worn the whole day would crack. He closed both his hands around hers. "I want to forget everything. I want us to have a normal life. But that's not going to happen while we're still down the rabbit hole. I have to take the fight right to Jargo, and I've got a way to stop him cold, but I need your help. I have to get to Florida. I need you to stay here, out of harm's way."

"Evan..."

Bedford opened the door. Walked in without waiting to see if their conversation was done. Palmer and one of the MI5 officers followed him into the room, the officer carrying Evan's luggage. He set it down and left, shutting the door behind him.

Carrie mouthed, *He won't let you go.*

"Evan," Bedford said. "What do I have to do to regain your trust?"

"It's gone. You've got leaks, and those will get me and my dad and Carrie killed. Now we can talk about a deal or you can let me go."

"You're not going anywhere, Mr. Casher." Now Palmer spoke. "Would you open your bag for us, please?"

Evan did, deciding to let them think they were still in charge for another minute. He saw the bag had already been searched. It held only a few clothes that he had bought and a few thousand in American cash. He had left Khan's gun with Razur.

"Your carry-on, please," Palmer said.

Evan opened up a small briefcase bag. Palmer reached in and pulled out a laptop computer.

"What's this?" Bedford held up the computer.

"A laptop."

Bedford opened up the laptop, powered it on. "It's passworded."

"Yeah."

"Enter the password, please, Evan."

"I don't know it."

"You don't know your own password."

"That's Thomas Khan's computer."

"How did you get it?"

"Doesn't matter," Evan said. "I did what I said I promised, which is get the files my mother stole. Khan is Jargo's moneyman. Or was. He's dead." Evan raised his hands in mock surrender to Palmer. "It was self-defense. In case you're prosecuting me."

Palmer shook his head.

Evan turned to Bedford. "Here's the deal. Let me go get my dad. I guarantee I'll still give you what you need to take down Jargo, but my dad and I, and Carrie, if she wants"—he turned to her, and she nodded—"we vanish on our own terms."

Bedford sank into his chair. "Evan. You know I can't agree to your request."

"Then I get a lawyer and I talk a mile a minute about CIA officers carrying explosive devices into Kensington bookshops. Your choice."

"Don't threaten me, son," Bedford said.

"I have an alternate suggestion," Carrie said. "Maybe one that will make you both happy."

Both men waited.

"If Evan trades his dad for this laptop, it requires a meeting. That brings Jargo out in the open. I know him—he'll handle this himself."

"Where is this exchange, Evan?" Bedford asked.

"Miami. Read my ticket, Bricklayer."

"I'm not your enemy. I never was," Bedford said.

"I pick the meeting site," Evan said to Carrie. "Once I'm in Miami."

Carrie turned to her boss. "This meeting pulls Jargo into the light. It's our best chance to stop him."

"And he'll be lightly guarded. Maybe just Dezz. He won't tell his operatives a word about this if he can avoid it," Evan said quietly. "No way his network knows they're on the verge of being exposed. He would face a mass, very fatal defection."

"You really think," Bedford said, "that you're running the show now."

"I am. And I don't want my dad put at risk," Evan said. "Anything happens to him, you get nothing."

"I envy your dad, having your loyalty," Bedford said. "But your dad's already at risk, because I'm quite sure Jargo has no intention of letting you leave that meeting alive."

"I've considered that possibility. I have a fallback. We're doing this my way."

Bedford put his hands flat on the table. "Would y'all please excuse me and Evan for a moment?"

The others got up and left, Carrie shaking her head. She waited for Palmer to step out, then said to Evan's back, "If you love me, you'll trust me. It's not a complicated equation. Don't fight us. Let us help you."

He didn't look at her. She closed the door behind her.

Bedford said, "This room isn't bugged. But it is sound-proof. Just so you know."

"Palmer's not taping?"

"No, he's not." Bedford took a sip of water. "If you've arranged a trade of these files on this laptop for your father, I assume you've spoken with your dad."

Evan nodded.

Bedford said, "Tell me what he said to you. Word for word."

"Why?"

"Because, Evan, I have had a contact among the Deep operatives for the past year. No one else in the CIA even knows I had a contact, including Carrie. I don't know his real name. Your father might be my contact, and he might have sent me a message through you. He knows we would be searching for you until we had conclusive evidence that you were dead."

Evan listened to the silence in the room: his own heartbeat, the hum of the heater fending off the wet cold outside.

"You're lying. You're just trying to get me to cooperate with you."

"Remember I asked you about what your father said on the tape Jargo played at the zoo. I wasn't so interested in the story Jargo peddled to your father; I was listening for code words. Just in case your dad was my guy."

"No." Evan's voice rose. "If Dad was your contact, you would have already known about Goinsville. About the other Deeps. About how to find Jargo and Khan."

Bedford shook his head. "The contact approached me. I've never met him. We spoke on the phone; he mailed me cell phones, to be used once, then destroyed. He was extraordinarily careful. I don't even know how he knew to find me, that I was the one charged with finding the Deeps. But he did. He agreed to work with me on a highly limited basis. I wanted to force his hand to do more—to tell me who he was, to tell me more about the Deeps—but he refused. I didn't even know his location, where he lived. I tried to trace him; he always hid his tracks. He gave me nuggets that proved his good intentions: a warning about an Albanian terrorist cell planning an attack in Paris; the location of a Pakistani nuclear scientist who wanted to sell secrets to Iran; the hideout of a Peruvian criminal ring. Every bit of evidence he gave me was correct. There was never face-to-face contact. We never paid him for his services."

"Why would he help you?"

"My contact said he disagreed with certain missions Jargo assigned him. He thought they were harmful to American interests. It seemed like he had a complicated relationship with Jargo; he wanted the operations to fail, but he didn't want to hand Jargo over. So he contacted me. I provided him with disinformation to feed back to Jargo's clients." Bedford shook his head. "My contact doesn't know where the other Deeps are to be found. The network remains highly compartmentalized. But he fed us valuable information about what kind of work Jargo did, the nuances and shifts in the underground market for corporate and government secrets." Bedford poured himself and Evan glasses of water, pushed a glass toward Evan. "I had an escape clause with my contact—that when it was time to run, he would identify himself to me and I would get him and his family out. Away from Jargo. To safety. It's what your mother wanted for you. I can't help your mother but I can help you."

"You could have told me about my dad before."

"I don't know if your dad is my contact, Evan. And I wasn't going to let anyone know I had a contact close to Jargo unless I had absolutely no other choice. We've reached that point. Tell me whatever your dad said. Word for word, if you can."

Evan pulled the PDA from his pocket, unlocked it with

his thumbprint, tapped the Voice Memo application. The conversation with Dezz, then Jargo, then his father, spilled out from the PDA, loud and clear. The two men stared at each other while Mitchell Casher's voice filled the small room. When it was done, Bedford closed his eyes.

"Look at me," Evan said. "Is he your contact? Is he?"

"Yes."

A tightness seized Evan's chest. "If Mom and Dad had just trusted each other..." He didn't finish the sentence. Mom would have known Dad was helping the CIA. Dad would have known Mom had stolen Jargo's client list as a shield to protect their son. They could have stopped Jargo without a shot being fired, and Mom would be alive.

"Lies were integral to their lives," Bedford said. "I'm so sorry, Evan."

Silence filled the room until Evan spoke. "Okay. So he's your contact. He's in trouble. What do you do to help him?"

"Did he give you those Graham Greene novels?" Bedford asked.

"What?" The question wasn't what he was expecting. "Yes. Before I started at Rice. He said I should read really brilliant books before I had to wade into the boring junk you read in college."

"Did he ever mention the 'if one loved, one feared' line?" Bedford leaned forward.

"I don't remember it if he did. But Greene is his favorite author, so he always talked about the books with me. The line sounds vaguely familiar."

"The quote is from *The Ministry of Fear*. It's a bitter truth. We always risk when we love. It's also a code phrase I established with your father." Bedford folded his fingers over his lips.

"Tell me what it means."

"It means, *Forget me. I can't be rescued.*"

Evan felt his poker face crack. "No. No. Your code doesn't matter now. You have to help him."

Bedford straightened his stance, with a quiet confidence that suggested the battle between them was over. "Evan. In this business you lose people. It's war. It's sad. I would have liked to have met your dad face-to-face, to have known him. I believe that I might have even liked him. But he's telling me to walk away. I don't know if he believes Jargo, that the CIA killed your mother. It may not matter what he believes. He expected if the CIA caught you, you'd be brought to me, and I'd ask you about anything unusual that he said. Whatever Jargo is setting up in this meeting is a trap. I can't risk it. My team is too small. We'll have to wait for another chance."

"You can't abandon him."

"I can't risk resources to save a dead man. He's warning me off. I'm sure to save you from being anywhere near Jargo." Bedford stood. "My sympathies. We'll head to Washington instead of Miami. We'll get you in a protection program. The government is extraordinarily grateful for what you've done."

Evan stayed in his seat.

"I know this is hard for you to hear. You've lost your mother. But, son, you have Carrie."

"I know." Evan stared at the warm mahogany of the tabletop.

"I give you every assurance we can hide you successfully. Think about where you might want to live. Ireland, or Australia, or—"

Evan looked up at Bedford. "No. We're going to Miami."

"I'm sorry, Evan, but no. Out of respect for your father—"

"The laptop. Through my film connections, I found a very good hacker. We already removed and hid the files. You'll never find them. You try and access the laptop without the right password, it reformats itself. Only I know where Jargo's client list is. And I'm not telling you unless you get my father back."

"Evan, listen to me—"

"The discussion is over." Evan stood. "Are we going to Miami or not?"

40

<hr/>

Y OU'RE WORKING A SCAM ON ME, Evan," Bedford whispered so he wouldn't be overheard on the CIA jet. They flew miles above the Atlantic, arrowing south toward Florida. Evan sat in the back, Bedford next to him. Carrie sat at a front window. A fourth passenger, a beefy-necked older man who Evan presumed was a CIA officer Bedford trusted, chatted with her. He'd introduced himself as Frame, no first name mentioned, so Evan was unsure if Frame was a code name like Bricklayer or his real surname. Frame made small talk about the Washington Redskins, apparently his preferred subject. Carrie smiled and nodded and kept glancing at Evan. "I know a scam when I see it."

"Excuse me?" Evan asked.

"I don't think you really have the files, at least, not all of them. You're a responsible kind of guy. If you could take Jargo down in an instant, you would. So you're not telling me everything you know about these files."

Evan remained silent.

Bedford gave him a crooked smile. "You are a piece of work, young man. Blackmailing the CIA."

"Not the whole Agency. Just you, Bricklayer."

"Piece of work," Bedford repeated. "I could use a young man like you, Evan."

"No, thank you." He knew Bedford meant it as a compliment, but he wanted no more of this world. "I don't think I'm conning you any more than you're conning me."

Bedford looked hurt. "I've been totally straight with you about our plan of attack." Bedford had outlined a simple scheme: get Evan to a safe house where he would call and arrange the meeting. He would take a laptop that looked just like Khan's; Bedford assured him Jargo would never get close enough to it to spot any differences or check a serial number. Evan would suggest an immediate rendez-vous at a secluded spot where Bedford and his team would take cover, not giving the Deeps time to set up their own counteroperation. Jargo and Dezz would be taken alive if possible, dead if required.

"Yes, and your plan sounds thorough," Evan said. "Just like Pettigrew taking us around London was."

Bedford leaned back. "Everyone on the team has been vetted. They're clean. Pettigrew wasn't a team member, he was a decorated field officer who wouldn't ask too many questions."

"Jargo's worried about his CIA contacts being exposed. He eliminated one by getting rid of Pettigrew."

"I suspect he was a client, not an operative. He was one of the most senior CIA officers in Europe," Bedford said. "You see the challenge I face. How deep Jargo's reach can be. But I promise you, Evan, I'll honor our deal. I'll bring your dad home. This is the best chance we've ever had to get Jargo. We'll have additional personnel in Florida to help us. I'm finally getting every resource I need."

Evan glanced toward the front of the plane. Carrie watched him. Frame was reading the *Guardian*'s headlines to her and commiserating about the state of the world.

Evan might not get another chance. He leaned in close enough to Bedford to smell the mints on the man's breath. "There's a reason Jargo's been able to infiltrate you, and that's because he knows you so well. The Deeps are a CIA problem, aren't they?"

Bedford frowned.

"Indulge me for a minute. Spy networks don't spring up out of orphanages. They have to be cultivated. The Agency spawned them. Alexander Bast set up the Deeps for the CIA. You could have agents on American soil who you would never have to acknowledge. A ready-made group of agents you could use for all sorts of clandestine jobs you don't have to explain to Congress, or to anyone. No paper trail of their involvement with the Agency. No blame if anything ever went wrong."

Bedford said, "I think that's an incorrect hypothesis."

"So who set up this network?"

"Alexander Bast, for his own reasons. I suppose he wanted to make money. Freelance spying. Mr. Bast was a man ahead of his time." Bedford stared ahead.

"You'll never, ever admit it was the CIA, will you? I'm wasting breath asking you."

Bedford smiled.

"You'll kill Jargo, even if you don't need to kill him to save my dad. You don't want him talking about your deals with him, the fact he was pinch-hitting dirty jobs for American intelligence. And you can take over the network. Worm your way into every intelligence service and business that uses the Deeps."

"When you and your dad are safe, the Deeps are no longer your concern."

"They have families like mine. And Carrie's. Kids and spouses who have no idea what they do. You'll hunt them down, won't you? Or use them for your own agenda."

"Evan. Please. Not your concern. Your only worry is getting your dad back. As soon as we have him, the two of you are on a plane to a warm, distant paradise, new names, cash, a fresh start."

"What about Carrie?"

"Her, too, if she wants to go with you."

Evan closed his eyes. He did not sleep. He heard Bedford rise from the chair, cough, pour a drink of water, go talk on the jet's phone, presumably to check on arrangements in Miami. Then Evan heard Carrie slide into the leather chair next to him.

"So. You've gotten everything you want."

"Not quite yet." Kept his eyes closed.

"The past day has been a nightmare. I thought you were dead. I thought I had made a mistake, that I had failed to protect you."

Evan opened his eyes, tilted his head close to hers. "I don't blame you. I trust you," he said in a low whisper, his mouth a bare inch from hers. "So you should know I don't have the files yet."

Her eyes went wide. "But you told Bedford—"

"I told Bedford I had the laptop, with the files on it. My hacker did crack the password on the laptop. But all the files are encrypted. My hacker hasn't been able to break the encryption yet. He may not be able to. We could be at a dead end."

"So the laptop we have—"

"—isn't Khan's. It's just a new one, the same model, bought this morning in London. It's my decoy, my fake-out. We put a program on it that will appear to reformat the hard drive if anyone attempts to crack the log-in password. My hacker has Khan's laptop back in London, and he's trying his best to unlock the files. But he hasn't yet. So I'm trusting you. Tell Bedford and maybe he'll break his deal with me to hide me and Dad. I'll only give him the real laptop once Dad and I are clear and gone. And I mean, gone under our own terms. In identities we've set up. Once we're gone, I don't want Bedford or the Agency to ever find us. Ever. My family's involvement ends now and forever. So you have to choose, Carrie. If you want to come with me and Dad, you can. I want to be with you. If you don't, if you want to stay with the Agency, that's your choice. But I'm trusting you with this information."

"What if we can't get your dad back or if Jargo has already killed him?"

"I think my dad is Jargo's weakness. I can't be sure, but..." Evan paused—remembering Jargo's cryptic words the first time they'd spoken on the phone: *We're family, in a way, you and I*; hearing Dezz's taunt: *We'll all be like family*—seeing two boys in a faded photograph who shared similar features. "I don't think Jargo will kill him."

"He killed your mother."

"But Jargo could have killed him when he found out Mom stole the files, and he didn't. He's kept him alive, fed him a whole story about the CIA killing Mom."

"Will you give the CIA Khan's laptop if your hacker can't break it open?"

"Yes. I still vanish, under my own terms, and I'll arrange for Bedford to get the real laptop. Maybe the CIA can crack the encryption if we can't. I don't want Jargo running free. I want him taken down just as much as you do. If I die today, the hacker turns over the laptop to MI5 in London, with a letter explaining what's hidden on the system."

She looked at him, then looked at Bedford.

"I keep wishing we had met in that coffee shop, just like regular people," Evan said, his voice still a whisper. "That we had our dates and got to know each other, without you already knowing everything about me. That we built trust the way everyday people do. I trust you now. But you have to trust me."

Not a moment's hesitation. "I do."

He put his arm around her. She closed her eyes, leaned into his shoulder. He closed his eyes, and this time he slept, heavily. When he woke up, she was asleep, nestled against his shoulder. For a moment the nearness of her broke his heart. Then the plane began its descent toward Florida, toward Fort Lauderdale.

I'm coming, Dad, and they won't know what hit them.

SATURDAY

MARCH 19

41

—◆◆◆—

FLORIDA AT MIDNIGHT. The air hung heavy with damp, the clouds blotted out the stars. The CIA jet shuttled to a remote hangar at the Fort Lauderdale–Hollywood airport, and two cars—a black Lincoln Navigator and a Lincoln Town Car—waited for the passengers. A woman and a man, dressed in dark suits, stood by the cars. The woman stepped forward as they approached.

"I'm McNee, out of the Mexico City office. This is Pierce from HQ." She handed Frame their credentials. "Who's Bricklayer?"

"I am." Bedford didn't introduce the others.

"Sir, you have several calls to return...regarding the bombing in London yesterday. If you take the Navigator, you can talk privately." She gave *privately* the subtlest stress.

Frame nodded at Carrie and Evan. "They can ride in the Town Car with McNee and Pierce." He handed Carrie her Glock; they had all given their weapons to Frame before boarding the plane.

"Do you have a piece for Evan?" Bedford asked. "I don't want him unarmed until our target's in the morgue." As if he didn't even want to say the word *Jargo* aloud, in a crowd.

"You know how to use?" Frame asked.

Evan nodded. Frame went to the Navigator, brought back a Beretta 92FS, showed Evan how to check, load, unload, and put on the safety. Evan put the gun inside the laptop bag and kept his grip on the decoy laptop. "I'd like to keep hold of the goods, if you don't mind."

"Fine," Bedford said.

"Where are we headed?" Evan asked.

"A safe house in Miami Springs. Near the Miami airport. Courtesy of the FBI. We told them we had a Cuban intel agent willing to defect," McNee said.

"Then you'll make your phone call," Bedford said.

McNee gave Evan a kind smile. "I promise when we get to the house, you'll get a good meal. I like to cook." She popped open the trunk, and Carrie and Evan put their luggage inside. Evan kept the decoy laptop clutched against his chest, as though it were the dearest object in the world to him, and McNee held the back door open for them. Pierce, the other CIA operative, got in the front seat.

They slid onto the cool leather of the backseat. McNee shut the door, got in the driver's seat, and started up the car. "We'll shake any shadows first." She powered up the dividing window between the front and rear seats so that Carrie and Evan could talk in private. Evan glanced back; Bedford was in the passenger seat of the Navigator behind them, already talking on a phone.

Evan stared out at the night. The air felt as warm as a kiss. Billboards, palm trees, and speeding vehicles flashed by. The two cars made a long series of turns and backtracks around the airport, stopping and checking and ensuring no one followed, and then McNee headed onto I-95 South. Even after midnight it was a busy highway.

They rode in silence for a few minutes.

"You shouldn't go to the rendezvous point," Carrie said. "I'm the bait."

"No. Your call is the bait. I don't want you near Jargo. You can't imagine...what he would do to you if he catches you."

"Or to you."

"He'd give me to Dezz," Carrie said. "I'd rather die."

"I'm going. End of story." Evan read the signs. An exit to take to the Miami airport. McNee wheeled over fast, taking the 195 East exit toward Miami Beach. But the airport, and the safe house, was to the west.

He looked through the rearview window; Bedford's Navigator swerved around two cars, horns blaring, staying with them, narrowly avoiding a pickup truck.

"What's wrong?" Evan said.

McNee flashed a look in the rearview mirror, gave a shrug. She pointed at the wire in her ear, as if to suggest she'd been radioed new instructions.

Pierce—the CIA guy in the front seat—unhooked his earpiece, fidgeted with a frown. Then he slammed backward into the passenger door and slumped down. McNee raced around a truck, putting distance between her and the Navigator.

Pierce wasn't breathing. A bullet hole in his throat. McNee stuck the pistol in the drink holder.

Evan kicked at the reinforced divider as McNee swerved across more lanes of traffic. It didn't budge. "She's kidnapping us," he told Carrie.

Evan stared through the back windshield. Bedford's Navigator vroomed up next to them, a black Mercedes in fast pursuit behind him. Bullets pinged against the driver's side of the Town Car as McNee tore away from Bedford's Navigator. Bedford, from his passenger window, shot at McNee. Flashes, the Mercedes firing at Bedford. But beyond the Mercedes, Evan spotted another car, a BMW, revving up next to the Navigator.

McNee cranked it to ninety, heading for Miami Beach. The towers of downtown Miami glittered beneath the clouds.

"Stop or I shoot!" Carrie ordered. McNee shot her the finger. Carrie fired at the divider, at a point between the dead man and McNee's head: the glass was bulletproof, and the slug hammered flat into the faintly green material.

Evan tested the locks. They'd been stripped; the controls didn't work. He kicked at the window. It was reinforced.

Bedford's Navigator accelerated close to the Town Car, like a lion chasing down a gazelle, looking for the battle-ending tenderness of throat. The Mercedes roared on the Navigator's other side in pursuit. Bullet fire from the Mercedes peppered the side of the Navigator's windows, the glass popping into small concentric circles but holding.

Evan slid back the cover on the sunroof, framing a gleam of the moon as it slid between two heavy clouds. He thumbed the control. Sunroof stayed still. He pulled the Beretta from his laptop bag and fired into the sunroof's glass. It held. The boom hurt his ears inside the closed car.

"We have to get out," Carrie said. The Mercedes nicked the Navigator, sparks flying up between the cars like a fountain of light. Gunfire erupted from the Mercedes and the side windows in the Navigator shattered.

Evan saw Bedford return fire from the front passenger side of the Navigator. The Mercedes answered with a burst of bullets and Bedford collapsed, half out the Navigator's window, a smear of blood along the door and the front window.

Bedford. Gone.

McNee's voice crackled to life on the intercom: "Quit shooting, and you won't get hurt."

There has to be a way out. Not the windows, not the roof. The seats. Evan remembered a news report he'd seen about a trend in recent models, to make backseats more easily removable to accommodate the constant American hunger for trunk room. *Don't let the Agency have modified everything or we're in a death trap.* He dug his fingers into the seat and pulled. It gave a centimeter. He yanked again.

He glanced over his shoulder: McNee's eyes burned into his in the rearview, otherworldly, distorted by the pocks in the bulletproof glass. He heaved again at the seat, and now he saw the Navigator veer behind them, its side crunched, Bedford's limp body dangling over the shattered glass, with a horrifying percentage of his head pulverized away. The Mercedes approached to attack the driver's side.

Frame wasn't surrendering. He wasn't abandoning them.

Around them, other late-night Miami Beach traffic sped and spun out of their way, cars steering to the shoulder, drivers reacting in alarm and shock to the war waging in the lanes. With bay on both sides, the highway offered no place to exit until Alton Road and the residential neighborhood edging South Beach.

She has to slow for the exit. Our chance to get out. Evan eased the seat back, exposing the dark of the trunk.

"Go!" Carrie shouted.

Evan wriggled through into the pitch-black. He swept his arm in the darkness ahead of him. Looking for the thin wire and handle that would release the trunk door from inside. Assuming there still was one. Maybe the CIA or McNee had removed it.

Bullets dinged above his head, hitting the trunk's top.

The Town Car careened to the right, then again to the left. Evan lay wedged in the narrow opening, and the charging rocked him back and forth. He twisted, pulling himself through the tight gap, pushing their small luggage out of the way. Carrie pushed his feet and he popped through the leather canal into the full dark of the trunk. She pushed the laptop bag into the trunk after him.

Evan found and jerked the release cord.

The trunk popped up and the wind of traveling at ninety miles an hour boomed in his ears. The night lay vacant of stars, the clouds low and heavy over the city like a pall, and the Navigator drove up close to the bumper, ten feet from him, Frame's face a white smear behind the dazzle of the lights.

McNee urged more from the engine, the speed surging past one hundred as she barreled onto the South Alton Road exit, blasted through a green light, standing on her horn, cars screeching as drivers slammed brakes to avoid crashing into the Town Car.

The Mercedes charged close and a man leaned out of the passenger side, gun leveled at Evan. Dezz. Grinning, hair flying around his face. Gesturing him back into the trunk.

Evan hunched down. Reached back into the rear seat, groped for Carrie's hand. Nothing.

"Come on!" he yelled to her.

The Mercedes rammed the Navigator again and a second burst of gunfire flared. The Navigator flew over the median through a gap in the palms and flipped. Bedford's body flew from the wreck and tumbled along the asphalt. The Navigator slid on its side in a shower of sparks, nose-diving into a darkened storefront, metal and glass splintering and shattering.

The Mercedes retreated to the right, then revved forward, coming up close behind the Lincoln. Dezz leaned out the passenger side, fired into the trunk hatch. The bullet hit above Evan, ricocheted into the night. Warning shot; he didn't doubt Dezz could put a bullet through his throat.

Evan steadied his gun and fired.

Missed. He was no pro. He fired again and the bullet popped into the Mercedes's hood. The Mercedes backed off twenty feet. He didn't know the pistol's range, but he wasn't about to waste another bullet. And too many people around; he could miss, kill an innocent bystander.

McNee lay on the horn, driving with insane abandon, powering down Alton Road, through the maze of beautiful people in their beautiful cars. She would kill people, he couldn't stop her.

But he could shoot out the tires.

The idea occurred to him with almost eerie calm. Before she killed innocent people, before she got back on a highway. It was the only way he could take command of the situation.

Evan leaned out again, aimed the gun at the tire below him. He wondered if the tire's exploding would kill him, if the car would somersault into the night sky and kiss the unforgiving concrete. In the car, Carrie might survive. He wouldn't have a prayer.

He held the gun steady and the Lincoln slowed.

They see me and they radio McNee. It's like having a gun to her head.

He fired.

The tire detonated. The blast of pressure and the car's swerve threw him back into the trunk. The Town Car spun into the oncoming lane; a banner for Lincoln Road passed above his head. Then the car stopped, amid a shriek of brakes.

The passenger window shattered from inside, Carrie emptying her gun onto the same fracturing point, firing the clip empty. Carrie went out, feet first, hitting the concrete in a tight roll, her arm out of the sling, and the Mercedes skidded to a stop thirty feet from her, crashing into a Lexus.

She held the decoy laptop in her good hand, raised it like a trophy. And ran. Away from both cars, into the snarl of traffic.

Dezz and Jargo came out of the Mercedes and fired at her. Evan took aim but two people got out of the Lexus, between him and Dezz, and he stopped, afraid of hitting them.

Dezz fired once at him, pinging the trunk lid, and Evan ducked down. People on the street, in the cafés, fled and screamed. He risked a look.

But Dezz and Jargo ignored him; they saw Carrie had the laptop. Carrie bolted toward the western end of the street; she hurtled into the parting crowd, into traffic, and the two men followed her.

They vanished around a corner.

Evan heard a police siren approach, the spill of blues and reds racing along the scorching path they'd taken. He grabbed the laptop bag and jumped out of the trunk; McNee's door was open, she ran hard in the opposite direction, her gun out, aiming at anyone who tried to stop her.

The BMW—that had been behind the Mercedes on the highway—headed straight for him. Braked. The window slid down. "Evan!"

His father behind the wheel, dressed in a dark coat, a bandage on his face.

"Dad!"

"Get in! Now!"

"Carrie. I can't leave Carrie."

"Evan! Now!"

Clutching the laptop bag, Evan got in. This was not what he had expected; he thought Jargo had his father locked in a room, tied to a chair.

"Here." Mitchell Casher pulled away from the Mercedes, tore along the sidewalk, steered off the chaos on Alton, took a side road. Then another side road.

"Dad!" He grabbed his father's arm.

"Are you hurt?"

"No. I'm fine. Carrie—"

"Carrie is no longer your concern."

"Dad, Jargo will kill her if he catches her." Evan stared at his father, this stranger.

Mitchell took a street that fed back onto Alton, two blocks away from the chaotic mess of the crash, then cruised up to the speed limit on the stretch of road that cut through the bay. On one side, giant cruise ships shimmered with light. On the other, mansions crowded a spit of land, yachts parked on the water.

"Carrie. Dad, we have to go back."

"No. She's not your concern anymore. She's CIA."

"Dad. Jargo and Dezz killed Mom. *They* killed her."

"No. Bedford's people did, and we've taken care of them. Now I can take care of you. You're safe."

No. His dad believed Jargo. "And Jargo just let you go."

"He made sure I had nothing to do with your mother stealing the files and running to Gabriel."

"You were CIA, too. Bedford told me. *If one loved, one feared.* I know the code."

Mitchell kept his eyes on the road. "The CIA killed your mother, and I didn't want Bedford coming for me. All that matters now is that you're alive."

"No. We have to be sure Carrie got away from them. Dad, please."

"The only person I work for now, Evan, is myself. The only job I have is to keep you safe, where none of these people can ever find us again. You have to do exactly what I say now, Evan. We're getting out of the country."

"Not without Carrie."

"Your mother and I made enormous sacrifices for you. You have to make one now. We can't go back."

"Carrie's not a sacrifice I'm willing to make, Dad. Call Jargo. See if they got her."

His father drove the BMW past the emergency vehicles racing toward Miami Beach, eased them back onto I-95 North. "Where are we going, Dad?" Evan still had the Beretta in his lap, and he imagined the unimaginable: pointing the gun at his father.

"Not a word, Evan, say nothing." His father tapped at his phone. "Steve. Can you talk?" Mitchell listened. "Evan ran into the crowd. I'm still looking for him. I'll call you back in twenty." He didn't look at Evan. "They have Carrie. Dezz winged her in the leg. They carjacked a ride, they escaped from South Beach. But he has Khan's laptop."

"The laptop she had is a decoy," Evan said. "Call him back and tell him I'll trade the files for her safety."

"No. This is over. We're getting out. I did what you asked."

"Dad, stop and call them back."

"No, Evan. We're talking, just you and me. Right now."

42

HIS FATHER DROVE EVAN TO a house in Hollywood. The homes were small, with metal awnings, painted from a palette of sky: sunrise pinks, cloudless blues, light eggshell the shade of a full moon. Fifties Florida. Stumpy palmettos lined the road. A neighborhood of retirees and renters, where people came and went without attracting attention. Evan remembered reading, with a chill in his chest and spine, that a group of the 9/11 hijackers had lived and gone to flight school in Hollywood because no one got noticed there.

Mitchell Casher steered into the driveway and doused the lights.

"I'm not abandoning Carrie."

"She ran. She abandoned you."

"No. She drew them away from me. She knew the laptop was empty, she knew they'd follow her. Because I can still bring down Jargo."

"You put a lot of faith in a girl who lied to you."

"And you put no faith in Mom," Evan said. "She wasn't leaving you. She wasn't running without you. She was coming to Florida to get you."

Mitchell's mouth worked. "Let's go inside."

As soon as they stepped in the door, Mitchell closed his arms around Evan. He leaned into his father's embrace and hugged him back. Mitchell kissed his hair.

Evan broke down. "I...I saw Mom...I saw her dead..."

"I know, I know. I am so sorry."

He didn't break the embrace with his dad. "How could you have done this, how could you?"

"You must be hungry. I'll make us omelets. Or pancakes." Dad was always the weekend cook, and Evan sat at the island counter while his dad chopped and mixed and skilleted. Saturday breakfast was their confessional. Donna always lounged in bed and drank coffee, left the kitchen to the men and stayed out of earshot.

He thought of that kitchen, his mother's strangled face, him hanging from the rafters at the end of a rope, dying, stretching his feet toward the counter before the hail of bullets cut him free.

"I can't eat." He stepped away from his father. "You're really not much of a captive, are you?"

"Be happy I'm free."

"I am. But I feel like I've been played for a fool. I risked my life...so many times in the past week, trying to save you..."

"Jargo only agreed to let me talk to you this way today. Just today."

"He made it sound like he would kill you."

"He wouldn't have. He's my brother."

Evan's stomach twisted. It was the truth of a fear that had lurked in the back of his mind since he'd seen the photos from Goinsville. It explained his father's gullibility, his torn allegiance. He looked in his father's much-loved face for echoes of Jargo's scowl, Jargo's cold stare.

"I don't know how you can claim him as your brother. He's a vicious murderer. He tried to kill me, Dad. More than once. In our home, at Gabriel's, in New Orleans, in London. And just now."

Dad poured them both glasses of ice water. "Let me ask you a few questions."

This was worse than being interrogated with a gun at your head. Because this was reality given an awful twist. Acting normal, talking normal, when nothing was normal.

"Do you know where the files your mother stole are?"

"No. Dezz and Jargo erased them. So I went to the source."

"Khan. What did you actually take from him?"

"Plenty."

"That's not an answer."

Evan knocked the water glass out of his father's hand. It shattered on the floor, sprayed cubes and liquid across the carpet. "I don't even know you. I came here to rescue you, and you want to grill me, Dad. We need to go out, get in the car, and get Carrie. Then we run. Forever. Jargo killed Mom. She wanted to protect me from this life, and you know it."

"Just tell me exactly what evidence you have against my brother."

A horrible thought occurred to him. "You told Brick-layer to stay away. You didn't want to be rescued. If you couldn't get me back . . . you want to stay with these people. You really do believe Jargo. Not me."

"Evan." Mitchell looked at his son as though his heart were an open wound. "It doesn't matter now. We can both go. Both hide. I know how. We never have to worry again."

"You answer me, Dad. You were Arthur Smithson. Mom was Julie Phelps. Why did you have to vanish?"

"None of that matters now. It won't make a difference."

Evan gripped his father's arm. "You can't keep any more secrets from me."

"You won't understand." Mitchell bent as though in physical pain.

"I love you. You know that is true. Nothing you can say will make me not love you." Evan put his arm around his father. "We can't run. We can't let Jargo win. He killed Mom, he'll kill Carrie. Doesn't that matter?" Evan's voice rose. "You don't even act like you miss Mom."

Mitchell stepped back in shock, grief twisting his face. "My heart is broken, Evan. Your mother was my world. If I lost you as well..."

The cell phone in Evan's pocket vibrated. Evan opened it. "Yes?"

His father stared at him, looking as if he wanted to reach for the cell phone. But he didn't.

Razur had provided Evan with the phone, and only Razur had the number.

"They really should name a computer after me," Razur said. "Or an entire programming language."

"You did it."

"I decoded the files. Bloody hell of a job. The files even had passwords against them when decoded. One file was triple-locked, so it must be the grand prize. It's just a list of names and pictures. It's called CRADLE."

Probably a code name for the client list. That would be the file most carefully guarded. "How can you get it to me?"

"I'm uploading copies to your remote server account.

You can download the files and the encryption software all at once. Can I delete the originals or trash the laptop?"

"No. I may need them. But I would suggest you hide them someplace very safe."

"And here I was all tempted to mount that laptop on my wall. Like a tiger I'd brought down." Razur was merry with his triumph.

"Thank you," Evan said. "Enjoy the money."

"I shall."

"You just saved lives."

"That's a bonus, then," Razur said.

"Drop out of sight for a while."

"I'm going on holiday. But you know how to reach me."

Razur hung up and Evan erased the number from his call log. He folded up his phone. Time to decide if he could trust his dad.

"Is there a computer and Internet access in this house?"

"Who was that?"

"Never mind. Tell me."

Mitchell licked at his lips. "Yes. In the back bedroom."

Evan went to the bedroom, found a PC connected to broadband. He fired up the computer, accessed the remote server account Shadey had set up for him when he'd called Shadey in Goinsville. "Where will Jargo take Carrie?"

"To a safe house. For questioning."

"Call them. Tell them to let her go. Or Jargo's client list is on the front page of the *New York Times* tomorrow morning."

"If you hurt him, he'll just go underground and he'll hunt us."

"Is it that you're afraid of him or that he's your brother?"

"Both," Mitchell said. "But listen to me. You release that

list, we'll be hunted by far more than the Deeps. Intelligence services, criminal rings around the world, will put bounties on our heads."

"Stop with the global guilt trip. You got us into this, I am getting us out of it." Evan tapped on the keyboard, downloaded Razur's uploads. There were several. He opened the first one. Account numbers, a good three dozen, in various Swiss and Cayman banks. He clicked open a folder called Logistics: a file inside, one of many, held the requirements for his mother's last assignment in Britain. A third held arrangements to meet with the Israeli Mossad and hand them a Hamas accountant who had reneged on a deal to provide information to Jargo. Photos of the murder of Hadley Khan, his slow torture, taken by Thomas Khan to prove his fealty, to document his loyalty to Jargo over family. And so on. Every document a page in the diary of a secret world.

A document that listed clients. For all the fear and death it had caused, the file was a simple spreadsheet. A few names at the CIA—including Pettigrew's—at the FBI, at Mossad, at both Britain's MI6 and MI5, at Russia's SVR, at the Chinese Guoanbu, at the German and French and South African intelligence agencies. The Japanese. Both the Koreas. Fortune 500 companies. Military commanders. High-ranking government officials.

"His reach—" his father said behind him.

Evan clicked back to the folder file for Logistics. He opened a subfolder named Travel. He read the last three entries. A chill rose on his skin.

"Dad. How did Jargo grab you when you came back to the States?"

"I flew into Miami on Wednesday night—he called me

back from my job early. He said there was a problem, he had to hide me. They took me to the safe house and he locked me up."

"Wednesday. Then what?"

"He and Dezz went to Washington to get a lead on Donna's contact at the CIA."

"No. They went to Austin." He pointed at a listing in the logistics file. "Khan arranged for a charter flight for them, from Miami to Austin on Thursday. They went to see Mom. Or to watch her. Maybe she spotted Dezz or Jargo, knew she was being trailed. That's what triggered her to run Friday morning."

His father stared at the screen.

Evan clicked down to another spreadsheet. UK operations. Money funneled into an account in Switzerland, from one to another. "Dad. Look. This transfer. Who is Dundee?"

His father had found his voice again. "An agent's code name."

"Paid the day I arrived in London and Jargo tried to bomb me. Dundee is probably the bomb maker."

Mitchell sank to the floor, still staring at the computer.

The final document—titled CRADLE—sat alone at the window's bottom. Evan clicked it open as his father grabbed his hand and said, "Don't, son, please, don't."

43

Too late. Evan opened CRADLE. It held old photos—of children. Sixteen children. One of his father, with his wide smile. His mother was a blonde wisp of a child, high-cheekboned, her hair twisted in a garish, girlish braid. Jargo at seven already had the flat, cold eyes of a killer. A sweet-faced girl looked like a childish version of the driver McNee. Names lay underneath each photo. He stared at his parents and Jargo. And Carrie's father.

Arthur Smithson. Julie Phelps. John Cobham. Richard Allan.

"Those were your real names," Evan said. "What happened to your parents?"

"They all died. We never knew them."

"Where were you born?"

His dad didn't answer. Instead he asked, "Did you download the encryption software?"

"Yes."

His father leaned over and clicked buttons. Dropped the CRADLE document on it again and the file reopened.

Not the CIA. Not an independent organization that Alexander Bast had started and Jargo had hijacked. New names lay beneath each schoolchild photo.

His mother. Julija Ivanovna Kuzhkina.

His father. Piotr Borisovich Matarov.

Jargo. Nikolai Borisovich Matarov.

"No," Evan said.

"We were a great, great secret," his father said behind him. In tears. "The seeds of the next wave of Soviet intelligence. The gulags were full of women, political dissidents, who were not allowed to keep their children. Our fathers were either other dissidents or prison guards who impregnated the women. Our mothers got to see us—once a month, for an hour—until we were two and then never got to see us again. Most of the children ended up in labor or reeducation camps. Alexander Bast went through the camps. He found the female prisoners with the highest IQs—giving them legitimate tests, because the Soviets claimed dissidents were mentally damaged and had low IQs—and he tested their two-year-olds, and then he took a group of us away."

"Bast was CIA."

"And KGB. He was a KGB-dangled double agent. His loyalty was to the USSR. He played the CIA for fools."

Evan touched the screen, the photo of his mother. "He transformed you into little Americans."

"In Ukraine, the Soviets built a replica of an American town. Called Clifton. Bast had another complex near it. We had the best English and French teachers, we spoke it like natives. We were even taught to mimic accents: Southern, New Englander, New Jersey." Mitchell cleared his throat. "We even had American textbooks, although our instructors were quick to point out Western falsehoods in favor of Soviet truth. And from an early age, we were taught tradecraft. How to fight, if needed. How to kill. How to lie.

How to spy. How to live a completely double life. We grew up in constant training, programmed for success, for fearlessness, to be the best."

Evan put his arm around his father.

"At the time, Soviet intelligence was in disarray," Mitchell said. "The FBI and the CIA kept rolling up and shutting down Soviet operations and agents in the States, because so many of the American-born agents had ties to the Communist Party before World War Two. And if you were a Soviet diplomat, the FBI and CIA knew you were also likely KGB—it tied the spies' hands, constantly. The illegals—spies living under deep cover—were more successful. Or at least Bast sold the upper echelon of the KGB on this idea. Very few knew of the program. It was identified under a training program called CRADLE on budgetary documents and reports, and given an extremely low profile. No one could know. The investment that would have been lost was too much, much more than training an adult agent."

"Then Bast brought you to the orphanage in Ohio."

"He bought it. Set us up in our new names and identities—"

"—and then promptly destroyed the orphanage and the courthouse. Giving you a fallback position if your identity papers were ever questioned. And a source for new identities when needed."

Mitchell nodded.

"To grow up and be spies." Evan pictured his parents as children, drilled, trained, groomed for a life of suspicion and deceit. In the photos they looked as if they just wanted to go outside and play.

Mitchell nodded again. "To be sleeper agents. But we were to attend college—our scholarships paid from an orphans' fund run by a company that was a front for

Bast—and then he, as a longtime trusted CIA operative, would smooth the road for recruitment."

"Into the CIA."

"Yes. Or land us jobs in defense, energy, aviation… wherever would be useful. We were to be flexible. To focus on operations. To wait for opportunities. To serve when summoned."

"And as the Smithsons, you got a job as a translator for military intelligence, and Mom worked for the navy. You were perfectly placed. Why did you become Mitchell Casher?"

"For you." Now his father seemed to draw strength from the moment. He stood before Evan, his hands folded in front of his waist like a penitent, his eyes moist with tears, his voice strong. Not trembling.

"I don't understand, Dad."

"We saw what America was. Freedom. Opportunity. Honesty. For all its warts, its problems—America is a paradise. We wanted to raise our children here, Evan, without fear. Without worry that we would be caught and killed or summoned back to Russia, where our parents had been in jail and we'd never been given a choice in our lives. Did you know at Clifton, we had to be taught how to make choices? How to deal with real independence?" Mitchell shook his head. "We had freedom; we had interesting work; we had food in our stomachs and no lines to stand in. We knew we had been lied to. Completely lied to."

Evan put his arm around his father once more.

"The only thing that shielded us from the KGB was Bast. He was our sole handler, our sole contact. We were not listed in official KGB files. We were not acknowledged. We were not even given credit for the operations we ran that were successful. If I stole computer-networking technology, Bast invented a fictitious traitor or onetime agent who had stolen it. The KGB command never knew I existed. Otherwise those fools in the KGB—more like a black hole than a bureaucracy—would have gotten impossibly greedy; asked us for the moon and stars and destroyed us all by giving us impossible jobs. The Soviets had just invaded Afghanistan; Bast told Jargo that he might be reassigned to run the networks the Soviets were building in Kabul. If he was moved out of position, it would have exposed us all to the greed and incompetence that was rife in the KGB's American operations."

"You would have had to work according to the KGB's rules. Not Bast's."

"In a strange way, we were like his children." Mitchell closed his eyes. "Your mother was pregnant with you, a few of the other Deeps had married, started having children. Building real lives." He swallowed again. "We were not supposed to be in contact with each other, but we were. My brother saw an opportunity. We would finally be real Americans. We'd be capitalists about our work."

"So the Deeps killed Bast. Two shots from two different guns. Jargo and another Deep."

"Me," Mitchell said in a soft voice. "Jargo and your mother and I went to London. Shot him. Jargo first, then me. It was like killing my own father. But I did what I had to do. For you. To give you a chance." Mitchell swallowed. "We killed him and the few we could reach in Russia who knew about CRADLE. It was less than ten men at that point. That file of us as children, it looks like a scanned paper I saw once of all of us, back in Russia. It belonged to Bast."

"And Khan kept it. For insurance, in case you all betrayed him the way Jargo did Bast," Evan said.

"I think you're right. We created the evidence and fed it to one of Bast's KGB handlers, that he had been murdered by the CIA, his fictional agents eliminated by the CIA. We all vanished from the lives we had lived. You were only a few months old then."

"But once the Soviet Union fell...you could have stepped forward."

"We had been spying for years by then, Evan. For the CIA. Against the CIA. We were freelance and we were very good. We could hardly step forward and say, 'Hey, we're a very successful network of former KGB agents, we've been doing the jobs too dirty for your own budgets, for your own people.' We would have been seen as the ultimate loose cannons, hunted by every intelligence service. Some of our clients, they've been using us for twenty-five years. They've risen far in their careers. We couldn't come forward. We had...built wonderful lives."

"So you did deals with everyone and their brother."

"We were the town whores of intelligence work. We stole from the Israelis for the Syrians. We kidnapped old Germans in Argentina for the Israelis. We stole from German scientists and sold to KGB agents who never knew we were once their colleagues. Corporate espionage because it's fast and lucrative." Mitchell ran his hand along his face. "Espionage is illegal in every country. There is no clemency. Even ex-KGBers that are working as consultants now in the U.S., they had not done what we had. They had not committed murder. They had not lived under false names. They had not sold their services to the highest bidder."

"And this noble work was done for my sake."

"For you. For Carrie. For ourselves and all our children. We didn't want you to never have choices. We didn't want to take you away from everything you had ever known. We"—here Mitchell's voice broke, that of a boy torn from a mother's arms—"we didn't want you to be taken from us. We wanted to be alive and free."

The shock of his statement made Evan's bones feel like water. "This isn't freedom, Dad. You haven't been able to do what you wanted. Be what you wanted. You just traded one cage for another."

"Don't judge me."

Evan stood. "I'm not staying in the cage you built for yourself."

Mitchell shook Evan's shoulders. "It wasn't a cage. Your mother got to be a photographer. I got to work with computers. Our choices. And you got to grow up free, not afraid, not with us rotting in a prison, just like our mothers." Mitchell's mouth contorted in fury and grief; rage fired his eyes.

"Dad..."

"You don't know the evil you were saved from, Evan. I don't mean the evil of murder. I mean the evil of oppression. Of your soul suffocating. Of constant fear."

"I know you think you did the right thing for me."

"There's no 'think' about it—I did, your mother and I did!"

"Yes. Dad." Evan drew his father into a long embrace, and Mitchell Casher shuddered. "It's okay. I will always love you."

His father hugged back, fiercely.

"You did the right thing at the time," Evan said. "But this life killed Mom, and it has nearly killed me and you both. Please. We have a chance to end it. We can go any-where else. I'll dig ditches, I'll learn a new language. I just want what's left of my family to stay together."

Mitchell sank down in the chair in front of the computer and put his face in his hands. Then he sat up, quickly, as though he'd assumed an unnatural posture.

He has to be ready all the time. Every moment that he's awake. Then Evan realized he had moved to that same edge of life, in just a week. He went to the computer, stud-ied the faces of the lost children. He took Khan's PDA from his pocket, wirelessly moved all the client names and agent names from the files on the computer onto the PDA.

"What are you doing?" Mitchell said.

"Insurance." Evan erased the downloaded files from the PC. Erased the browser history so it wouldn't point back at the remote server. He shut down the laptop and closed the lid. He could redownload the files from the Internet again. If he lived.

"The files paint a target on our backs. You should destroy them," Mitchell said. Evan wondered which face his father wore now: the protective dad, the frightened agent, the res-olute killer. Evan's skin went cold with shock and with fear.

"I'm afraid of you," he said.

Piotr Matarov, Arthur Smithson, Mitchell Casher, looked up at him.

Evan walked out of the bedroom. In the small breakfast nook, his father's raincoat lay over the back of a chair. Evan dug around in it, pulled out a satellite phone. Clicked it on, paged through the few numbers listed. One for J. He car-ried the phone back to his father.

"You did what you did to have your life. I have to stop Jargo to have mine. I cannot let him kill Carrie, and I cannot let him get away with killing Mom. He gets stopped in his tracks. Now. You can either help me, or not. But before you walk away, I need you to make this phone call." Evan put his hand on his father's arm. "Call. Find out if Carrie's all right. You haven't seen me. I got away."

Mitchell clicked, rang. "Steve." A pause. "Yes." Another pause. "No. No, he got away from me. He has a friend or two in Miami. I might try them." A pause. "Don't kill her. She might know where Evan would go. Or if I find him, she could be useful in bringing him in. We still need to know how large Bricklayer's group is." Mitchell spoke with a soldier's brisk tone. Weighing options, offering counter-moves, speaking like a man comfortable in shadows. "All right." He clicked off. "They're at the safe house. Our final stop on our escape route. She's still alive. He's...questioning her. He wants the password to the laptop."

What had she said in the car? *He'll give me to Dezz. I'd rather be dead.*

"She doesn't know the password. That computer's empty, anyway." *Except for my fallback, my poker bluff for Jargo, if he ever cracks it.*

"I bought her time," Mitchell said. "But it won't be pleasant for her."

"Where is she?"

Mitchell shook his head. "You can't save her."

"I can. If you help me. Just tell me where Jargo has her."

"No. We're running. Just you and me. Never mind Carrie. You and me."

Evan took the Beretta from his coat pocket. He didn't raise it. "I'm sorry."

"Evan, put that away."

"You made the tough choices, Dad, for me. Because you

loved me. But I'm not leaving Carrie. Tell me where she is. If you don't want to go, it's your choice."

His father shook his head. "You don't know what you're doing."

"I absolutely do. Your choice."

Mitchell closed his eyes.

44

‒‒◆‒‒

*I*T WILL END TONIGHT, Evan thought. *One way or another, all the years of lies and deceit end. Either for my family or for Jargo.*

Mitchell drove north to 75 West—nicknamed Alligator Alley. As they headed west, the night cleared and the adrenaline settled into Evan's flesh and bones like a permanent high. They listened to a news station out of Miami; McNee was dead, shot by a police officer as she tried to flee the scene in Miami Beach.

"Jargo won't kill Carrie right away. They'll want to know everything that the CIA knows—they'll take their time. Jargo can't afford to let the CIA work another mole into the network."

"Will Jargo torture her?" *Torture.* It wasn't a verb you wanted within a mile of the woman that you loved.

"Yes." The answer sounded flat in the dark space between them. "You cannot dwell on Carrie, Evan. If you go in thinking about Carrie...or your mother...you'll die. You must focus on the moment at hand. Nothing more."

"We need a plan."

"This isn't my forte, Evan. Rescue operations. We're not a SWAT team."

"You kill people, right? Consider it a hit. On Dezz and Jargo."

"I don't usually have an untrained person to protect, either."

"This is my fight as much as yours."

Mitchell cleared his throat. "I go in alone. You'll stay hidden outside. They'll expect me to return here, if I can't find you. I'll say you're still missing, no report that the police have found you. I'll tell them that I've heard the news report that McNee is dead, but that I heard on the Miami police band that she's alive but captured. Since Jargo stole a civilian car, he won't have heard any police-band reports."

"We hope."

"We hope. They'll know if McNee is alive, the FBI and CIA will bring extraordinary pressure to bear on her. We need to run." Mitchell glanced at his son. "That movement creates an opportunity of weakness. They will want to shut down everything in the house before they go."

"The decoy laptop. They'll take that with them?"

"Yes, unless they've already broken it with an unlock program."

"They won't have," Evan said.

"What did you put on the decoy?"

"Let's just say I learned a few tricks from the poker champs when I filmed *Bluff*. The importance of mental warfare."

"When they come out of the lodge, Jargo will be walking alone, Dezz probably will have Carrie in cuffs. Both will be armed and ready. I'll drop back and get them both in my kill zone. I will shoot Dezz first, because he will have the gun on Carrie. Then Steve." His voice wavered.

"Don't hesitate, Dad. He killed Mom. I promise you it's true."

"Yes. I know he did. I know. Do you think knowing makes it any easier? He's still my brother."

Silence hung between them for a long moment before Evan spoke. "What if they want to kill Carrie before leaving? The Everglades—you could make a body vanish forever."

"Then," Mitchell said, "I'll lie and say I want to kill Carrie myself. But slow. For turning you against me."

The cool calculation of his father's voice made Evan shudder. "I don't think it's right you go in alone. You don't have to fight my fight."

"The only way this will work is if they believe you and I are *not* together and have not been together."

"All right, Dad. Can I ask you a question?"

"Yes."

"Did you love Mom?"

"Evan. Yes, with all my heart."

"I wondered if maybe the marriage was arranged, to give you cover."

"No, no, son. I loved her like crazy. My brother, he was in love with her, too. It was the only time I beat him in anything. When Donna chose me."

The night was dark and vast. Evan had never seen the Everglades before and it was both empty and full, all at once. Empty of the human touch other than the highway, filled by a plain of dirt, water, and grass that throbbed with life. Mitchell headed south onto Highway 29, on the edge of the Big Cypress National Preserve. No lights of a town or business, just the curve of the road heading into black.

In the darkness by the side of the road, his father stopped the car.

"Hide in the trunk. Break the trunk light so it won't shine."

A jolt of panic hit his chest. So much unplanned. So much to do to try to prepare, but no time.

"The driveway goes around to the back of the lodge, where there's a large porch. I'll park with the trunk aimed away from the lodge. You'll see a gray brick building toward the back of the property. It's a garage and houses the generator. Run as fast as you can for it. Stay behind it until I come for you. If we come out and I miss a shot, you should have a clear line at Dezz or my brother."

"Dad. I love you." Evan took his father's hand in the darkness.

"I know. I love you, too. Go get in the trunk."

45

INSIDE THE TRUNK—FOR THE SECOND time in a night, and he hoped for the last in his life—Evan felt the BMW come to a stop. He heard his father get out of the car. No call of greeting broke the still quiet, and he heard his father go up the stairs and onto a porch, then a door open. Then he heard a murmur of cautious hellos, his dad's voice sounding actor-pitch perfect in its weariness and fear, and then the door shut.

He eased the trunk open, rolled out the back. The night air was cool and moist, but his palms were drenched in sweat. He held the Beretta that Frame had given him a few hours ago. No spill of lights glowed in the night to show him his way. He lay flat for a moment on the concrete, waiting for a door to fly open, shots to fire. Nothing.

He ran, keeping the cars between him and the lodge's back porch.

Blackness. He didn't have a flashlight; his dad had said not to risk using one. He ran into the pitch-dark and hoped that he wouldn't trip and plunge into wet or a hole or a stack of trash cans that would set off a din. He stumbled against the garage, eased around its corner. Evan stayed still. Every rustle sounded like a snake or a gator—he did not want to see alligators again—slithering closer.

He thought he heard a click: probably an alarm system, reactivating after his dad was inside. He stayed still as stone, the sweat oozing down his ribs, his breath sounding huge in the silence. He had a gun. He had Khan's PDA, with its fancy alarm deactivator, which he had no idea how to use. Now he needed patience.

Five minutes. Ten minutes. No blast of shots. No creak of a footfall on the back porch. He peeked past the corner of the garage, past his father's parked car, up to the lodge. Only the sound of his breath, of the ocean of life around him.

Then he heard the slightest crush of a heel on tall grass. Fifteen feet away. He froze.

"I . . . see . . . you," a voice called in singsong. Dezz. "Sitting so still . . ."

A bullet smacked into the brick wall ten feet to his right. Evan lurched backward. Another shot hit the corner, well above his head. Shards of brick pelted his face.

Evan pointed the gun in the direction of the shots. He'd seen a moment of flash, but he was shaken and he hesitated.

"I see you sitting, pointing a gun. You're not even close," Dezz said. "Put the gun down. Come inside. Or I'll march back inside and I'll break your father's spine. He won't die; it'll be worse than death, because when we roll out, we'll just dump him, freshly quadriplegic, in the swamp. The choice is yours. It's over, Evan. You decide how nasty it gets for your dad and Carrie."

Evan dropped the gun. The clouds parted for a moment and he saw, in the dim moonlight, Dezz hurrying toward him, gun stretched out. Then a savage kick hammered him into the wall. Brick cut the back of his head.

Dezz drove the heel of his boot into Evan's cheek.

"You took me away from my game with Carrie," Dezz said, bending to retrieve Evan's gun from the grass. "And I was just getting warmed up."

46

"I HEAR AN IDIOT PISSING HIS PANTS." Dezz pushed Evan up the back-porch steps, his gun nestled at the back of Evan's head. Pressing against his scalp, maybe the same gun Dezz had used in Evan's mother's kitchen a week ago.

Evan's head throbbed and his face ached. He kept his hands up.

Dezz grabbed his arm, shoved him through a doorway. Evan tried to stop but he splayed out on the tile floor.

Dezz flicked on lights. He trained his gun—the same one he'd smashed Evan in the face with—on Evan.

Then Dezz pulled the goggles free from his face and tossed them on the counter. "Night vision, with an infrared illuminator," Dezz said. "Nowhere you can hide from me. Not that it matters anymore. You are quite the fearsome mercenary. It's like watching a Special Forces bloopers tape." Dezz clicked on a light, and now, close to him, Evan saw a twisted, compact version of himself: the same dirty-blond hair, the same slim build, but Dezz's face wore a harsh thinness, as if life had short-changed him on the flesh. A pimple sprouted at the corner of his grin.

Dezz jerked Evan to his feet and locked the gun on Evan's head.

"Please run. Please cry. Please give me a reason to shoot you."

Evan blinked against the bright lights. The lodge opened up into a broad foyer. Dim lights shone, but none of the glow slipped past the boarded-up windows. The furnishings of a lobby had been stripped clean, except for a wagon-wheel chandelier that hung from the ceiling. It had the air of an expensive building trying to look rustic, aimed at the ecotourist or hunting crowd.

"I'm surprised you came out looking for me," Evan said. "Since you're so scared of gators."

Dezz drove a hard punch into Evan's stomach, ramming him against the wall. He collapsed, fought to stay conscious. Dezz grabbed Evan's throat, pulled him back to his feet.

"You're"—he slammed Evan's head against the wall—"a"—slammed it again—"nothing," Dezz said, finishing with another head pound. "Famous filmmaker. That counts for nothing in the real world. You thought you were smarter than me, and you're just so unbelievably dumb." Dezz opened a piece of caramel, shoved the wrapper into Evan's mouth.

Evan spat the wrapper out. Blood coursed down the back of his neck. "I talk with Jargo. Not you."

A scream, born of terror and pain, broke from upstairs.

Evan froze; Dezz laughed. He prodded Evan with the gun. "Get up there."

He pushed Evan up the curving grand staircase. "Girl Scout's a screamer. I bet you knew. I bet you scream, too. I bet you cry first, then you piss yourself, then you scream your throat raw. When I'm done with you, I'll have to take notes so I don't forget." The staircase led to a wide hallway with four doors, all but one shut. Boards covered the window at the end of the hall. Dezz pushed Evan into a room.

The room had once been a conference space, where people sat with open binders, fought off meeting fatigue, watched droning presentations about sales projections or revenue figures, and probably all wished they were out fishing or hunting in the Everglades instead of deciphering a pie chart. They would have drunk coffee or ice water or sodas cold from a bowl filled with ice. Muffin tray in the middle.

Now the table and the drinks were gone, and Jargo stood, holding a red-stained knife and a pair of pliers. He stared at Evan with a cold, fierce hatred, then stepped aside so Evan could see.

Carrie. She lay on the floor, her top torn off her shoulders. The bandage on her shoulder was ripped free, the shoulder and her leg both bloodied. Pain fogged her eyes. Her right arm was thrown over her head, handcuffed to a steel hoop in the floor, installed where carpet had been pulled away.

Then Evan saw his father. Mitchell sprawled on the floor, his face bruised and bleeding, the fingers on his right hand broken into twisted shapes, handcuffed to a metal bar that ran the length of the room.

Mitchell's face crumpled when he saw his son.

Jargo rushed forward and slammed his fist into Evan's face.

Evan hit the floor. He heard Dezz giggle, heard him step aside, make room for his father.

Jargo kicked Evan hard, in the spine. "I kicked a man to death once." Jargo kicked Evan in the neck. "I kicked Gabriel until he was nothing but paste and shreds."

"Don't smash in his face yet," Dezz said. "I want him to see me do Carrie. Especially when I stick it in her, and she loves it so much that she's screaming. That'll be cool."

Evan said, past the blood in his mouth, past the agony in his neck, "I came here to make a deal with you."

Jargo kicked him again, in the stomach. "A deal. I don't care about any deal. Give me the files, Evan. Now."

"Okay," Evan whimpered. "Please stop kicking me so I can...tell you."

"Get him up," Jargo said, tucking the knife back into his pocket. Dezz yanked Evan to his feet.

"Steve, don't, he's my son, don't," Mitchell said. "I'll do whatever you want, just let him go, please."

Jargo glared back at his brother. "You traitor. Don't you beg to me."

"What I'm offering," Evan said with a calm assurance that surprised him, "is a deal that lets you stay alive." He looked past Jargo's shoulder at Carrie; her eyes opened.

"Well, this I can't wait to hear," Jargo said, a trace of cold amusement in his voice.

"We could have brought the police. We didn't," Evan said. "We want to settle this. Just between the four of us."

"Give me the files. Right. Now." Jargo raised his gun. "Or I take you outside and I shoot out both knees and I start kicking the flesh off your bones."

"Don't you want to even hear my offer?" Evan asked. "I think you do."

47

FOR A MOMENT JARGO'S FACE WAVERED behind the gun sight.

"Because if you kill me, there is no deal. No files for you," Evan said. "No more Deeps. I didn't come to kill you. I came to deal."

"Then why'd your father come in alone?"

"His idea. Not mine. He's overprotective. I'm sure you're the same way with Dezz, Uncle Steve."

Jargo smiled.

"Or should I just call you Uncle Nikolai?"

The smile faded.

"You're running out of time," Evan said. "You want the files on Khan's laptop, I can give them to you." Evan stepped around the gun. He knelt by his father. "I told you this wouldn't work, Dad. We're doing it my way."

Mitchell nodded. Stunned.

"You broke his fingers," Evan said to Jargo.

"Dezz did. He gets carried away. Mitchell didn't tell us you were outside, though, if that's what you're wondering."

"I don't doubt him," Evan said. "I'm sure I can trust him completely, the same way you can trust Dezz."

"What is that supposed to mean?" Dezz said.

Evan's gaze met Carrie's. His back was to Dezz and Jargo and he mouthed, *It's okay.*

She closed her eyes.

"I can give you the files now," Evan said.

Jargo put the gun back to his head.

Evan leaned down to the decoy laptop's keyboard. The laptop was powered on, a prompt screen awaiting the password.

Evan leaned down, typed the password, and stepped back.

"There you go," Evan said.

The laptop digested the password, the prompt screen disappeared, a video application started automatically, a film file loaded into the application and ran.

"What is this?" Jargo said.

"Watch," Evan said.

The film opened with the Audubon Zoo on last Monday morning, the sky gray with the promise of rain. The camera zooming in close on Evan's face, then Jargo's. Jargo in full profile, talking rapidly, his cool starting to break.

Then Evan's voice began to speak on the film. "That angry man in the picture is Steven Jargo. You've been doing business with him for a long time. You've hired him to kill people you don't like, steal secrets you don't have, commit operations that your government or your bosses don't approve of. You may not have seen his face before—he hides behind other people—but here he is. Take a good look."

On the screen, Jargo's face turned toward Shadey's hidden camera. Angry, almost frightened. Vulnerable.

"Mr. Jargo's operations have been compromised. He lost a list that had the name of every client who used his freelance spy network. Officials in every major intelligence agency. Government ministers. High-ranking executives. If you have received this e-mailed message, your name is on this list."

Jargo made a noise in his throat.

Then the scene fell apart into gunfire, Evan punching Jargo, Evan and Carrie fleeing into the depths of the zoo, Jargo pulling himself up from the ground, he and Dezz giving chase.

"Why am I alerting you to this problem?" Evan's voice resumed. "Because we value your business. Your loyalty to Mr. Jargo's network. But every organization needs to grow to meet new challenges. Our time for change is now. I understand this may make you uneasy about conducting additional business with us."

Dezz said, "You can't."

"Please, have no fear," Evan's voice said. "There is no need for you to order your intelligence services to kill Mr. Jargo. We are his associates, we have taken command of his network, and the situation is now under control. You will be contacted in the near future by a new representative of our company regarding your future business with us. Thank you for your attention."

The screen faded as the crowd in the zoo continued to run past Shadey's station. Then the film started again. Evan let it play. Let it work under their skin.

Jargo stood frozen. A man whose world had vanished. Dezz grabbed Evan's throat.

"Back down," Evan said. "I'm not done laying out the deal for you."

"Let him go. Let him talk," Jargo said in a cracked voice.

"Your clients," Evan said in an even tone, "are powerful

people who don't want their dirty laundry aired. Maybe they'll work with me and Dad, maybe not. They have reason to stick with the Deeps. We can hurt them, they can hurt us, but if we all hold our noses, they get what they want and we'll make a lot of money."

"*We'll?*" Jargo said.

"Yes," Evan said. "Dad and I are taking over the Deeps."

48

THE ONLY SOUND IN THE ROOM was the looping video and the whisper of Evan's recorded voice. Mitchell and Carrie stared at Evan, Dezz looked ready to murder, Jargo's mouth worked as though struggling to form words.

"That still cool with you, Dad?" Evan called. "You want Jargo in or not?"

Mitchell found his voice. "I don't want my brother dead. But, no, he can't stay in command." Playing along with Evan, stepping into his son's charade.

"Okay, Dad." Evan gave Jargo a smile; the hardest gesture he'd ever made. "I'm not cutting you entirely out of the family business. I mean, if you want to retire, it's your choice." He pulled Khan's PDA out of his jacket pocket. "I took this from Thomas Khan. A copy of that film we're all enjoying is also sitting on a computer, preset to e-mail in less than ten minutes. To every client. And to every Deep. Those kids you were raised with, endured hell with. I know you've killed at least two of them. That leaves twelve who don't know what a piece of trash you are. They'll find out in ten minutes."

"So I just hand over the reins to you?" Jargo said.

Dezz bounced on the soles of his feet.

"Yes, you do. Sound familiar? You pulled a similar stunt on Alexander Bast twenty-odd years ago. But I'm not killing you." *Not yet,* he thought. He gripped the PDA, willed his hand not to shake. "I can stop the e-mail program from scaring your whole network and every client of yours. Only I have the key. You kill me, you hurt my dad or Carrie, the files go, and you're history. The Deeps will hunt you. The clients will hunt you. And when they find you; you'll be the one kicked to death."

"Dad," Dezz said in a strained voice, "you cannot cave to him."

"I had a hacker break all of Khan's files open for me," Evan said. "I know your name, Uncle Nikolai, I know who you are and who pays you. It's done for you. Over."

"He's lying!" Dezz screamed.

"Am I? I have Khan's laptop. I have his files, his PDA, and that film footage." Evan narrowed his stare. "You messed with the wrong guy."

"It's all a bluff," Dezz said. His reddened face sweated, he grimaced showing small white teeth.

Evan kept his gaze on Jargo, unlocked the PDA with his thumbprint. He tapped open a file on the PDA. Held it out for Jargo to read. A long list of names. Clients. Deeps.

"Do I look," Evan said, "like I'm bluffing?"

The glow of the PDA played along Jargo's face. He read the names. Closed his eyes. "What . . . do I have to do to get you to not send the e-mail?"

"Put your guns on the floor. Unlock my father and Carrie. Leave. Immediately. Just go."

Dezz raised his gun. "No!"

"Kill me and it goes," Evan said. "Decide."

"You could still send the e-mail," Jargo said.

"You'll just have to trust me," Evan said. "Dad still wants to run the Deeps—I won't destroy his business." The lie tasted fine in his mouth, with all the other lies. He held out his hand. "Your gun."

Jargo said, "Mitchell. You know I never would have hurt you. I gave you the life you wanted. The life we dreamed about. I cannot believe you would turn on me."

"You just broke his fingers," Evan said.

"Not me. Dezz did. Dezz . . . did." Jargo took an unsteady step. "You're doing this because you think I killed your mom. I didn't. I did not." A stress on the *I*. "I just wanted to find out what she had taken, why she had taken it. I . . ." He shuddered, uncertain in his sudden weakness.

"Shut up and give me your gun. Eight minutes."

Jargo handed him the gun.

"Unlock Carrie. Unlock my dad."

"Do it," Jargo said to Dezz.

"No way, no way, no way!" Dezz's voice morphed to a high shriek. "It's a lie, he's just telling us a story, it's what he does!"

Evan aimed the gun at him. "Seven minutes. You want to get down the road, I imagine." He wanted to shoot Dezz, shoot him right through his lying eyes. But he just wanted them gone, his father safe, Carrie safe. The police could pick them up on Alligator Alley, whether they fled back to Miami or headed northwest to Tampa.

Jargo grabbed the keys and knelt by Mitchell. Mitchell pushed himself away from the wall. In pain.

Dezz closed the laptop, cut off the reel of video, and swung the gun toward Evan. "Dad, this is a bad idea. He's bluffing. There's no wireless around here for him to connect to, to stop an e-mail."

"I can do it with a phone call, too," Evan said. "You're running out of time."

"Dezz. Shut up." Jargo clicked loose the cuff that held Mitchell to the iron bar and glared at his son. "If not for your lack of self-control..."

Mitchell climbed to his feet, one circle of the handcuff open, the other dangling from his left wrist. He stared at his brother. Anger, hate, hurt, a kaleidoscope of emotions built over the years of deception, played across his face.

Evan saw it, keeping his gun trained on Dezz, thinking, *Dad, just let them go, we've got the upper hand, play it out, they're gone and we're fine...*

"You killed my Donna," Mitchell said. His mouth sounded as if it were full of gravel. "You flew to Austin and killed her."

Then he swung the heavy cuff.

The open circle of steel caught Jargo in the face, sliced through skin, hooked hard into his cheek. Jargo screamed. Mitchell yanked the cuff and tore his brother's face open.

Dezz swung his gun toward them, but Mitchell spun with a kick and caught Dezz's arm. The bullet blasted into the cypress flooring.

Evan ducked back to cover Carrie, who was still bound to the floor.

Dezz retreated to the door and fired. Twice. The first bullet caught Jargo in the back of the head as he staggered, his hooked face chained to his brother's wrist. The second hit flesh with a wet pop as the two brothers collapsed together.

Evan fired. Dezz fell back from the doorway. Evan heard footsteps pounding in retreat, a howl of pain. Evan kept his gun trained on the door, frantic with fear for his dad. He knelt by the crumpled bodies. Jargo lay atop his father, and he pulled him off. Jargo was dead, the back of his head a wet mess. Unseeing eyes bulged in disbelief.

Mitchell looked at his son. He moaned and closed his eyes. A circle of bullet gouged the middle of his shirt.

"Evan!" Carrie's voice cut through the haze of shock. She pulled hard at the cuff that bound her to the floor.

"Dad is shot—" he started, then his head cleared. Get her loose. She could help Dad, he could go finish Dezz. If Dezz came back, he couldn't leave her bound to the floor.

"Jargo's got the key," she said.

He found the keys under Jargo's dead arm. He hurried to her, keeping the gun aimed at the doorway, jabbed the key into one lock. It popped free.

"Keep aiming," she said. "I'll open the other lock."

"Babe, he shot my dad." All the bluster, all the confidence bled out of Evan's voice.

"We're . . . going to get help right now." She sat up, shaking. "I'm shot, Evan, he shot me in the leg."

"I'll kill him—" Evan started.

She put a hand on Evan's mouth. Silence.

"I think he'll run," she whispered.

"I'll get help for you and Dad. Then I'm going to go kill Dezz." Evan heard a coldness in his voice he had never heard before.

Carrie touched Mitchell's throat. "Evan . . ."

All the lights went out.

49

IN THE DARKNESS EVAN CLOSED HIS hand over Carrie's.

Silence again. But then a groan of the cypress staircase.

"He's coming back," Carrie whispered.

"Is there another gun up here?" Evan whispered.

"I don't know . . . they took your dad's when they brought him in."

Another creak of a footfall.

Dezz. Dezz killed the power, plunged them into darkness. Evan's PDA, abandoned on the floor, gave off the barest gleam. Evan groped for and found his father's face. A slight trickle of breath tickled Evan's fingers. Alive.

Another step below. Dezz was coming.

"Can you walk?" Evan asked.

"Not far. Not fast."

He fumbled along Jargo's body and found the knife. Evan stuck it in the back of his pants, pulled his shirt out over the waist. In case he lost Jargo's gun.

He handed her his cell phone. "See if you can get a signal in here. Call."

"I have no idea where we are."

"A mile or so south off Alligator Alley, Highway 29 south. Abandoned lodge on the right side of the road."

The footsteps against the cypress stopped. Dezz inching along the carpet. Or simply waiting for them to run out into the hallway.

"He's coming," Carrie said. Evan heard the panic rise in her voice. A dim glow shone when she switched on his phone.

The bullet smacked hard into Evan's right hand, where he held the gun, and he screamed and fell back. In the first few moments of shock there was no pain, then agony flared straight up his arm to his brain. He dropped Jargo's gun, blood gushing from his palm.

"Drop the phone," Dezz ordered, "or he dies."

She obeyed.

"I . . . see . . . you . . ." Dezz called. "Still."

No. Couldn't be. But then he remembered the goggles. Dezz had worn them outside, tossed them on the counter. Dezz's retreat was simply to douse the power and get the goggles. Lights out, with only him seeing. Heading back upstairs to kill them.

The bluff—Evan's only way to defeat them—had failed. Gone. It was over.

His hand throbbed in pure pain. The gun was gone. He ran his other hand along his fingers. All still there, but his right hand was a pulpy mess of flesh, a hot hole in the back of his hand.

"You . . . you killed my father." Dezz's voice sounded disembodied in the darkness.

"You shot him," Evan managed to say. The knife. He had Jargo's knife, tucked in the back of his pants. He reached for it, then froze. Dezz could see him.

Bring him to you. Close enough to stab.

"Dezz. Listen. We can talk, can't we? Can't we?" Evan said. *Let him think you've reached the end of the rope. Let him think you're that scared boy again he almost killed in Austin.* He pushed Carrie away from him. She tried to draw close to him but he shoved her away harder. "This is between you and me, Dezz."

"You don't have to worry about Carrie." Dezz's voice floated in the black. "I'm not killing Girl Scout. Yet. We'll have a lot of quality time alone."

Evan tested the bluff again. "You have to let us go, or those files break the Deeps."

"I'll just start all over again. Running a network's a hassle. I'll do just fine on my own."

Evan kicked himself up against a corner of the room, held out his bloody hand for mercy. *Keep coming, you freak, keep coming.*

"A guy like me, I can always find work." Dezz's voice cracked. Evan heard the crinkle of an unwrapping caramel.

Evan closed his good hand around the knife.

"But a guy like you..." A flash of brilliance blinded Evan. The bullet struck the wall above his head. A hoot of laughter. Dezz, toying with him as he had outside. Evan put out his mangled hand, groped the wall. The gun fired again, above his head. He cowered to the floor. Begged in ragged cries for his life, thinking, *He wants to play, just let him walk by Carrie and keep coming.*

Gunfire erupted again. A series of flashes. Downward. The sound of bullets hitting flesh and flooring. Carrie screamed.

"Bye now, Mitchell," Dezz said. Now the flash of light

faded, just a repeating pattern in the black, an echo of death.

But Evan saw where the flashes were, ten feet away, a constellation burned against his eyes. Evan ran forward, the knife in his good hand, listening for a huff of breath. To his left. He stuck the knife out straight in front of him and slammed full force into Dezz.

Dezz screamed. Evan flew into him. They fell to the floor. Evan brought the knife down, felt it pierce fabric and skin. Dezz screamed again.

Evan's torn hand found the goggles and he stabbed below the lenses. Once. Twice. A fist slammed into his jaw, a hand closed around his shattered hand and twisted.

The pain was beyond reason. Crippling. But he smelled caramel, felt warm breath near his face. He raised the knife and drove it downward.

Dezz stiffened and gasped, died, the breath sliding out of him.

Evan yelled for Carrie. He unhooked the goggles from Dezz's face and put them to his own eyes.

Eerie green. Dezz below him. Dead. He raised his head. Carrie crouched in the opposite corner, near his father. Her eyes clenched shut, then opened wide in the blackness. His father, his face gone.

Evan stared at his father in the greenish otherworldly light. "Carrie, it's over . . ." He staggered to Carrie and knelt before her. He put the goggles on her so she could see him. She touched his hand and started to cry.

Evan turned and placed his hand on his father's chest. He felt the silence and closed his eyes. Behind him Carrie leaned into his back and her tears touched his shirt.

Finally he stood and helped Carrie to her feet, careful of her wounded leg. She held his injured hand tight to her chest.

Guided by the goggles, he and Carrie walked downstairs into the blackness.

TWENTY DAYS
LATER

50

⬤

"YOU HAVE A DECISION TO MAKE," the man said.

Evan stood on the wet sand, watching the tide dance around his feet. Carrie stood on the porch of the rental house, arms crossed, watching them.

"I wanted to talk to you alone, Evan." The man was the new Bricklayer, Bedford's replacement. "My proposal is simple. The film you made to bluff Jargo actually has a wonderful idea sewn up in it. Taking over the Deeps network. It's brilliant in its simplicity."

"I only made the video to scare Jargo if he caught me."

"You could take over the Deeps," Bricklayer said. "There's no one alive on Jargo's team who knew about you to contradict you." Evan glanced at him, but Bricklayer's smile was neutral. "The rest of the network wouldn't question you were the heir apparent if you told them your parents and Jargo trained you for the role should they die. Your knowledge of the network and its finances will be very convincing. And we can feed their clients—at least the unfriendly ones—whatever information we want."

"Or blackmail them into doing your bidding," Evan said. "I'm not the right guy for the job."

"But you are." The new Bricklayer lacked Bedford's

charm; he spoke, instead, with a quiet arrogance. "Evan. We've made a sizable investment in you." Because he was a bureaucrat, he started naming the favors of the Agency: "Set you up here in Fiji, gave you new names. Provided funerals for your mom and dad. Paid a large sum of money to your friend Shadey for the help he gave you in bringing Jargo down. We've given you your life back."

The life Evan had had was gone, but he said, "I appreciate all you've done." He didn't want to talk to this Bricklayer—this thin shadow of the decent man Bedford had been—anymore. But he was curious. "The other Deeps. You've located them all."

"They're being watched." Watched. Not arrested. Because they might still be useful in their ignorance if Evan said yes to Bricklayer's proposal. Bricklayer gave him a lazy smile. "Their next orders could come from you."

Evan drew a line in the sand with his toe. "They have lives like my folks did? Kids?"

"Yes. Lots of kids. And if we leave that network in place...well, none of their kids have to suffer." Bricklayer smiled at Evan, pretending that he wasn't using guilt to shame him into stepping back into the world of shadows.

Evan stared out at the water. He counted to ten. "Let me think about it. Let me talk to Carrie."

"There's really only one answer to give, Evan." Bricklayer cleared his throat.

Evan turned away from Bricklayer and walked back to the porch. His head and his heart filled with grief for his parents, for a mother bravely defying a dangerous secret world to save him, for a fearless father who sacrificed himself for his son. He needed them more than ever right now, but all he had left of them was their love and courage.

He hoped it was courage enough to do what must be done. So they didn't die in vain.

Bricklayer still stood on the beach, glancing out at the white of the waves, turning his gaze back to them. Waiting for an answer.

"What does he want?" Carrie asked in a whisper.

He told her and her face fell. She put a hand over her eyes.

"But I'm making a different choice than my mom made," Evan said, "when she had to choose how to use the files. She used them as a shield. I'm using them as a battering ram."

"How? They'll never leave us alone. They'll force us to help them."

"It ends today." He paused. "I still have a copy of the list Razur hid for me."

She took her hand down from her face.

He turned his back to Bricklayer, leaned against the porch railing. "We'll release the files to every major media organization in the world." It was what his mother should have done. What Gabriel should have done. What the CIA should have done. "Running didn't work for my parents. We're going to have the lives they wanted for us. We're not looking over our shoulders anymore. Are you with me?" He tried to smile. "You want to buy a ticket?"

Evan saw all the pain and loss Carrie had suffered cross her face. "It's a risk, Evan."

"No. It's a choice." He took her in his arms and she hugged him with all her strength. "And I choose you."

ACKNOWLEDGMENTS

This book is fiction. That means it's made up, entirely a product of my imagination, is conjured out of thin air, and bears no reality to the actual world or any person or organization in it.

I owe great thanks to Peter Ginsberg, who embraced the book, from initial concept to final draft, and, like the fantastic business partner he is, helped me keep my eyes on the prize; and Mitch Hoffman, who brought a brilliant and laserlike editorial insight to a weighty manuscript and truly helped me find the heart of the story of Evan and Carrie. I am also indebted to Carole Baron, Brian Tart, Kara Welsh, Susan Schwartz, Erika Kahn, Lindsey Rose, and Genny Ostertag for their enthusiasm and support for the book.

For their help in researching and completing this novel, I thank many people:

My sister-in-law Vicki Deutsch, my brother-in-law Michael Deutsch, and my niece Savannah were considerate hosts in Florida.

Phil Hunt, MD, answered my questions regarding medical trauma, and Charlyne Cooper facilitated our talks.

My in-laws Rebecca and Malcolm Fox offered encouragement during critical junctures.

At the Audubon Zoo in New Orleans, Louisiana, Roberto Aguilar, DVM, senior veterinarian, and Sarah Burnette, public relations director, kindly gave me a detailed behind-the-scenes tour. Dr. Bob and Sarah answered even my clumsiest questions with grace and humor. The Audubon Zoo is one of the jewels of the South, and I encourage you to visit it the next time you're in New Orleans.

Shirley Stewart, my UK agent, and Jennifer Wolf-Corrigan answered questions and kept me laughing. Jennifer's fellow book-club members Martha Ware, Joanna Dear, Jo Shakespeare-Peters, and Sarah von Schmidt also provided welcome opinions regarding the London settings.

Marcy Garriott, director of *Split Decision* and president of the Austin Film Society, patiently answered my questions about the craft and practice of documentary filmmaking.

I owe thanks to three of my fellow writers in particular. Christine Wiltz was a generous guide to New Orleans and allowed me to use her good name to open doors. Elaine Viets kindly drove me around Miami and Fort Lauderdale and suggested locales for the book's South Florida chapters. Jonathon King pointed me to the perfect location for the Everglades scenes.

As always, my deepest appreciation goes to my wife, Leslie, my sons, Charles and William, my mother, Elizabeth, and my stepfather, Dub, for their encouragement and support.

When a beautiful woman asks for his help, ex-CIA agent Sam Capra becomes caught in a battle with the most dangerous enemy ever—a man who owns the people who run the world...

Please turn this page for a sneak peek at

DOWNFALL

1

—•◦⊙◦•—

Wednesday, November 3, afternoon

San Francisco, California

The simplest beginnings can unravel a life. A family. A world.

In this case, chewing gum.

Diana Keene reached into her mom's ugly new purse in the middle of their argument to snatch a slice of spearmint. She saw three cell phones hidden at the bottom of the purse.

One pink, one blue, one green. Cheap models she'd never seen before, not like the smartphone Mom kept glued to her side at all times, befitting a public relations executive.

"And since you'll be running the company while I'm gone," Mom was saying, her back to her daughter while she stuffed a sweater into her luggage, "no sauntering into the office at nine, Diana. Be there by seven thirty. Give yourself time to scan the news feeds from the East Coast."

Diana grabbed the gum, stepped away from the purse, and considered whether or not to confront her mother in her little white lie. She decided to dance around the edges.

"I don't think it's healthy to go without a cell phone for two weeks." Diana crossed her arms, staring at her mother's back. She unwrapped the gum, slid the stick into her mouth. "What if I need you?"

"You'll survive." Her mother, Janice, zipped up her small suitcase, turned to face her daughter with a smile.

"What if a client throws a fit? Or I do something wrong?"

"Deal with it. You'll survive." Janice straightened up and smiled at her daughter.

"Mom—what if I need—" and then Diana broke off, ashamed. She stared past her mother's shoulder, out at the stunning view of San Francisco Bay, the hump of Alcatraz, the distant stretch of the Golden Gate. It was a cloudless day, the early haze burned away, the blue of the sky bright. *Need what? Need you to keep running my life for me?*

"Need money?" Mom, as she often did, finished the sentence for her but misinterpreted what she meant. "Diana, you're a grown woman with a good job. You can survive for two weeks without any"—and here Mom did her air quotes, bending her fingers—"emergency loans."

"You're right." *Why are you lying to me, Mom?* she thought. "Where is this no-contact retreat again?"

"New Mexico."

"And I have no way to contact you—none at all?" *Like on these three cheap phones?*

"Cell phones are forbidden. You could call the lodge and leave a message, I suppose," Janice said, but in a tone that made it clear that she didn't want her Bikram yoga or her bird-watching or her organic lunch interrupted. "The whole point is to get away from the world, sweetheart."

Mom stuck with the lie, and Diana felt her stomach twist. "This just isn't like you, withdrawing so completely from the world. And from your work. And from me."

"Yes, I'm a workaholic, sweetheart, and it's made me tired and sick. I'm ready for a break, and I'm ready for you to be fine with it."

Diana thought, *Confront her with the lie. And then she knows you snooped in her purse like a kid would, and you're twenty-three, not thirteen, and...maybe Mom has a good reason.* She thought of the hours her mother had worked, everything she'd done for Diana. In the car. She'd ask her about the phones in the car.

"I'm ready."

Diana jingled her keys. "Fine, let's go."

Mom's town house was the entire top floor of the building. They took the elevator down and walked across the building's small lawn (a rarity in San Francisco), through the heavy metal gate to Green Street. Diana put her mother's bag in the back of the Jaguar that Janice had bought her for her last birthday. Diana drove out of the lovely neighborhood of Russian Hill. Janice talked about what needed to be done at work while she was gone: account reviews, pitching stories on clients to the leading business publications, preparing for client product launches in January. Diana kept waiting for her mom to stop lying.

They were ten minutes from the airport and Diana said, "Why are you taking three, yes three, cell phones to a place that forbids them?"

Her mother looked straight ahead and said, "So when they confiscate one, I'll have extras hidden away."

Diana laughed. "You troublemaker. Give me the numbers and I'll call you or text you."

"No. Don't call me." She looked out the window. "Just let me go do what I need to do and don't call me."

Her tone was far too serious. "Mom..."

"Do not call me, Diana, and frankly, I don't appreciate you rooting around in my purse. Stay out of my business."

The words were like knives, sharp, and to Diana's ears not like Mom.

The drive turned into a painful silence as Diana took the exit for the airport.

"I don't want this to be our good-bye, honey," Janice said.

"Are you really going on this retreat?" Diana pulled up to the curbside drop-off.

"Of course I am." Steel returned to Mom's voice. "I'll see you in two weeks. Maybe sooner if I get bored." Janice leaned over and gave Diana a kiss on the cheek, an awkward sideways hug.

You're still lying to me, Diana thought. *I don't believe you.*

"Love you, honey," Mom said. "More than you can know."

"Love you, too, Mom. I hope you have a great time at your *retreat*."

Mom glanced at her. "Two weeks will let you make a splash at the office while I'm gone. Be smart, show everyone you deserve to be my successor. You'll be running it when I'm dead and gone." Janice's voice nearly broke on the last words, like she needed to clear her throat. She squeezed Diana's hand.

Diana didn't care for talk like that—for any suggestion of a Mom-free world. "I'll keep everything running smoothly."

Then Mom stepped out of the car, grabbed her small suitcase, and walked toward the terminal entrance.

Diana thought of jumping out of the car, running to her for one more hug, and thought, *No, I won't, because you're clearly lying to me and I want to know why.*

Her mother had never lied to her. The reason had to be big. Two weeks where Mom didn't want anyone to know where she was. She headed back toward the city. But not to her own apartment. Back to Russian Hill, back to Mom's.

Diana felt a cold tapping of terror down her spine, her imagination dancing with the possibilities behind her mother's lie.

Janice Keene watched her daughter, the only true good thing she had done in her life, drive away until Diana was gone from sight in the eddying swarm of cars, cabs, and limos.

Inside her purse the pink phone rang. She answered it.

A voice of a man, with a soft mixed accent of an American who'd spent much time in London, said, "You'll be traveling under the name Marian Atkins. Inside the lining of your purse is an appropriate ID. There'll be a package for you at your hotel when you arrive with what you need. Call me on this phone when the first job is done, and then destroy the phone. I'll call you then on the green phone. The blue phone for the last job."

"I understand."

"Remember you're doing it all for your daughter, Janice. And then you can rest easy."

"I know."

The man hung up. Janice Keene went to the ladies' room and tore open the lining of the purse and yes, there was a

California driver's license and a credit card in the name of Marian Atkins. Attached was a sticky note with an airline and a confirmation number and a hotel name with another confirmation number. The purse had been delivered to her house yesterday via an overnight courier, from an address in New York.

Janice walked to one of the airline's self-service kiosks and tapped in the first number. The screen brought up an itinerary that informed her she was booked on a flight to Portland, Oregon. It spat out a boarding pass for Marian Atkins.

She collected the pass and walked with resolve toward the security lines.

Janice Keene was going to do what she must to ensure the world—that uncertain, awful, wonderful place—could never hurt her Diana. To be sure her daughter had a perfect life, just as perfect as the last seven years had been for her mother.

No matter who had to die.

2

"Sam! I want to get married here!"

"Of course you do, darling," I said. I smiled at the venue's event planner as we walked through the large marble atrium of the Conover House, one of the grander spots to host a wedding or conference in San Francisco. The romantic grin on my face was the kind I'd worn when I got married for the first time. Mila's hand was clenched in mine, and her smile was dazzling. Pure bridal joy.

"Well, let me give you a tour," the planner said. She was a tall woman, fortyish, in a smart gray suit. She'd sized us up the moment we arrived—sans appointment with that hurried disregard of the truly moneyed—and we were dressed to kill. No pun intended.

"One thing first," I said.

"She will show us a cost estimate later, darling," Mila said, ever the impatient bride. She leaned in close to me, her hair smelling of lavender, her eyes dancing with mischief. "Whatever it is, I'm sure it will be worth it."

"My question isn't cost. It's security," I said. "You have security here, yes, during events?"

"Yes, of course, if that is a concern."

"It is." I didn't elaborate on a reason. I just kept my fake smile in place.

"We have a contract with a topflight security firm here. And a system of monitors and cameras throughout the building." She gestured up at a small camera in the top corner of the atrium. I flexed the smile for the camera's benefit.

"He is such the worrywart." Mila looked stunning in her dark, snug dress, every inch the giddy bride. She wore a ring on her hand, a lovely diamond, that sparkled grandly on her finger. "Now the building."

"One more question," I said. "You have cameras monitored, yes?"

"Yes. Our on-site team can respond. Or they're happy to work with your own security team, if you should have one."

"That's very reassuring," I said, and off we went on the tour of the beautiful old building, which had once been a very grand bank, the planner pointing out the venue's features and facilities.

"I am thinking," Mila exclaimed as we walked along the marble floors, "of a 1920s theme for the wedding. Sam, is that not brilliant?"

"Brilliant," I said. The architecture and decor certainly fit her idea. We were on the second floor by now, and I spotted a men's room as we headed toward a grand staircase leading to the third floor. "I'm feeling a bit unwell, please excuse me. You all go on, I'll catch up."

"He is so nervous to marry me," Mila said to the planner as I went through the men's room doors. "We have been through so much together, you see."

That was true. The door shut behind me. No cameras in here. I went into a stall, counted to sixty, and then I walked out and headed downstairs. The planner had already told us that most of the food service and administrative offices were on the first floor.

I assumed security was there as well. There might be a guard on duty, but there were no events being hosted right now, one conference having ended at noon. I tested the door marked SECURITY, lockpick at the ready.

But the door was unlocked.

I stepped inside. A small chamber, because they needed the real estate for food and rentals. Nine monitors set up to show various rooms and entrances of the Conover House. But no guard. Bathroom break?

One monitor was tuned to a cable news channel. The vice president of the United States had died last week from a sudden stroke, and conjecture about who the president would appoint as his successor was rampant. To me it sounded like a festival of endless talking heads. On the security monitors I saw Mila and the planner strolling on the third floor, and Mila pantomimed excitement to keep the planner focused on her, not on wondering where I was at or why I was taking so long in the bathroom.

A stack of DVDs stood on the rack, each in a jewel box, with a date and time range written on it, tied to a particular camera. The dates went back for a week. Liability issues, I thought. The venue wanted to protect itself. Because even among a well-heeled crowd, fights break out, people get drunk, tumbles happen down the stairs.

Or someone tries to commit a murder and fails.

I pulled one disc out of its jewel box for an evening three nights ago, from 8:00 P.M. to 10:00 P.M., for the main ballroom. I replaced it with a similar disc. The discs got reused, I figured, at the end of the week. I slid the jewel box home and slipped the original video disc into the small of my back, against my belt. My jacket hid it.

On the screen, Mila bounced on the tiptoes of her elegantly shod feet, enraptured with the thoughts of the perfect wedding reception.

The door opened. A guard, midtwenties, about my age, stepped in. He looked annoyed but not angry to see me. "Sir, you're not supposed to be in here."

"Sorry. I was getting a tour with my fiancée"—I pointed toward Mila on the screen—"and I had a security question that I didn't wish to ask in front of her while we're getting the tour for our wedding reception. The door was unlocked."

"Yes, sir?"

"Are your people armed?"

The guard blinked. "No. We've never needed to be."

"Thank you." I didn't explain my question. I knew my intrusion would be mentioned to the planner, and they'd wonder why I was so obsessed with security. I didn't need to give an answer since Mila and I wouldn't return here. I nodded and I walked past him, and I was entirely sure that as I went up the two flights of stairs he watched me on the screen. I rejoined Mila and the planner and made sure to give Mila a convincing kiss for the benefit of the security guard. Her mouth was tight under mine, firm and warm.

We finished the tour, discussed possible booking dates eight months from now, and promised to call back soon.

Then we headed out into the busy Financial District, walked to the car, and drove back toward my bar in the Haight. I told Mila what I'd found, handed her the stolen disc.

"You asked if their guards were armed? I suspect every date I mention to the planner now, the venue will be booked," Mila said. "I am so disappointed."

"I could kill you," I said.

"What, the wedding is off?" she said in mock surprise.

"I got caught. I had to talk my way out."

"You have gotten lazy and sloppy," she said. She slipped off the diamond engagement ring—I had no idea where she'd gotten it—and put it in her pocket.

"I told you I didn't want to do . . . *this* anymore."

"Do what?"

"Be your spy, your thief, your hired gun." I kept my hands steady on the wheel. "I have a son now."

"And the reason you have him back is me," she said. "I've given you much and asked for little."

"Mila . . ."

"Fine. Let's go see your son. And"—she held up the disc I'd stolen—"let's see who our would-be killer is."

My bar in San Francisco—one of thirty plus I own around the world—was called The Select and it wasn't open yet; I'd decided while my son Daniel was here not to open until five in the afternoon. It gave me more time with him. I parked behind the bar in a shared lot and opened the door with a key. The bar itself was silent. Upstairs, I could hear laughter and music and my heart melted a bit. Call me sentimental. I'd fought far too hard to get my son back to ever feel embarrassed by emotion.

Upstairs, in the office/apartment above The Select, my son Daniel, ten months old, was on a blanket, crawling and laughing, while Leonie played with him. I'd been lucky. Leonie hadn't enrolled yet in art school, so she had the time to travel with me, bring Daniel along as I went to several of my bars over the past two weeks: New York, Austin, Boston. We'd flown down from my bar in Vancouver yesterday, at Mila's insistence, because there was a problem.

Mila knelt to tickle Daniel's nose, earned a giggle from him, and then she completely ignored Leonie. Leonie ignored her back. They don't like each other and I'm not entirely sure why. Leonie is not Daniel's mother; she is, well, a nanny of sorts, an art student-turned-forger. She'd lost a lot in her life, and I'd saved Leonie from a criminal syndicate called the Nine Suns. The same syndicate that kidnapped Daniel and his mother, even before he was born, and destroyed my CIA career. Leonie had been good to Daniel and taken care of him when no one else would. She was deeply attached to my son, and so I'd asked her to stay in his life. We'd had a brief fling—under highly stressful circumstances—and were back to being just friends. Leonie had been nothing but perfect with Daniel, but I knew Mila thought I'd made a mistake, asking a former criminal to watch over my son.

I hoped Mila was wrong.

Mila slid the disc into a laptop on the desk.

"Here he is." She pointed. "Dalton Monroe." She clicked with the mouse and a red dot appeared on Monroe, a tall, rangy man in his sixties. He wore a suit and seemed determined to meet and greet everyone in the room, which was at least two hundred people.

In his right hand was a glass of bourbon.

"It's no easy thing to poison a man in front of two hundred witnesses," Mila said. "I admire the nerve."

I picked up Daniel and sat next to her. He squirmed a little on my lap, eager to watch the red dot, like it was a game. Leonie stretched out on Daniel's blanket and began to sketch in a pad aimlessly.

"Two hundred people, but it gets pared down pretty fast," I said. "Look. He has a bodyguard near him. Maybe five admirers in a knot around him. Beyond that, a few people watching him directly, angling for their chance to talk to him. Maybe fifteen, at any given second, looking at him. And looking at that same moment at the poisoner."

She accelerated the feed; forty minutes into the video, Dalton Monroe stumbled badly, clearly ill. He dropped the bourbon glass. The bodyguard hurried him out, Monroe smiling, waving off concerns from the other guests. He had then been taken to a private medical clinic, where it was diagnosed that he'd ingested a nonfatal dose of digitalis. The press were told he'd simply become ill at the party and had to leave. Dalton Monroe was worth a billion dollars and did not care to have it known that someone tried to poison him at a reception celebrating his latest business acquisition, a local software company he'd bought to fold into his empire.

"He's Round Table, right?" I asked Mila. The Round Table. My secret benefactors. A network of resource-rich and powerful people who want to be a force for good in the world, behind the scenes. They have Mila as their face to me; they gave me the bars to run, a web of safe houses around the world.

They helped me get back my son. I know little about them, except that they started off as a CIA experiment that finally broke free to pursue their own agenda.

"Yes," Mila said. "Someone tried to kill a Round Table member. I want you to find out who."

"I said I'd run the bars for you all. Nothing more." I settled Daniel on my knee.

"Sam, perhaps Leonie wouldn't mind taking Daniel for a walk," Mila said. "The day is so lovely."

"I don't mind." Leonie was normally chatty with me, but always quiet around Mila.

"No, would you leave him, please?" I got down on the blanket with him, wriggled fingers at him. I felt like I never got to see him enough, even when he was traveling with me.

"Fine," Leonie said. "I'll go get an iced coffee." I thought she already had the ice in her voice. She left. Mila stood at the window while I played and made bubbling noises at Daniel, and I figured she waited until she saw Leonie on the street below.

"You need to be nicer to her," I said. "You can trust her to keep her mouth shut about the Round Table." And I knew we could—we'd given Leonie a far safer, brighter new life.

"I will never trust her."

"I do, end of discussion."

"I understand you want to be with your son," Mila said. "I do. But the bars, a very good livelihood for you, were not free. There was a price attached."

"I'm not ungrateful. But I'm also not a police detective."

"The Round Table never wants the police involved. If this poisoning attempt on Monroe was because he is a member of the Table, then we must know without involving the police. Felix will help you." Felix was the manager of The Select. The senior managers of my bars know about the Round Table and were recruited to help with their work.

"What about you?"

Daniel grabbed my wiggling fingers and laughed. Sweetest sound ever.

"I have to return to Los Angeles tomorrow on other business. I'm sure you can handle this."

"And what do I do when I find out who tried to poison Monroe?"

"Give me their name. Then the Round Table will decide how to proceed." She got up from the laptop, gave me a smile dimmer than her fake bridal one. "Don't pretend you're not itching for some action. A man like you doesn't like to sit and play with a baby on a blanket for long."

"Actually, I like nothing better." I made a face at Daniel. "Don't we? Don't we like playing on the blanket?" Daniel concurred with laughter but then gave me a rather serious frown, as though a more detailed answer required thought.

Mila didn't smile. "I know you love Daniel. But I also know you, Sam. You cannot sit at a desk; you cannot play on a floor. You need something more."

I looked up at her. "No, I don't."

"Sam. Send Leonie and Daniel home to New Orleans. They've been traveling with you for two weeks; a baby needs routine and order, not bars and airplanes. I'll even give Leonie and Daniel a ride to the airport, get them their tickets. Then you go home when you've cleared up this little case for me, yes?"

I was a former undercover CIA agent, not a detective, but I nodded. Anything to get her to go. If I found Monroe's poisoner, fine. If I didn't, then maybe I could make a new deal with the Round Table. One that kept me out of trouble. One that let me play on blankets. Then I could go home to New Orleans for a while. I had to find a way to make this balance work.

"That planner will be so disappointed that we're not getting married there," I said. I don't even know why I mentioned it. The words felt odd in my mouth, and I was glad Leonie wasn't there, even though we were just friends now.

Mila crooked a smile at me. "Maybe if you find our poisoner," she said, "I'll throw you a big party."

ABOUT THE AUTHOR

JEFF ABBOTT is the *New York Times*–bestselling, award-winning author of thirteen novels. His books include the Sam Capra thrillers *Adrenaline* and *The Last Minute,* as well as the standalone novels *Panic, Fear,* and *Collision. The Last Minute* won an International Thriller Writers award, and Jeff is also a three-time nominee for the Edgar award. He lives in Austin with his family. You can visit his website at www.jeffabbott.com.